# Bao Bao's Odyssey

# From Mao's Shanghai
# to Capitalist Hong Kong

## Paul Ting

In **BAO BAO'S ODYSSEY: FROM MAO'S SHANGHAI TO CAPITALIST HONG KONG**, mischievous adolescent Song Bao Bao grows up devoted to his country under the stringent eyes of the Communist Party. Precocious for his age, he has strong innate curiosity and discovers many truths that others may not wish him to know. Conscientiously fulfilling his daytime duties to the Party, the boy also leads a busy nightlife. He follows Communist doctrine obediently and enthusiastically to pursue his dream of becoming a Nobel Prize winner. When required to engage in such activities, he writes the largest number of Da Zi Baos (Big Character Posters) in the least amount of time, makes the most impressive paper heart in class, energetically kills sparrows, and assumes the role of leader in group discussions. His enthusiasm is partly based on his assumption that a bright future lies ahead of him. Then, one day he realises that, because of his background, he is and always will be ineligible to attend a good university in his home country. Bao Bao is devastated. All his dreams are shattered. There is no future ahead of him. Then, mustering all his courage, he racks his brains to find a way out of this impasse. Finally he makes a fateful decision, which will change his life forever.

Born in Fuzhou, **PAUL TING** left China when he was a student. Paul Ting has lived in Hong Kong, Germany, Spain, Canada and France and has a good command of English, German, Spanish and French as well as of his native language, Chinese. He graduated from the University of Western Ontario, Canada with a B.A. (Hon.) degree in German literature. He has worked in very different locations, including an oil-rig near the Alberta-Saskatchewan border, Canada and a logging camp in British Columbia, Canada. His occupations have varied greatly, including working for Lufthansa, as a computer salesman and as the chairman of a publicly-listed company in Hong Kong. He has travelled to over ninety countries and participated in various adventurous trips, ranging from hitch-hiking across Canada (from Vancouver Island to Newfoundland), and taking survival courses in the Amazon, Brazil. He is married with a son and a daughter.

# Bao Bao's Odyssey

# From Mao's Shanghai
# to Capitalist Hong Kong

## Paul Ting

## Proverse Hong Kong

**Bao Bao's Odyssey: From Mao's Shanghai to capitalist Hong Kong**
by Paul Ting.
5th edition.
Paperback published in Hong Kong by Proverse Hong Kong, June 2017.
Copyright @Proverse Hong Kong 18 June 2017.
ISBN: 978-988-8228-07-2
Available, among other outlets, from https://www.createspace.com/7268721

1st published in Hong Kong by Proverse Hong Kong, 23 March 2012.
Copyright © Proverse Hong Kong, 23 March 2012.
ISBN 978-988-19934-9-6

Distribution and other enquiries: Proverse Hong Kong, P. O. Box 259, Tung
Chung Post Office, Tung Chung, Lantau Island, NT, Hong Kong SAR, China.
E-mail: proverse@netvigator.com Web site: www.proversepublishing.com

The right of Paul Ting to be identified as the author of this work has been
asserted by him in accordance with the Copyright, Designs and Patents Act
1988.

Cover photograph by Vincent Zhu. Cover design by Artist Hong Kong
Company.
Page design by Proverse Hong Kong.

Proverse Hong Kong

British Library Cataloguing in Publication Data (1st edition CIP Block)

Ting, Paul
  Bao Bao's odyssey : from Mao's Shanghai to capitalist Hong
  Kong.
  1. China--Social conditions--1949-1976--Fiction. 2. Hong
  Kong (China)--Social conditions--20th century--Fiction.
  3. Bildungsromans. 4. Young adult fiction.
  I. Title
  813.6-dc23

ISBN-13: 9789881993496

# TABLE OF CONTENTS

**Note on the spelling of Chinese place and personal names**
In general, pinyin has been used except for the names of famous
people – e.g. Chiang Kai Shek (not Jiang Jie Shi) – and
organizations – e.g. Kuomintang (not Gau Min Dang) – that are
well known in non-pinyin versions.

*For my amazing family*
*Especially for Kathleen*

CHAPTER ONE

# WRITING DA ZI BAOS

Bao Bao, a boy of medium height with a slim build, was a quiet teenager who possessed a serious look that made him appear more mature than his actual age of fifteen. He was having dinner at home when someone shouted his name outside. It was a sharp and high-pitched female voice. Quickly the boy put down his chopsticks and rice bowl and ran to the window. He opened the window swiftly and stuck his head out. Underneath the window stood classmate Zhou, leader of the class, a plain teenage girl with a narrow frame.

"All students are requested to return to school immediately and to spend the rest of the evening and possibly the night writing Da Zi Baos,"[1] shouted Zhou. Bao Bao nodded reluctantly in response to her order. "Da Zi Baos?" He shuddered at the thought, as he went back into his room.

As soon as Bao Bao returned to the dinner table, Auntie said, "You must eat more. You might have to spend the night at school. Nowadays we are all driven to insanity, as we can no longer spend our nights at home. Look at Uncle, he comes home after midnight and leaves home at six in the morning every day. It makes sense that workers come home late due to working overtime at the factories. But when students and teachers are occupied with writing Da Zi Baos late into the night, I am at a complete loss. I don't understand why the Party[2] doesn't let you teenagers rest at night." Auntie sighed. Bao Bao stared at his auntie, who looked more tired than usual. Auntie fell into silence as she stared blankly at her rice bowl.

Auntie suddenly turned to Bao Bao and shouted, "Come on now, hurry up and eat more! I don't want you getting hungry later in the night!" Auntie added more rice to Bao Bao's bowl as she spoke.

Bao Bao stuffed so much rice into his mouth that he could barely breathe. He tried to eat as much as he could so he could avoid responding to Auntie. The Party's habit of calling students to work late into the night was an opportunity for the students to demonstrate their enthusiasm and revolutionary spirit to the

7

Party. So far the Party and Chairman Mao[3] had received much revolutionary support from the workers, farmers and soldiers. However, the Party and Chairman Mao still needed confirmation from intellectuals, including the students.

As soon as Bao Bao had forced all the rice down his throat, he swung his schoolbag across his shoulders and leapt out of the door. Bao Bao quickened his steps to school to show the new regime that he was on call at all times and that the Party could count on him whenever he was called upon. His usual leisurely pace to school would not do for tonight, as he needed to be at school immediately.

Battling the chilly evening breeze, Bao Bao dashed across Huai Hai Road to Shanghai High School the famous school that he attended. Tonight, he was dressed in a simple dark blue cotton padded jacket, which was tailored bigger than his actual size. He grew so quickly that his Ma Ma resorted to buying bigger coats. A larger jacket would enable him to wear it for two or even three more years; at least that was his Ma Ma's hope. The young boy continued to walk in the cool air under the cloudy grey sky.

Bao Bao wore a small blue cap on top of his short jet-black hair. His mouth and nose were covered by a cotton facemask, leaving only a third of his face to battle the wind. Facemasks had become fashionable following the Communist takeover of China in 1949. The cotton mask protected one from infectious diseases and also served to keep one's mouth warm. But like most "new things" in life, the mask was highly uncomfortable at the beginning, so it took a while for Bao Bao to grow accustomed to the feeling of having his mouth covered. Like a scarf and winter gloves, the mask had become a winter necessity for him.

Bao Bao was slightly annoyed that the class leader had called him from home for such nonsense. "All this fuss for nothing!" Bao Bao grumbled.

Soon he arrived at school. Unusually, the lights were on. As he set foot in his classroom, Teacher Ma handed him a bamboo writing brush and said, "Song Bao Bao, we are all gathered here tonight to spend the evening and the rest of the night writing tens of thousands of Da Zi Baos to show our revolutionary zeal for the Party."

Teacher Ma was about fifty years old. He was slender and his frail-looking shoulders drooped on both sides. His silver-grey hair was cut short to his ears. A pair of thick-rimmed glasses framed his small eyes. Despite his stern appearance, Teacher Ma was one of the more approachable teachers in school. Similar to millions of other Chinese, he wore a blue cotton uniform.

"Our class has set the goal of writing two thousand Da Zi Baos tonight," Teacher Ma announced. "Of course, the more the better! The topics are free, but must be in line with the Party's most recent campaigns. This time, the focus of our writing is quantity. Over there are stacks of rice paper, a pile of brushes and plenty of black ink. Jump right to work!"

At this moment, Bao Bao did not know what to write about. He briefly recalled that the current movements targeted money squandering and conservative thinking. Bao Bao regretted that he had not paid attention in class to current issues and did not know where to begin. His mind was completely blank. Bao Bao slowly turned his head and surveyed the class. – Papers were being shuffled, brushes were being taken firmly into hands, and heads were beginning to tilt downwards as everyone got down to work.

Suddenly, it occurred to Bao Bao that many articles had been published on the most current political campaigns. "Why not just replicate or paraphrase the newspaper articles?"

Bao Bao swiftly put down his calligraphy brush and organized his desktop materials along an imaginary line across his desk before getting up to make his way towards the library. The library was usually closed at four in the afternoon, but tonight was a special occasion and the library had been kept open to assist the students.

Without a person in sight, the library was unusually quiet. Bao Bao could hear his own breathing with every step that he took. He helped himself to a stack of newspapers on the bookshelf and flipped through the pages rapidly. His heart pounded heavily as if he had won the lottery as he spotted valuable articles that would solve his headache once and for all. He rolled up the newspapers and locked them safely between his armpits as he scurried back into his classroom.

Back in his seat, Bao Bao sat at the very tip of his chair with his back as straight as a board and his chest sticking out. He felt refreshed and bursting with confidence with the help of his new weapon. He smoothed out his jacket and hair as he collected himself. Suitably poised, the boy gracefully dipped his worn calligraphy brush into the thick black ink placed on his desk and gently pushed the brush downwards as he rotated his brush from side to side. Holding his breath, he carefully pulled the brush out of the ink, tapping it lightly with his fingers as he rubbed it on a black stone inkpad to squeeze out the excess ink.

The boy was amazed at his newfound composure and vowed to keep his aura of sophistication for the night. He shut his eyes, inhaled deeply as he drew all of his energy into one focal point in his mind as his fingers slowly crawled across his desk to pick up his ready-to-use brush.

The results were stunning. It was as though his body, his arm, his wrist, fingers, the brush, desk, paper and ink were all one. Each vertebra, each muscle and joint responded swiftly to Bao Bao's each intention. His upper body became loose and open, his wrist supple with movement, the brush was transformed into a part of his body. Stroke after stroke came spilling out of the brush as his shoulders rounded themselves and his arm moved in and out like the wings of a seagull in flight. Following the swift rhythm of his breath, one character after another began to appear neatly on the rice paper before his eyes. Within a few minutes, Bao Bao had completed his first Da Zi Bao. He set his brush against the ink pad before him and looked fondly at his work:

"In Shandong Province, there was a professor who neither had interest in teaching nor in helping his students. Within one year, he had signed contracts with eight publishers. He was after fame by publishing his books. He confessed in public that the publishing of his books had contributed to his income. He encouraged his students 'to be industrious and show what you can achieve'. The authorities revealed that he had produced nothing, yet had accepted 1700 yuan in advance. How shameful!"

This time the authorities were after quantity and not quality. The Party wanted proof of the students' enthusiasm by producing an enormous number of Da Zi Baos. The Da Zi Bao that Bao Bao had just finished would eventually be added to the finished rice paper pile tomorrow morning and thrown aside no matter what.

Bao Bao shook his head and picked up his bamboo brush once again.

"In Beijing, a Physical Education teacher contaminated the thinking of many sportsmen. He urged young sportsmen to, 'work hard so that they could make it to the national team'. Sportsmen on the national team would receive new clothing and an abundance of food. Being part of the national team, he said, would, 'ensure that every sportsman received new clothing and an abundance of food', which one could not obtain otherwise. What a thirst for fame! It is unbelievable that our young sportsmen were educated in this way."

"In Nanjing, a teacher had mastered phonetics, but regarded his expertise as his own property. Whenever he gave out recordings, revealing his immaculate pronunciation, he shamefully asked for money as a reward. What a degraded character!"

And so, in one session, Bao Bao finished three Da Zi Baos, one after another. "Time for a break!" he thought as he put down his brush and looked around. He glanced around his classroom, which was a triangular room with five rows of desks. In each row, three wooden desks were placed parallel and each desk was equipped with two wooden chairs, one for each of two students. In the last row, the fifth row, there were two unoccupied desks. At the front part of the classroom was a small stage for the teacher and behind him there was a large blackboard. On the wall above the blackboard hung a huge colour portrait of Chairman Mao. Every classroom had a colour portrait of Chairman Mao. "Perhaps the authorities entrust Chairman Mao to watch over us students all the time?" thought Bao Bao.

Bao Bao glanced over his shoulder to observe the classroom. Holding his breath, he listened intently and took in the sight before him: dozens of fingers were busy shuffling papers, arms were moving in all directions, heads were bobbing up and down, as the students toiled away at their writing. Every movement and every sound was so intense that Bao Bao felt as if he was sitting in a boat in the middle of an ocean, surrounded by harsh rippling waves.

After a couple of minutes, Zhou, the head of the class, came in and announced in her high-pitched voice, "Friends, comrades, and classmates, I have just heard that the students in Class Three have increased their goal to reach two thousand five hundred sheets by early morning. We must now increase our goal. We must be better than the other classes and exceed their output. Now is the time to show our revolutionary fervour. Do you all agree with me?"

"Yes!" the class shouted in unison.

Zhou was a small girl with a round, beady face. She had been named head of the class due to her pure communist family background and because she had denounced her neighbours for playing mahjong[4] in a hidden room in the basement, the previous year.

Wang Ming, a tall and handsome boy with wide shoulders and a strong neck, shouted, "We must produce two thousand and six hundred Da Zi Baos to beat Class Three. It won't be difficult, if every one of us writes one hundred of them! With twenty-six students in the class, this amount is completely achievable!"

"Yes! This is an excellent idea, Comrade Wang! Without a doubt, every one of us can reach this goal! I myself will write a hundred and ten!" shouted Zhou.

"I am going to write a hundred and eleven!" cried someone from the back corner of the classroom.

"One hundred and twelve! One hundred and thirteen!" yelled others, one after another.

The quiet classroom suddenly turned into a noisy auction sale as they shouted out one number after another.

"Quiet!" shouted Zhou.

"Quiet!" she repeated as she tried to calm her classmates.

"Let me give my opinion first: I understand that we all want to show our enthusiasm for the revolution and are eager to prove our determination and commitment by working hard into the night in response to the Party's invitation. Now let us settle for a total of three thousand – meaning that each student will write one hundred and fifteen Da Zi Baos. Certainly, the more, the better! With three thousand as a minimum, we will be well ahead of the other classes; that is most important! Of course each of us can set a personal goal of more than one hundred and fifteen. Bear in mind that one hundred and fifteen is the bare minimum for each and every one of us. Have I made it clear?" Zhou gave her warning loudly and excitedly.

"Shi! – Yes!" everybody cried aloud as they punched their right fists into the air. Zhou was overwhelmed with joy and pride at the sight of such zeal shown by her class.

"Long Live the Chinese Communist Party!" shouted Zhou.

"Long Live the Chinese Communist Party!" cried the class after Zhou.

"Long Live Chairman Mao!"

"Down with the bourgeoisie!"

"Down with individualism!" shouted Zhou and the entire class followed her slogans after her.

The calling out of slogans awakened all the classmates and everyone continued writing their Da Zi Baos. By now Bao Bao had managed to write ten Da Zi Baos by copying from the newspapers, though he still had a long way to go.

Li Yong, Bao Bao's good friend, was half an inch shorter than Bao Bao. He had a shaved head and a short stubby neck. Whenever he spoke, he made excessive gestures with his thick fingers. He stood up and came over to Bao Bao and whispered into his ear, asking him for ideas about topics to write on. Bao Bao said to him, "Come out to the toilet, so we can talk." So Li followed Bao Bao to the toilet. "Why don't you copy Da Zi Baos from the newspapers?" suggested Bao Bao.

"How can I? Where can I get newspapers at this hour?" questioned Li.

"You can get newspapers from me. You may use the stack of newspapers on my desk."

Li was hesitant and asked, "What happens if they find out that I am copying from the newspaper?"

"Don't worry about copying. Actually you are not copying. You can paraphrase the articles and say that you simply borrowed the newspapers' ideas. There is nothing wrong with borrowing good ideas. Excuse me, I must get back to work now," said Bao Bao and he rushed back to his desk and continued writing. Bao Bao was careful not to let people see him talking to Li in private because Li was now labelled an "obscure element" in the new society, due to his poor family background.

Back in the classroom, Bao Bao handed Li the newspapers that he had copied from earlier. By the time Bao Bao had reached his thirtieth page, he felt exhausted. His right hand was trembling from fatigue and he could no longer hold the writing brush upright any more, nor could he write as energetically and beautifully as he had when he began. He could not find an excuse to go home. In fact, nobody was allowed to go home.

"Psst, what time is it?" Bao Bao asked his classmate, Li Shan, who sat across the aisle on his left.

"Nearly eleven o'clock," Li replied.

Normally at this time, all students and teachers, as well as the city of Shanghai itself, were fast asleep. Bao Bao would also be deep asleep but, tonight, sleep and a quick nap were completely out of the question. In front of Bao Bao's eyes was the harsh reality that he had to write eighty-five more Da Zi Baos. So far he had achieved fewer than one third the number of what was asked of him. The thirty pages had taken him four hours to complete. How many more hours will I need, to complete the rest? Bao asked himself. Even dwelling on a simple arithmetic question such as this was far more interesting than copying words from newspapers.

"Thirty pages in four hours – two hundred and forty minutes – equals eight minutes per page. At this writing speed, eighty-five pages would require six hundred and eighty minutes – eleven hours and twenty minutes. This means that the rest of the eighty-five pages must be completed by 10.20am tomorrow. That is much too late!" Bao Bao grumbled softly.

But how can I do it? Bao Bao asked himself. If quality is not the issue right now, perhaps I can simplify each Da Zi Bao, omit some sentences, and write in bigger Chinese characters? Then I can reduce the length of time I take for each, from eight minutes to six per page.

So Bao Bao started to write his Da Zi Baos with bigger characters and less content. It still looked quite good considering it only took six minutes! Six minutes times eighty-five was five hundred and ten minutes or eight and a half hours, meaning that by 7.30am Bao Bao would be finished! Bao Bao was ecstatic and felt that he was following Chairman Mao's famous teaching that if we want to win the war, we must plan it carefully. Upon this satisfying revelation, he decided to take another break. This time he wanted to ask his close friend Wu Hai Bin to come along.

Wu was a tall fellow, about an inch taller than Bao Bao, sitting a few rows behind in the far corner from Bao Bao. He was built like an athlete – tall, handsome and strong looking. His eyes were wide and his thick eyebrows gave him a strong presence. His lips always seem to be locked in an upward slant – giving him a friendly, cheerful look.

Bao Bao took out a sheet of paper from his schoolbag and quickly scribbled down some words. He folded the paper in the form of an aeroplane and shot it with an elastic rubber band to Wu's desk, in the far left hand corner of the room, behind Bao Bao. Wu unfolded the paper aeroplane and read Bao Bao's message inside. Wu stood up and walked to the corridor and Bao Bao followed him to the toilet. Bao Bao said, "You haven't taken any breaks tonight! You must be working very hard."

"Yes, I am working hard. But it's ridiculous. It looks like we'll spend the entire night here for nothing. How awful! I am so sleepy now."

"Me too! I'm also very sleepy. I have been thinking – how nice it is to sleep in a bed. I've never appreciated a bed so much until now. I honestly miss my bed!" Bao Bao continued, "If I miss a night's sleep, it will take me a of couple days to recover from it. My mind won't function properly tomorrow. Why does the Party do this to us? The country will gain nothing if we lose our health."

Seeing that these complaints were leading nowhere, Bao Bao changed the topic and said, "Suppose every class reaches its goal of producing two to three thousand pages each. Tomorrow morning our school will have a huge pile of two hundred thousand sheets of garbage. Who will read them? Not the students, nor the teachers, nor the students in neighbourhood schools, as they will be producing their own Da Zi Baos at the same time. There are over several hundred schools in Shanghai. If we take one hundred schools, for easy calculation, then twenty million rice paper sheets, many tons of black ink and an enormous number of brushes, not forgetting two to three hundred thousand students' sleepless nights will be wasted. What for? Just so the Party Secretary can report to the Central Committee in

Beijing that students in Shanghai have shown their revolutionary zeal to the Party and Chairman Mao!"

Wu did not know what to say and took a pack of cigarettes out of his pocket and flashed it before Bao Bao's eyes. "Look! To keep me awake, I have brought something."

"You smoke? How dare you do so?" Bao Bao asked, as he stared at his friend in astonishment.

"I stole the cigarettes from my Dad. He's a chain-smoker like Chairman Mao. But I don't smoke normally. Only on special occasions, like tonight, when I have no alternative to keep myself awake. The cigarette helps," Wu shrugged.

"I have never tried a cigarette, because it's forbidden for teenagers. May I borrow one from you to give it a try?" asked Bao Bao.

"Of course you can, but not here in the toilet, nor in the corridor. If they catch us smoking, we'll be in big trouble. We can smoke in a dark corner in the playground downstairs. But now we must go back and write Da Zi Baos. If we are absent for too long, they will begin to suspect us. Let's meet in an hour in the playground, just around the end of the staircase. When I leave the classroom, you can simply follow me."

"Sure, I'll see you in an hour," said Bao Bao and returned to his desk to review his work. The idea of giving cigarettes a try within an hour's time excited the boy. Suddenly, he did not feel so sleepy any more. "I have already written thirty sheets! From now on, I can copy my own Da Zi Baos with a little modification here and there for the next thirty pages. If I do this, I will need only four minutes per sheet. That means that I can finish the rest of the eighty-five sheets in three hundred and forty minutes, five hours and forty minutes! Now it's about eleven o'clock and it looks as though I may be able to go home before dawn, at around five o'clock!"

Ugh no, he discouraged himself. If I finish early, when the others are only halfway through, then the teacher may become suspicious of my work and may examine its quality. It could be a disaster! If they don't check my work, then they will increase my workload, since it looks as though we will all be going home at the same time. So I'd better spend six minutes on every sheet and take more breaks. Bao Bao decided that this was the best solution.

Seeing that all the students were yawning with fatigue, Zhou stood up and announced that it was time to shout out slogans again. The class then obediently cried out the slogans as loudly as they could. When they had finished, Zhou said that they would repeat the shouting every hour. This would cheer everyone up and prevent anyone from falling asleep. At the same time, the loudspeakers were tuned to maximum volume so that the students could hear revolutionary songs and marching music relayed from the city's broadcasting station. Bao Bao then realized that it was not just his school and all the other schools in Shanghai, that were spending a similar night, but that all the work units across Shanghai were doing the same. Every student and work unit member was displaying his or her enthusiasm for the revolution by responding to the Party's call to write as many Da Zi Baos as they could.

After shouting for about ten to fifteen minutes, Bao Bao was parched. He felt like a water-buffalo, toiling endlessly in the fields. Each slogan and each song that blasted through the speakers felt like a whip lashing against his bare skin. He longed for a drink of hot, strong tea, to keep him awake. He looked around the classroom. There was neither hot water nor a place to boil water anywhere. No-one had dared even to bring a thermos bottle to school, as using a thermos bottle was a habit of the bourgeoisie, who constantly sought after comfort and luxury in life.

Bao Bao did not dare to inform anyone of his cravings. Otherwise all his classmates would turn against him and would write Da Zi Baos denouncing him for his malicious, materialistic outlook. Bao Bao quivered at the thought of the repercussions. He dared not think of a cup of hot tea any more.

He put down his calligraphy pen and excused himself to go to the toilet again. In the toilet, he guzzled down cold water from the sink and imagined it to be hot and tasty tea. He splashed some water on his face to freshen up a little and to keep his eyes open. The thought of being able to try his first cigarette excited him.

Returning to his seat, Bao Bao felt much better. He was not as tired as he had been earlier. He continued listening to the loud march music from the overhead speakers and felt rather inspired. Everyone was immersed in his or her writing, including Teacher Ma, who kept on writing, without using any reference materials, such as newspapers.

"Hmm. I wonder how quickly Teacher Ma is writing and what he is writing about," Bao Bao thought. But he dared not check his teacher's work.

He turned to look at Zhou. "Goodness! Zhou looks so tired! Yet soon, before the hour is over, she will jump up and begin a powerful slogan-shouting session." It had become Zhou's primary job to encourage the students every hour with slogan-shouting, to keep them, as well as herself, awake.

"What time is it, Comrade Li?" Bao Bao turned to his classmate.

Li Shan was becoming impatient and snapped, "Why don't you ask your parents to get you a wrist-watch? They're in Hong Kong and they can easily send you a watch." Bao Bao remained quiet.

Uncle did promise Bao Bao a watch as a New Year's gift, but Bao Bao would have to wait. He was embarrassed to ask his uncle for it again, nor did he want to trouble his parents. Moreover, if Bao Bao's parents sent him a watch, the People's customs would levy a heavy duty on it. It was known across China that all good watches were produced in capitalist countries, such as Switzerland and Germany.

Li Shan suddenly turned towards Bao Bao, took off his watch from his wrist and placed it on the upper left corner of Bao Bao's desk and said, "Help yourself!" Bao Bao smiled with gratitude for Li's generosity. Now it was much easier for him to keep track of the time.

It was three o'clock in the morning and Bao Bao was ahead of schedule. At that moment, he saw Wu standing up and walking towards the corridor. Bao Bao followed him hastily. In the playground, Wu lit up a cigarette for Bao Bao, who inhaled the smoke abruptly and began to choke. Wu patted Bao Bao's back to release the tension in his throat. Wu said, "I guess you have never tried smoking before."

"Yes, it's my first time."

"In this case, just draw the smoke into your mouth and blow it out without inhaling it."

"I saw in a movie that Chairman Mao inhaled smoke deeply into his lungs and waited a while before exhaling the smoke slowly through his nostrils."

"That is not for you. That is for an experienced smoker. As a beginner, you inhale a little smoke in your month only and quickly exhale it. Don't let the smoke go beyond your throat."

"Are you sure? I may waste your cigarette if I do so."

"Don't worry about wasting my cigarette. It takes time to learn everything, including smoking!"

"If that is the case, I'd better not start smoking. I'll have to think it over. Thanks a lot for your cigarette, Wu."

Upon returning to his classroom, he was curious to find out how much his peers had written, especially the ones who had shouted out the more ambitious goals. On second thoughts, Bao Bao decided against acting upon his curiosity because he knew he would accomplish his goal by early morning. If his fellow peers found out that he was ahead of them, they would become jealous and begin to struggle against him. They would denounce him for his bourgeois thinking and for turning the writing of Da Zi Baos into a contest, and aiming to win it. They would then examine the quality of his work and find out that he had copied his first thirty pages from newspapers, repeating the same content over and over again in subsequent pages. Misfortune would fall upon him. Tomorrow's struggle meeting would be summoned against Bao Bao and his dream of becoming a scientist would be forever ruined.

Bao Bao continued to write until his entire arm was numb. Gradually, fatigue and the desire to sleep overcame his revolutionary spirit. Even blinking to keep his eyelids open was useless. Bao Bao's round forehead smashed loudly onto the glistening black ink before him.

"Song Bao Bao!" shouted Teacher Ma and tapped Bao Bao's shoulder. Bao Bao looked up in bewilderment. The fresh black ink began to drip down his forehead and nose. Bao Bao reached up to wipe his sullied face when he saw that even the back of his hand was smeared with blotches of ink.

"Look at you! What have you done to yourself?!" Teacher Ma asked him sternly.

Ashamed, Bao Bao stood up and walked towards the toilet and rubbed his face and hand with soap in cold water. He tried his best to remove the black ink stains from his shirt. He came back and apologized to Teacher Ma for falling asleep. Teacher Ma did not blame him, as he understood that the students were extremely tired from staying up the whole night. Some other classmates also had fallen asleep. Bao Bao even heard some people in the class snoring. Bao Bao looked at the watch on his desk. "What! It's five o'clock now and I have about twenty more pages to reach my goal!" Now all Bao Bao needed was to muster up his courage and give the remaining pages his utmost concentration; tiredness and sleepiness were his number one enemy.

At six o'clock sharp, Zhou straightened herself up from her desk and began to lead the class in a slogan-shouting session once again. With his eyelids half-closed, Bao Bao slowly looked up from his desk. The darkest moment of the night is right before dawn, he thought. So I just need to pull my last bit of strength together to finish off the last few sheets, just like a runner approaching the finishing line." He visualized a grim and cruel picture of the Red Army[5] fighting against Chiang Kai Shek's[6] soldiers in the snow where they had to endure many sleepless nights with no food and little water to survive. This gave Bao Bao energy and hope. After all, he thought, what is this compared to what the soldiers of the Red Army did? If they could do so much for our dear Motherland why can't I finish my assignment? I must not give up! I am nearing my goal!

At half past six, Bao Bao finished his one hundred and fifteenth sheet. Since nobody had announced the completion of their Da Zi Bao writing, Bao Bao did not want to be the first. So he tried to kill time by rearranging his sheets and placed his best thirty sheets on top. He glanced at his watch. It said "6.40am". "The minute hand on the watch doesn't even seem to be moving forwards!" Bao Bao sighed. He was growing fidgety, while waiting anxiously for time to pass.

Finally at 6.45am, Bao Bao collected himself, stood up and walked towards Teacher Ma and asked him politely, "Is it sufficient to write one hundred and fifteen sheets?"

Despite Bao Bao's best efforts to speak as softly as he could, the entire class of students all jerked their heads up and peered curiously at Bao Bao, trying to eavesdrop on Bao Bao's and Teacher Ma's conversation. Some of them started to count their pages, while some other students walked over to Bao Bao's desk, to see his accomplishment.

Zhou began to count Bao Bao's sheets and then said, "It is indeed one hundred and fifteen sheets that you have here. Now you must show your revolutionary spirit by helping your peers so that our class can reach our goal together. Don't forget, we are not individualists!" Bao Bao paused for a second and mumbled, "That was my intention anyway."

Bao Bao cursed himself silently. You idiot, Bao Bao! Ugh! Now look what you have done! You have many more pages to write now! You should have known that to finish earlier only meant that you would have to help others! You are still not allowed to go home early!

Now Bao Bao realized that the other students were smarter than him, as they had no intention of reaching their targets; because they would all have to go home at the same time anyway. He turned his head to Li Yong, whom he wanted to help the most, since Li was not interested in the Party's nonsense and was always behind in class.

Bao Bao peeked at Li's papers. "At the speed that Li Yong is going, he is going to be one of the last comrades to finish writing his Da Zi Baos." As Bao Bao was about to call out for Li, he warned himself that Li was an "obscure or grey element", because his father was blacklisted for being a criminal. If Bao Bao offered to help him, he would be making a mistake, giving assistance to the family member of a Counter-revolutionary! He was not allowed to do so in public, although Li Yong was his good friend. Bao Bao felt sad.

So Bao Bao remained at his desk and just wrote more for the class as a whole. Bao Bao was so engrossed at writing additional Da Zi Baos for the class that he failed to notice Teacher Ma standing over him.

"Song Bao Bao. How did you manage to finish all of this on time? Did you plan it according to the number of minutes you would need for each page?" Teacher Ma inquired, as he snatched a couple of dozen sheets from Bao Bao's desk and started to flip through them aggressively.

Bao Bao gazed at Teacher Ma with trepidation and thought, "How come Teacher Ma was so smart as to see through what I was doing? Perhaps it's because I am the only one who reached the target on time." Then he saw Teacher Ma's eyes flicker around his desk until they settled upon Li's wrist watch. The answer occurred to Teacher Ma in a flash. Bao Bao quickly uttered, "Uh...I was thinking of Chairman Mao's teaching that we should never go into a war when we are not sure that we will win; and that preparation is one of the single most important factors in winning a battle. Therefore, in my case, my preparation was to calculate the required time for writing one single Da Zi Bao. That is why Comrade Li generously loaned me his watch." Teacher Ma hesitated for a minute and said, "So, if we had all followed the sayings of Chairman Mao, the whole class would have reached our target on time."

At that moment Teacher Ma was interrupted by an announcement from the loud speakers, "Friends, comrades, and students, we are going to report your extreme enthusiasm to the Central Committee of the Communist Party and say that you have spent the entire night at school writing Da Zi Baos to show your extraordinary revolutionary zeal for the Party as well as for Chairman Mao. Now it is seven o'clock in the morning and we suggest that you return home and come back for classes at one o'clock this afternoon. Of course we will not discourage those of you who refuse to go home for a break. You are welcome to stay at school to continue producing more Da Zi Baos or to help the school authorities count the number of Da Zi Baos that our school produced last night. Don't forget that your normal classes will resume at one o'clock this afternoon. I repeat, at one o'clock sharp."

As soon as the announcement came to an end, the most popular revolutionary song praising Chairman Mao, "The East is Red", was broadcast at maximum volume across the entire schoolyard.

The east is red,
The sun rises,
In China emerged a Mao Ze Dong,
He seeks welfare for the people,
He is the great saviour of the people

Bao Bao left school and made his way home. Zhou, Wang Ming and a few other revolutionary enthusiasts remained at school. Outside on the street, Bao Bao inhaled the fresh morning air and saw the real "East is Red", as the fiery sun was rising from the east and shining dazzlingly at daybreak.

Slowly he made his way home. His legs felt as light as paper and he could no longer walk in a straight line. All he could think of was to snuggle into bed as quickly as possible. He blinked his eyes several times to fight back his drooping eyelids.

Gradually, the scent of the fresh air from the large plane trees lining the streets awoke his body bit by bit. His right arm and hand were still suffering from severe cramp. Walking in the dewy morning air gradually awoke him. He desperately needed to return home and gain a few hours' sleep but his legs refused to cooperate, so he continued on, walking slowly. As soon as he arrived home, Auntie brought out his breakfast and told Bao Bao that Yuan Yuan had come back a while ago, Lin Lin came home at midnight but Uncle had not yet returned from school.

Auntie told him that there were very few pedestrians on the street and – according to the radio – the cinemas and theatres were only half full because people were busy writing Da Zi Baos. Bao Bao shook his head at the absurdity of what he had just heard. Imagine how many hundred tons of paper, ink and writing brushes had been wasted! China was always been short of paper, and frequently imported paper-pulp in large quantities from Canada. What are Da Zi Baos good for? Just to show that people are obedient and willing to respond to the Party's absurd requests? Why is the Party so insecure? Instead of wasting tremendous resources, aren't there better ways for students to express obedience to the Party and Chairman Mao? Bao Bao had no-one to ask for answers to questions such as these.

The alarm-clock rang like a trumpet. Bao Bao woke up frightened. It was already half past eleven and he had to hurry to school for a class at 1.00pm. Three hours of sleep had passed in a flash; as if he had just lain down to sleep and then had to get up right away. A few months ago students were treated like human beings. Now they were treated like robots. Without a doctor's certificate or a body temperature above thirty-eight degrees centigrade, they would be treated as deserters if they missed participation in any of the Party's campaigns. The quick nap had given Bao Bao a sharp headache. He put a thermometer in his mouth, but there was no fever, as he had already supposed. If he had gone to the doctor's, the doctor would tell him the headache was caused by a lack of sleep.

Revolutionary enthusiasts like Zhou and Wang Ming had not slept at all, as their revolutionary spirit had overcome their fatigue and their headaches. Bao Bao dared not think of his own aching head. He took his lunch hastily and rushed out of the door. He walked swiftly along the same road to school that he had walked along last night.

As announced, normal classes were to resume at one. But, to Bao Bao's disappointment, he found that all normal classes had been cancelled. Instead everyone was sitting on the ground in front of loud speakers listening to the results of last night's Da Zi Bao writing. The students had attained absolute victory. The total number of Da Zi Baos achieved by each class was announced to the students. Bao Bao's class, Class Four, had delivered three thousand two hundred and fifty sheets. "Impossible!" Bao Bao thought. From his observation, he was the only one who had reached the target. He believed the maximum they had completed was two thousand or less. He was sure three thousand was a lie, a naked lie!

Perhaps Zhou and Wang Ming and other enthusiastic revolutionary students like them finished off the balance during the time when we were at home sleeping, thought Bao Bao. No. No way, he answered his own thought. Three or four students could not have completed a couple of hundred pieces in the last few hours. Besides, they were all worn out and exhausted. Three thousand is absolutely out of the question. Why did we exaggerate?

Zhou was delighted that her Class Four had beaten Class Three and other classes. Class Three must also have exaggerated their amount to avoid losing face. It was without doubt that the secretary of the school had inflated the figures, otherwise Bao Bao's school would no longer be considered a politically advanced school. Perhaps this was the same reason for overstating China's output of grain. Every day, Bao Bao read and heard from news reports and media sources regarding China's rapid increase of grain and rice, but farmers had less and less to eat. The supply of food and groceries had declined so sharply that there was nothing left in the marketplace. Bao Bao had never cared too much for the exaggerated grain figures, but to observe lies and exaggeration amongst his teachers and classmates disappointed him.

Suddenly he heard his name mentioned by Teacher Ma. "Comrade Song Bao Bao put Chairmen Mao's spirit into practice by arriving at his goal on time. Chairman Mao has taught us the importance of preparation for a war. Song Bao Bao put this into practical use by calculating how many minutes he would need for one single Dai Zi Bao and how many hours he would need for one hundred and fifteen. In this way he worked sheet by sheet until he completed his quota on time..." All the students in the class turned their heads to look at Bao Bao. He blushed and felt uneasy. He was a quiet student. He was one to feel hurt easily when criticized and uncomfortable when praised.

Bao Bao felt uneasy with all the attention. In reality, he had followed Chairman Mao's saying in order to speed up his work, so that he could go home early to get some sleep.

Teacher Ma added, "Song Bao Bao also showed his revolutionary spirit by helping his peers out, so that our class reached the goal in unison."

"But had I stayed home this afternoon, nobody would have praised me and it would have been better for me. But why did the school lie about classes resuming at 1.00pm? Why am I constantly surrounded by lies everywhere? If the political campaigns go on like this, when will we have time to study and acquire knowledge? Without knowledge, how will I become a scientist?" Bao Bao wondered.

Bao Bao turned his head around and gave Wang Ming a quick look. Wang's face was pale and his hair dishevelled. He seemed completely worn out. Sitting near Wang, Li Yong also looked dejected and exhausted.

All of a sudden a high-pitched female voice came from behind Bao Bao. "Objection, Teacher Ma!" It was Zhou. "I disagree that Bao Bao is a good model for us, as he was cheating with his Da Zi Baos. It's true that he delivered his Da Zi Baos on time with the right quantity. But you should read what he has written. He copied articles from the newspaper, then repeated the same thing over and over again a dozen or so times. While Song Bao Bao went home to sleep, Wang Ming and I checked his work thoroughly and it is totally unacceptable."

Teacher Ma was totally unprepared for this confrontation, and stood dumbfounded for a few seconds. Then he said, slowly, "As I mentioned before, this time we were aiming at quantity in our Da Zi Bao writing, as we needed to report to the Party Secretary of the District a reasonably large number of Da Zi Baos. The Party did not emphasize the significance of the content of the Da Zi Baos. So I still believe Comrade Song Bao Bao did a good job."

Zhou stared speechlessly at Teacher Ma. She was so angry that Bao Bao thought her eyes were going to pop out.

CHAPTER TWO

# NOBEL PRIZE-WINNER OR A DR BETHUNE?

The next morning Bao Bao was exhausted, but he had to go to school nonetheless. On his way to school, Bao Bao saw people gathering at the newspaper kiosk outside Fu Xing Park. He rushed to the kiosk and pushed himself forward with all his might towards the front of the crowd. He quickly snatched up a copy of the newspaper. His eyes darted swiftly across the top of the paper, "Two American-Chinese scientists living in the United States have received this year's Nobel Prize on account of their discovery in Physics."

Bao Bao could barely keep the newspaper open with his hands as he was shaking with excitement. To become a famous physicist was his dream. Bao Bao's eyes shone when he saw the photo in the newspaper. He leaned closer and peered at the photo of the two scientists shaking hands with another man. His pupils dilated with his growing enthusiasm. "To be awarded the Nobel Prize is my dream too! By the time I am thirty years old, I will be awarded the prize as well! But I shall not receive the Nobel Prize as a US Citizen, since America is not a peace-loving country. I will keep the entire prize to myself, instead of sharing it with other scientists. I shall prove to the world that fifteen years of struggle has been worthwhile.

Across Bao Bao's left shoulder hung a dark green schoolbag that he had purchased from a thrift store. Although secondhand, it was of excellent quality. The bag was produced by "the enemy" – the US imperialists, for their very own soldiers. In order to support Chiang Kai Shek's [7] efforts against the Chinese Communists, the bag was shipped alongside weapons and ammunition as army supplies to China. Sprawled across the insides of the bag – in a miniscule font, read the three forbidden words, "MADE IN USA."

Though simple and terse, these three words brought immense stress into Bao Bao's life. He was annoyed, "How could such a fine creation be tarnished by these three little words?" After much thought, Bao Bao decided to smear black ink all over the label until he had covered up every single letter.

The thought of winning the Nobel Prize invigorated him so much that no longer felt tired from his sleepless night, spent in writing Da Zi Baos. Now he felt as though he was already a prize-winner. The youngster began to daydream. No longer will I have to walk through the boring streets! My chauffeur will drive and escort me to wherever I wish to go in my shiny black sedan. Bao Bao's eyes gleamed with exhilaration. From time to time, I will receive invitations from the Chinese government. Prime Minister Zhou En Lai will ask to dine with me. He will tap my shoulders and say, "Good job, you have shown the world the brilliance of the Chinese race!" The Prime Minister and his fellow officials will raise their glasses of Maotai[8] in a toast to me, as if I were a dear old friend. I will have the honour of sitting next to Chairman Mao who will praise and flatter me because I am a world renowned scientist. With Chairman Mao, we will sip Longjing[9] tea while he smokes.

Bao Bao's light skipping came to a halt when he arrived at the school gate; he glanced up at the gate which was dwarfed by the two cement columns that stood on either end. On top of each column, there rested a large sculpture of a worker, a farmer and a soldier carrying the Communist flags while running forwards in unison. This served to illustrate a rapidly developing China. Seeing the deserted playground, Bao Bao noticed that he was late. Bao Bao sprinted across the playground and leapt up the cement staircase to the correct floor. He stuck his head into Classroom 12. "Phew! The teacher isn't here yet," he thought as he hurried over to his seat. He plonked himself down on his wooden seat, quickly tucked his shoulder-bag underneath his chair, and waited patiently.

As soon as Teacher Ma entered the room, the students fell silent. All students stood up in unison and immediately sat down together at once – this was the new way of greeting without having to say "good morning" or "good afternoon". In the new era, all forms of greeting were curtailed to a minimum, as salutations were considered to be excessive in the old bourgeois society. Teacher Ma managed to retain his usual composure, though his eyes were dark and puffy from the night before. Similar to any other day and to the millions of Chinese, he wore his usual blue cotton uniform. He greeted the class with a tight smile and proceeded to lecture the class on the most widely accepted topic of the time – the topic of Dr Norman Bethune.

Dr Norman Bethune was a famous Canadian surgeon. He moved to China in 1938 and joined the Chinese Communist Party. As a surgeon of China's Eighth Route Army, – the Ba Lu Jun[10] – the main army of the Communist Party of China, he saved countless Communist soldiers' lives in the battlefields. He died in 1939 due to blood-poisoning from a cut that he picked up while performing surgery on a Communist soldier.

Not again! Bao Bao thought. This must be the one hundred and tenth time I am listening to the story of Dr Norman Bethune! Bao Bao could not help but glance up at the ceiling and begin to daydream. He wondered why the same story was repeated over and over again. He later found out that the repetition was deliberate – a technique applied so that the material would penetrate the heads of the young students. Possibly Chairman Mao was well aware of the inherent selfishness of human beings and wanted to implant selflessness into all Chinese minds. Thus, Norman Bethune was chosen as an exemplary citizen for millions of Chinese. As Mao said, "The death of a man can weigh as heavy as Mountain Tai,[11] or as light as a feather. It all depends on his contribution to the country." Although Dr Bethune had lived for only eighteen months in China, he was already an unforgettable hero in the hearts of seven hundred million Chinese.

Bao Bao could not help but compare Dr Norman Bethune to the winners of the Nobel Prize in today's newspaper. The former led a harsh life, but was worshipped by millions of Chinese after his death, whereas the latter had found instant fame and glory. But Bao Bao realized that the two could not be compared; after all, Dr Bethune's legacy and the Nobel Prize are two distinct honours. Earlier in the morning, Bao Bao had settled for the Nobel Prize as his lifelong goal; but following Teacher Ma's lesson, Bao Bao now had another icon from which to choose.

Subsequent to Teacher Ma's lecture followed the usual class discussion. Only through class discussions could Teacher Ma discover each student's opinion regarding Norman Bethune. In Bao Bao's opinion, the easiest way to get through this type of a discussion was to repeat more or less what Teacher Ma had said before. So Bao Bao continued on with idolizing Dr Bethune, so that he could get out of class discussion with flying colours. He, however, remained silent about his discovery in the newspaper earlier that day.

Teacher Ma seemed quite content with the class discussion and asked if anyone had any questions. Li Yong raised his hand quickly and asked, "What was Dr Bethune's 'si sheng huo' – his private life – like?"

As soon as the words, "si sheng huo", spilled out of Li Yong's mouth, over a dozen pairs of eyes darted across the room towards him. Bao Bao was annoyed, "Why does dear Li Yong ask such a question? Li Yong should know that 'si sheng huo' does not exist in our society nowadays, as it belongs to a capitalist society. Doesn't Yong know our society well enough? Is he doing this just to show his enthusiasm in Ma's class? His approach is wrong!"

Teacher Ma threw Li Yong a displeased look upon hearing his question. Seeing Teacher Ma's bewildered expression, Bao Bao quickly found a way to help his friend Li by saying, "Li Yong meant: 'Was Dr Bethune's wife also so great that she accompanied her husband to China?'"

Teacher Ma frowned at Bao Bao's paraphrase of Li Yong's question and squinted through his thick glasses as though deep in thought and said, "No, his wife left him less than two years after they got married. His wife did not share the same vision. Dr Bethune, as a famous surgeon, could have had as many beautiful women as he wanted, but he chose none. Dr Bethune could have afforded a luxurious life, a house full of servants, delicious food, fashionable clothing – which is the goal of every person in capitalist society. But instead, Dr Bethune dedicated his life to revolutionizing the world. Isn't that something? Isn't that unique, isn't that great?" Teacher Ma pressed his ideas home.

"Ding Dong!" The bell sounded right after Teacher Ma's passionate speech. Bao Bao hastily stuffed his books into his shoulder-bag as Teacher Ma called out in the front of the room, "Don't forget to read Chairman Mao's essay entitled, 'In memory of Norman Bethune' on page 57 of your textbook!"

After class, Bao Bao's mind was like a ping-pong ball in the midst of a match – bouncing back and forth from one side to the other. No matter how hard he tried, hundreds of images of his winning the Nobel Prize competed against hundreds of loud orders from Chairman Mao commanding him to commit his life to his Motherland like Dr Bethune.

By the end of the school day, Bao Bao felt ashamed of himself for seeking personal glory. Now, he began to admire Dr Bethune for his selflessness and lack of interest in fame. He thought back to Chairman Mao's valuation of Dr Bethune, "A man who was above low interests." Finally, the spirit of Dr Bethune outweighed, for Bao Bao, the fame and glory of the Nobel Prize winner.

Earlier during class discussion, Bao Bao had proclaimed Bethune to be his hero, though he did not mean it. He had said this merely to please the Party and Teacher Ma, as numerous political campaigns had taught him to suppress his personal opinion and simply to repeat what the Party had said. The Party only wanted echoes and allowed no opposing opinion. Bao Bao was not the only one who had learnt to fall in with what the Party wanted. Most Chinese had acquired the skill in order to survive under the new regime for the past decade. After Bao Bao's internal debate during the day, Chairman Mao had won. Now Dr Bethune had replaced the Nobel Prize in Bao Bao's mind.

CHAPTER THREE

# THE PARK

Bao Bao and his younger sister, Yuan Yuan, lived with their Uncle, Auntie and their cousin, Lin Lin. But where were their parents?

Up to two and half years after the Communists took over China in 1949, the Chinese border to Hong Kong, then a British Colony, remained open. Bao Bao's father suffered from a business failure in Shanghai and was forced to leave for Hong Kong in 1950. At that time he carried very little money with him, just about twenty US dollars in total to the strange city.

A few years later, Bao Bao's father made a small fortune and bought two flats in the Hongham area of Hong Kong. His father then wanted Bao Bao and his whole family to join him immediately in Hong Kong. Bao Bao wondered how his father had managed to make a fortune in a foreign place. Unfortunately, he had never had the opportunity to ask his father, face to face.

In 1952, about two years after his father left Shanghai, the border to Hong Kong was suddenly closed. Anyone who intended to travel to Hong Kong needed to obtain an exit visa from the Gong An Ju – the Public Security Bureau, or PSB – and an entry visa from the British authorities.

To obtain an exit permit from the Gong An Ju in China was no easy task, because nearly all applications were turned down. Even Bao Bao's Ma Ma, his father's lawful wedded wife, had great difficulty getting an exit visa permit to join her husband in Hong Kong. Bao Bao's father, who suffered from failing health in 1955, wrote to his wife every day, urging her to put pressure on the Public Service Bureau by visiting them daily. However, despite her best efforts, the answer from the PSB was always the same. – Time after time the PSB replied, "No"; a deep and resounding, "No".

The frequent visits lasted about two years until Bao Bao's Ma Ma finally met a sympathetic officer who gave her the honest advice that she would never be granted a visa for the whole family. As the new regime was very short of hard, foreign currency, she should leave one or two children in China so that the remittance from abroad could continue. She would then have a better chance of leaving China. The very next day she went to the PSB again and this time she demanded to see the head in person. After a long wait, she finally talked to the head and made a deal with him that she would leave her fifteen-year-old son, Bao Bao, and her thirteen-year-old daughter, Yuan Yuan, in Shanghai as "collateral", and would be granted an exit visa for six months to visit her sick husband, and to take with her their two younger sons of five and seven years old.

Immediately after returning home she wrote this to her relatives:

*Dearest Ying Ying and Song Ping,*

*According to your promise, should I leave Shanghai, you would come over to look after Bao Bao and Yuan Yuan. Today I have finally received my exit visa for Hong Kong. Please come to Shanghai immediately and move into my apartment to take good care of my children as they are still young.*

*You may take the living-room facing the street and convert it into your bedroom while Bao Bao and Yuan Yuan will sleep in the bedroom facing the interior courtyard. I am sure your daughter, Lin Lin, will find a good school. The education in a cosmopolitan city such as Shanghai is better than in Fuzhou.*

*Your affectionate Sister-in-law,*
*Da Sao*

As soon as Bao Bao's and Yuan Yuan's Ma Ma finished writing to her brother and sister-in-law she started to pack for Hong Kong frantically – throwing all necessary items into her suitcases. She packed all her clothing into three big suitcases as if she had no intention of returning soon. Bao Bao stood at the doorway, hands behind his back, as he watched his Ma Ma throw one item after another into her open bags. She was ecstatic to have received an exit visa. Although she promised Bao Bao that she would return quickly, he was sceptical about this.

Ma Ma will never come home, he thought. Even though I am only fifteen and Yuan Yuan is only thirteen, she thinks that we are old enough to take care of ourselves. And now that Yuan Yuan and I are offered as "hostages", we may have to remain in China for decades to come. We will never be able to leave China! Hmm...But, on a brighter note, as long as our parents are living outside China, there is still a glimmer of hope that one day – just maybe – one day, we will be able to join them abroad! Despite the many thoughts running through Bao Bao's head, the young boy still secretly wished that his Ma Ma would soon return. He hoped that life could be like the good old days once again.

In the meantime, their Ma Ma gave Bao Bao and Yuan Yuan some important advice. "I shall send you money every month and write to you regularly. I expect to receive only short letters from you and Yuan Yuan twice a month. You may write anything concerning your daily life, but nothing about the government, as the police will monitor our correspondence. I don't want either of you getting into any trouble!"

A few days after Ma Ma's departure, Uncle and Auntie arrived in Shanghai from Fuzhou by long distance train. They had brought with them several suitcases, since they were relocating to the big city. Auntie was astonished to see the enormous number of tall buildings in Shanghai – it looked completely different from the small city that she had grown up in. She was impressed by the wide roads and the high apartment complexes – everything seemed to be so compact and congested at the same time. But living quarters were packed closely next to one another and a sense of gloom hung over the big city. Despite its architectural splendour, the city appeared barren. The skies were grey and there were no children to be found running in the streets or farm animals roaming about.

It was not long before Auntie and Uncle finally arrived at Bao Bao's father's apartment in Huai Hai Road. Auntie glanced up at the building. "This is one of the busiest places I've ever lived in," she thought as they began to walk up the stairs.

Uncle Song guessed that his brother-in-law must have purchased the apartment with a great many gold bars, although the unit was not the best in the complex, Auntie took a deep breath as her eyes darted up the lengthy staircase. She gripped the handrail firmly as she began to make her way up the steps.

As she laboured up the staircase, Auntie Ying studied the apartment complex curiously. "This building was put up in the thirties, well-built with cement and steel. The staircase is made of something very hard, almost crystalline." She glanced back at her husband and asked, "What is it made of, Song Ping?" Uncle stooped down, brushed his middle finger across the step and felt the cold floor. "Ai! Lots of dust! This place hasn't been cleaned in years! But it's made of marble. Can you imagine? It must have cost a fortune!" he exclaimed.

"Why," said Auntie Ying, "It's beautiful! Look! If you wipe off all the dust, you can see white with streaks of beige and pink!"

"So he did do it!" Uncle exclaimed. "Brother did make his fortune and purchase a house with marble floors, as he described in his letter!"

They continued up the stairs as Auntie kept on examining the condo. Towards the landing on the top of the stairs, a faint glimpse of light showed through a dusty window above. Holding the windows together were thin, brownish-red coloured frames that were rusting away overhead. "My goodness, if only someone had cleaned this place!" exclaimed Auntie.

For the past decade, people had hardly ever discussed the idea of maintenance. Everyone had been preoccupied with political campaign after political campaign. Rarely did the thought of maintenance enter people's minds. Bao Bao's apartment occupied about one hundred and ten square metres. Past a thick wooden door, a corridor led to the living-room, kitchen and bathroom. There was a bedroom at the other end of the corridor, with walls papered with a once-intricate pattern of intertwining gold and red flowers. The paper had peeled because of the intense heat and humidity present throughout the spring and early summer in Shanghai.

In the darkly-lit living-room, a number of handsome looking pieces of furniture were scattered randomly about. Upon careful inspection, it became clear that the dining and other tables had all been hand-crafted from expensive rosewood. Neither the furniture nor the wooden floor had, however, been polished with wax for many years. In the bedroom, the left corner of the dressing-table mirror was slightly damaged. The black bed-post

35

been treated as blackboards by Bao Bao, who had written mathematical formulae on them in white chalk.

The curtain was no longer in its original place. Someone had taken it down and deployed it as a bedcover. Cotton material had become very precious and was rationed. Each man was entitled to only one shirt or one pair of trousers each year.

With no vacuum cleaner for domestic use, all the carpets were filthy with the accumulation of decades of dust and dirt. Later, Bao Bao discovered that Uncle had cut the carpet into several smaller pieces, washed and dried them, and spread them out as mattresses for the night.

The chandelier, which consisted of six lampshades, had only one complete lampshade left and the remaining five were damaged: Three shades had been broken and two were missing light-bulbs. To find replacements for such luxurious lampshades and their special light-bulbs had become an impossible task in the new era. The government's first and second Five-Year Plans[12] focused only on "heavy industry", and left no room for "light industry", such as textiles, home appliances and furniture. Items such as lampshades and special light-bulbs were no longer produced, as they represented a bourgeois lifestyle. Thus, the apartment of one hundred and ten square metres was lit by only a few 25-volt light-bulbs, as opposed to the minimum of 240 volts needed for one single chandelier. The whole apartment was gloomy. In fact, the whole city of Shanghai was gloomy.

Soon Uncle and Auntie had settled in. As instructed by the children's Ma Ma, they slept in the living-room, while Bao Bao and Yuan Yuan shared the queen-size bed in the bedroom facing the courtyard. Being on the first floor the former was an extremely noisy room because pedestrians, buses, cars, and trams passed by from early morning to late in the night, while the latter was an absolutely quiet room. For Uncle and Auntie, it was hard to adjust to the hustle and bustle of city life. For the entire first month they had difficulty sleeping. They had to stuff cotton balls into their ears to block out the noise. However, Lin Lin adapted quickly and soon slept well in the noisy room.

It had taken a couple of months for Uncle Song Ping to complete his transfer to Wu Ai Middle and High School in Shanghai. Relocating from the countryside to a city was not allowed, but due to the need for an English teacher, coupled with being guardian for Bao Bao and Yuan Yuan, the authorities made an exception and granted Uncle temporary permission to teach in Shanghai.

Bao Bao was approaching fifteen and his sister thirteen. They both occupied the old queen-sized bed in the quiet bedroom facing the courtyard. One day, Yuan Yuan told Auntie that Bao Bao sometimes exercised in bed at night, moving his body in a rhythmical beat for frequent "military drills", so that he could one day shoot down the American spy-plane which invaded Chinese air territories frequently during the night these days.

"How is it possible?" Auntie asked curiously.

"Bao Bao told me", Yuan Yuan whispered, "Below his abdomen, in his groin area, he is in possession of a cannon, which he exercises from time to time with his hand in a rhythmical movement in order to gun down an American or Chiang Kai Shek spy-plane. Even though he is only fifteen, he will be glorified as a national hero!"

Auntie's jaw dropped in shock and her pale cheeks turned scarlet red as she could not believe her ears. As soon as Uncle returned, she shared this embarrassing story about Bao Bao with her husband. Together, they decided that the children were growing up and that they should no longer sleep in the same bed. That same evening, a folding bed was quietly placed in the bedroom and Yuan Yuan was moved away from the queen-sized bed, though Bao Bao never found out why.

The following morning, Bao Bao went to school as usual. Today, there was no special news at the kiosk. Only a few pedestrians were there buying their daily newspapers. When Bao Bao was about to make a turn at Huai Hai Road, he saw Li Yong, his best friend, walking across the street.

"Li Yong!" Bao Bao shouted.

As soon as Li Yong heard him, he ran over to join Bao Bao so they could walk to school together.

Bao Bao was glad to see Li Yong as he could not find him yesterday after Teacher Ma's class. "Li Yong!" enquired Bao Bao, "Why did you ask such a silly question during our political lesson yesterday?" "Aren't you aware," he continued, "That there was no 'private life' for Dr Bethune,as he devoted all his time and energy to saving Chinese Communist soldiers' lives? Don't you know that there is no private life but only collective life in our new society? The question you asked branded you as a backward element. You certainly don't want to remind them of your weak family background and your father."

Li nodded in agreement and said: 'Thanks, Bao Bao. Thank you for helping me out yesterday, in class. I promise to pay good attention to what I say in future."

Though Li Yong grew up under the red flag, his family background was disastrous. Five years ago, Li's father Li Kang Ming was sentenced to fifteen years' reform through labour and sent to gaol in Qinghai province in northwestern China. After the arrest of Li's father, life for Li Yong and his Ma Ma became unbearable overnight. Since they were now a tainted counter-revolutionary family, all their friends and relatives avoided them. Neighbors and acquaintances looked down upon them and pretended not to know them when they met in the street. When it came to voluntary work organized by the neighbourhood committee, or by school authorities, Li and his Ma Ma were often assigned the dirtiest and filthiest work, such as sweeping the dirty streets on a frigid winter's morning and mopping the stinking toilets. Above all, it was highly unlikely that Li would ever be admitted to a university.

In Bao Bao's opinion, Li Yong should be grateful that he could still remain in a big city like Shanghai and that their famous high school did not expel him. Li should keep his mouth shut at all times. If he expressed the slightest dissatisfaction against the new regime, disaster would fall upon him and his Ma Ma. At all times, Li should reiterate his gratitude towards the Party, even in his dreams. The Party would like to invent a 'thought detector' to find out what Li Yong really thought of the new society deep down in his heart. But since such a machine was unavailable, the regime created a terrifying environment in which everyone spied on him. Li knew anyone could denounce him and, if they did, the authorities could arrest him. In fact, the authorities preferred to eliminate all suspicious elements in society, so that the new regime would have fewer enemies.

Living as second-class citizens, Li and his Ma Ma had no right to complain. In accordance with Chinese tradition, a family member had to share all living experiences with his family, be it fortune or misery. For thousands of years, Chinese mandarins put their family members in important positions and it was well-accepted by society because nepotism was part of the fabric of Chinese culture. Familial ties were so extreme that if an emperor were to execute a high ranking official, his entire lineage would have to die with him in order to avoid possible revenge by a family member of the beheaded person.

On the other hand, had Li denounced his father, his social status would have been elevated instantly. The Party would have praised him for his heroic act and guaranteed him a bright future. He would immediately have been invited to join the Communist Youth League and membership of the Communist Party would have been extended to him as soon as he reached adulthood. He would not have to live under such terrible discrimination. Instead he would lead a good life for having proved to the Party that he considered the Party was above all and much more important than his own father. Now he had missed this unique opportunity. But Li had not the slightest regret.

As soon as the two youngsters approached the school gate, Li winked at Bao Bao and they went into school separately. Bao Bao was glad that he was not seen beside Li. Otherwise people would postulate that Li was contaminating Bao Bao. Bao Bao regretted that Li had to live under such discrimination. The Party's propaganda proclaimed New China to be a classless society where everyone enjoyed equal rights under the red flag. "But how come Li isn't treated equally, along with everyone else? Surely Li is as good as others are!" Bao Bao thought. He wished that family background did not play such a significant role in people's lives. His friend Li had little control over his fate; little say as to whether his father was a Communist hero or a Counter-revolutionary whom the Party condemned.

From time to time Bao Bao and Li Yong would sneak into the park to observe lovers in the darkness. This evening they met at the gate of Huangpu Park at seven o'clock when it became dark. Due to the electricity-saving measures prevailing in Shanghai, the lights in the streets as well as in the park were very dim. If it were summer, the park would have been packed with people. However, on a cool evening like today, only a handful of people were in the park. The darkness coupled with the emptiness of the park had transformed the venue into a paradise for lovers.

As much as love and sex in public were condemned and deemed immoral by the new society, Bao Bao found it difficult to withhold his curiosity. Even in a big city such as Shanghai, with millions of inhabitants, one was unlikely to spot a pair of lovers kissing in public. For lovers there was no café, no bar, no nightclub. If a pair of lovers asked for a room at a hotel reception desk they would be rejected unless they produced a marriage certificate; for love and sex were regarded as exclusive to married couples. Therefore unmarried lovers had no choice but to convene in the darkness – underneath trees, inside bushes and shrubs in parks. This was of course very inconvenient, but to whom could the lovers complain? No-one dared to bring this issue to the attention of the authorities.

Bao Bao and Li Yong shared much amusement and laughter whenever they frightened couples with an unexpected flashlight, before running away as quickly as their legs could carry them. They thought it was fun to scare couples kissing or embracing each other in the darkness.

Now again the two youngsters groped around in the darkness for this purpose. Bao Bao and Li Yong were careful not to make a sound, not to give any hint of their presence. They crept along behind a two metre high hedge. Through the hedge they could see bare ground, and on the other side of the ground stood a three metre high wall, separating the park from the city.

Li placed his ear close to Bao Bao's. Suddenly, they heard a female groaning. Her voice came from the ground between the hedge and the wall. The moan sounded as if the woman was suffering! Li looked at Bao Bao and grinned wildly. They had found a couple! Quickly, the two boys crawled through the hedge, their hearts pounding as they were about to discover what was happening.

They continued squirming their way through the bushes, towards the noise, to try to spot the culprits. Finally, they reached the place where the groaning was at its loudest. Bao Bao jumped to his feet, whipping out a torch from his lower pocket, as blood raced through his body. He leaned back against the hedge and switched on the torch.

A flash of bright light engulfed the area, enabling Bao Bao to catch a glimpse of a woman lying underneath a man. Alarmed by the sudden flash of light, the man jumped up. Bao Bao could not believe his eyes: the woman was lying on the ground naked! From head to toe, she was lying there, completely exposed. Each of her breasts was bigger than a Da Tang Wan - Big Soup Bowl . This monstrous sight Bao Bao had seen only once before in a painting and he had found it too ghastly to be true.

Bao Bao looked to his right and to his left for Li, but heard his friend scurrying away from the scene. What with Li running away and the angry man getting up, Bao Bao was forced to give up his desire to give the naked female body a second and more intense look. He reluctantly switched off his torch and began to chase after Li.

After running non-stop for about fifty metres, they slowed down. "Well," laughed Bao Bao, "We don't need to run so quickly, because the man can't chase after us. Not without his trousers and underwear on!"

"For goodness' sake! I think we saw too much tonight! It really was too much. I didn't expect to see such an awful scene. It was disgusting!" cried Li.

Bao Bao agreed with what Li had said. "It was far, far, beyond our imagination. I never expected to see such a scene! It was really disgusting," he added. But, Bao Bao went on, "What were they doing on a cool autumn night with their naked bodies next to each other? Could this be what is called, 'sexual intercourse'?"

"I have no idea," sighed Li. Obviously he was not interested in continuing this conversation, walking faster than Bao Bao.

Under the dark night sky, they continued to walk silently home. I still regret not having taken a better look at the naked woman, Bao Bao thought to himself. But what could I do? I didn't want to be beaten by the man after he leapt up! I had to run.

When Bao Bao returned home, it was half past nine and the family was asleep. Nowadays, people slept early and woke up early in order to save electricity for the government. The last movie show at the cinema house ended at nine o'clock in the evening. After the last movie, the whole city went to sleep. Bao

41

Bao entered the apartment quietly. He was careful not to wake anybody up. Normally he would have been asleep at this hour, as he had to get up at six for school. But tonight was a special night, because the sight of the real, naked female body, encountered for the first time in his life, had excited him and made him restless. Curiosity in the female sex overwhelmed his mind.

"Why do women have big breasts? What for? Only for feeding babies? But not all babies are breast-fed. What were the naked man and woman doing on the cold ground behind the hedge? Could this have something to do with the forbidden topic? Everything relating to the word 'sex' is forbidden to be discussed in public. If it is not considered a sin, it certainly is known as ugly and dirty. In our society, only married couples are allowed to have 'sex', even though they don't utter the word 'sex' openly. Instead they use other words to indicate 'having sex', such as 'fang shi' which means 'matters of bedroom'. Does it have something to do with where a child comes from?" Bao Bao's head was bombarded with hundreds of questions.

When Bao Bao was younger, he was told that a baby came from an egg. "But how can a human baby evolve from a tiny egg?" Bao Bao thought, as he could not imagine what an egg-sized baby would look like.

When the woman moaned and screamed in the bushes, was she in pain? Bao Bao wondered, as he tossed and turned in bed. He regretted that under the torchlight he was unable to see the female's lower abdomen. He wondered what female genitals looked like. Growing up, he had often seen pregnant women with swollen bellies and he had been told that a baby was growing inside them. But why did the grown-ups lie to me about babies and their affiliation with eggs? Does the swollen belly have something to do with a man and a woman? Can an unmarried young girl be pregnant? he thought wildly.

Impossible! A girl cannot be pregnant when she is not married. At least I have never heard of it, Bao Bao thought. To whom can I ask such questions? Auntie? Uncle? Teachers? Or our neighbours? But the answer he gave himself was negative. No, they will never give me an answer. They will all avoid answering such questions or brush me off and say that these are "adult matters". Yes. They will tell me that, at my age, my focus should be to study hard. If I ask these questions more than once or twice, the adults will think that something is wrong with me. Perhaps they will suggest that I need to clean my brain to get the dirt out! But his questions continued. How have I profited from the park scene tonight? Why did I go there?

Bao Bao was becoming annoyed with the insomnia that he was suffering from. Tomorrow is a big day for my school. All pupils in Shanghai are to demonstrate on the streets in the afternoon to protest against American spy-planes invading our air-space, Bao Bao thought with his eyes half closed. I regret going to the park, I hate myself. I shall tell Li Yong, "No more parks in the future!" I, Song Bao Bao, am a good Youth Pioneer.[13] And now I am a good candidate for the Communist Youth League and...and a good student of Chairman Mao. I will wait until I am old – much older – to consider marriage...and to know "fang shi" – matters of the bedroom – it is then that all related doubts will be cleared away. This is how Bao Bao reassured himself as he dozed off to sleep.

It wasn't long until the first cock crowed at the crack of dawn. Bao Bao ignored the cry and continued sleeping. Finally Auntie came in, "Bao Bao! Hurry, it is time to get up!" Bao Bao let out a loud grumbling, "Coming". He continued to sleep until his auntie came in for a second time to shake him. Bao Bao lay in bed, thinking about whether or not to lie to his auntie by telling her that he was sick. But this morning's class discussion and afternoon's demonstration were too important to be excused from. If Bao Bao did not show up, it would be detrimental for his image as a politically advanced student. The Party and Chairman Mao entrust in our hands the future of our Motherland, Bao Bao thought, as he touched his forehead with his palm to feel if he had a fever. No, his forehead was cool. "I am not really sick. Now I have no excuse, but to get out of bed. I have no-one to blame but myself for not having slept enough last night!"

Finally and reluctantly Bao Bao slipped off his mattress. While throwing on his clothes, he reminded himself, "Now, now! It is a privilege to attend school. School is something that only pupils in Chairman Mao's New China can enjoy! Poor children in America, Africa, the Middle East, India and the rest of Asia can only dream of going to school. The doors are closed to them!"

Bao Bao's ambition was to attend university – a famous university – and in time become a Nobel Prize-winning scientist. With this thought in mind and feeling less tired, he walked into the kitchen for breakfast.

As usual, Bao Bao ate his breakfast in a hurry. Today, he swallowed his congee and gulfed down his mantou – white Chinese steamed bread made of wheat – as quickly as he could. He glanced over at Auntie, who was busy washing dishes. He examined her from her shoulders down and then focused on her chest. Are her breasts bigger than a Da Tang Wan - Big Soup Bowl ? Bao Bao wondered, as he recalled the bras that Auntie hung on the balcony to dry from time to time. Did the woman at the park have bigger breasts than my Auntie? Auntie's breast size is difficult to discern through her bra, underwear, shirt and sweater. Why have I never paid attention to Auntie's breasts before?

"Bao Bao! What are you doing? Hurry up and go now or you'll be late!" said Auntie. Obediently, Bao Bao grabbed his schoolbag, swung it over his shoulder and rushed out of the door.

CHAPTER FOUR

# EVILS OF AMERICAN IMPERIALISM

The morning class began with Yin Yin, Bao Bao's classmate, delivering her findings from the American News Agency regarding a speech given by Richard Nixon at the Detroit Economic Club. Yin Yin said, "According to US Vice President Nixon, the American economy achieved the world's best living standard as the result of its high GDP..." Her voice trailed off as she gathered herself together and shouted, "But that is a lie!" Bao Bao complained silently to himself. "Why do our lessons always feel like drama classes?"

Teacher Fang, a mother of three children and in her late forties, reacted with delight and clapped her hands together. Although short, Teacher Fang had a chubby body and a broad face. Her bouncy personality was matched by straight cut hair cropped to her chin; whenever she turned to look at her students or the blackboard, her bob would bounce up and down.

She looked at her student Yin Yin eagerly, "And why? Where is your proof?"

Yin Yin smiled proudly at her teacher and said, "There were five million unemployed and an additional four million so-called mobile workers whose employment fluctuated on a daily basis. This means they were only employed for the day. The next day, they would have to line up at the manpower office to try their luck. The unemployment figures have soared fifty percent from last year."

Teacher Fang nodded at Yin Yin and said, "Excellent! Now can someone describe to me the life of an unemployed person?"

Dan Dan raised her hand quickly and said, "An emaciated and unemployed woman told a journalist that her husband had been jobless for three years and that she had survived on nothing but potatoes and beans. For three years, she had not consumed any meat. Today, she has nothing to eat except the same beans and potatoes".

"Bravo! Bravo!" Bao Bao wanted to exclaim, but he refrained from making any noise as this was a serious political lesson on a sensitive subject, so he decided to keep his mouth shut. Instead, Bao Bao's hand shot up as he leapt to his feet and addressed his classmates, "In comparison with America, life is much better in China! After all, in China, every family is entitled to a ration of one catty (about 500 grams) of pork every month!" Bao Bao smiled broadly at his classmates, feeling very proud of himself as he sat down.

In his seat, Bao Bao shuffled his papers until he found a blank sheet. He wrote a few words to praise Dan Dan's wonderful statement on a piece of paper and folded it into a paper aeroplane. He waited patiently for Teacher Fang to turn her face towards the blackboard. He stood up and leaned forward to throw the paper aeroplane onto Dan Dan's desk, where she sat two rows in front of him.

Bao Bao's fun came to a stop as he turned his attention back to the class discussion. Yin Yin was complaining that she had not finished her statement, so Teacher Fang nodded to let her continue, "Senator JF Kennedy from the Democratic Party said in spite of food overproduction, there are more than 1.7 million Americans going to bed with an empty stomach. In 1958, agricultural overproduction increased to nearly three times that of 1953. Instead of distributing food to the hungry workers, the overproduced food has been dumped into the ocean so that the price of grain can remain stable."

Before Yin Yin had finished, another classmate, Xiao Lan, interrupted, "Over fifteen million Americans today live in slums. In a tiny basement, three double-beds are placed adjacent to each another. One cannot breathe properly due to the lack of windows and any other form of ventilation. When it rains, water seeps through the walls. Six families share a small bathroom. Everything is covered in dirt and filth. Rats run all over the place. Can you imagine it? Not long ago, a baby was attacked by rats and died!"

During Xiao Lan's vivid description, Bao Bao remembered another ghastly story from the newspapers and could hardly contain his disgust as he thought about it. – He had read a woman's confession that it had been ten years since she had taken a bath and her baby has not been washed for an entire year! He had also read that the smell of heroin, mixed with decaying wooden furniture, rubbish and the rotting smell of human bodies made living in the slums unbearable. – But Bao Bao also thought about conditions at home. We do have many people in Shanghai living in poor conditions, he considered, but such destitution as in America is unimaginable.

Mei Ling raised her hand to interrupt Xiao Lan, even though the student had not finished his gruesome description of the slums. Teacher Fang was delighted with her students' enthusiasm and agreed to let Mei Ling proceed, but suddenly she changed her mind. Teacher Fang pointed her index finger at Li Yong and asked him to talk about the poverty in American slums.

There was no response from Li Yong for thirty seconds. The entire classroom fell silent. Bao Bao turned his head backwards to look at his friend. In fact all eyes were gazing at Li, whose face and neck reddened. Apparently, Li was caught unprepared for this discussion. Teacher Fang's sweet smile disappeared from her face as she asked Li Yong to stand up and step forwards toward the front of the classroom.

Teacher Fang interrogated him, "Why didn't you do any research for today's discussion?"

Li Yong hesitated for a while and murmured, "My friend asked me to go out last night."

Bao Bao became nervous and hoped that Li Yong would not mention last night's visit to the park as he was involved.

"Why did you go out last night? It was not a Saturday and you should have your lesson prepared for days in advance! You know that today's political lesson is a continuation of last week's class discussion of 'the evils of American Capitalism and Imperialism', in line with the Party's current anti-American Campaign. Last week I gave your class an assignment to gather information from newspapers, magazines, books and radio broadcasts on the said topic and then share your research results in class with your peers this morning. If you continue to show no interest in class and refuse to do your homework, I will have to pay your Ma Ma a visit at home. Now your punishment is to stand in the corner on my left until the end of class."

Li Yong was very embarrassed and lowered his head to look down at the floor. There was nowhere he could turn to hide his blushes. Bao Bao wished that he could help him, but there was nothing he could do now. My friend Li, he thought, you could have easily said something as this topic is so open. Are you crazy this morning? What's the matter with you? Bao Bao was annoyed and he regretted that he had asked Li to go to the park last night.

Now Bao Bao felt uneasy and nervous, "What should I say? I'm also not prepared for today's discussion!" Bao Bao had done no preparation for today's topic, as he believed it to be a waste of time to research the evils of America, as any three-year-old child in China could tell you that 'America is bad'. Therefore, now he had to listen attentively to what his peers said and paraphrase a suitable version for his use. Bao Bao had already spoken as part of his share for the class, so Teacher Fang paid no specific attention to him. "But I must say more!" Bao Bao urged himself.

Mei Ling continued, "More than sixteen million American citizens are well over sixty-five and are living in poverty. Although they all receive a pension, inflation is slowly eating away their pension income. So everywhere in America, you will find the elderly complaining about their poor living standard. The situation is exacerbated when a senior citizen falls ill because they have no medical insurance. It is often said that a family becomes broke when someone in the family falls sick."

Mei Ling went on, "The life of retired professors is not much better. Some of them eat only once a day and others are employed as night watchmen. Among these professors are some famous writers and scientists. They despair of their future and fear falling ill one day. When President Eisenhower was asked about the security of American citizens, he replied: 'When Americans are only after security, they find gaol to be the best place to live. There, one gets enough to eat and a bed plus a roof over his head'. In China, one can sum up America in one short sentence, "America is a paradise for children, a battle ground for adults and a cemetery for old citizens".

Suddenly Wang Ming raised his right hand and interrupted, "As to what you just said about President Eisenhower, allow me to add a few words." Teacher Fang nodded, so Wang Ming continued, "I have read in a journal that President Eisenhower himself, in sharp contrast to the man on the street in America, enjoys an extraordinarily luxurious life. His salary plus his bonus amount to two million US dollars a year Additionally, taken together, the high cost of maintenance of the White House and the salaries of his personal staff exceed two million dollars." Teacher Fang interrupted, "How can the cost of maintenance of the White House amount to two million dollars? I can't believe it. This is an unbelievably huge sum of money for maintenance. Can you give us some explanation?"

"The garden of the White House is eighteen hectares and the gardening team consists of seventy-two skillful gardeners, plus an additional maintenance team of thirty-two, including mechanics, electricians, carpenters, painters and cleaning ladies. The White House also has a private swimming pool, a private golf course, a library and a private cinema that screens the latest films exclusively for the President and his family members! His means of transportation consist of the most modern ships and the biggest aircraft, Air Force Number One and hundreds of bodyguards! The air force fleet accompanies his aeroplane whenever he travels!" Wang Ming had hardly finished when Zhou interrupted, "President Eisenhower is only an official, but the genuine bosses in the US are the monopolistic capitalists who spend money in monumental amounts. Henry Ford, owner of Ford Enterprises, sometimes spends a quarter of a million dollars on hosting a party! Thus, in a capitalist society, one lives either in heaven or in hell."

Bao Bao raised his hand and Teacher Fang looked at him and smiled. She was proud to see her students expressing their hatred towards the United States and no time being wasted. This proved that her pedagogical method was successful. Bao Bao mentioned that senior citizens in China were much better off than their counterparts in the United States: firstly, they could retire early, males at sixty and females at fifty-five and receive 80% of their last salary as pension. There was nearly no inflation in China so that even those who lived as long as eighty, or ninety years on pension need not worry about money. Secondly, when they retired, Chinese workers were rarely worn out since their jobs were less demanding. Thirdly, the elderly enjoyed immense respect in society and usually lived with their children, so loneliness is unknown to most of them. Last and foremost, senior citizens enjoyed good medical insurance so that they need not worry about sickness.

"Very good," Teacher Fang said. "Song Bao Bao is right. The elderly are highly respected in our society and elderly leaders hold the most important positions in the Central Committee of the Chinese Communist Party. Yes, China is definitely much better than America in all aspects."

Bao Bao exhaled in relief, as he had passed this discussion with flying colours and no-one had noticed that he had not done his homework.

The Central Committee that Teacher Fang had mentioned was a committee exercising the highest authority in the capital, Beijing. It was where top leaders, including Chairman Mao, gathered to implement policies for China. Bao Bao's impression of the Central Committee was of a host of old but powerful leaders. Chairman Mao was among them, but he was not so old. All of a sudden Bao Bao raised his hand again to ask, "How long is an American president's tenure? How long will Chairman Mao continue to lead our country? He is already sixty-five years old and well beyond the retirement age for males in China!"

"The American Constitution allows the President to serve his presidency for eight years maximum, in two terms," answered Ms Fang. Bao Bao immediately followed up, "Does our Constitution restrict Chairman Mao's tenure?"

Teacher Fang was taken aback by Bao Bao's unexpected question. She was perplexed and bewildered, as nobody in China was allowed to discuss the Chairman's tenure. "The Chinese Constitution does not stipulate how long Chairman Mao can hold the position as our country's supreme leader. But our Constitution is still very young and will be amended as our country grows. Song Bao Bao, don't forget we are in class discussing 'evil America' today – let us not deviate from our topic."

Teacher Fang turned to Shan Yu, the girl with the ponytail, and asked her to present her research. However, Bao Bao could not help but continue thinking. Perhaps Chairman Mao will one day announce the length of a Chairman's term, as George Washington did. Hopefully, one day the older members of the Central Committee will be replaced by younger leaders. Bao Bao had nothing against old men leading the country, but at eighty years old, the old men's minds surely were not as nimble as were those of young people. Will Chairman Mao retire soon and set an example for the future leaders in China, he wondered. But then, all the Chinese emperors had remained on the throne until death came upon them. Would Chairman Mao follow in the footsteps of the emperors? Bao Bao was very curious, but he dared not ask more.

While Bao Bao's mind was wandering, Shan Yu was asked by Teacher Fang to go ahead. She said, "American agriculture has been monopolized. Between 1945 and 1948, more than one million small farm-owners went bankrupt and sold off their lands to wealthy landowners. In 1954, 18% of the American population were farmers. In 1955, this figure was reduced to 13% and in 1958, to 12%. Because of this reduction, more than half of farm equipment, machines and animals had to be sold in auction. As a result of monopolization, 31.3% of all agricultural products are produced by 2.8% farm workers belonging to large corporations, whereas 56% of individual farmers and workers only produce 9% of agricultural products. Consequently many farmers have left their homes and gone into the cities in search of jobs. This pushed the number of unemployed up drastically."

Teacher Fang clapped excitedly and said, "Bravo, bravo! Comrade Shan Yu has presented us with facts backed up by statistics. When we say that America is bad, we must show the facts and nothing is more convincing than true facts represented by hard figures. Shan Yu must have done extensive research to arrive at these numbers. Congratulations on a good job well done," Teacher Fang gushed. Bao Bao could have sent Shan Yu a few nice words by paper aeroplane to congratulate her on her excellent report, but he was not interested in her.

Next Teacher Fang asked Cao Qin to talk. Cao Qin said that she had no figures at hand but she had a true story to tell. She spoke of the poorly dressed American children who ran around on the streets. There was a severe shortage of nutritious food for them and they did not attend school nor could they visit doctors when they were ill. They wore dirty and smelly clothing because their mothers could not afford to buy soap. Bao Bao nearly burst out laughing. He thought the soap story must be Cao Qin's own invention. Fortunately, Bao Bao did not laugh out aloud. It would be bad if he did so, because the purpose of this discussion topic was to treat America as the number one enemy and no statement would be treated as joke. In a solemn discussion such as this one, it was necessary to put on a stern face all the time, or at least pretend to be serious. Soon Cao Qin fell silent. Apparently she had nothing more to say.

Bao Bao came to Cao Qin's rescue. He said, "Not only do Chinese elders enjoy their lives, but also children and teenagers benefit from our Communist ruling. On 1 June 1953, the day of the International Children's Festival, the first "Shao Nian Gong" – Children's Palace – opened in Shanghai. The huge Children's Palace was a former wealthy merchant's residence. After the Liberation, [14] the regime confiscated the colossal mansion and converted it into a 'Children's Palace' where children and teenagers can gather after school and during weekends to participate in a myriad activities such as dancing, drawing, painting, singing, acting, playing musical instruments, boxing and fencing, etc. It also contains a cinema, stages for drama perfomances and orchestral performances and halls for concerts and art exhibitions of the children's painting and calligraphy."

Bao Bao continued, "At the Children's Palace, children have the honour of meeting renowned writers, scientists, war heroes and role-models from our work force. Only in the Children's Palace can a few thousand children assemble together under one roof. In the various rooms, children can attempt to build radios, and assemble aeroplanes and motorcar models. Only in Chairman Mao's era can children have the privilege of enjoying life at the Children's Palace, at school as well as at home."

Bao Bao's statement pleased Ms Fang and he was thrilled with his ability to participate in class discussions easily without any preparation. Bao Bao was satisfied with himself for earning extra points from his teacher while helping out Cao Qin.

Wang Ming, a tall boy, raised his hand several times, huffing and puffing impatiently. Finally, Ms Fang gave him a chance to present his findings. He told the class that the US dollar would soon be devalued and that inflation threatened many western countries. "Our currency, the Renminbi is the strongest and most stable currency and we do not suffer from inflation," he commented proudly.

Approaching the end of class, Ms Fang took the opportunity to share a few words with the students. "It seems as though

America wants to conquer the world," she announced. "She has waged war here and there, as making wars is good for her business. If there was no war, capitalist America would be nervous as they would have nowhere to dump their oversupply of weapons, ammunition, and such. In 1950, America attacked Korea. Even today, ten years after the establishment of New China, the Americans are still supporting Chiang Kai Shek, who retreated to the Chinese island of Taiwan, by sending her famous Seventh Fleet and best warships to defend Taiwan. Up to now, American spy-planes have invaded Chinese territory more than a hundred times!" Teacher Fang exclaimed, ending the class with those words.

After lunch, all regular classes were cancelled for the afternoon and instead they all had to go to an organized demonstration. All students assembled at the school playground at one o'clock sharp. Then they started to march towards Hua Shan Road where they would rendezvous with students from other schools in the same district. As soon as they had marched out of the school gate they began to shout, "Down with US Imperialism!", "Long Live New China!", "Long Live Chairman Mao!"

The government had blocked off the entire road for the students' demonstration against America. This time it was, for the one hundred and twenty-first time, a demonstration to criticise American spy-planes invading Chinese territories. It had become customary for Bao Bao and his schoolmates to march in the streets at least once or twice every week. So it was no longer unusual to see hundreds and thousands of youngsters marching to protest against America's evil practices.

Why is America always against us?" thought Bao Bao. First, she refused to recognize us as a nation because we are Communists, and contrary to our will, they have formed an alliance with our enemy Chiang Kai Shek in Taiwan. Then, they banned China from joining the United Nations and now, they are constantly sending over planes to spy on us! Despite our one hundred and twenty-one protests, America continues to spy on us. Do they not see the power of the Chinese population? If a spy-plane were to come now, the pilots would certainly be surprised to find hundreds and thousands of Chinese underneath the aeroplane in every corner of Shanghai, shouting against America." Bao Bao shook his head in disbelief as he continued marching and yelling, "Down with America!" while pumping his right fist in the air.

At half past four, the rally came to an end. Students left their designated groups and gradually made their way home. Nowadays students were frequently required to participate in demonstrations, rallies and public meetings that the new regime had come up with. This was in strict adherence to Mao's doctrine that students should not bury their heads in books, but actively be involved in all political movements.

After the demonstration, Bao Bao was exhausted, not only because of the long meeting and demonstration, but also from last night's lack of sleep due to the shocking scene at the park. However, Bao Bao did not want to return home, even though he had homework assignments waiting for him. He had other plans for the rest of the afternoon. As soon as the rally ended, he left his classmates. He was alone now and he felt fresh and energetic again, as he was planning to visit a bookstore on the Bund. Since he was at the People's Square, not too far away from the Bund, he hopped onto a bus heading to the Bund to visit the bookstore, a place that he had been looking forward to visiting for quite some time. While many the bookstores in Shanghai forbade customers from browsing through books, this bookstore was different. The huge bookstore had many open shelves where customers could browse openly.

The moment Bao Bao entered the bookstore he started to get fidgety. His mouth suddenly felt dry, while his hands became cold and clammy. His usual craving for knowledge suddenly disappeared as he glanced around the bookstore and gazed at the "Health Section", where he found many youngsters busily flipping through pages. Most of them were male teenagers. Bao Bao hesitated for a second and decided to go ahead because he was alone and thus had nothing to fear. Seeing the male readers browsing the books in the "Health Section" he was encouraged to go ahead with his plan. Perhaps they are looking for the same thing, Bao Bao thought to himself while picking up a random book. He quickly flipped to the index page and ran his finger down the list of topics. Since he found no mention of human sexual organs, he hastily restored the book to its rightful place. He continued to search, flipping through his second, third, fourth and fifth book, until he finally found a book that contained what he was looking for.

When Bao Bao saw an image of female genitals, he was taken aback. "Huh? It looks like a bright hibiscus flower!" he thought. The "vulva" and the "vagina" looked so different from the male penis and testicles. "Wah! So women do not have penises and scrotums, instead they have vulvas and vaginas!" Bao Bao's hands were shaking and his cheeks turned cherry-red. He put the book away and quickly scanned the room behind him. "Phew, nobody is paying attention to me! Everyone seems to be busy, doing their own thing." Finding no-one looking at him, Bao Bao felt less nervous and returned to his thought. What he saw was merely a diagram. "What do they look like in real life?" he wondered. He continued looking for more diagrams until he found a sketch of many human bodies. There, he saw the penis and scrotum of a man, which looked very much like the Greek sculptures that he had seen in a book when he was younger. "Why are the Greeks so obnoxious? Why do they constantly show off their secret parts? We Chinese would never do such a thing! We Chinese are more civilized!" He flipped to the female section and saw pubic hair in the groin area and realized that it was labelled the "vulva" and "vagina" that was invisible to the human eye when a woman stood upright or lay down on a bed. Bao Bao regretted that he had not seen the pubic hair of the naked woman under the flash light in the park. It was because of his haste that he saw only her naked breasts.

After this astonishing discovery, Bao Bao realized that there was nothing left in the "Health Section" for him today. So he stepped out of the bookstore. He was in desperate need for fresh air. He felt as if he were a culprit. He dreadfully needed to be alone and find a quiet spot to hide. But in the crowded Bund how could it be possible? Suddenly, he felt as though his peaceful life has been destroyed. Bao Bao worried that this discovery and his forlornness would show on his face. Fortunately he was alone and nobody recognized him on the Bund. He reprimanded himself for his curiosity. Why couldn't I wait until I was thirty to discover the differences between men and women legally? Now I am so ashamed of myself. Why doesn't school teach us about gender differences? Why do adults keep sex as a top secret? What about bedroom matters? Must I wait for fifteen years to know about them? Fifteen years is a long time! In fifteen years' time I shall already have obtained the Nobel Prize! Bao Bao looked down in disappointment. The words "Nobel Prize" shot through his head like a bullet. What am I doing here?

Do I have a lot of valuable time to waste if I have set either the Nobel Prize or Dr Bethune as my goal in life? Bao Bao questioned himself.

He crossed the street and walked towards the shore of the Huangpu River. Seeing the busy river changed Bao Bao's mood instantly. A few ships were parked across the earth-coloured river water. In the middle of the river lay a motor ferry, a shuttle ferry and a tug with cargo ships positioned closely behind. A few Chinese junks moved slowly towards a platform set up near the other end of the shore. Bao Bao kept looking. Flashes of crimson red embellished the spectacle before him. Everywhere he looked, red banners and propaganda posters fluttered in the breeze; bright red banners flapped above the ships, over junks and on buildings proclaiming "Long Live Chairman Mao!", "People of the World Unite!", "Down with American Imperialism", "Long Live the Chinese Communist Party!"

Everywhere, people seemed hard at work along the river; men of all sizes were loading and unloading goods at the dock; boats, cars and trucks were all moving in different directions. Heavy, grey smoke released from chimneys clouded the skies. Bao Bao stood silently on the shore, studying the scene in front of him. What am I doing here? Bao Bao questioned himself. I have so much homework to do tonight! Another voice inside him yelled, "Don't you see that everyone is hard at work to build up our country? Can't you see the red flags everywhere? The red flag, our national flag, symbolizes the blood of countless Communist soldiers who sacrificed their lives to fight against Chiang Kai Shek's Nationalist soldiers and Japanese aggressors! It is at the cost of their lives that we are living happily and freely in our New China today!"

Bao Bao looked up at the sky through the thick smoke; he could make out the red orange-like sun sinking gradually down the horizon. He headed for home in a hurry. He knew Auntie would not appreciate him being late for dinner. He quickly took his place at the end of the long bus queue and waited his turn.

The bus was packed at rush hour. By chance Bao Bao found himself standing close to a young girl in a blue Mao jacket. She had large breasts and long shining black hair. As the bus moved and made a turn, everyone was knocked over to one side of the bus. The young girl's bosom accidently pressed tightly and firmly against Bao Bao's chest and upper left arm. The warmth of her young feminine body electrified Bao Bao. For him it was a shock. He should feel fortunate, but he cursed in his head, "No, no. Leave me alone, you seductive breast! Leave me in peace! For the next hundred years, I must have nothing to do with breasts and nothing to do with anything female! You, devil, stay far away from me!" He abruptly pulled his body away from hers as he elbowed his way forwards through the heavily congested bus.

CHAPTER FIVE

# SHANGHAI NIGHT-LIFE

Bao Bao came home about half an hour later than the usual dinner time and the whole family was waiting for him. At the dinner table they chatted as usual, about the future of the children. Uncle spoke excitedly about Bao Bao's future. Auntie said, "Bao Bao will grow up to be a successful man. Without doubt, he will become a famous scientist one day." Then Uncle chipped in. "Bao Bao will not only become a famous physicist; he will win the Nobel Prize some day!" Bao Bao felt uncomfortable with all the pressure that Uncle and Auntie were putting on him. Does Uncle see no future in his own life? Has he transferred his own dreams onto me? Did our grandfather subject Uncle to similar pressure? Does the older generation always exert such pressure on the younger generation? Or am I the only guinea-pig? Bao Bao wondered. I must find out one day."

Now Uncle raised Bao Bao's favourite topic, "Bao Bao, have you heard that two of our Chinese scientists, Zhen Dao Li and Zhen Ning Yang, both American citizens who work in the USA, have been awarded the Nobel Prize? I believe they're the first Chinese to win such a high honour." Bao Bao was excited and listened attentively to what Uncle had to say.

"It was a sensation among us teachers at my school, because one of the teachers knows the father of Zhen Ning Yang, a professor at the famous Fudan University in Shanghai. Can you imagine how fortunate and proud his father is to have a son winning the Nobel Prize? It's a remarkable achievement, not only for the family, but for our nation and our race. Yang's father is now being treated as a highly honourable person in our society. His Nobel Prize has not only made his father and his immediate family members of the elite, but his relatives are also benefitting from his success. No longer will they have to wake up at four in the morning to queue up in the market for a slice of meat or a catty of fish. From now on, not only meat and fish, but most groceries – rice, eggs, milk; fruit, vegetables and lard – will be delivered to their doorstep everyday! For thousands of years, the rich and powerful Chinese looked after their relatives; and it seems unlikely that such a custom can suddenly disappear."

Bao Bao thought that he wouldn't mind sharing his fortune with his relatives, as he believed, "It is better for them to rely on me, instead of me having to rely on them". He remained silent and then the idea of winning the Nobel Prize took possession of him again. Perhaps Yang will come back to China, he thought, at least for a visit to see his old father some day and to enjoy his own fame and glory. He will definitely be treated as a super super VIP, so that when he returns to the United States, he will speak highly of China.

"Bao Bao, you are definitely not less talented than the Nobel Prize winner!" Uncle continued. "You must get on the right track! To be on the right track is the keyword for you. Please always bear this in mind!" Uncle urged. "Starting tomorrow you must devote all your energy and concentration to mathematics and physics. Other subjects, such as political history, literature, geography and languages can take a backseat on your priority list." Uncle took a few more mouthfuls of rice from his rice bowl and added, "Beginning tomorrow, you will have more food to eat. Even if our family starves, you will have enough to eat, so that you will have sufficient energy for your studies!"

Bao Bao grimaced and looked at his uncle silently. Why doesn't Uncle ever mention Dr Norman Bethune? As a teacher, he must know the story of Dr Bethune very well. Can it be that Dr Bethune is not acceptable in the minds of ordinary Chinese people, because he had neither a son nor a family? Being without a son meant that Dr Bethune was not a perfect human being according to Chinese tradition. To have no son means the discontinuation of the family name, Bao Bao thought. How could Dr Bethune be responsible to his father, his grandfather and his great-grandfather for the discontinuation of his family name? It was lawful in old China for a man to have concubines, if his wife failed to deliver a baby son for the family. Furthermore, Dr Bethune gave up his luxurious life in Canada and led a miserable life in China. If I was miserable, how could my Uncle benefit from me? thought Bao Bao.

After dinner, most families would remain at the dining-table to kill time by chatting. Families would sip tea together, one cup after another and men would smoke one cigarette after another. The room was full of smoke, but nobody felt bad about the smoky air. It was as though everyone in China was accustomed to living with cigarette smoke. They chatted and gossiped about this and that. They could talk about any subject as long as they did not criticize or offend the new regime. The adults were especially cautious about what they said in the presence of children, as denouncing adults was highly encouraged by the government.

The older people missed the fun of playing mahjong, an entertaining game played by four people for hours, even throughout the night. Mahjong had been a traditional Chinese game for thousands of years, but it was now forbidden by the Party. The People's government condemned it as gambling, because in most cases, mahjong involved winning or losing a big or small sum of money, thus making it an exciting pastime. Many elderly persons were denounced by their children, servants and neighbours for playing mahjong and were detained at the police station – Gong An Ju – where they were ordered to self-criticize through writing confessions. If they repeatedly ignored the warnings from the new government, they would eventually be sent to thought reform through labour – *lao dong gai zao*. Bao Bao's classmate had successfully denounced her neighbours for playing mahjong secretly in their basement and was promoted to the position of head of the class.

There was not much to do at night. Life was dull and monotonous, as the Party had shut down all bars, nightclubs and dance halls. Bao Bao thought of Chairman Mao when he started the farmers' revolution. Mao lived in a cave where there was nothing, not even electricity, and in the night one either went to sleep or studied Party doctrines under dim oil lamps. "Perhaps Chairman Mao experienced nostalgia for the good old times and wanted to bring our cosmopolitan city, Shanghai, back to that era," Bao Bao thought.

The only club that still existed was the Seamen's Club on the Bund, but this was open to foreigners exclusively. The only bar operating was the one in the Peace Hotel lobby, to which admission was granted to foreigners and overseas Chinese only. The latter had to show their foreign passports at the entrance to prove their non-Chinese nationality. The last show at the cinema house ended at 9.00pm. Only on Saturdays did the final show last until 11.00pm. The showing of foreign films was limited to films from Russia and Eastern Bloc countries. Films from capitalist countries were strictly forbidden.

Bao Bao heard that, prior to the revolution, the American film, *Gone with the Wind* was shown in cinema houses in Shanghai. He asked the older people about it and they all praised the film as a great sensation. Now for years, the cinema houses had been repeatedly showing the same Chinese films, films such as the "The White-Haired Girl", a film about a young girl who refused to become the concubine of her old landlord and who took refuge in a mountain cave. After a decade, the Red Army finally liberated her. As she stepped out of the cave, it was seen that her hair had turned as white as snow due to the lack of light and sunshine. Bao Bao had nothing against "The White-Haired Girl". However, watching the same film over and over again was boring.

Other Chinese films were similar to "The White-Haired Girl", so that the Chinese public had seen much the same film many times. Bao Bao walked by the Guang Ming Cinema House that morning and saw a poster of the Indian Film, "Awara" (*The Wanderer*), which was coming back to Shanghai soon. The poster showed a picture of a young man in a short-sleeved shirt and rolled-up pants, hair dishevelled, walking freely under the bright sun. Behind him was a woman. It had been four years since Bao Bao had seen this movie. He was delighted to see the announcement and was eager to see this foreign film again. Perhaps he could invite Dan Dan, the most beautiful girl in his class, to the film.

"No, No, I can't do that!" He shook his head vigorously. "If someone were to see me at a film with Dan Dan, they would spread vicious rumours about my having a girlfriend. At fifteen years old, I am much too young to have a girlfriend! Uncle, Auntie, my teachers, my parents, the Party, and Chairman Mao would certainly disapprove of it!"

Sometimes Bao Bao strolled by the Seamen's Club on the Bund, which was the only luminous place at night in dark Shanghai. Tonight, Bao Bao found himself in front of the

Seamen's Club once again. At the entrance stood two Sikh guardsmen with turbans on their heads. One had a tattooed arm, while the other had a gold chain around his neck. The two terrifying men paced back and forth in front of the club, ensuring that no Chinese entered.

I wonder, what do the foreigners do inside? He studied the front of the club curiously. It was an old Gothic-style building built in the thirties. Bao Bao was told that foreigners drank wine, beer, spirits and liquor, instead of tea. He could not fathom what kind of pleasure there could be in drinking. The taste of alcohol was unknown to Bao Bao and he wished that he could taste it someday. He was told that it was wise not to drink, as alcohol would eat away his liver and strip away his wallet.

Every time Bao Bao wandered to the Bund, he wished that he could enter the Seamen's Club to see how the foreigners killed their evenings by drinking. He also wanted to enter inside to see the impressive display of foreign goods.

They say many top-quality foreign and Chinese goods, such as bicycles, watches, sewing-machines, tape-recorders, cigarettes and cigars are on display in the club, but they're sold exclusively for foreign currency, as Chinese yuan are not accepted at the club.

Bao Bao was eager to see foreign goods, but it was impossible for him to enter the Club. Bao Bao saw foreigners walk into the Club freely and he wished he could approach them and ask them to take him in with them. But he was too shy to ask such a favour from strangers. Also, he was unable to speak a single word of any foreign language so he would not be able to communicate with them in any case. Bao Bao felt sad at not being allowed to go in. "Why won't they let us locals in?" he thought.

Before the revolution, it was said, there was a signboard outside a park entrance reading, "Chinese and dogs not allowed inside the park". – The park was in one of the foreign concession areas. – Hearing about this, the entire Chinese nation was furious at the foreign imperialists for treating Chinese people like dogs on Chinese territory. Bao Bao could remember vividly that the Communist Party condemned this evil behaviour of the foreign imperialists. But now, why does the Chinese government, our people's government, forbid us Chinese from entering the clubs and bars in China? This does not make sense to me! thought Bao Bao.

As for the currency, why does the Seamen's Club refuse to accept our yuan? Bao Bao wondered, recalling the class discussion when Wang Ming had asserted, "Chinese currency – renminbi – yuan – is the strongest currency, because we don't use gold as a reserve to back it up. We have a population of six hundred million Chinese to guarantee the value of our currency. Therefore the value of our yuan will increase, while the US dollar will lose value!"

"Ding! Ding! Ding...!" The massive clock atop the customs building in Shanghai chimed nine times.

"Aiyaah!" It was getting late! Bao Bao woke up from his fantasy and hurried to the bus-stop in the humid summer's heat.

On midsummer days, the temperature in Shanghai soared to thirty-five to thirty-eight degrees Celsius. It was impossible to stay at home because the living space was so small that four, five, six, or even seven or eight people were all crammed into one room, with no fan or air-conditioner. Only a very few private hotels, cinema houses and theatres were equipped with air-conditioners. Most public venues, however, had ceiling fans for ventilation. It was customary for everyone to carry a fan. In the evenings everyone walked up and down the dark streets and in the parks, trying to catch a breeze. Once they found a well-ventilated spot, people would stay there. Sometimes, they even brought with them a folding bed, couch or mat in order to sleep overnight in the open streets. Quite often one would find teenage girls sleeping alone outside on the streets. The security was so good that young girls did not need to worry about being harassed or raped.

When a person lost his or her wallet, there was a ninety-nine percent chance of finding it. One foreign tourist threw away a pair of old shoes in a hotel room. To his surprise a few days later, the same pair of old shoes was brought back to him at his new hotel, as someone thought that he had forgotten to take them when he checked out of the first hotel. A few days later, he travelled to another place and the pair of used shoes was brought to him again and again. He found it impossible to get rid of his old shoes in China.

In the streets, vendors sold cookies, preserved fruits and soft drinks under the dim streetlight and all shops remained closed, while the whole city was enveloped in darkness. Television was unknown. Although it had passed the government's assessment, the current technology in China made mass production of television sets impossible. People showed interest only in more accessible goods such as bicycles, watches, sewing-machines and radios rather than in the revolutionary television. So before television sets were available in every household, everyone lived on the streets.

People went to sleep early and woke up in the early morning. Because everyone woke up so early, the official lunchtime had been moved forwards to 11.00am and correspondingly dinner time was set at 5.00pm. For housewives, it was not a bad idea, since the earlier they began to queue up in the markets, the better their chance of being able to purchase a piece of meat or fish with their ration coupons.

Bao Bao found that dinner table conversation at home was usually quite tedious since Uncle's only topic was Bao Bao's future. So Bao Bao always excused himself from the table to take a walk. Previously, he had sometimes gone with Li Yong to the park, to investigate what men and women were doing behind the shrubs in the darkness at night. However since the awful scene of the naked woman in the park, Bao Bao dared not ask Li Yong to go to the park any more.

Sometimes, he visited his classmates' homes. However, he rarely found satisfaction in talking to teenagers of his own age. He would rather talk to old people as he discovered that they had wisdom and a lot of experience in life. The old people in China had endured different turbulent times: the time of the Qing Dynasty under the Dowager Empress Cixi, the young Republic under Dr Sun Yat Sen, the invasion of the Japanese, the Foreign Concessions, the era of Chiang Kai Shek and the Kuomingtang and now, under Chairman Mao, the Communist regime.

Bao Bao felt very lucky that he did not have to live through such tragic and turbulent epochs in China. He was grateful to Chairman Mao and the Communist Party that he had a good life and that ahead of him was an easy path leading to a bright future. All he needed to do was to follow Chairman Mao's doctrines obediently, "To learn, to learn, and again, to learn", and, "Do what the Party asks you to do".

Bao Bao found it rather easy to finish his homework within one to two hours after school. In a rare case he would spend three or four hours doing his homework at the weekend. He had basically nothing to do after dinner. His secret to attaining good grades was to listen attentively during class and to review his textbooks thoroughly a couple of days prior to a test or examination. In subjects such as mathematics and science, he listened carefully to what the teachers taught in class. Once he understood the concepts, he would hold onto the knowledge for a long time. As for politics and the literature class, he would just have to regurgitate the Party's words and sentences and he would be fine. In the eyes of the teachers and the school authorities, Bao Bao was a good student with a great consciousness of Party doctrines. He was classified as a "politically enthusiastic" student despite the fact that his parents were of the bourgeois class and lived in exile, something that was unacceptable to the Party. But Bao Bao had no way of changing his destiny or his family background. He admitted that either you are born with a silver spoon in your mouth or you were not.

Bao Bao's unfavourable family background had given him a lot of headaches. He wondered how to tackle this problem. It was clear to him that Chairman Mao was perfect and that his orders were and would be followed by all seven hundred million Chinese. When the Chairman said that family background was essential, no-one dared to deny it. This included Bao Bao. In fact, Bao Bao wished that one day he could become a Party member as well, since all good things and leading positions only went to Party members. However, to become a member of the Communist Party was a long way off for Bao Bao. At his age, he would first have to join the Communist Youth League, and when he became an adult, if his behaviour met the Party's expectations, he could be recommended by three Party members to join the Party. However, to gain acceptance by the Communist Youth League was problematic for Bao Bao due to his weak family background. The Communist Youth League only took in children from good family backgrounds; or in other words, the children of peasants, farmers, workers and soldiers. It was unlikely that the Communist Youth League would take him.

Suddenly a superb idea struck Bao Bao. Once he was awarded the Nobel Prize, he would be invited to join the Communist Party. And if he was invited to join the Party, all he would have to do would be to sign an application form and swear an oath, and no questions would be asked. Bao Bao was satisfied with this solution and was able to sleep better.

Apart from his devotion to homework, political campaigns and Communist doctrines, his insatiable appetite for discovering the past and present of the outside world made him restless. He felt as though this was a huge mosaic and that his job was to gather the bits and pieces that would eventually form a grander, fuller picture of the world. At this time, Bao Bao felt that old people were his source to finding these bits and pieces. Thus, in the evenings, Bao Bao went to different neighbourhoods to chat with old men. After a few visits, he realized that the old men had little interest in talking to a young boy like himself. Perhaps they were suspicious, thinking that Bao Bao was sent by the people's government to monitor their conversations and relay their complaints on the new regime to the Party.

Furthermore, the old men were not lonely, as they usually lived with their children, grandchildren and relatives. "Why would they want to chat with a stranger like myself? It is always dangerous to speak to strangers nowadays. That must be why they are reluctant to chat with me," muttered Bao Bao to himself.

Whenever time allowed, Bao Bao would stop by the kitchen of the Coffee House, which was located in a converted garage in the back lane behind Bao Bao's building. There, he would peer through into the kitchen at Chef Wang, who whipped flour, eggs and sugar together into a bowl to bake lovely cream-coloured cakes for the Coffee House. Chef Wang was plump and stubby and around fifty-years old. His belly was quite big, so his pants sat below his stomach. His balding head was clean and shiny, as though he waxed his head every morning. In the evenings, Bao Bao had often seen him taking a stroll in the backyard alley with his pet, a tame duck with snow-white feathers.

*From Mao's Shanghai to Capitalist Hong Kong*

One day, Chef Wang saw Bao Bao standing outside his kitchen watching him cook and he offered the boy a slice of cake and a cup of coffee. This was Bao Bao's very first taste of coffee and cake. One whiff of the freshly brewed coffee was all it took to catch Bao Bao's attention, putting him into a trance. Mmmm, he thought. This smells heavenly! Ah! And the cake! It is so fluffy, so smooth, yet so thick, creamy and rich at the same time! With every bite, the pieces of cake seem to melt away in my mouth! From then on, whenever Bao Bao wanted to feel happy, he would recall the tantalizing aroma of the coffee, the silky texture of the cake and sometimes he would even make his way over to the backyard of the Coffee House for a visual treat.

# CHAPTER SIX

# DAN DAN

Maths Teacher Feng looked unhappy these days, because about thirty percent of the students in Bao Bao's class failed the last geometry exam. He could not understand why the class standard was so low whereas the exam results in other classes were much higher, though he had used the same teaching method. He tried in vain to improve their level in geometry; but at the end of the day, the good students remained good and the weak students continued to be weak. The gap between the two extremes could not be narrowed. Whenever Feng introduced challenging problems, the bright students were always excited to show off their talent and ability to solve the problems whereas the poor students were always lost. They remained silent and shared the same emptiness in their eyes as they stared helplessly at the problems written on the blackboard. They dared not utter a single word, as they did not want the teacher and classmates to detect their weaknesses. Teacher Feng had little idea how he could help them. Repeating the same lessons did not guarantee a better grasp of the material. He had no way of finding out to what extent the students had digested his lectures.

Teacher Feng had neither the interest nor the patience to be a teacher. At the time of his graduation, the University asked him to jot down his preference for career paths for himself. He replied in all honesty that any profession other than teaching would be fine with him, as he hated teaching. Nevertheless contrary to his wish, six weeks later he was assigned to a Shanghai high school as a teacher. He was annoyed and he complained to the Party Secretary who replied that by assigning jobs to graduate students, personal interests were never taken into consideration. One just had to do what was assigned because every job played an indispensable role in serving the country and the people.

The Party Secretary further added that teaching was great. Chairman Mao had many titles as the great leader of our country, but he most preferred to be recognized as a teacher. The Chairman himself had started his career as a high school teacher in Hunan Province.

As soon as the name Chairman Mao was mentioned, Feng was left speechless as nobody could challenge the supreme leader. Nevertheless, it continued to bother Feng that when he was asked to write down his career preferences no consideration was give to his request. Perhaps only the favoured children of the Party had their wishes fulfilled. How could one become a Party favourite? Feng really wanted to find out.

Feng had been teaching Mathematics for three years, but he still hated teaching. Today, he decided to experiment with a new method by dividing the twenty-six students in Bao Bao's class into five small groups. He intentionally mixed the good and the weak students in each group to let the students help one another. As a talented student, Bao Bao was appointed leader of the group with Zhou, Wang Ming, Li Yong and Dan Dan. Teacher Feng hoped that Bao Bao and Li Yong would help Wang Ming, Zhou and Dan Dan with their homework assignments. The small group had accidentally brought Bao Bao and Dan Dan together, which delighted Bao Bao tremendously, as it gave him an opportunity to be close to Dan Dan, who, in Bao Bao's opinion, was the most beautiful girl in the school. Bao Bao had always wanted to find an excuse to approach her, but he had been too timid to do so.

On the first day of school, when he saw Dan Dan for the first time, he wanted to approach her. However, it was unlikely that a timid young man of fifteen would have the courage to talk to a female stranger. Even if he had had the courage, he would have been turned down by her, as it was not customary for young females to accept any form of contact with male strangers without a proper introduction. But the forming of the study groups had brought Bao Bao close to Dan Dan and from now on he could approach her on any geometry-related problem and later on any other matter of the class. Bao Bao was grateful that Teacher Feng had accidently done him such a great favour. Now Bao Bao was sitting next to the beautiful Dan Dan. This was better than anything he could have dreamt of! Soon Bao Bao's group came to an agreement that three times a week, they would spend one hour after school to give Zhou, Wang Ming and Dan Dan extra help in geometry.

Bao Bao realized that Zhou and Wang Ming were very good in politics but very weak in mathematics. He studied his classmates carefully and arrived at the conclusion that most of the students with good grades were from bourgeois backgrounds while whose with proletarian backgrounds struggled academically. He recalled the Communist Party's official explanation of this. – "The bourgeois class has enjoyed many generations of educational privilege while the proletarian class has lived under constant suppression, always with no education at all. Therefore, children from the proletariat class are weaker academically." – Now, the new regime had turned the situation upside down and allowed more proletarian students to study in universities in the hope that within a short span of time, the majority of those holding key positions in the government would be replaced by those from the proletarian class.

Bao Bao looked at Li Yong, who was busy helping Zhou and Wang Ming and thought, Zhou and Wang Ming are academically weak, but they may have a better chance than Li of getting into a university. Despite his intelligence and excellent grades, Li may never be accepted by a university in China because of his family background. It was a question that puzzled Bao Bao. Why does the Party tell us that we are living in a classless society where equal rights supposedly exist? But he shook off this idea. Oh, stop it! Stop thinking of politics and focus on pretty Dan Dan. She is right next to me! I must talk to her, and Bao Bao turned his face to her.

Teacher Feng was pleased to see the group discussions proceeding well. He was about to thank God – but no, he should thank the Chinese Communist Party instead – for it was the Party's that had introduced and constantly preached the importance of helping one another in a group. Chinese tradition had it that every man worked for himself and his own family. – But this came to a halt in Mao's era. Now, everyone had to think of the group, the unit, the commune and the community that he or she belonged to. Seven hundred million Chinese were no longer scattered all over the place like before but were like sand dissolved into a water basin, unified under the rule of Mao. Teacher Feng's new method of allowing students to help one another saved him much time and energy. He considered his new pedagogical method a success.

Bao Bao's group left school at half past four, an hour after the class was dismissed. Zhou, Wang Ming and Dan Dan felt pleased with the amount of work that they had accomplished. By being together in a small group, they were more able to ask and answer questions, especially Zhou and Wang Ming, who felt more comfortable to speak their minds, whereas in the big class they were afraid to ask stupid questions. As far as learning was concerned, Bao Bao had not gained anything from the small group. However, to be able to sit legitimately next to Dan Dan was amazing, totally unexpected and much better than anything in the world that he could hope for. As for Zhou, who had denounced Bao Bao during the night spent writing Da Zi Baos, Bao Bao paid no attention to her. And what had Li Yong gained? Neither knowledge, nor a girl, but through helping Wang Ming and Zhou, he had demonstrated to the Party that he was willing to follow the Party line. The more enthusiasm he showed, the more leniently he would be dealt with by the Party, even after taking account of his poor family background.

At the school gate, Zhou and Wang turned left, whereas Li, Bao Bao and Dan Dan turned to the right. Li walked with them for a short while and then took French leave and disappeared. Bao Bao and Dan Dan were left to walk together alone. Normally, it would be alright for Li to disappear, but today Bao Bao felt that it would be better if Li had stayed. He felt embarrassed to be left alone with a pretty girl on the street. Finally, Bao Bao murmured to Dan Dan, "Why did Li Yong leave us without saying goodbye?" She lowered her eyes and her face turned rosy. She did not answer, but kept on walking down the road with him.

Perhaps she felt embarrassed. It must have been unpleasant for her to be left alone on the street with a boy. Usually Dan Dan walked to school with her brother or girlfriends; sometimes she even held onto her girlfriends' hands. But she did not know how to behave when walking with a boy alone in public. She prayed that she could disappear into an alleyway just as Li did, but that would be very impolite.

At this moment, they were passing a department store. Dan Dan felt this was a great opportunity for her to get away from

71

him and so she said, "Excuse me, Bao Bao. I must go inside to buy a few things."

Unexpectedly, Bao Bao said, "Good idea! I need to buy some toothpaste myself! Let's go together." Dan Dan started to feel uneasy. She was afraid that people would see them shopping together and begin to gossip.

Bao Bao sensed her uneasiness and felt that it was probably improper for him to follow her into the store. Thus he found a random excuse and said, "Perhaps my Auntie has already bought toothpaste. It's better for me to wait for you outside the store". So she went into the store alone.

After a while, she came out with empty hands. Bao Bao asked if she had bought what she wanted. Dan Dan shook her head and replied, "No". Bao Bao looked at her big eyes, her straight nose and rosy coloured cheeks and found her very attractive. He thought it would have been better not to have waited for her, yet he wanted to stay with her as long as he could. They continued to walk in silence. He looked down at her dark brown head bobbing up and down.

In order to break the awkward silence, Bao Bao cleared his throat and tried to say something, "What kind of difficulties are you encountering with geometry?"

"I find geometry somewhat abstract with fictitious lines being used all the time!" answered Dan Dan and added, "I never know when and where to apply a fictitious line!"

Bao Bao smiled and asked, "Have you ever seen people playing billiards? Basically geometry is like a billiard game. Before one uses the long billiard cue to hit the hard and small ball, one has to identify the direction in which the ball will move after the hit. The ball travels only in one direction in a straight line and when the ball hits the the edge of the billiard table, it turns in different angle. Be it an acute angle, or an obtuse angle or an adjacent or right-angle, it all depends on the force and the angle of the ball being hit. Sometimes it takes a few straight hits to bring the ball to the hole. I always compare the indirect straight movements of the ball with the fictitious lines in geometry. In other words, similar to playing a game of billiards, one must assume that the ball will finally arrive at the hole. In order to achieve this, one must calculate the amount of force required to hit the ball. After a hard hit, or a few light hits, the ball in question will be brought to the desired hole successfully. The force one uses to hit the ball determines the distance that the ball will run. Of course, the more force one employs, the further the ball will travel forwards and backwards.

Billiard games were unfamiliar to Dan Dan, because after the revolution, this game had more or less disappeared, because it belonged to the bourgeois. Although billiards was not officially prohibited, the billiards clubs closed down one after another following the closure of ballrooms and nightclubs. Bao Bao had never held a billiard cue in his hand, but he had seen people playing billiards once, a couple of years ago. At that time, he did not know anything about geometry. Bao Bao was well aware that in fact billiards had not much to do with geometry, but associating a game of billiards with geometry made his conversation with Dan Dan less abstract. He spoke like a professor making things more comprehensible. Knowing that Dan Dan had no idea about billiards, Bao Bao seized this unique opportunity to impress her. Yes, she was amazed by Bao Bao. She knew that Bao Bao was the same age as her, or at most one year older. But how does he have so much knowledge? And why does he speak like a profound scholar? She dared not tell him that she had never seen a billiard game. She was afraid that he might laugh at her. She looked at him with admiration.

Soon, they approached Dan Dan's home. She felt relieved and said, "Here is my house. Thank you for your help. Bye-Bye," and turned towards the door of her building.

As soon as Dan Dan disappeared, Bao Bao felt ten pounds lighter. He felt as though he could jump up and fly like a feather in the air. He skipped along the street, his book-bag flapping against his bottom. His very first encounter with a female had left him with a blissful feeling, indescribable to his normal self. This was a type of exhilaration that he had never experienced before.

"How can a woman make a man experience such happiness? No, this cannot be true! I never see such happiness in Uncle, who has Auntie with him all the time," he thought.

"Can this be love at first sight? Perhaps it is love that is making me feel different. If it isn't love, then what is it that

73

makes me feel so great?" he wondered. "How does Dan Dan feel towards me? Why did she go into the department store and walk out empty-handed?! Did she want to get rid of me? Was she embarrassed to be walking with a boy in the street? Or was she bored with me?" Countless questions began to flood Bao Bao's mind. He could not stop thinking about Dan Dan. He kept on guessing about her feelings towards him.

Now Bao Bao noticed that he was near his home, so he turned right into the lane where his apartment was located. It will be another two days before I will be able to meet her in the small group again and I have to wait for two days to walk her home again. Two days are very long, but it's better than no meeting at all, he comforted himself.

Before getting close to Dan Dan, Bao Bao confessed that he had had no luck with girls. He thought of his classmate, Tao, who was a good-looking and aggressive boy, a year older than he. Tao had very many girlfriends. Among them was Miss Song, a well dressed, sophisticated girl with permed hair and polished, dark-red nails. Rumour had it that Tao had made her his girlfriend and had even kissed her. Bao Bao on the other hand was not so lucky with girls. "But then Tao and Song were both failing so many subjects that it looked like they might have to repeat grade 10," he comforted himself. "I am doing very well academically and I have passed all my exams with flying colours. If I were to get involved with a girl, I might suffer a setback with my grades in school," he reasoned. "This is after all, what my Uncle, Auntie and teachers have always warned me about.

CHAPTER SEVEN

# BUILDING A RADIO

After several trips to the kitchen of the Coffee House, Chef Wang invited Bao Bao back to his room. He was from Guangzhou and lived alone in Shanghai. He was pleased to have Bao Bao over as a guest. Bao Bao accepted the invitation cheerfully, as Wang was one of the very few older men whom he could chat with and from whom he could gather pieces of small coloured stones to help him complete his mosaic. As soon as Bao Bao stepped into Chef Wang's small room, Bao Bao felt at home. Bao Bao sat down on a wooden chair while Chef Wang lay on his single bed. The furniture was plain; it consisted of a bed, a wooden chair, a small closet and a wooden desk, where a hot-water thermos and a radio rested. Like most Chinese families, photos were hung on the walls. One photo showed his deceased wife, while the other showed his two sons who both lived in Guangdong province. Looking at the old radio, Bao Bao thought that it must contain at least eight tubes, meaning that it could receive shortwave transmissions.

"What kind of a radio is this?" asked Bao Bao.

"It is a powerful radio with ten tubes, an impressive Zenith product made in the thirties in the USA, before the Liberation, I bought it from a soldier. It still works well." Chef Wang smiled proudly.

Bao Bao was startled. Chef Wang must have been listening to foreign broadcasts. That's why he seems to know so much! Does he know that it is strictly prohibited? At night, police cars patrol every corner of the city using special equipment, to detect whether people are listening to foreign broadcasts, especially Voice of America broadcasts in Mandarin! Whoever is caught doing so is arrested immediately and sent to gaol right away! But, he reassured himself, I'm sure that Chef Wang must know what he is doing and so I should keep my mouth shut!

"Sir, can one listen to shortwave broadcasting through this?" Bao Bao blurted out. But immediately he realized that his question had been too direct and he quickly attempted to rectify it by adding, "I mean, can you listen to broadcasting from Russia,

75

the German Democratic Republic, Poland, North Korea, and Vietnam?" Listening to broadcasts from other Communist countries was acceptable to the People's Government.

"Certainly, with the antenna I have, I can receive broadcasts from the whole world, including America and Taiwan," he replied.

Bao Bao was in shock, as he could never imagine someone being so open and so straightforward to a stranger like himself on this forbidden subject. Did Chef Wang not realize that listening to broadcasting from America or Taiwan was a serious crime and that one would be sentenced to prison for many years? Bao Bao felt very concerned.

In the meantime Chef Wang stood up and opened the window to show Bao Bao his antenna which was not long at all, only three to four metres long outside the window. Chef Wang added, "If I eavesdrop at night, no police car will drive by to catch me because this is a backyard inside an alley."

Bao Bao was delighted to hear Chef Wang's comment about being undetectable. However, he did not want to dwell on the subject of eavesdropping, as he had by now collected sufficient information from Chef Wang regarding listening to shortwave broadcasting.

Quickly Bao Bao changed the subject to his major interests. "Sir, since we are living in an 'egalitarian society' or 'equal rights society', why does family background matter so much?! Why does our new regime discriminate against those who do not belong to the farmer, worker or revolutionary class? There is nothing we can do to change the family we are born into. Now, university admissions and good jobs will all go to those with proletarian backgrounds. Is that fair? What do you think, Chef?"

The Chef answered, "My boy, men are not equal from birth. One person is more or less intelligent and another is stronger or weaker. In our population of six hundred million, there are thirty million intellectuals – five per cent of the whole – who are not from proletarian origins and whom Chairman Mao has never trusted. In order to please the entire population, the regime has to discriminate against this five-percent minority, in case one day they regain power and take control of the entire country. Adolf Hitler adopted a similar tactic during World War Two. He was well aware of the Germans' hatred of the Jews, so he suppressed the Jewish minority by driving them out of Europe and exterminating them to win the favour of the German population. His aim was to ensure that his Nazi troops would support his dream of becoming a world conqueror by invading Poland, Denmark, Norway, France, Belgium, Italy and finally Russia."

Bao Bao felt uneasy when he heard Chef Wang attacking the new regime. He stood up and left abruptly. He wished that he had brought a pocket tape-recorder with him, so that he could listen to the chef's words again. Too bad! But this was merely a figment of Bao Bao's imagination, as an actual tape-recorder was as big as a water basin!

Back at home, Bao Bao continued to think obsessively about having a radio that received shortwave broadcasting from overseas. Now he had learnt from Chef Wang that he could manouever his way around police surveillance and avoid being detected, he too wanted a powerful radio at home. At Chef Wang's place, Bao Bao refrained from discussing the Voice of America, because he did not want to let Chef Wang know that he was interested in listening to shortwave broadcasting from capitalist countries. However, deep down his heart, Bao Bao had always been fascinated about life in other countries, especially China's number one enemy, the USA, whom Bao Bao and his schoolmates had been attacking day in and day out. He was eager to hear what the enemy USA would say about his dear Motherland, China.

Although Bao Bao welcomed the thought of listening to the Voice of America, it scared him to think of how serious a crime one would be committing if one listened to foreign broadcasts. Immediately, images of patrolling police cars and people charged with felonies were conjured up in his mind. He recalled how the police locked up all of those who disobeyed the rules or who had the slightest intention to betray the Motherland, sending them off either to gaol or to places where they would have to slave away for the rest of their lives.

Tonight Chef Wang has taught me how to listen to shortwave broadcasts without getting caught, thought Bao Bao.

Chef Wang was right. If one were to listen to shortwave in a room facing a backyard, he would never be detected by a police patrol. Bao Bao had never seen a police patrol entering a small alleyway. Occasionally, he would see a taxi or a car waiting in the backyard, but never at night. In order to enter the backyard, one had to open a heavy iron gate at both ends. This usually required two people to push the gates apart simultaneously. But at night, who would bother to go to such trouble? Furthermore, if Bao Bao planned to listen in to a broadcast, he could first look down from his bedroom window to observe whether any strange vehicles were in the backyard. He clapped his hands in delight at realizing that he could listen in after all! However, one problem remained: Where would he find a powerful radio and antenna? His uncle's radio picked up only long waves; he needed something similar to the chef's ten tube Zenith for shortwave, but he could not ask the chef to lend him his radio.

After much contemplation, Bao Bao came to the conclusion that he must build his own radio and set up his own antenna. As a matter of fact, he had built a radio two years earlier at the Children's Palace with his friend Kai Kai. But it was a long-wave radio with three tubes only. Kai Kai was two years older than Bao Bao. He was known in the neighbourhood as a radio fanatic, who devoted most of his time to building different types of radios. However, Kai Kai was not a role model for Bao Bao, as he neglected his studies.

The idea of building his own radio excited Bao Bao so much that he could not fall asleep. He would have to force himself to do so, as it was getting late. Nevertheless, before he put much effort into falling asleep, he got up and made his way to the toilet down the corridor. He heard a noise, took a step back and listened intently. Why are there whispers coming from Uncle and Auntie's room? Bao Bao wondered. He could not figure out what they were whispering about so late in the night, so he pressed his ear closely to the swinging door that led to Uncle's room. Normally he could hear clearly everything that was said inside the room. But tonight the soft murmuring, mixed with light giggles from Auntie, made Bao Bao curious. Why are they whispering and not speaking out as usual? Why are they still awake at this hour? Bao Bao continued to stand outside their door, perplexed.

Soon he heard rhythmical sounds from the mattress. What are they doing now? His hand shot up to his mouth, in attempt to stifle his cry. No…it can't be! Auntie is such a decent and austere woman, could it even be possible that she too, is lying underneath Uncle, naked?!

Now his body trembled from tension. I have to find out more, he determined as he slowly pushed open the door and crawled into their bedroom, cautious not to make any noise as he aimed to reach the edge of their bed. He could not see anything in the darkness. The noise from the mattress continued. Now he heard no more whispers, nor laughs from Auntie, but only the rhythmic noise from the mattress mixed with increasingly heavy breathing from Uncle. Suddenly the noise from the mattress stopped and Bao Bao heard a loud flop on Uncle's side of the bed.

Being so close to them, Bao Bao wished that he could touch Auntie's lower abdomen to feel with his hand what female genitals were like. But he dared not, because as soon as he touched her body with his small hand, Auntie would surely scream with surprise. He would be caught and there was no way to escape. Life would then become disastrous for me. It would be too embarrassing for me to live with Uncle and Auntie. I would have to move out. Where would I go? Bao Bao wondered. His body shivered from fear and his feet were cold. Gradually he crawled back towards the door.

"I have to get up early for work tomorrow morning." Now Bao Bao heard a whisper from Uncle.

"You always leave me in the lurch," he heard Auntie reply. Now you are satisfied and I am halfway through. It would be much better for me if you had not started such a game with me."

"I didn't want to leave you halfway through, but I could not last. I had no control of myself. You know we don't have nutritious food nowadays. To do a good job I need to eat eggs, pork, and beef, and drink chicken soup. Without decent food I am too weak to perform!" retorted Uncle.

The whispering stopped. Silence dominated the bedroom. Soon Uncle began to snore. Bao Bao continued to crawl until he reached the swinging door. Being as careful as he could, he slowly pushed open the swinging door.

Bao Bao crept back to his own bed. Now he was more confused than before. The conversation such as "leave me in the lurch," "halfway through," "nutritious food, chicken soup, eggs, pork, beef", "satisfied", "lasted long", "a good job" "no control of myself" went over his mind. To the best of his knowledge he could not fatham their meaning, nor could he find any association amongst these words and sentences.

In bed Bao Bao took a deep breath and closed his eyes. The scene from Uncle and Auntie's room had left him restless. He could not let dirty thoughts enter his pure mind. He had to maintain his good reputation as a good student of Chairman Mao. "One, two, three, four, five, six, seven...," the youngster counted, trying to sleep. It was his favourite method for falling asleep. It has always proved a useful and effective way for him to shut down his thinking. However, tonight when he got to, "One hundred and seventy," the question came back to attack him. Why did the woman in the park moan loudly whereas Auntie kept silent? Perhaps Auntie suppressed her voice for fear of waking up our neighbours? Now another question popped up. Was the naked man in the park also out of breath as my uncle was? "No! No! I must continue counting!" he silently yelled. But what number was I at? He could not remember, so he started from one hundred and one all over again, "One hundred and one, one hundred and two, one hundred three...", until he finally dozed off.

The following day, as soon as school was over, Bao Bao went to see Kai Kai, who lived on the third floor of a four-story house, which was left behind by his relatives. The owner of the house had fled to Taiwan shortly before the Communists took over Shanghai. Kai Kai shared a tiny room with his brother. Over ten radios were on display in his room everywhere, from his desk to the floor near his mattress.

Kai Kai told Bao Bao that the most powerful radio was one with ten tubes which could pick up short waves from every corner of the world. Bao Bao was amazed and said, "I would like to build a powerful radio, such as this, to satisfy my ego!"

"Haha. I know, I know that feeling!" said Kai Kai. That is why I have built so many radios myself! I have always dreamt of being the King of Radios one day," he said. "The proudest moment in my life was when I turned on my small hand-made radio in the park and loud music came out of my speakers. A crowd surrounded me and watched me with great amazement.

"You will need about thirty yuan, Bao Bao," Kai Kai continued, "to build a ten tube radio, about eighteen yuan for an eight tube radio."

Bao Bao repressed his desire to ask about the price of an antenna. If he did, Kai Kai would immediately realise what he intented to do. Instead, Bao Bao decided to calculate the price of an antenna in his mind. To build an extensive antenna, Bao Bao thought, which stretches from the window of my bedroom to the roof of the three-story townhouse across the backyard, I would need a thirty to forty metre cable. Based on the average cost of twenty cents per yard, I would need at least seven to eight yuan for the antenna. With such a long antenna, I would be able to receive short-wave broadcasts from everywhere in the world, even with only eight tubes. Yes, an eight-tube radio is what I need! It will cost me about twenty-five yuan in total.

My Goodness, how can I find so much money? Bao Bao asked himself in disbelief. Could he borrow the ten tubes from Kai Kai? No, no way, he thought. The ten tube set is Kai Kai's gem. He would never let anyone touch it. However, Bao Bao was sure that if he could buy all the tubes and accessories, Kai Kai would gladly help him build an eight-tube radio. With an extensive antenna I would not need a ten-tube radio, he decided. So Bao Bao did more sums in his head. It would cost twenty-five yuan – that's five yuan less than thirty. Every yuan matters to me, as I do not even have even one yuan now. Furthermore, an eight-tube radio is much less suspicious than an expensive ten-tube radio in the eyes of the Communist Regime. But where can I find so much money? Bao Bao started to panic. Twenty-five yuan was nearly half a month's salary for a worker or teacher. If it was approaching the Chinese New Year – the Spring Festival – which took place around February each year, he could, following Chinese custom, collect red envelopes from his older relatives, with money inside. But that usually amounted to only ten or twelve yuan in all – if he was lucky! But the New Year was far away! He did not have pocket money or any allowance. On some occasions, he received one yuan – a hundred fens – from his uncle or Auntie to buy a Popsicle on a hot summer's day. To get twenty-five yuan seemed too daunting of a task for Bao Bao!

Before going to bed, Bao Bao set his alarm clock. At eleven in the night he quickly pushed the off button before the noise of the alarm could wake his sister up. He slipped out of bed; sneaked out of his room and carefully tiptoed his way across the corridor towards Uncle and Auntie's room. He shut the swinging door behind him and proceeded to enter their room without making any noise. He peeked at his uncle, auntie and cousin who were all sound asleep. Uncle was snoring loudly like a locomotive. Bao Bao crept to his uncle's bedside, to the jacket hanging off the clothing rack and hastily stuck his hands into the pockets. To his disappointment, there were no large bills. Finding empty pockets, Bao Bao had no choice but to head back to his bed.

How stupid I was! Bao Bao silently reprimanded himself. How could I believe that a person would carry twenty-five yuan in his pocket when he makes only sixty a month? Furthermore, today is not the end of the month, nor his payday. Even if it were his payday, the money goes straight into the bank! How stupid I was to think that I could borrow twenty-five yuan from Uncle!

In the days that followed, Bao Bao had nothing else on his mind but to get the money and build the radio. After school one day, Bao Bao sprinted to the three-story building where Kai Kai lived. Bao Bao knew that the former owner had stored some construction materials in the basement of the four-story building that could be worth some money. Bao Bao sneaked into the building, but instead of running upstairs to visit Kai Kai, he went down to the basement to a pair of large dusty French doors. He quickly tugged at the door handles, only to find that the doors were locked. His eyes darted back and forth, inspecting the place. Seeing no way to enter, he picked up a stone from the ground and shattered part of the window close to the lock; then he stretched his arm through the window to turn the lock from the inside.

"Yes!" he silently cheered as he entered the storage room. It felt as though his heart was pounding five hundred beats per minute as he hoped that no-one had heard or seen him breaking in. He scanned the basement briefly, finding tiles and wooden plates all covered heavily in dust. Finally, he found a box of door and window handles made of copper. Paying no attention to the dust, he quickly dumped the books out of his schoolbag and stuffed his bag full with all the copper handles and bars that he could find. He then swung his schoolbag across his left shoulder, scooped the textbooks into his arms, and and left the storage room in a hurry.

Bao Bao rushed home to drop off his books and left again shortly after, with his schoolbag overflowing with copper handles and bars. Bao Bao marched determinedly towards the metal-dealer shops, despite the hefty weight that hung on his thin frame.

The dealer weighed Bao Bao's articles and gave him a ten yuan bill in exchange. But ten yuan would not solve his problem. He desperately needed an additional fifteen yuan to accomplish his mission. But what can I sell? he asked himself. There are no more copper handles left in the basement.

Hmm, he suddenly remembered something. About a year ago, Bao Bao had started collecting his nail-clippings in a box. – He had heard people say that human nails are worth a lot. – But after a whole year of collecting his nails, they still weighed very light, as though there was nothing there at all! With such a tiny mass of nails, he thought in disappointment, it is not worthwhile even to approach a nail-dealer.

Then one day when Bao Bao was doing his homework, he heard a bell ringing. Ding-ding! Ding-ding!

"All of you at home look around you! Look for old furniture! Give me your furniture and I'll give you cash!" an old man called out.

Why! It's the old furniture collector! He has come to our apartment lane! Bao Bao thought excitedly. His heart was racing wildly as he frantically surveyed his room. I could easily raise enough money for my radio if I sold a piece of used furniture! But what can I sell? Everything seems so useful!

"Ah-ha!" Bao Bao yelled out loud, clapping his hands together in glee. He knew exactly what piece of furniture to get rid of! He dashed into the corridor, went to a monstrous-looking hall-wardrobe and began to toss out every single shoe,every piece of clothing and every other item it held. I've never liked you! You hideous thing! Bao Bao thought mischievously.

It was an awful-looking piece of black furniture. It was built like a shrine, with a triangular top, held up by two slender columns, each containing three small drawers. There was no storage unit inbetween them. But long, finger-like hooks protruded downwards from the top of the frame for hanging coats. Bao Bao had always thought it looked like a beast; a dark black beast, towering over him. It was mouldy and had specks of white from old age. To make matters worse, there was a filthy rectangular mirror between the two flimsy pillars. At night, it looked like an enormous open mouth, ready to gobble up anything that came its way.

"Wei! Wei!" Bao Bao hollered as he stuck his head out the window. "Hello! I have a splendid piece of furniture for you!" he lied enthusiastically. "Come up to the second floor!"

The furniture-dealer arrived at Bao Bao's apartment, took a good look at the hall-wardrobe, and offered Bao Bao ten yuan.

"Ten yuan? Why! This is worth much more than that! Not only can you hang up your coats, but you can keep all your precious items in its six drawers, store your shoes, and use the mirror to keep your hair tidy by!" Bao Bao argued as he pulled open a drawer, trying to show off the good points of the piece of furniture. Bao Bao knew that ten yuan would still not buy him his radio and continued, "Surely this is the most versatile piece of furniture in all Shanghai!"

The furniture-dealer thought for a little while and said, "Alright. Fifteen yuan and that is all I am going to pay. If you want more than that, you can find yourself another buyer!" The furniture-dealer handed over fifteen yuan and said, "Take it or leave it!"

Bao Bao beamed at the furniture-dealer. Fifteen yuan was what he needed to build his radio. "Done!" called out Bao Bao, as he stretched out his arm and eagerly took the money. The furniture-dealer called down to his assistant to remove the heavy hall-wardrobe from Bao Bao's home right away.

Yes! Yes! Yes!! Bao Bao cheered silently. As soon as the furniture collector left, Bao Bao sprinted out of the apartment to buy all the necessary parts for his radio. Life is good! Life is sweet! How wonderful this is!" thought Bao Bao, as he skipped along towards the shops.

That evening, when Uncle and Auntie had returned home, they were startled to find that Bao Bao had sold their furniture. Uncle was furious that Bao Bao had sold a big piece of furniture without seeking his permission, whereas Bao Bao thought that it was his father's house so he had the right to do so. So they argued. Uncle wanted to beat him but Bao Bao was too active to be tied down. They continued to yell at one another until Bao Bao explained that he needed the money to build himself a radio.

Upon hearing his explanation, Uncle felt sympathetic towards the boy. He asked Bao Bao why he had failed to consult Uncle and Auntie for the money, as they still had money left in a savings book from his Ma Ma's monthly remittances from Hong Kong. Bao Bao didn't have to sell his father's possessions which were under the custody of Uncle. Bao Bao felt bad and apologized. He fell to his knees and started to kow-tow,[15] but Uncle pulled him up and consoled him, telling him that everything was fine and that he could build his radio tomorrow.

The next day, Bao Bao brought a forty-metre long cable home after school. He climbed to the roof of the three-storied townhouse across from his housing block. The residential police cadet, Bai, happened to be roaming around, and stood there watching Bao Bao installing his ridiculously long antenna. The people's government encouraged youngsters to be innovative and to explore the world of science and technology, so Cadet Bai was not in the least suspicious of Bao Bao's extensive antenna.

With all the accessories Bao Bao had bought, he went to see Kai Kai, who pulled out a drawing for an eight tube radio and right away he and Bao Bao started to assemble the radio piece by piece.

Bao Bao was anxious to test the capability of his newly built radio. The very same night, before going to sleep at nine o'clock, he set his alarm clock to wake him up again at midnight.

At that time of night, China was deep into the night and everyone was sleeping like a rock. Bao Bao went to the window, pulled the curtains behind him and peered through into the backyard. It was pitch dark outside. He stood there for a time, waiting patiently to see if he could distinguish any movement or noise. After a while, he pushed open his window and stuck his head out to look around.

Great! There's no police patrol vehicle out in the lane! he told himself. So Bao Bao set his earphones over his head and started to test how capable his new radio was to receive shortwave broadcasts. At first the radio was fuzzy. Also there seemed to be a loud noise in the background that blocked his reception. This was a disappointment. It's too bad the regime blocks reception like this! But Bao Bao continued to tune the radio. Suddenly he heard a powerful voice. Wah! This is it! This is the moment that I have been waiting for, for a long time! This is my chance to learn about the outside world! He turned to other channels. "This is the voice of Taiwan!" he heard. And he also heard something called "BBC", resonating through his earphones. They are all available! He became excited. With all this shortwave, and access to foreign transmissions in Mandarin, I will be able to gather many more pieces for my mosaic!

Suddenly, he heard Chinese from "The Voice of America". Now that the radio had ushered him into a whole new world, he decided to take his time and gradually explore everything foreign to him. "Go to sleep! You have an exam tomorrow!" Bao Bao warned himself.

Bao Bao was going to switch off the radio when he accidentally tuned into "The Voice of Taiwan", which seemed to be broadcasting some staggering news. Despite some hazy interruptions and noise in the background, Bao Bao listened intently.

"...recent strike of over one hundred workers at the Shanghai Phoenix Bicycle Factory!" the voice said.

Bao Bao continued to listen. "Workers sat outside their factories peacefully and silently protesting. In response, the people's government immediately dispatched over one thousand armed soldiers to remove the strikers from the streets!"

One thousand armed soldiers? That's ten times more than the number of the harmless workers! Bao Bao was amazed.

Bao Bao admired Chairman Mao. If the news from the enemy's broadcast is reliable, then Chairman Mao is not only a real genius, but also the most brilliant political leader on the earth! When Mao started his Communist Party with a handful of people in the 30s in Shanghai, he encouraged his colleagues with his famous motto, "A tiny spark can start a prairie fire". Now under his rule he has extinguished any possible spark before it emerged.

Bao Bao was proud of China because he had been told that Chinese workers would never go on strike. This was due to the unique Chinese socialistic society that turned all workers, farmers and soldiers into owners of their country. The workers were all aware that they worked for themselves. The more they contributed today, the more their offspring would harvest tomorrow. For a brighter future, they had to work hard today. It is logical that the owners would never strike for more wages, shorter working hours, or better working conditions. This was the fundamental difference between Chinese workers and western workers, the latter being exploited by capitalists whose workers go on strike ceaselessly.

There were a few other possible reasons for Bao Bao to believe why there were so few strikes in China. Firstly, the Chinese news agency would never report news to the public, with its potentially bad example. Secondly, the Chinese had lived submissively under the rule of the emperors for the past four thousand years. They were used to being tolerant as long as they had food and a place to live. Thirdly, Chinese culture had been heavily influenced by Buddhist teachings, which counselled people to be patient; to welcome suffering, and to accept their fate, in order to receive in exchange a good life through reincarnation.

Bao Bao thought that he should verify the news of a workers' strike with Chef Wang tomorrow, but after second thoughts he changed his mind, "I'd better not share this news with Chef Wang. The moment I mentioned strikes, he would know that I had listened to our enemy's broadcasts, as nowhere in China could one learn or even hear about such dreadful news. I'd better keep this secret to myself!"

Bao Bao looked at his alarm clock. It was already past one in the morning and he had to get up at six. Normally, at his age, he required eight to nine hours sleep. Tonight, he could get a maximum of only five hours' sleep. Tomorrow there was another hectic day ahead of him, since he had to take an exam in the morning and attend a street demonstration against American Imperialism in the afternoon. Without any hesitation at all, he made a resolution for himself that he would eavesdrop on his shortwave radio only on weekends. He would not listen to the radio during the week days as it would destroy his health. Also, he must be careful not to wake up Yuan Yuan who slept in the same room. "Even Yuan Yuan should be excluded from this secret," resolved Bao Bao.

# CHAPTER EIGHT

# TENSION IN THE TAIWAN STRAIT

The usual school lesson was in process when the loudspeakers overhead suddenly announced, "Attention, all teachers and students, you must discontinue your lessons immediately and proceed to the playground where we have an important announcement to make."

All the students shoved their books into their schoolbags and left the classrooms. The corridors and staircases were packed with students. Each form-teacher led his class to the designated area on the playground for the emergency meeting. Within half an hour, more than two thousand students had assembled on the playground. It was a relay of Premier Zhou En Lai's speech, made the day before yesterday, 9 June 1958, in Beijing. The school's loudspeakers were linked up to the national broadcast, so that the students could listen to the relay of the speech at the same time as many millions of Chinese people.

Bao Bao suspected that the speech would be about the political situation in the Taiwan Strait, which was becoming more and more tense every day. Certainly Bao Bao and his fellow students would have preferred to sit comfortably in their classrooms to listen to the broadcast. Nevertheless, the school authorities demanded that the students should stand outdoors to show their respect to the Honorable Premier. Furthermore, standing in the playground would make the students feel that there was a nerve-racking crisis imminent.

A week after China had started shelling the Quemoy Islands,[16] on 4 September, the US Secretary of State, John Foster Dulles, instructed by President Eisenhower, announced in public that the US would harass the People's Republic of China because of increased aggression in the Taiwan Strait from the Chinese side. The United States of America had gathered many warships in the Taiwan Strait close to Quemoy and Matsu – two tiny islands belonging to Taiwan, but located very close to the Chinese province of Fujian – and it was preparing to enter into war with China. The students listened to the Premier's speech through the loudspeakers for over an hour and then marched in groups in the direction of the People's Square in the city centre.

"Down with American aggression and the war menace!"

"Down with the American imperialists" shouted Bao Bao loudly and vigorously, in unison with his classmates as they marched.

"We will never give up if Taiwan is not liberated!"

"We support our Premier's Announcement with all our heart!"

"Get out of our Taiwan Strait, you monstrous Americans!" shouted everyone.

The participants in the parade consisted of not only students but also men from all walks of life. According to the newspaper reports on the following day, two and half a million people participated in the march. The People's Square itself was not large enough to accommodate that many people, so they marched from North to South, from East to West and vice versa. The people of Shanghai were infuriated.

"Unconditionally liberate Taiwan!" yelled Zhou.

"Unconditionally liberate Quemoy and Matsu!"

The next day over two hundred and fifty thousand people gathered again at the People's Square to listen to Mayor Chen Yi's speech, "For thousands of years, we Chinese have loved peace. It is our tradition to resist attacks from the outside. Today, however, two and a half million people in Shanghai and millions in other cities are participating in this campaign, to support our Premier's declaration to reject American intervention in our domestic affairs. We are here to show our strength – the strength of six hundred million people – to annihilate American intrusion of any kind." Mayor Chen Yi continued, "The political tension in the Taiwan Strait has been caused by US Imperialists, who must take full responsibility. Our actions are only a means of self-defense and are nonetheless justified. Truth and fairness are on our side!" shouted the Mayor.

Two and a half million inhabitants gathered in the People's Square in Shanghai and the adjacent streets. Despite heavy rain, everyone listened attentively to the Mayor's speech, which was followed by the speech of Ko Chin Sze, the First Party Secretary of Shanghai. The People's Square was packed with people.

Standing in the crowd, one could see nothing but red posters with white Chinese characters splashed across them, expressing hostility to American Imperialism. The rain continued but no-one dared to leave the Square. It was an honour for those who stood inside the square, as a great number of people were standing outside on the streets.

Bao Bao was lucky to be among the ten percent inside the square. But he was not happy at all. The rain soaked his and others' clothing, but no-one complained. At this critical moment, one had to demonstrate the spirit and zest of the revolution. The red posters were soaked by the rain and the white words cut from paper and glued on the red posters were no longer legible.

The students had no right to complain. They were constantly reminded of the Red Army – the Chinese Communist army – which, in rain and snow, and under burning sunshine, had fought against the Japanese and Chiang Kai Shek's soldiers for twenty-two long years. The rain was an opportunity to show to the new government the determination of the Chinese people to resist the American Imperialists. Even so, Bao Bao hoped that after the Mayor and the First Secretary's speeches, he could go home and change out of his wet clothes.

But, oh no! Bao Bao saw the President of the Labour Union Mr Chen Ming, take the microphone after the First Secretary of the Party had spoken. To Bao Bao's dismay, Mr Chen Ming's speech was followed by the army spokesman, the Communist Youth Leader, and then the representatives of farmers, of the women's union and of writers, one after another. Bao Bao was dripping with rain and bored because all the speeches were similar. "What a huge waste of time!" he murmured. But of course Bao Bao he did not complain loudly. If he was caught criticising anything revolutionary he would be labelled a Counter-revolutionary for the rest of his life. Finally, it became dark and the big meeting came to an end. The people marched in different directions out of the Square.

On the following day it was reported that three million people had participated in the parade and the meeting in Beijing in Tian An Men Square, where the honourable Premier Zhou En Lai and Chief Party Secretary Deng Xiao Ping had appeared on the stage to greet the public.

In the days that followed, fewer classes were conducted. Students spent most of their time in the playground where they aimed to build up their bodies, to learn shooting skills and to throw stones as if they were grenades. Since only a few air rifles were available, most of the students ran instead, to build up their bodies physically. In order to defend the Motherland, it was crucial that everyone should become physically fit. The female students also showed their enthusiasm, though they were more conservative. One day over one million four hundred thousand females flooded the streets, lanes, alleyways, factories, hospitals and communes to demonstrate against American Imperialism.

The political science teacher, Teacher Ma, read out to the class from a newspaper, that on Long Life Road, a ninety-six-year-old lady had led a parade, yelling out, "After the Liberation, the position of women in our society finally turned around! Now we live happily and with joy in life. But American Imperialism prevents us from leading a good and peaceful life! We must annihilate the Americans and we must liberate Taiwan and liberate the women there, living in suppression under the Chiang Kai Shek regime!" In his heart, Bao Bao doubted that a woman would be able to walk on the Long Life Road when she was ninety-six years old."

Teacher Ma continued, "The women of Ping An Road in Yu Lin district marched to the steel factory with wheelbarrows full of used steel and metal parts, demanding that the old steel be melted down to produce canon-shells to defend the Motherland.

"The female students of the First Normal Institute carried rifles while parading. After intensive training for three days and three nights, thirty-five of them became qualified shooters and eight of them became excellent shooters. In the afternoon, a parade of women arrived at the People's Square and a similar meeting on a large scale took place. In the evening, women marchers carried torches on the streets."

Auntie spent the whole day outside on the streets, marching and protesting and displaying posters. She was so busy these days that the only time of relaxation was when she took a quick nap or siesta in the hot afternoon. – The siesta had become quite popular in China. Although China is not a tropical country, not only housewives but men of all walks of life had grown accustomed to spending half an hour or so at their desks or in a public area to take a quick nap, to gather more energy for their afternoon and evening activities. This was due to the lack of nutritious food.

After taking a nap Auntie attended studies organized by the residential women's association. They discussed political developments in small and big groups and marched in parades, according to instructions given by the Party. This morning she left home very early without preparing breakfast for the family. The political demands of her appearance in the parade against America weighed much more with her than private household chores. Bao Bao went out to buy some *da bing* – some baked Chinese cakes[17] – for the family's breakfast. At noon, as well as in the evening, Lin Lin and Bao Bao would return home and find nothing to eat in the kitchen. Uncle would put some noodles into boiling water and the whole family would eat the noodles with soya sauce.

This particular day happened to be Bao Bao's sixteenth birthday. Uncle promised to celebrate his birthday on a later day at a restaurant when the political tensions eased. There were only a few restaurants around, and even in the restaurants one needed ration coupons to buy rice or noodles and the choice of dishes was limited. Who could afford to go to a restaurant? – Definitely not an ordinary teacher like Song Ping and his family. – However, for Bao Bao it was possible to visit a restaurant once a year, as he received regular remittances from his Ma Ma abroad.

While eating the plain noodles, Bao Bao thought of his previous birthday with his Ma Ma. In celebration of the special occasion, his Ma Ma had cooked a couple of Bao Bao's favourite dishes. The shortage of food was not severe a year ago, but this year the situation was completely different. They ate the plain noodles silently and Bao Bao reminisced about the old days when one could eat noodles with a big piece of pork. Now they had only 500 grams of pork for the whole household for an entire month. What could Auntie do with such a small amount of meat?

While she was crying out loudly, "Down with the Paper Tiger of American Imperialism!" Bao Bao's auntie was asking herself, "What am I doing here? It is Bao Bao's birthday! What have my daughter, husband, Bao Bao and Yuan Yuan had to eat today?" The guilty feeling made her cry. The parades seemed idiotic to her and it was absurd that she, a housewife, had to attend them so often.

Another of the parades, Auntie would never forget: It was to welcome the Indonesian President Sukarno on his state visit to Beijing and Shanghai. [18] The organizer of the welcome committee had explicitly instructed all women to dress colourfully, as opposed to their usual dark blue uniforms. Auntie possessed a long, silky evening gown that was made for her wedding in the old days. Since the Liberation she had not dared to wear this elegant rosy-coloured evening gown because it was a symbol of corrupt, bourgeois life. But on the occasion of welcoming President Sukarno, she took it out of her suitcase and ironed it.

Prior to the visit of President Sukarno to Shanghai, documentary films had been shown all over the city, documenting how the splendid and magnificent Sukarno had been received in Beijing. Crowds of people, cars, bicycles, fresh flowers, paper flowers and flags of all colours flooded every street from the airport to the downtown area. People were dressed in colourful clothing as if they were celebrating at a carnival. They happily marched along while men banged gongs, women waved flags and youngsters carried banners and posters bearing President Sukarno and Chairman Mao's photos. Crowds stood close together on two sides of the more than twenty kilometre long road from the airport to the State Guest House. Posters with big Chinese and Indonesian slogans could be seen everywhere. "Long live President Sukarno!" "Long Live Chairman Mao!" "Merdeka" – "Independence in Indonesia" – "Bung Karno" – "Brother Karno".

At 1.00pm, all the prominent leaders arrived at the Beijing airport. Among them was Chairman Mao. Four Chinese aeroplanes had escorted the President's aeroplane from the Mongolian border. When the President emerged from his plane, the thunderous cheers of a million people broke out. President Sukarno was dressed in an army uniform of the highest rank with the black angular hat of the common man. He stepped down from the aeroplane with an erect carriage, and with a smile plastered across his face. Chairman Mao walked towards him and they shook hands warmly. Then they walked together towards the crowd. The deafening cheering and roaring continued. Then the President and Chairman stepped into a black limousine, which drove away, followed by hundreds of cars. "What a sensational sight! Certainly Shanghai is putting up a magnificent welcome for the President!" Bao Bao thought, watching the film.

All of a sudden, Indonesian folk dances became very popular in China. All across China cinemas showed Indonesian scenery. This was the first time that a tropical country's pictures had been introduced to China. For a whole week, many people in Shanghai were busy making paper flowers, writing posters and hanging portraits of President Sukarno and Chairman Mao across the city.

On the day of the President's arrival in Shanghai, Auntie, like millions of people, was called on in the early morning by her women's association to participate in the parade. Bao Bao, Yuan Yuan, Uncle Song and Lin Lin on the other hand all went respectively to their school or work unit to form part of the grand parade.

In the beginning, Auntie was quite happy that she finally had the chance to dress beautifully. For the first time in years, she was allowed to wear her long silk gown. However, towards noon she grew impatient and asked herself, "When will the President arrive? People are becoming tired under the hot midday sun, wandering around the streets!" She had been happy in the morning when she found that the evening gown still fitted her well and that she still looked beautiful in the mirror, though for many years now she had been forbidden to think of beauty. Now she frowned because, wearing the long silk gown, she could not sit on the dirty pavements with the other women. Her legs were wobbly and her feet were sore from hours of standing. Even before leaving her house that morning, she was already exhausted from her active participation in the welcoming preparations.

A vendor came by with a basket of mantou – soft white steamed bread made of flour. Auntie rushed to pay five fens and was lucky to get a mantou for her lunch. In a few minutes the whole basket of mantou was sold out and most people had nothing to eat. Auntie quickly wolfed down her first bit of food for the day. It was a funny sight to see in the street a lady dressed in an elegant silk gown biting so eagerly into a mantou. But at the moment, nobody in China paid attention to etiquette.

Their neighbour Mrs Tang offered Auntie a cup of tea. Auntie Ying was grateful and said, "Thank you so much for your tea. This morning I left home in such a hurry that I forgot to bring my thermos flask with me, although I had filled it with tea."

Behind Auntie Ying and Mrs Tang came a whisper from a stranger, "The Government should buy us a free lunch at least."

Immediately a cold voice replied, "Are you crazy? It would cost the government a couple of million yuans if everyone had a free lunch. Don't forget we are volunteers here and we do it for our country!" Auntie turned her head around and saw that the speaker was Mrs Liu, assistant to the secretary of the Women's Association.

Mrs Liu looked at all of them and added, "Comrades, we should be overwhelmed with gratitude to our dear Party and to the honourable Chairman Mao that we women have the great honour to receive a President. After the Liberation, housewives such as ourselves are no longer slaves, confined to the kitchen all the time. I know most of you have not brought lunch with you, but the fact that the President's flight is delayed is beyond our control. You can have your lunch when you return home in the late afternoon, or even in the evening. Now is a great time to show your revolutionary zeal! Long Live Chairman Mao!" she shouted, simultaneously raising her right arm. All the people present were obliged to raise their arms and shout after her, "Long Live President Sukarno!" "Merdeka!" "Selamat Datang Bung Karmo!" – "Welcome, Brother Kano!" Shouting slogans enlivened them and they soon forgot about their hunger.

"The President's aeroplane will land in one hour. It won't be long!" remarked a responsible young man. Auntie was pleased that she had eaten a mantou. She was sure those who had not got a mantou were not happy. But any unpleasant feeling had to be suppressed. Outside they had to keep their mouths shut and put on a smiling face. The fresh flowers which they had brought for the President looked tired. And so did the people. The flowers did not need to demonstrate a revolutionary spirit. They did not experience thirst after shouting slogans. Fortunately only a small number of them were fresh. Most of the flowers were hand-made.

Finally Auntie put her handkerchief on the pavement and sat on it. Her neighbour Mrs Tang also sat on her handkerchief beside Auntie.

"You are lucky that you have eaten a mantou," said Mrs Tang with envy.

"How about you? Have you eaten something?" asked Auntie Ying.

"No, nothing, except a cup of tea. Now my stomach is growling from hunger. I did not expect it to last so long and there is no toilet that we can use," said Tang, feeling uncomfortable.

"But you may go into any shop and ask if you can use their toilet. They dare not refuse you!" answered Auntie.

Seeing that nobody was listening to their conversation, Tang added, "We women are very unfortunate to be dragged out of our homes to take part in such nonsense. In the old days, when the old government asked us to do things, they would pay us. Now we get no pay, no free meal, not even a cup of water. This is really ridiculous! We are no better than slaves now."

Auntie tacitly agreed, but was careful not to say anything which might offend the new regime. "To be frank with you I really wanted to go to the market to prepare food for the family and then stay at home. Now my husband, daughter and relatives will come home and there will be no lunch for them. They will be starving. I don't know how they will survive. I feel so guilty! You see, today is my nephew's birthday! I really wanted to go to the market this morning," Auntie Ying repeated with tears welling up in her eyes, "to find something special for the occasion."

Mrs Tang complained, "What can you buy in the market nowadays? It's empty. We are wasting our time here, waiting for the President and we waste time in the market as well. Yesterday I arrived at the market at five in the morning and found many big stones, beer bottles, an old chair and dirty clothes, one after another, forming a long line on the floor in front of the meat stand. Shortly before they started to sell the meat, all of a sudden there were many people in front of me, because the night before they or their friends had placed these items on the floor to identify their position in the queue. Ten minutes before sales at the meat or fish stand started, they appeared at their front positions in the queue, as represented by the stones, beer bottles, old chair, and dirty clothes. Because so many people used this dishonest method of queuing, by the time I arrived at the stand from my place in the queue, the meat was sold out. I wasted one and a half hours and I came home with nothing but a catty of vegetables. This is our life in this happy, socialist society. We should be grateful to the Party and to Chairman Mao for giving us such a wonderful life."

"It's not fair. It happens to me too, every day, "Auntie said in reply. "I really hate it and I always want to remove the bottles and stones."

"No. It's impossible," Mrs Tang replied. "Those who play those tricks are usually either rogues or friends of the sales-girls who sell the meat and fish. If we moved the stones or the bottles, they would beat us, or kill us.

"It's ridiculous. Even with money and a ration coupon, there is no guarantee that we can buy food.

"The bad thing is that our government knows only how to drive us out to parades and political campaigns. They don't look after us. Everywhere we need connections, even to buy food."

"What was the market like in the old days?" Auntie Ying asked, curiously. "I ask this because I am a newcomer in Shanghai."

"Before, in Chiang Kai Shek's time, everything that you could think of was available in the market. All you needed was money. Now under the new regime, money is not enough. You also need a ration coupon and connections! My recent experience of wasting an hour and a half, queuing in vain, was not unusual!"

Then Auntie Ying asked another question. "Where is the beef? Why don't we get ration coupons for beef?"

"Beef goes to the Muslims in place of pork. There is no beef for us. The cows have to work hard in the rice fields." Mrs Tang wanted to continue but suddenly they heard people applauding and cheering loudly about one hundred metres away.

A man in a blue cotton suit came up on a bicycle and cried out loudly, "Everybody stand up! The President is visible! Applaud! Smile! Cheer! Shout!" Everyone did as the comrade had commanded, but there was no President in sight. Only after ten minutes of continuous cheering, shouting and applauding did a black limousine drive by. People applauded fiercely and shouted as loudly as they could, throwing paper flowers at the moving car. Auntie pushed herself forwards with all her might to the front, as she wanted to take a good look at the President. When she finally got to the front, the black limousine whizzed by and she had only a brief look. The President wore a prestigious uniform and a black angled ordinary person's hat just as they had seen in the film. His sunglasses covered part of his face. Next to him was Mayor Chen Yi.

Coming back home, Auntie was exhausted and annoyed. She said to Uncle, "I have been standing from six in the morning until six in the evening, but I saw the President only for a few seconds in the far distance. Was this worthwhile? On top of those twelve hours, we spent more than a week in preparation." Uncle looked around out of habit to make sure no stranger was in the room and said, "Our New China was born a few years ago and we have been endeavouring since then to join the United Nations. Our application has always been rejected, because the small island of Taiwan is representing China. The last time twelve countries voted, 'Yes' for us, and forty-two countries said, 'No'. Sukarno voted in our favour and besides, he is one of the very few presidents of a capitalist country willing to visit us. Therefore we need to impress him by giving him the warmest of welcomes. "But who knows? Perhaps we will condemn him in a few years time. In politics, everything is possible. To the State it was better for you to stand under the burning sun, waiting for Sukarno rather than sit at home, thinking funny things."

Bao Bao had been annoyed when he found nothing to eat for dinner, particularly considering that he had not eaten any lunch. Now his uncle's explanation pacified him, as he was eager to do everything for his country. Auntie had no more questions and promised, "Tomorrow, I shall prepare breakfast and leave it on the table before I go to the market. I hope to find food and make a good meal for you all."

The following evening Bao Bao remained late at school because of shooting practice. In the school grounds, a few gas lamps were lit so the students could work during the night. The political tension rose from day to day and the islands of Quemoy and Matsu were shelled from the mainland at least a few thousand times daily. The train service to Fujian Province, which is close to these two small islands, was cancelled. All those with a bad personal profile or a bad family background, such as former land owners, family members of Counter-Revolutionaries and capitalists, were ordered by Beijing to leave Fujian Province, where the battle front would be. It looked like war would break out at any moment.

All classes were temporarily suspended. The Lao Wei System was set up. "Lao" represents physical exercise and "Wei" means, to defend the Motherland. The standard of Lao Wei was set very high, similar to what is required of a professional sportsman. For example, the running speed for men should not be more than thirteen seconds for a hundred metres and not less than one point five metres for the high jump. Since the goal of Lao was so high, the majority of students could not reach it. Fortunately one heard no more about Lao Wei later on. However, the school reported to the responsible authorities that every student had passed the Lao Wei test and was ready to go to the front. Bao Bao knew it was a lie.

Tonight after shooting practice, Bao Bao's class remained in the playground, where every one of them was asked to swear, in front of the red national flag, in the dim gas-light, that he was willing to join the Communist Youth League and ready to be sent to the Front. They lined up one by one to take this oath. Now it was Bao Bao's turn. He stood up, walked forward a few steps, raised his right arm and, holding in his left hand the paper he was given, read out, in a trembling voice. "I, Song Bao Bao, swear that I am determined to join the Communist Youth League. With my life, I will defend my Motherland and I am ready to go to the Fujian battle-front now." After he finished reading, he put his arm down, went back to his position, and handed the paper over to the next student who stepped forward in turn. Matching his trembling voice, Bao Bao's inner confusion was beyond description.

It was too much for him. Bao Bao would never have made such a solemn declaration if he had not been forced to do so. Things went too fast for Bao Bao to cope with; he had no time to think and make a decision. In Bao Bao's class, five members of the Communist Youth League forced the entire class to swear the oath that night. Tomorrow, they would report this to the Party Secretary and get credit for it. Had Bao Bao had sufficient time to think it over, it would have been a slow and painful decision. He would never have made such a decision so quickly. Now he was angry that he had not had a chance to determine the course of his own life. He found it cunning of the Youth League members to force him to swear an oath right after shooting-practice in the dim gas-light, when they were hungry and exhausted. In the end, twenty-six students in the class swore the oath. The five members of the Youth League had accomplished their mission and they let everyone go home.

Bao Bao did not realize it was nine in the evening. Now he felt hungry as he had not eaten dinner yet. The revolutionary spirit had outweighed his hunger. Now on his way home he was released from his political burden, so he could allow himself to feel hungry. As soon as Bao Bao went out of the school gate, someone tapped him on the shoulder. Bao Bao turned round. It was his close friend, Wu Hai Bin.

"Hi, Bao Bao! What do you think of tonight's event? Aren't you happy that you have sworn an oath and that you can become a member of the Youth League?"

"I don't know how to describe my feeling. I don't mind becoming a member of the Communist Youth League, as it will lead to Party membership when I grow up. As you know, to become a Party member is the ultimate goal for everyone, otherwise we will have no future."

"So you are determined to be sent to the front and to die there?"

"No. I am not ready to carry a heavy rifle and use my body to block the non-stop shooting of the enemy's machine guns. In other words I am not ready to die. I have many plans for my life."

"In this case you are not a good Communist. Do you know what it means to be a Communist?" Wu challenged Bao Bao.

"Yes, of course I know. As Vice-Chairman Liu Shaoqi said, it means 'Immediate readiness to offer one's personal interest, even life for the Party'," replied Bao Bao fluently.

"Since you are not ready to die, why did you swear the oath tonight?" Wu continued to challenge him.

"And why did *you* swear?" Bao Bao retorted. "Don't bullshit me that you are ready to die and that your political consciousness is higher than mine. I know you as well as you know me. We are good friends. When we talk to each other we can take off our masks. Tonight we were both morally blackmailed by those five huai dan bastards, those bad eggs! Tomorrow they will get credit, but we are no longer in charge of our own fate."

"What do you mean by not being in charge of our own fate? A few minutes ago you confessed that you would like to be in the Youth League and even join the Party later. Now according to the solemn declaration we made under the red national flag we are already members of the Youth League. You should be happy that they did not do a background check on you, otherwise..."

Bao Bao interrupted him. "Otherwise what? Do you mean they wouldn't let me join the Youth League, because of my parents? Is that what you are trying to say?" Bao Bao was annoyed and continued, "I don't think the authorities have overlooked my family background. They just need people to go to the front. I can imagine that they might send inexperienced youngsters to fight at the front during the first part of the battle. After a million youngsters die, than the professional soldiers will follow to attack the enemy. This strategy will distract the enemy and as a result the professional soldiers will be able to hit them badly and win the battle easily. Hai Bin, my dear friend, I hope you don't think that your family background is much better than mine," Bao Bao warned his friend. "Your father is a writer, an intellectual, and I don't think Chairman Mao will like this very much, although he himself is a scholar. Don't forget that Mao gave the order to clean up the city of Shanghai by burning an enormous number of books. This was the first thing he did after he took over control in China. Perhaps you might end up going to the battle-front with me. Certainly, I hope I'm wrong. As I just mentioned, I'm not ready to die."

"Don't worry, Bao Bao! China is huge. We have a population of over six hundred million. If Chairman Mao wishes, he can send half of the entire population to the front. He doesn't need to send us teenagers to the war. We are hardly able to carry heavy rifles as yet."

"You are right, Hai Bin. I worry too much. In these past few days they have trained us to shoot, to do physical exercises, and to fight. They have asked us to swear oaths. All of this might simply be just a test to see if we are absolutely obedient to the Party and at the Chairman's disposition."

"I hope the tension in the Taiwan Strait will ease soon, so that our lives will go back to normal," said Hai Bin.

"I hope so too," added Bao Bao. "We have wasted about two weeks on the Taiwan issue and I hope normal classes will resume soon, as I really miss school."

"Me too. It is disgusting to take part in ridiculous campaign after ridiculous campaign, but we have no choice."

"If the political situation goes on like this, we will miss too many classes. In that case I'll never become a scientist."

"Who wants you to be a scientist? Chairman Mao wants us to become farmers or workers."

"Yes, Hai Bin, you are right. That is precisely my problem. How about you? What is your ambition?"

"I don't have a specific ambition to be this or that at this time. I will just take what life offers me."

"Anyway let's hope this Taiwan Campaign will soon be over and that the regime will not be so silly as to send us to the front," Bao Bao said, concluding the conversation.

At home, before Bao Bao went to sleep, he switched on the radio. He tuned into the Voice of America, but it was in a foreign language. He recalled that the Voice of America in Mandarin was available only at midnight. Now it was half past ten and he could not wait for so long as he was worn out. He browsed through different channels and suddenly found Chinese Mandarin from an overseas broadcasting station. The news was horrifying. It said that Mao's intention, when he started the trouble by shelling Quemoy and Matzu, was to induce American's largest fleet, the Seventh Fleet, to come to the Taiwan Strait for a direct confrontation. Nikita Khruschev, then the Prime Minister of Russia, was nervous that, once the war broke out, Russia would be obliged to protect China, according to the Sino-Russian military defence agreement. Through many interferences in the transmission, Bao Bao could make out the news that Mao's intention was to create a nuclear war between America and

Russia in the Taiwan Strait. The outcome of an eventual nuclear war would be that three hundred million Chinese would die and the remaining three hundred million Chinese would be the ultimate winners. Bao Bao was panic-stricken. He could not believe what he heard. He would like to see Chef Wang tomorrow because it was extremely important to find out whether the news was reliable or not.

After school Bao Bao strolled along the street for a while. He looked in the shop windows and found that most shops did not have many things to offer. The colourful fashion dresses that were usually on display had disappeared; instead there were monotonous dark blue Mao suits in the store windows. Why does everybody wear the same Chinese jackets in dark blue, grey and dark green? Could this be the Chairman's idea that the entire people should think and dress in the same way as prescribed by him? Bao Bao was curious about this. The shoe shops no longer exhibited ladies' multicoloured high-heeled shoes, but in their place only cotton, rubber-soled shoes were for sale. As high heels and beautiful dresses belonged to the extravagance of bourgeois society, they must all be eradicated.

Bao Bao continued walking and turned the corner where Fuxing Road and Ruijin Road met. He glanced into the window of the pharmacy store at the corner and found that much of the pharmacy displays had been changed. Usually in the showcases, the pharmacy exhibited all kinds of different birth control methods including pills, condoms and plastic appliances, but now it showed only toothpastes, toothbrushes and hand creams. Bao Bao was always curious to see the birth control products, as he wondered how adults used them to accomplish their secret mission in bed.

About a year ago, China's Health Minister, Li De Chuan, started a Birth Control Campaign by stating, "Our country is currently big and over-populated. This over-population will hinder China's progress to become one of the world's most prosperous and powerful nations. China's over-population is suicidal to its own endeavours."

From then on, radios, movies, fliers, and posters all carried the words, "birth control" and "family planning", to propagandize the importance of practising birth control. All types of methods and appliances were displayed in the showcases of department stores, convenience stores and pharmacies. Propaganda groups frequently visited offices, factories, farms and individual household units, to introduce and promote birth control methods across China. Countless lessons were given on this subject. Bao Bao had often heard these popular words, "birth control", but did not know how it worked, as he lacked any fundamental knowledge about sex.

A few months ago, during the Birth Control Campaign, Bao Bao was told that the expansion of population across China must be curbed. It was explained that the recent population spike was due to several reasons. The new regime had not only advanced in the use of effective medicines to reduce the spread of epidemics, but had also been engaged in many water improvement works and safety measures to reduce the death rate. They said that the annual increase in the birth rate was 2.5% or fifteen million people, while the death rate was currently1.5% or nine million people.

Russia had only one-third of the population of China, yet Russia possessed 230 million hectares of agricultural land, double China's agriculture land. There were 2.5 million farmers working on 110 million hectares of agricultural land in China, whereas the Soviet Union had only four hundred thousand farmers on 170 million hectares of land. Yet Nikita Khruschev, then the Prime Minister of the Soviet Union, complained that the number of Russian farmers was four times more than their counterparts in the USA. Bao Bao wondered how machinery would affect China's infrastructure. If manual labour in China was replaced by machinery, what would the regime do with the two million plus unemployed farmers?

Professor Ma Yinchu, the Chancellor of Beijing University, the most prominent advocate of birth control, warned the National People's Congress about the population explosion, which at that time amounted to an increase of 23 million a year, equal to the entire population of Canada. If the government subsidized each baby in China with the sum of one hundred yuan, then China would have to spend a minimum of 2,300 million yuan to take care of her newborn population. This amount would increase exponentially as the population expanded and more children were produced. Furthermore, the 2,300 million yuan would not be a one-time expense for the government. For each additional year of life, every child would need clothing, food, accommodation, education, health care, doctors, and as they grew up they would need nurseries, schools, universities, teachers, professors, dormitories, books, stationery, medicine, transportation, jobs, etc. If the population expansion continued, how could China improve her living standards? If one day China were to become an industrial country, what would her people do?

After dinner, Bao Bao went to see Chef Wang, whom he had not seen for a couple of weeks.

When Bao Bao entered Chef Wang's small room, he found Chef Wang listening to local Shanghai opera. He switched off the radio and asked, "My son, what is in your mind?" Chef Wang knew Bao Bao came always with questions.

"I have noticed that the pharmacies have removed their displays of birth control pills and appliances from their showcases. Does this mean the Birth Control Campaign is no longer in effect?"

"My son, what do you know about birth control? You need to have a lesson on sex to understand fully the matters of the bedroom. Birth control is only a part of the picture. When we have more time to spend together I would like to give you a lesson on sex."

Bao Bao was cunning enough not to ask directly whether or not Mao was aiming at nuclear war as he did not want Chef Wang to suspect that he was listening to shortwave radio broadcasts. He began with the minor question of birth control and hopefully, as they chatted, they would eventually discuss the question he was really interested in.

"I am not interested to know about bedroom matters. I have time. I would rather wait until I'm thirty, just before marriage, to find out about the whole thing. Please tell me now why our government has slowed down its birth control propaganda, after giving it so much attention for over a year?"

"I guess you have heard about the importance of birth control for China," Chef Wang said, as he opened a drawer and took out a magazine. He flipped through it, then stopped at a certain page and started to read:

*Nevertheless, at the Eighth Congress of the Communist Party, held in May 1958, Chairman Mao expressed his views about the issue of the Chinese population, "Our ever fast-expanding population is an objective fact and our asset. If China were to have a nuclear war today, the aftermath would include half the population dying and the other half living. Thus, half of the six hundred million Chinese would survive from the war and would then be able to dominate the world."*

Chef Wang had hit on the precise point that Bao Bao had had in mind. Chef Wang continued, "Since the statement came from Mao, the Almighty God of our time, the government has stopped the Birth Control Campaign. Mao's China is going back to Confucian times when one's ultimate goal was to produce hundreds of sons and thousands of grandchildren, as there were no pensions in ancient China. When they grew up, every child was obliged to contribute something to his parents' living expenses. So, the more children a family had, the more income the parents would get."

"How did Health Minister Li De Chuan and Professor Ma Ying Chu react?" Bao Bao was curious to know the answer.

"When they were so active at promoting birth control, they were severely attacked by a contemporary group of scholars, who believed that Mao was accurate in advocating monumental population growth and pointed out that for thousands of years the Chinese have had pride in their enormous population. A massive population is after all the engine of human development. China could never be overpopulated. The more people, the better for China. These scholars also severly attacked the English eighteenth century scholar, Thomas Malthus, who in 1798 had published a paper, "On the dangers of population expansion".[19] Their argument was that he represented the interests of the bourgeoisie. After all, who dares to challenge Chairman Mao?" Chef Wang paused.

Bao Bao said, "I recall that I read somewhere that China suffers from a shortage of agricultural land. She has only 110 million hectares of farmland, whereas Russia possesses 230 hectares. And the Russian population is one third of China's."

"Yes, you are right, but let me show you what pro-Mao scholars have argued on this issue," answered Chef Wang, and he flipped through his official magazine. He paused at a particular page and read:

> Pro-Mao scholars argued that China is a huge country with space for any size of population. For example, Jiangsu province has a density per square metre of 384 people – 105 more people per square metre than Belgium and 72 more people per square metre than Holland – and we should note that both Belgium and Holland have the highest density per square metre in the world. Both countries together amount only to a third of Jiangsu in land-size. On the other hand, Xinjiang province is seventeen times bigger than Jiangsu in land-size with a population of five million. If Xinjiang were to have 386 people per square metre as Jiangsu Province does, it would house seven hundred million people, more than the entire current population of China. And Xinjiang is only one of the twenty-six provinces in China.

"I don't understand how living standards in China can improve if our population expands as Chairman Mao wishes," Bao Bao reflected.

"My son, you are switching the topic," Chef Wang said.

On the following day, the Defense Minister Peng De Huai announced that the daily bombing of Quemoy and Matsu from the mainland would be suspended for two weeks, so that the people of the islands could receive food supplies from Taiwan. This would be under the condition that no American war ships would be allowed to accompany cargo ships into the Taiwan Strait. Xiao Wang, Bao Bao's classmate, whispered in Bao Bao's ear. "The bombing is nonsense! We have been bombing the barren land of these two tiny islands for months. Do you know how much we have wasted every day, yet our farmers have nothing to eat. The government boasts that we have a good life, but in reality we don't."

Bao Bao did not reply for a while, because he did not know what to say. He was not well acquainted with Xiao Wang. He did not want to say something which Xiao Wang could eventually use to denounce him one day, although certainly he would never denounce anyone for sure. Finally Bao Bao replied, "Nothing can go wrong if we follow strictly Chairman Mao's instruction to shell Quemoy and Matsu a thousand times a day."

However, eight days later, the bombing resumed because American ships were caught sight of in the Taiwan Strait. Five days later, Minister Peng changed his plan into shelling the two islands on alternative days. Bao Bao agreed with what Xiao Wang had said. The new regime could no longer afford to waste so much money. It made no sense to throw money into the water.

A few weeks later, Bao Bao heard less and less about the Liberation of Taiwan. Meetings, parades, discussions and theatre shows were no longer focused on the topic of "Taiwan" and posters regarding the "Liberation of Taiwan" gradually disappeared, faded, or were washed away by the rain. The solemn declaration of Bao Bao and his peers, to go to the front to die for the country, was not mentioned by anyone any more. Apparently the Taiwan Campaign was over. Bao Bao received no confirmation of his membership of the Communist Youth League. Bao Bao had been right when he thought it was merely the Party's test to find out whether the youngsters had any objection to joining the Communist Youth League and dying for the Motherland during their teenage years.

# CHAPTER NINE

# BRAINWASHING

After two weeks of regular classes, the senior high school students gathered again in the assembly hall. Instead of regular lessons in the classrooms, the school authorities had invited a hero – the son of a proletarian family – to tell his own story to the students. For those who were not serious about their studies, life at school in Mao's era was full of excitement, as unexpected events took place one after another. Students went to school every day, but not necessarily to attend classes. Chairman Mao was aiming to change everyone's thought, so he launched one campaign after another.

Right after the Communists took over China in 1949, the Land Reform Movement was launched to discriminate against landowners and to distribute the land to poor farmers in the countryside, and this was followed by a series of Thought Reform Movements targeting intellectuals across China. The Three-Anti Campaign was introduced against Communist Party Members, to combat waste, corruption and bureaucracy. The Five-Anti Campaign – against bribery, theft, inside information, fraud and tax evasion – aimed primarily at businessmen. In 1956, the Socialization of Capitalist Enterprises Campaign was introduced for the government to take over private enterprises. In the same year, Chairman Mao launched the slogan, "Let a Hundred Flowers Bloom and Let a Hundred Schools of Thought Contend!", encouraging tens of thousands of intellectuals to speak out their grievances against the Communist Party. A year later, Chairman Mao swung his policy round, launched the Anti-Rightist Campaign, labelling as Rightists those who had critized the Party.

By 1954, the Three-Anti and Five-Anti movements were approaching an end. Many people had been arrested and sent to gaols or to labour camps in distant, remote places for Thought Reform. In the Thought Reform camps, they were treated as prisoners and forced to endure hard labour for long hours. In the evenings they had to study Communist doctrines and Mao's work. But those who denounced their bosses, parents, relatives, friends or neighbours in favour of the Communist Party were put on a pedestal and worshipped as heroes.

Today, the guest speaker was Comrade Gao Si Yan, who came from a proletarian family. Gao was at one time corrupt However, after brainwashing by the Party, Gao returned to denounce his former boss and became an instant superstar in the new society. Now Gao was employed by the municipal government. His job was to deliver his own story to the public. In the past few years, he had given countless speeches to schools, factories and work units. Today, Gao Si Yan had come to speak at the famous Shanghai High School. In the morning the assembly-hall was fully packed with students and teachers. In the eyes of the school authorities, today's attendance by students weighed much more than a regular lesson. At half past eight, Comrade Gao appeared on stage. He was a tall man, over one point eight metres, clothed in a grey-blue Mao suit, like millions of Chinese on the street. As soon as Gao walked up onto the stage, Bao Bao was perplexed, for Gao looked quite familiar. Bao Bao had seen him somewhere before, but could not remember where.

Gao began his presentation by telling his experience of writing confessional essays towards the end of 1953. He had been chosen by the new regime to write his self-criticism at one of the Confession Centres located in Pu Dong, a suburb of Shanghai. At the Centre, he was assigned to a group of eight under the supervision of Cadre Pei. Gao was asked to write his confession beginning from the age of seven onwards as from that age he had begun to comprehend his surroundings and events.

Bao Bao was sitting in the middle of the assembly-hall. He was sleep-deprived from the night before, because he had been listening to the shortwave broadcast. Sitting in the middle row amongst hundreds of students, Bao Bao felt at ease because he was not being watched by teachers or activist students. He was so relaxed that he soon dozed off.

Suddenly Bao Bao heard in his sleep the name of Li Guo Ming mentioned by Gao Si Yan. He was shocked and woke up. Isn't Li Guo Ming the father of my best friend Li Yong? Bao Bao thought and he turned his head around to look for Li Yong. He found him. Li Yong was sitting also in the middle, two rows behind him. Li's face reddened, and Bao Bao knew he was right. The person whom Gao Si Yan had attacked was Li's father. Bao Bao was bewildered. Is Li ashamed of his father's sin, or does he hate Gao who betrayed his father and is now elevated to the stage as a hero? Bao Bao had great sympathy for Li Yong, who was in an embarrassing situation that day. Had Li Yong known today's guest speaker was Gao Si Yan, certainly he would never have come to school! It was too bad no-one knew beforehand who the invited guest speaker was. With Communism you can never predict anything! How horrible that my friend has to put up with this! What a pain in the neck for Li Yong! Bao Bao saw that nobody around was paying attention to him and fell asleep again.

In the midst of his deep sleep, he felt someone tugging at his arm; his fellow classmate was trying to wake him up, as Gao's speech had come to an end. "What time is it?" Bao Bao asked as he jolted upright. "It's lunch time," answered his classmate. At this moment, Party Secretary Huang stepped up onto the stage. He thanked the hero Gao for coming to the school and for his speech. He then proceeded to give a homework assignment to all students. "In the next political session there will be a class discussion on Comrade Gao's speech, which will be conducted by the class teacher of each class."

Bao Bao was astonished. My God, why will there be a class discussion on Gao's speech? When did they add this session? The class discussion was not planned, nor announced beforehand. How come? What am I going to say to my class teacher, Teacher Fang, the day after tomorrow? I listened to nothing that Gao said. How awful! Today's speech isn't similar to familiar topics such as Dr Bethune and American imperialism, which I can easily spin out! I know nothing about this Gao!

Then he thought of a solution. I'd better catch up with Li Yong right now. I'm sure he knows every detail of Gao's speech. I'd better walk home with him and ask him to tell me everything. Bao Bao looked for Li Yong among the students who had been dismissed. Bao Bao found him and followed a couple of metres behind him. As soon as they stepped out of the school gates, Bao Bao hastened to catch up with Li and said, "Li Yong, tell me everything about today's meeting. I was sleeping for the entire session. I was exhausted this morning because I went to bed late last night. I understand what your feelings must be towards that huai dan bastard, Gao. But can you summarize his speech without bias for me? I need it for the class discussion the day after tomorrow."

"Of course I can! You're my best friend. I would do anything for you. Don't worry, Bao Bao!"

Bao Bao did not mention that he had been listening to shortwave radio broadcasting late in the night and that this was why he lacked energy this morning. Bao Bao treated listening to the enemy broadcasting in the night as his top top secret. He would never share it with anyone, not with his best friend or even with his sister, Yuan Yuan. Bao Bao thought, "It wouldn't work if I leaked my secret to Li. Li might tell the next person to keep it a secret and the next person would tell another next person to keep it a secret. Soon many schoolmates would know it and it might come to the attention of the police. One day the police would come to put handcuffs on my wrists and send me to gaol. The radio equipment and the antenna would be the best possible evidence of my crime. I would be speechless to defend myself during interrogation. One wrong move would ruin my life completely. Life can be so cruel!"

"Bao Bao, you have not missed much. The meeting was very boring. If my father had not been directly involved with Gao, I would have taken a nap as well. I believe one third of the students fell asleep this morning. Perhaps this was the reason Party Secretary Huang scheduled a class discussion at the last minute to challenge those like you who did not pay attention to the speech in the assembly-hall. You are very fortunate to have me to tell you everything. I don't think there is anyone else at the school who knows Gao's case better than I do."

Li Yong continued, "Basically Gao told us that he came from an extremely poor family and was taken home by my Dad who sent him to school. Then he worked at my Dad's office. His speech focused on the story of how the writing of numerous confessional essays changed his gratitude to hatred towards my Dad."

Bao Bao was pleased and said, "Gao should have been very grateful to your father. What happened after that?"

"Then came the Five-Anti Movement in 1951-53. The regime was looking for someone to denounce my Dad and they chose his former employee, Gao, who in the eyes of the authorities was the best person to file suit against my father, the man who had saved his life."

"How could the regime choose Gao, knowing that Gao owed your father so much? How could the Party demand Gao, specifically, to stab your father in the back? Gao is definitely the wrong person to carry out this mission, as under normal circumstances Gao would never do such an ungrateful thing to your Dad who had saved his life."

"But in the meantime the Party converted him into an enemy of my father and made him accuse my father publicly."

Bao Bao asked, "Tell me, what did the Party do to change Gao from a grateful person to an enemy of your father?"

"It will take quite a while to explain."

"Then explain it to me briefly!" Bao Bao was getting impatient.

"First of all, Gao was sent to an isolated place called a "Confession-Centre" in Pu Dong, a Shanghai suburb, and there he was surrounded by many strange participants who were gathered there for the same objective of writing a confessional essay or self-criticism."

"What is a self-criticism?" Bao Bao asked.

"Gao was asked to write his life story with serious remarks about all his wrongdoings that were not in line with the Party's policy."

"What was his story? Can you briefly outline it?" Bao Bao requested.

"Gao came from a very poor family. At the age of seven he witnessed his Ma Ma's death from cholera. His sister was sold to a landowner as a slave-maid. He and his father suffered from constant starvation. They endured several floods and droughts and witnessed the Japanese invaders killing innocent Chinese people. Later on, he and his father begged their way to Shanghai, where his father became a rickshaw driver and Gao was a beggar. One day my Dad saw Gao begging in the street and out of sympathy, my Dad took him home and sent him to school."

Bao Bao commented, "That was Gao's life story, not a self-criticism nor a confessional essay."

"Yes, you are right. That was his first essay, which was immediately rejected by Cadre Pei, who demanded that Gao's writing should emphasize his life after the Liberation in 1949, particularly with my Dad. He also pointed out to Gao that my Dad was a criminal merchant and a Counter-revolutionary."

"What was Gao's reaction?" questioned Bao Bao.

"Gao initially had a difficult time. He hoped to see my Dad or give him a phone call to find out how much of the past could be revealed, so he and my Dad could give a consistent account. But this was impossible, as he was not allowed to make any phone call, nor could he leave the Centre. Cadre Pei asked Gao to write a critical confessional essay and assigned him a private room, isolated from other participants."

"Did Gao encounter difficulty in writing about his business life with your father?" asked Bao Bao.

"Extremely difficult! Gao said in his speech that he racked his brain for two days in the cell."

"What made it so difficult?"

"Because Gao did not know whether he should write all the wrongdoings or just part of them. If he confessed that he had helped his boss, my Dad, to change a medicine label from a cheap to an expensive one, doubtless Gao would be charged and arrested, and my Dad would be imprisoned too, due to Gao's declaration. Gao hesitated to admit everything, because he knew that my Dad was smart enough not to say much in an interrogation."

Gradually the two youngsters were approaching Bao Bao's home. Li said, "Song Bao Bao, how about you go home and I shall pick you up on my way to school in the morning, so that we will have enough time to continue with Gao's story?"

"Great, shout for me or send me a signal in the morning and I will come down," said Bao Bao as he made a turn into his alleyway.

During lunch, Bao Bao was obsessed with Gao's dilemma. On the one hand, if Gao did not write down all his wrongdoings, Cadre Pei would not let him go. But on the other hand, if he did, the regime could convict him and legitimately send him off to prison. Furthermore, Gao's admission of guilt would directly affect Li Yong's father and he would be arrested immediately on account of Gao's confession.

What would I have done if I were Gao? Bao Bao asked himself. Hmm, it's a tough question. He thought for a while and came up with an answer. I would condemn my former boss Li for actions in which I was not implicated, such as bribing Communist cadres in various ways to win commercial contracts. As for the adulteration of medicine labels, I would not mention it at all, as it is a big crime, in which I was actively involved.

Bao Bao nodded as he was quite sure that the authorities were not aware of the adulteration, otherwise both Gao and Li would be in gaol right now and Gao would not be here at the school to deliver his speech to the students. However, Bao Bao was confused as to why the authorities had wasted so much time and effort to let Gao write one confessional essay one after another. Bao Bao felt at a loss.

Nevertheless, on second thoughts, Bao Bao was no longer sure of his own judgment. Things may not be as simple and straightforward as I think. I'd better be careful and not fall into a trap, Bao Bao warned himself.

At this moment, Gao's lanky figure and melancholy face popped into Bao Bao's mind. No wonder he seems so familiar! Bao Bao thought excitedly. I have seen him before at Chef Wang's coffee house! He had a vivid image of Gao standing up to bid Chef Wang farewell one afternoon. Bao Bao had seen Gao two or three times at Chef Wang's coffee house in the late afternoons when it was less busy, chatting with Chef Wang over a cup of coffee. Ah! Bao Bao thought as he clapped his hands together, I knew he looked familiar the moment he walked onto the stage of the assembly-hall. Why don't I go to Chef Wang to ask him about Gao! Perhaps Chef Wang and Gao are well acquainted with each other! I won't have to wait until tomorrow morning to get the information from Li. – What's more, Li might be biased, since Gao has caused so much suffering to Li's father. Perhaps Chef Wang can give me another side of the story! Bao Bao glanced at the clock on the wall. Two-thirty in the afternoon! Alright, I'll go later today after I finish my homework.

That evening Bao Bao went to see Chef Wang at his home. "My son," he said as soon as he saw Bao Bao, "Tell me, what is your new question?"

"Chef Wang, do you know a tall guy called Gao Si Yan?"

With no hesitation Chef Wang replied, "Of course I know him. Tell me, why do you ask about him?"

"Gao Si Yan was invited to our high school to share with us students his own story. In his speech, he told us how he had elevated himself from an associate of criminals to a proletarian hero."

"My son, you have found the right person to tell the true story of Gao Si Yan. Nobody can give you a better story of Gao than I can. I know him inside out. Tell me, why are you so curious about him? Were you unhappy with the lecture that he gave at your school? Or do you doubt him?" Chef Wang's small beady eyes searched Bao Bao's face for an answer, with much anticipation.

"Chef Wang, to be honest with you, when Gao was giving his speech I found it boring and I fell asleep. After his speech, the Party Secretary of our school unexpectedly asked us to participate in a class discussion. My failure to listen to his speech will prevent me from doing well in the class discussion. I urgently need some help!"

"No problem, my son. I can help you. Gao was a beggar. A few years ago he begged me to give him leftovers from my Coffee Shop and I did. So for two to three years he came to collect left-over food every day, until one day he met a kind gentleman who took him home and sent him to school. I must say Gao is a very handsome and hard-working young man. I like him very much. Whenever he has time he drops by to chat with me. He treats me like his own father."

Not wasting any time, Bao Bao asked, "You may recall that, during the Anti-Three and Anti-Five Campaigns, Gao was in deep trouble. He was detained at a Confession Centre, where he was asked to write confession after confession. Can you tell me how Gao Si Yan survived his confessional essay writing? – Particularly when he found himself in a dilemma about whether or not to confess absolutely everything." Bao Bao was not sure if Chef Wang knew such small details of Gao's life.

Fortunately and amazingly, Chef Wang remembered the case well and said immediately, "After a while Gao came to the conclusion that he would write only about how his former boss Li had bribed Communist officers, an act which Gao was not directly involved with. But absolutely nothing about the adulteration of medicine."

"Was his confession accepted?" questioned Bao Bao.

Chef Wang answered, "Of course not. The responsible officer flipped through Gao's self-criticism and yelled at him angrily. When Gao addressed the officer as 'Tong Zhi so and so' – as you know, the word *tong zhi* means 'comrade' or 'common goal' – the officer shouted 'Who is your Tong Zhi? Your goal is counter-revolutionary, whereas our goal is to love our Motherland.' The officer then continued, 'How many times have we brought it to your attention that you must uphold your proletarian roots and stance! Yet you still show sympathy for our class enemies. The struggle is not between Gao and Li, but between the working class and the bourgeoisie! Your main problem is that you are too shortsighted! You see only your personal advantages and comfort and forget about the bigger picture, our great proletarian China!'"

"Did the officer give Gao another chance to amend his confession?" asked Bao Bao.

"Yes he did, but it was his very last chance to write an honest confession," Chef Wang replied. He then told Bao Bao the warning that the officer gave to Gao. 'We will let you make your own decision,' he said. 'You may associate with the handful of Counter-Revolutionaries or, if you want, you can come back to us, to the family of over six hundred million Chinese. Your confession is crucial to us, as it is a written declaration, a document showing that you have broken off ties with your dirty past and have become a new person. To break off from the past can only be achieved through your own words and your own personal realization of your felonies. If you hide your sin, you will never become a new-born proletarian again.'"

Bao Bao was shocked that the authorities knew everything about Gao and he asked, "But why didn't they arrest him? I can't understand that."

"My son, it was a part of the brainwashing process. Soon you will see how the brainwashing method worked on Gao."

"What happened then? questioned Bao Bao. "Did Gao confess, this time around?"

"In the days that followed, Gao Si Yan found himself in isolation. His peers ignored him. It was as if he was already deemed a Counter-revolutionary. Everybody stayed away from him. Nobody dared to address him as Tong Zhi – comrade – and sometimes he felt that his peers were gossiping and speaking badly of him behind his back.

"How did Gao feel?" Bao Bao was anxious to know about this.

"Slowly, Gao began to change. He began to reprimand himself, saying 'Gao Si Yan, you are very different from your former self now. You think of nothing but the comfort, idleness and coziness of the bourgeoisie to which you don't belong. You have forgotten about your suffering in the past and your sister's miserable fate. You don't belong to the side of the exploited, but to the side of the class enemy. Think of what you did for Boss Li at night! The adulteration of medicine could have poisoned and killed injured soldiers.' Bao Bao stared at Chef Wang with admiration for his ability to remember the details so well.

Chef Wang paused a moment to emphasise what he was about to say and then added, "Gao finally woke up."

"Did he confess everything finally?"

"After five days in isolation and constant humiliation from his peers, Gao finally wrote everything down and tried not to leave out any small detail. He admitted his crime of changing medicine labels at night. Judging from his confession, he should have been arrested a long time ago. He felt very guilty and ashamed of himself. While he was writing, tears came from his eyes. He wished he had denounced Boss Li in public earlier. Now it was too late. He had missed his chance."

"I guess his confessional essay was well-accepted this time. Am I right?" Bao Bao said with confidence, as he wanted to show Chef Wang his wisdom.

"No. It was unfortunately contrary to what you thought, my son. Gao went with a long fifteen page confessional essay to the authorities. He thought the officer would be pleased with the absolutely true confession that he was presenting. Nevertheless, contrary to Gao's expectation, the officer accepted his essay with indifference and told him to wait. They would notify him of the Party's decision in a few days."

"Why was it so?" Bao Bao murmured. "As far as I know, all his previous essays got immediate feedback. How come, this time, when Gao had written to the Party from his whole heart, the authorities showed him such an indifferent attitude? I am really at a loss to understand what kind of game the officer was playing. It must have been torture for poor Gao!"

"Yes, you are right," Chef Wang agreed. "The irresolution of the situation made Gao Si Yan crazy. After admitting guilt, he could do nothing but wait for the sentence. Every day and every night felt like an eternity to him. How long would his gaol sentence be? Would it be two or three years, or four or five years, Gao wondered. Or would it be even longer? Perhaps the sentence would be death, if any soldiers had died from the adulterated medicine.

"At this time Gao was desperate and his body quivered. The more nervous he was, the more he hated Boss Li. Had Boss Li not stepped into Gao's life, things would not have been so bad for Gao. Though Gao would have remained poor, he would at least have led a peaceful life and enjoyed the respect of society. The officer was right that Boss Li had picked Gao up from the streets purely out of his own personal interest. For very little money, Boss Li had bought a faithful, reliable and hardworking 'slave'."

"How many more days did Gao have to wait until he received news from the authorities?" asked Bao Bao. "Could Gao run away from the Confession Centre? Did Gao ever give any excuse to take a day of absence, such as to visit his father?"

"Yes, but it was all useless. Shortly after Gao arrived at the Centre, he applied for one day's leave to celebrate his fiancée's birthday. But his application was turned down. Later, he applied again for a day off to visit his sick father. His request was rejected once again. Now, at this critical moment, Gao dared not raise the same issue."

"It was difficult for Gao to know how many more days of torture he had to endure," Chef Wang continued. "It all depended on the Party. Gao was like a piece of meat to be stewed in a slow cooker and the authorities would determine when the meat was ready for serving."

"If I were Gao, I would rather die than be left hanging around," said Bao Bao angrily.

"I agree with you. But soon the turning point came."

"What do you mean, turning point? Tell me quickly!"

"For several consecutive days Gao was in bad shape. He had no appetite to eat, nor could he sleep. He tossed and turned in his bed and waited for daybreak. He sat alone, as everybody stayed away from him. He was thinking of suicide, but soon he refrained from such thinking. He was still a bachelor. There was no son to carry on his surname 'Gao'. If he left no son, it would be a disaster for his father and his ancestors. Gao said to himself, 'I may be a criminal, a murderer, but my family surname cannot be eliminated because of my stupidity in seeking out death.'"

"Tell me about the turning point please!" Bao Bao demanded impatiently.

Chef Wang spoke calmly, "When Gao's stress had become intolerable, Director Liang, the boss of the Confession Centre, appeared outside the door of his room. Gao was shocked and he thought the director had come to deliver the sentence. For him it was the end of the world! However, contrary to what he feared, Director Leung called him 'Comrade Gao' and congratulated him for his excellent confession, which the Party Committee of the Confession Centre had unanimously approved and accepted."

Bao Bao said to himself in his mind, Ah! The Communist Party is impossible to comprehend. When Gao was awaiting good news from his confession it was in vain. But when he was waiting for punishment, he received commendation from the Party!

Chef Wang continued. "Then the Director invited Gao to his office. The moment that Gao entered the small office, Gao fell on his knees and cried, 'please forgive me!' The Director pulled him up, sat him in a chair, and said, 'For heaven's sake, we are all Tong Zhi – comrades – and we belong to one family, the family of the great proletarian class that is bringing China to socialism. The Party has chosen you to be trained in this Centre, because you originate from a pure proletarian family. Although you were contaminated by the evil bourgeoisie in the past, we are delighted that you have now broken off all ties with them. By writing confession after confession you have wiped away all your sins. Now you are a new-born person in our new society. Your past mistakes are generously forgiven by the Party. You should be grateful to the new government and to Chairman Mao. Our goal at this Centre is to help young people like you to return to their original class. Soon we will give you an opportunity to prove to the public that you are a new person; that you have drawn an immaculate line from your past and from the bourgeoisie. You may meet your enemy, your former boss, Li Guo Ming, in a struggle meeting and we would like to see how you put into practice then what you have written in your confessional essay. Please cherish this unique opportunity."

Again Bao Bao seized the opportunity to show his wisdom and impress Chef Wang, and said, "My guess is, that life after this turning point improved immensely for Gao. Am I right?"

"Of course you are totally right. An hour later his peers came out of their studies. They all congratulated him on his newborn life. They invited Gao to play football. Gao was ecstatic! For over a month at the Centre he had only stood at the sidelines, enviously watching them play football. Now he was taking part in the game, because now he belonged to this gigantic proletarian family.

"Less than a week after his release, Gao was notified to attend a thousand men's 'struggle meeting' to condemn his former boss, Li Guo Ming's, crimes. Gao did not feel uneasy about doing this. On the contrary he eagerly participated to show his loyalty to the Party."

When Bao Bao left Chef Wang's place, his mind was fully loaded with thoughts of the brainwashing technique used on Gao Si Yan and he was amazed that Chef Wang had such a vivid memory of Gao's experience – which dated back three years ago – as if it happened yesterday.

The next morning at seven thirty a tiny pebble hit Bao Bao's window. He knew it was Li Yong. Bao Bao hastened downstairs to meet him and they walked to school together. Bao Bao told Li Yong that he had met someone last night, who knew Gao Si Yan very well and had told him Gao's story. Now Bao

Bao was confident that he would be prepared for the class discussion.

However, he still wanted to know more, so he asked Li Yong, "Li Yong, did you attend the big struggle meeting?"

"Yes, I did, because I wanted to see my Dad for the last time before he was sent away to gaol in a remote place. The struggle meeting was the only place where Ma Ma and I could see him." Tears came from Li's eyes. Bao Bao was very sad and handed him his handkerchief.

"Was the big struggle meeting an appalling experience?" Bao Bao asked. "I have heard about such meetings very often but I have not been at one myself."

"It took place in a huge hall, bigger than our school assembly-hall, packed with at least one thousand people. The walls of the hall were plastered with countless combative Da Zi Baos directed against the Counter-Revolutionaries. Behind the stage in the centre hung two huge portraits of Chairman Mao and Chief Commander Zhu. In front of the portraits was a row of chairs for the Communist officials as well as three judges. The criminals were brought on to the stage one by one, like in an assembly line. When one was finished the next one would come up. When the soldiers brought my Dad up on to the stage, they forced my Dad to kneel down facing the public with his two arms stretched straight backwards parallel with each other. The soldier behind pushed his head further down. They called this gesture the "jet-plane position", which is extremely difficult for one to endure. Then Gao Si Yan, his former employee, walked up and pointed his index finger proudly at my Dad and started to accuse him…"

"What did you feel when you saw Gao on the stage accusing your father?" Bao Bao interrupted his friend.

"I wanted to kill him. If only I had had a gun!"

"Where would you get a gun?"

"Nowhere. You know it is impossible to get a gun nowadays. The new government confiscated all weapons right after the Liberation and made sure that no weapons were left among the public."

"Now that you are three years older, did your hatred towards Gao lessen when you saw him on stage yesterday?"

"When I saw him on stage giving his speech, I wished the same thing as I had three years ago. I wanted to find a gun and I wanted to kill him without compunction. But guns are strictly banned in our New China. I could carry a knife to stab him, but that would be very difficult and risky because he is much taller and bigger than me. I can only hope that one day, with my intelligence, I will find a way to take revenge."

"What happened to your father after Gao's accusation?"

"The chief judge announced the sentence; that my Dad would be sentenced to fifteen years of Reform Through Labour – Lao Dong Gai Zao – in the barren Northwest.

"Weren't there any lawyers to defend your father?" Bao Bao asked.

"No. No lawyers at all! My Dad was grabbed by two soldiers and pushed down from the stage while the audience shouted loudly and angrily, 'Down with Counter-revolutionary Li Guo Ming!' 'Down with the running dog of the capitalist class.' 'Long live our Great Leader Chairman Mao.'

"My Dad turned his face to give me a look for the last time. His face and his neck were red. That was the last time my eyes met his. And that was three years ago." Tears dropped from Li Yong's eyes again. The handkerchief which Bao Bao had given him was very useful.

"Have you seen your father at all since then?"

"No, not even once. He is now in the remote Qinghai Province, which is more than three days and three nights' train ride from Shanghai. I have no money to make such a long trip. Even if I were to make such a long trip, I doubt that I would be allowed to visit him, as he is a prisoner. In my dreams, though, I have seen him a couple of times." More tears poured from Li's eyes.

"How about Gao? Did he receive any sentence? After all, he was a conspirator in the adulteration of medicine."

"No. He got no sentence, nor punishment. On the contrary, he became an instant national hero. For the past three years, Gao has done nothing but give the same speech about his own story. I think the worst time for him was when he was detained at the Confession Centre."

"That's not fair!" Bao Bao complained.

"Where is fairness in our justice system? My Dad was not allowed to hire a lawyer, nor could he lodge an appeal."

Bao Bao did not know how to answer. To avoid further sorrow he switched the subject, "I guess you are not attending the class discussion tomorrow? But you have given me every detail I could need. You are really selfless, like Dr Bethune," said Bao Bao, as they walked towards the school gate. Li Yong hastened his steps, while Bao Bao slowed down his pace. As usual they wouldn't enter the school at the same time.

CHAPTER 10

# BEDROOM NOISES

For quite some time, people had been looking forward to the Moon Festival. In addition to the Spring Festival which westerners call Chinese New Year, two major festivals are celebrated in China. They are known as the Dragon Boat Festival and the Moon Festival, and take place on the fifth day of the fifth month and the fifteenth day of the eighth month respectively in the Chinese calendar (about one to two months behind the western calendar). As a result of the discrepancy between the Chinese and the western calendar, the Moon Festival is celebrated in October when the weather becomes cool and windy, and the leaves on the trees start to fall. – The Chinese believe that the falling of leaves is the best time of the year to give life a boost by holding a festival. – During the festival the government took care to feed everyone with a reasonable meal. Every family received special ration coupons for a small piece of meat, a small piece of fish, some eggs and a chicken. At this time, the queues were shorter as the supply was sufficient for every household.

In Bao Bao's household, Auntie went to the market to do her festival shopping at five o'clock in the morning. Outside, it was pitch-dark and she walked slowly towards the wet market, where she bought a piece of meat, a small fish, ten eggs, some green vegetables and a live chicken.

At home she jabbed a knife into the live chicken's throat to kill it. Then she let the chicken's fresh blood gush into a plastic container on the table. After a while the dark red chicken blood solidified into a jelly which was then placed aside to be cooked later. Auntie then dropped the dead chicken into boiling water and cleaned the chicken's innards by removing the liver, stomach, intestines and heart, which she later mixed with the blood "jelly" in the pot to cook her specialty dish. She then chopped the chicken into eight big pieces with a big Chinese knife and dumped them into a big pot. She added water and salt into the pot to cook for two hours, making a delicious chicken soup with great flavour.

The head and two feet of the chicken were not thrown away. Instead, Auntie washed them thoroughly and chopped the claws off the chicken feet. She then put them into a metal pot to be cooked together with the chicken pieces to add flavour to the soup. For another dish she cut the meat into small pieces and stewed them. Later on when she saw that the meat was ready to serve, she added her hard boiled eggs (having removed the shells) to the stew and cooked the meat and eggs together with dark soy sauce. Soon the eggs turned dark brown after absorbing the colour of the soy sauce.

This special occasion allowed Uncle to come home for lunch. Before he reached home, Auntie had already placed the food on the table for him. He happily chewed the chicken leg, swallowed two eggs and gulped down the chicken soup. To him, the food was unusually delicious. The last time he had eaten chicken was three months ago during the Dragon Festival. As soon as he finished eating, he stood up and hurried back to school. Auntie watched Uncle eating, but did not eat with him. After he left, she quickly ate some rice and one egg. She then went back to the kitchen where she poured some water into the pot and boiled the chicken once more for dinner.

Every festival meal was an opportunity for family and relatives to gather together. For today's dinner, two relatives from another province were invited. Uncle Li, as Bao Bao called him, was the headmaster of the school that Bao Bao's uncle Song Ping had taught at in Fuzhou before his relocation to Shanghai. Uncle Li was about sixty years old. His hair was grey and his cheeks were broad. In spite of his stern face he smiled all the time, which gave people an impression that he was an approachable person. Another guest was Auntie's brother, a Bare-foot Doctor named Wang. "Barefoot Doctor" was a new term used to describe farm doctors in Chairman Mao's era. Initially, they were family physicians exclusively serving Chinese farms. Now most of them had to walk from household to household bare-footed because their income as farm doctors was so low that many of them could not afford to wear shoes. Yet they served the commune members with their heart and soul. Barefoot Doctors were highly praised by the Party, as the spirit of Dr Bethune could be felt in them. Dr Wang was in his early forties. He was a tall and handsome man in the Chinese style. He knew so many jokes that he could tell them all night and make everybody laugh.

Today, the house was filled with festival spirit. The young and the old ate and laughed at the table. They smoked and drank spirituous liquor and they all had fun. Uncle Li had brought a bottle of Maotai, a rare drink, given to him by the housekeeper of the State Guest House in Beijing, who had asked Li as a favour to help his niece's admission to Li's high school. Auntie and Uncle said unanimously that Uncle Li should keep this scarce bottle for himself for a bigger occasion. However, Uncle Li insisted on opening the Maotai liquor, a potent drink distilled from fermented sorghum and wheat. Bao Bao had heard a lot about wine and liquor, but he had never had the opportunity to try it. Uncle and Auntie were against Bao Bao's trying, but Dr Wang said Bao Bao should try it, as sooner or later a teenager should taste liquor. So Bao Bao tried a sip. The moment the liquor with 53% alcohol went down his throat, Bao Bao choked and felt dizzy.

Soon Bao Bao's normally happy and tranquil face disappeared. His expression became serious and pensive. The sight of all the eggs, meat and chicken soup that littered the table reminded him of Auntie's and Uncle's whispering at night. Bao Bao recalled his uncle's complaint that he could not perform due to the lack of nutritious food. Now he watched his uncle eating nutritiously so that he could perform better later – but to perform what?

Suddenly his face blushed. "Was it from the Maotai or from shame, or from both of them?" he asked himself. He lowered his head and dared not look at anybody as if he was a culprit. He felt a surge of heat run through his body. He stood up and rushed to the toilet to use cold water to wash his face in the washing basin. He put his hand under the wash basin, cupped cold water into his palms and splashed his face and neck area..

"Aiyaah!" thought Bao Bao. "Why is the devil coming back to me at this inappropriate time, when we have guests at home? God, please help me to get rid of the devil!" Bao Bao grumbled.

His auntie had rushed to the bathroom after him, and said, from outside the closed door, "Are you all right? Are you throwing up?"

"I am fine. I am coming out right now!" Bao Bao replied.

Auntie went back to the table and told her guests, "The poor lad, it is the very first time in his life he has tried strong liquor and he has not had such a sumptuous meal for a very long time. His stomach cannot take it. Let him throw up and he'll feel better! What a pity to waste such good food!"

"He shouldn't have tried Maotai in the first place, as I warned," added his uncle.

After the rich meal, the family sat around and sipped green tea. The men smoked ceaselessly and praised Auntie for being such a talented cook. Every dish was excellently prepared. They chatted about this and that.

"How is life on the farm? I hear there is a lot of starvation nowadays. Is that true?" asked Uncle Song.

Dr Wang replied, "Yes, it's very bad indeed! Each farmer is entitled to a ration of only fifteen catties so they have to mix rice with tree bark, leaves and grass roots to fill their stomachs."

Immediately, Bao Bao, now back in the room with the others, raised a question like an adult, "How come? Even I as a teenager get thirty catties a month. But a farmer! Imagine how hard they work every day and only get fifteen catties. This is unbelievable and it doesn't make sense. Can this be true!"

Dr Wang explained, "The ration coupons are distributed according to region and province. The amount of rice varies from region to region and from city to city. It depends on many factors, such as the number of people in the province, the harvest, the taxes levied by the Central and local governments and corruption, etc. In big cities like Shanghai and Beijing people receive the most. In Fuzhou, a smaller city, you receive a smaller amount. Farmers receive less and I have heard that a million farmers have died of hunger."

"But why don't farmers move from the farms to the cities, where they can get more food?" Bao Bao asked seriously. In fact Bao Bao liked to be treated like an adult. This was a unique opportunity for him to behave like one.

"Yes, that was possible in the old regime under Chiang Kai Shek," explained Dr Wang patiently. "When there was a famine in Anhui, many of the starving farmers begged their way out to Shanghai. Now with the system of "Hu Kou Bu" – the registration book issued by the local authorities in the new regime – there is no more mobility. Not only farmers but also city dwellers may not move from one place to another. Also, the Hu Kou Bu is valid only in the place of issue. Without it, no ration coupon can be granted. Nevertheless, because of the recent severe famine, a hundred thousand starving farmers rushed to the cities. In their life-and-death struggle for survival, they didn't care about the Hu Kou Bu. But this time, tens of thousands of soldiers have been called out to block every possible passage into the cities. So inside the cities one does not notice the devastating state of the famine."

"When do you return home?" interrupted Uncle Song, changing the subject. Apparently he did not want the depressing news of famine to spoil the happy festival atmosphere.

Auntie brought out the moon cake. It was a Chinese tradition to eat moon cake during the moon festival. Because of rationing, Auntie received only one moon cake for the family. So she cut it into eight slices and let everyone have a small piece of the cake. The thin skin of the cake was made of flour and the inside was filled with sweet red bean paste.

After the moon cake was finished, it was traditional to watch the full moon, as Chinese people believe that, on 15 August in the Chinese calendar, the moon is at its fullest and brightest. From Bao Bao's apartment they could see no moon. So the two guests, accompanied by the whole family, went up to the roof terrace on the fourth floor to watch the full moon. On the terrace they came across Dr Sun and his wife, who lived in the apartment on the fourth floor. The Suns asked about Bao Bao's Ma Ma and sent their best regards to her in Hong Kong.

After enjoying the full moon, Dr Wang and Headmaster Li left. Bao Bao and his cousin cleaned up the dinner table and helped Auntie to wash the dishes, while Uncle sat on the bench and Yuan Yuan played the piano for them. The long-awaited Moon Festival was finally coming to an end.

In southern China, people believe that, with a full stomach, people can sleep better. Therefore, many people eat a Ye Xiao – a light meal – in the evening, before going to sleep, just to sleep better.

Tonight, Bao Bao had a full stomach, but he had no intention of going to bed early. He had taken a cup of strong tea to keep him awake. When he splashed cool water onto his face in the washroom, he thought that tonight could possibly be an exciting night. Perhaps Uncle and Auntie would put on a show in their bed since his uncle had eaten well today.

Bao Bao came out of the washroom and went back into his room. He found Yuan Yuan had fallen asleep in the folding bed in their bedroom. He went through the corridor and stood outside the door leading to his uncle's bedroom. He heard no movement, nor whispering inside. He went back to his own bedroom and put on his headset to listen to music on the radio for a while. Then he went back to the swinging door leading to his uncle's bedroom.

This time he heard a little noise from the old mattress of uncle's bedroom. He pushed the door open slowly and entered the bedroom. Opening the swinging door would make no noise now, because Bao Bao had oiled the door hinges in the afternoon. He steadied himself on his toes, pushed the door open slowly and carefully, and entered the bedroom. It was pitch-dark and he could see nothing. The noise continued to come from the mattress in a rhythmical beat and Bao Bao continued creeping up toward the noise of the mattress. He then sat on the floor, trembling. It was a cool night, but the excitement of witnessing something as unusual as this made him forget about the cold. Sitting on the floor, he thought, Can this be what is called, "Fang Shi" – matters of the bedroom? And he visualized his uncle's penis passing through the lips of Auntie's vulva and entering her vagina. Ew! No, impossible! The penis in the book was quite sizeable whereas the vagina was only a thin and narrow line! How could this be possible? I must go back to the Xinhua bookstore tomorrow and check the pictures again.

Bao Bao's thoughts were interrupted by Auntie's moaning. Why is she suddenly moaning? She didn't moan last time. I have never heard her moaning like this since she came over to live with us. She is moaning in a different way to the nude lady in the park. Is she in pain? Bao Bao tried to listen to every whisper attentively. "I want…I want…Give me more…more…more…" his auntie moaned.

131

Oh my! Is this painful for my poor auntie? Why does she keep asking for more? he thought, totally confused.

Bao Bao arched his neck left and right hoping that he would be able to see more, but in the darkness he saw nothing. His thin body quivered as he fell back onto the floor. Now his uncle's breathing grew heavier and heavier, while his auntie's moaning grew more and more intense. From the moaning and breathing he could figure out that his uncle was lying on top of his auntie. My God, is that what I saw with Li Yong at the park; the naked man above the naked woman? How awful! The action continued with louder and heavier breathing! Suddenly, Uncle collapsed and was completely silent! The noise of the old creaking mattress suddenly subsided and all huffing and puffing, moans and groans disappeared! Silence ruled the room.

He could not see auntie's female sexual organ in the darkness. Without thinking, Bao Bao stretched his right arm out and touched his auntie's abdomen. He moved his hand downwards until he reached her pubic hair. Like a bombshell, his hand was caught by his uncle's big hand. He was so shocked. He knew it was the end of the world for him.

Quickly he came to the resolution that the only way out was to run to the kitchen, grab hold of the big Chinese knife and cut his neck like Auntie did with the live chicken. "I'd rather die than live in disgrace," he thought. His whole body was quivering, yet he made an effort to calm his right hand which was held by his uncle's big hand.

In contrast to his worst nightmares, his uncle caressed his small hand and said, "Darling, your hand is cold". There was no response from Auntie. Perhaps she was indulging in the pain she had suffered a minute ago. Shortly afterwards, Bao Bao withdrew his lower arm slowly. He had cold feet and felt goose bumps spring up everywhere from his head to his toes but he felt calmer inside and relieved that he was saved.

Now came his auntie's whisper, "It was so nice! You have finally satisfied me! It has been such a long time. Do you know," her whispering continued, "tonight reminded me of the time we were young and just married. Now I feel content to know that you still love me," she babbled on. This time, Uncle was silent. Perhaps he had already fallen asleep. Bao Bao eavesdropped no more. He wanted to escape. He crawled along on tiptoe in the darkness as Uncle began to snore loudly. Returning to his own bed, Bao Bao felt psychologically and physically exhausted and collapsed into an uneasy sleep.

The following day, Bao Bao went on an excursion to the bookstore to try again to discover the secret between men and women. On the way there, he thought, I don't think I am asking too much? I just want to have a clear picture of the whole thing. Once I have seen a naked woman or I have been given an explanation of Fang Shi – matters of the bedroom – the devil will never bother me again. And I will not follow it so closely any more. My character is that I keep on discovering new things around me that I don't understand and I will not give up doing this. Why must I wait another fifteen years until I am married to find out the answers to this secret? Why must I always be attacked by the devil for the next fifteen years? I am a good student of Chairman Mao and I do not want to eavesdrop, nor do I want to submerge myself in adult affairs. How can I be liberated from the devil? I want to be free, and to be free from all indecent and immoral thoughts. I have got myself into a huge mess but the worst part is that I have no-one to share this uncomfortable feeling with, nor do I have anyone just to talk to about my curiosity and suffering. Why don't they teach this material in school? The lesson will not be for Song Bao Bao only, but for all youngsters at the age of puberty. Why is sex such a mystery? Shall I take up Chef Wang's offer to explain everything to me? Hmm, but that is too embarrassing – I cannot bring myself to approach an old man about such a sensitive topic.

Bao Bao shuffled along Nanjing Road in the direction of the Bund. He passed a foreign bookstore. It occurred to him that perhaps he could find something interesting there also, because he had heard of many attacks on foreign capitalist reading materials. Without hesitation, Bao Bao entered the foreign bookstore. He had always been fascinated by everything foreign. He flipped through art books and a few magazines and finally found a black and white photograph of a foreign woman in elegant female underwear. Unfortunately he had learnt only a few basic words in English.

Bao Bao came out of the foreign bookstore without disappointment as he had not expected much when he entered the store. Besides, it was not what he had in mind. His goal was to go back to Xin Hua book store which he had visited a couple of weeks ago. On the way over, he wondered, What does a naked foreign woman look like? Does she have bigger breasts? Is there also Fang Shi amongst foreigners? Is the colour of her pubic hair also blond like her other hair? Soon Bao Bao realized his imagination had gone too far because there were seldom any foreigners to be seen in China. It was as if none of them ever existed. Are there no foreigners in China?

Bao Bao suddenly realized that he was wrong, There are no foreigners on the street, but there is a settlement for a designated group of foreigners living in Shanghai." His memory went back to the special day when the school bus took them on an excursion to the outskirts of the city. Bao Bao spotted a white Russian settlement through his bus window. The Russians who refused to return to Russia after the October Revolution in 1917 had been living there ever since. Now, the second and third generations of that community remained in the settlement. What captivated Bao Bao most was the blond and blue eyes of the young girls who were skipping about. He wished the bus would make a stop so that he could jump out and talk to them. It would have been exciting to see and speak with people of other races. Unfortunately the bus had continued on and left Bao Bao longing for more familiarity and knowledge of other ethnic groups. Taking a good long look at the dirty and dusty settlement and at the shabby clothing of the foreigners, Bao Bao decided that, under Communist leadership, it was the Chinese who were the best off.

As soon as Bao Bao arrived at Xin Hua bookstore, he went directly to the "Health Section", where, as usual, many male youngsters were flipping through the books. Bao Bao was curious to know what these youngsters were looking for. He walked behind them and caught a glimpse of the pages they studied. Three young men were looking at the picture of a naked female body picture in a medical book. Ha Ha, I am not the only one! Bao Bao was pleased.

This time Bao Bao was less shy than the first time. He picked up the book that he had looked at before. He browsed through the book until he arrived at the female sexual organ page. He kept the place with his left thumb and continued to flip further through the pages until he arrived at the male sexual organ page. He compared the two drawings of the female and male organs. The drawings were about the same size, but the male penis looked much too large to enter the thin and small passageway. Bao Bao was disappointed that his guess was not working. The book explained nothing about sexual intercourse. It showed only the names of all human organs. He tried to read the explanations in the following pages, but they were exclusively on the topic of birth control. Bao Bao asked himself whether he should buy the book with the male and female drawings. No, for goodness sake no! What would happen if one day someone in the family discovered the book? At home Bao Bao had no private drawer with a lock, to secure his personal belongings.

In the chapter on birth control several methods were introduced. Among them were pictures of condoms. This reminded him of his adventure last year when he found a condom at home and blew it up to the size of his head. Uncle and Auntie had watched, amused, as it expanded and they laughed along with Bao Bao as he blew with all his might until it popped.

That night Bao Bao lay awake in bed. From time to time he got up and walked through the corridor close to the door leading to his uncle's bedroom. He stood there trying to listen to any whispers or any noise from inside, but no noise came. He was hoping, as soon as the whispers began, that he could push open the door slowly and crawl on the floor towards the bedside. He wished to gather more information about the couple's secret behaviour. He waited and waited, fearing that his wait might be in vain, as on previous nights. He imagined that it would be wonderful if there was another festival, so that Auntie and Uncle could have another big meal and then have the energy to put on a dramatic show. Hmm...but the next festival isn't until Chinese New Year, which is about four to five months away. Thinking about this, Bao Bao fell asleep.

In the middle of the night, he woke up and said, Why do I waste so much time on these dirty thoughts and scenes? Why am

I obsessed with this immoral and filthy spying on my Uncle and Auntie!? The devil is attacking me again! Why am I so curious and so persistent to find out things that I should not know at my age? Why am I not equally curious about science? There must be so much to discover in the field of science, more than in the old double bed. A discovery in science would be admired by all and bring honour home, especially for me, since my ultimate goal is to become a Nobel-Prize-winning scientist. A new discovery in science would put me, my family and my relatives in a privileged class. Abundant nutritious food would be delivered to our home daily. Uncle and Auntie would have a rich meal everyday and every night they could do gymnastics in bed.

Thinking of discoveries in the scientific field in the middle of night woke Bao Bao up even more, because a certain idea had struck him. He got up quickly and switched on the dim table light. He took out a piece of white paper and a pencil. The number "5" had always fascinated him and he wanted to investigate all the numbers ending in "5". He knew that he should sleep, but his drive for discovery was too strong. He began multiplying the number "5": 5 by 5 marks make 25, 5 by 15 marks 75, 5 by 25 marks 125. He saw no relationship between these numbers except that they all ended in "five". He continued multiplying five by numbers ending in five until the paper was full of numbers. He took another sheet of paper and continued.

Bao Bao had always enjoyed multiplying numbers manually as he believed the more he used his brain, the sharper it would be. He murmured, "I must keep my brain working all the time."

He took out another piece of paper and wrote: 5, 15, 25, 35, 45, 55. Then he thought, "If I multiply each number by itself, the results are $5^2=25$, $15^2=225$, $25^2=625$, $35^2=1225$, $45^2=2025$, $55^2=3025$." He discovered that all the results ended in 25. He also discovered that one could arrive at the first digits of the product by multiplying the first digit of the factor with a number greater than that factor by 1. For example: with $55^2$, he took 5 and multiplied it by six (5+1) to get 30, then wrote after the number 30 the number 25, arriving at 3025. It occured to him that, to know the result of $1125^2$, we could find the answer by the following method: 112 x (112+1) = 12656, followed by 25 which yielded 1265625.

Bao Bao was immensely pleased by this small arithmetical discovery. He wanted to jump in the air to rejoice and celebrate, but Yuan Yuan was sleeping in the same room. Furthermore, everyone else in the house was sleeping. Even though he had made a small discovery, he felt that he should not wake everyone up. He did not know whether any mathematician had published this formula before. I must say it is a tiny discovery. Nonetheless, this could lead to bigger things in the future for, as Chairman Mao had said, "A simple spark can start a prairie fire." He smiled.

Bao Bao felt victorious. Not only had he made a discovery, but he had also conquered the devil that had been lurking to engage him that night. Chairman Mao's famous saying, "Learning, Learning and more Learning", had always been a motto for Bao Bao. Had he strictly followed Chairman Mao's instruction, he would not have been haunted by the devil. But I am not the only teenager who has flipped through books in the Health Sections of bookstores! he argued. The other young men were attacked by the devil as well. We are all brought up with the proverb that, "An inch of time is as valuable as an inch of gold", So why do these other youngsters waste time in bookstores like I do?! They must be obsessed by the devil too! With these thoughts in mind, Bao Bao dozed off, a faint smile hovering over his face as he dreamed that he would win the Nobel Prize one day.

The following day in class, Bao Bao double-checked the theory that he had worked out on the previous night. It worked! Bao Bao had read a great many reference books on mathematics but he had never come across one with a theory such as the one he had proposed last night. He did not want to discuss his discovery with his teachers, nor with his peers. He would rather keep it to himself. This was perhaps due to his upbringing when, as a child, he was told, "If a plan is made public, it may fail easily. However, if you keep it to yourself, it will have a better chance to succeed."

Bao Bao also warned himself that he should not be proud of himself, on account of his arithmetical discovery. He recalled how humble Chairman Mao had been when he proclaimed the birth of the People's Republic of China on 1 October 1949 in Tian An Men Square in Beijing. He thought of the monumental success of the Chinese Communist Party in gaining total control of the Chinese mainland, "One step forward in China's long march of hundred thousand miles ahead."

Tonight Bao Bao was not in the mood to switch off the lights and wait for an eventual whisper from his auntie and uncle. Instead, he was busy at his desk trying to find relationships with another number such as "three".

"Bao Bao! You must go to bed early as you have to wake up early tomorrow morning!" called Auntie, seeing the light was still on in Bao Bao's bedroom.

Bao Bao was experimenting with all numbers ending with "three" and then later with all numbers ending in "four". He toiled for hours but found no association among them as he had done with the number "five" last night. He used many sheets of paper without result. Looking at the countless multiplications on the number sheets, one would be amazed at the diligence and perseverance of Bao Bao.

To praise the virtues of hard work by the Chinese, Mao drew attention to a legend from Taoism, "Yu Gong moved the mountain". As the Chinese characters indicate, Yu Gong, was "a foolish old man." In front of his shack there was a big mountain which blocked his path to the South. One day, Yu Gong made up his mind to move the mountain with the help of his offspring, using only spades and wheelbarrows as their primary tools. Once the mountain was removed they could reach the South directly from their shack. While Yu Gong and his offspring were busy moving the mountain, a clever old man passed by and laughed, "You are doing a stupid thing. How can a few people move a mountain?"

Yu replied confidently, "I cannot accomplish it in my lifetime, but I have children and grandchildren...If they all set this as their goal, the mountain will eventually be moved. Even if it takes a thousand or ten thousand years! The main point is that we are all striving towards the same goal and we will never give up until it is accomplished!"

The gods in heaven were touched by Yu Gong's will-power and persistency. Two angels were sent to earth to move the mountain for Yu Gong, and afterwards, he and his family were able to go to the South without having to go around the mountain.

After a few hours of multiplications by hand and brain, Bao Bao was now completely exhausted and deeply disappointed. He switched off the lights, which he should have done hours ago. He began to doubt whether or not he had the talent to become a famous scientist one day. Perhaps he needed to work harder although he regularly got straight "5"s (equivalent to "A"s).

The five point (1, 2, 3, 4, 5) system, now used in schools, was introduced from Russia. Bao Bao was told that it was advantageous for students to use this Russian system, as – with the old hundred points system – it was impossible to distinguish between 77 and 78, or 95 and 96. Before the new system was introduced, Bao Bao strove constantly for 100 and he was unhappy when he got 93, 94, or even 98. Now the maximum he could achieve was "five". This saved Bao Bao from his permanent struggle for a 100. He found the new grading system less challenging since he got straight "5"s easily in all his subjects.

I must continue to explore until I find something more in Math. Perhaps I'm no good now but I'm sure that I will be good in the future. Not every scientist is born a genius. The famous Thomas Edison tried a thousand times until he invented the light-bulb. I must sleep now, otherwise I will be very tired tomorrow.

Teacher Ma complained that Bao Bao was too tired in the morning as he often fell asleep in class. He promised his teacher that, in future, he would make sure to go to bed early. If the situation did not improve, the teacher would pay Bao Bao's family a visit to discuss this matter with his uncle and auntie. "Why do I work so hard in the night? Night time should be for sleeping and I am not on some intense nightshift regimen". In fact he was not doing anything for the school at night.

Subconsciously Bao Bao realised that his current fascination for devising mathematical formulas had driven the devil of adult sexual matters completely out of his mind.

CHAPTER 11

# SMALL COUSIN

The Greeks produced sculptures of naked men and women thousands of years ago. In the Tang Dynasty (618-907 AD), well-endowed women wore dresses with low necklines. Why must we wear dark blue uniforms? Perhaps Chairman Mao would like to protect our women in the same way as the women in the Middle East who wear long black costumes? When I was younger I used to play with young girls, but now female classmates are very shy and always avoid looking at me. If I tried to ask a girl something, she would simply run away. I know that I have not changed, but somehow teenage girls are now taught to have less or no contact with their teenage male counterparts. For this reason one would never find male and female teenagers holding hands and walking together in the street. Also, for this reason Dan Dan felt uncomfortable walking with Bao Bao on the street.

Again, Bao Bao warned himself that he should go to sleep. He turned his head to the other side of the pillow and hoped to fall asleep right away. But he failed. The park scene, his auntie's whispering and the illustrated diagram of female sexual organs came back vividly to him. He thought back to a year ago when his younger sister Yuan Yuan was sleeping in the same bed with him. He regretted that he had missed a good opportunity of investigating her body. A girl and a woman are of the same kind after all. "Why didn't that bother me a year ago?" After a while, he comforted himself that the opportunity was still there, because his young cousin Lin Lin was still around and he could approach her easily. Perhaps Lin Lin was better, because Yuan Yuan, being his own sister, was too close to him. He wanted to solve this mystery once for all and be freed from the devil forever.

The following day Bao Bao scrambled home as quickly as school was over. He opened the door and his eleven-year-old cousin, Lin Lin, was sitting at her desk just as he expected.

"Where is Auntie?" he asked her.

"She is at the daily afternoon political studies' meeting organized by the neighbourhood committee", Lin Lin replied.

Bao Bao smiled mischievously as he knew his auntie was away.

"Come here. I have something to show you," ordered Bao Bao.

His young cousin followed him into his bedroom. Bao Bao walked towards the windows facing the backyard and pulled the curtains shut against the broad daylight. Lin Lin asked, "Why are you closing the curtains and what do you want to show me?"

"We are going to play a special Ban Jia Jia, different from the one we used to play," said Bao Bao. – Ban Jia Jia was a children's game. Literally it meant "to set up a household". – Children wanted to imitate the adult life-style, so in the Ban Jia Jia game, boys played the role of father, who went out to work, and girls would take the role of a housewife, who cooked and cleaned the house while the husband was away at work. For children to play Ban Jia Jia, their mother usually bought them plastic toys such as mini home furniture and kitchen utensils, including tiny plastic plates, spoons, chopsticks etc. In the game, when the boy – the father – returned home from work, he expected the girl – his wife – to bring out food for dinner. In a big family, brothers and sisters gathered together for dinner. Simulating this, many children could play Ban Jia Jia at the same time. At the end of the game, the children received a little food to eat, which their mother usually prepared in advance. At this time, as there was a shortage of meat, children received dried bean curd in place of dried beef or pork.

Today Bao Bao wanted to play Ban Jia Jia with Lin Lin in a different way. Bao Bao said, "In the new Ban Jia Jia game I shall play the role of a family physician and you will be my patient. You come to my clinic for a physical check-up."

Children had another set of toys for playing doctor and patient, which consisted of a stethoscope, a needle set, a thermometer and some cotton balls. Children often used the doctor set to treat a doll. Usually the boy played the role of a medical doctor who first checked if the doll had a fever, then pulled up her shirt to check her chest using a stethoscope. Finally the boy would pull up the skirt of the doll and give her an injection in her thigh.

"Have you ever had a physical check-up?" asked Bao Bao.

Lin Lin had no idea what the new Ban Jia Jia would be like. Bao Bao added, "I mean, have you ever taken off your clothes and let a doctor examine your naked body?"

"No, not by a male doctor, but by a female doctor. Why do you ask? This has nothing to do with you," she retorted. "I am not allowed to be alone with you in your room. If people find out that I am alone with you in a dark room they will gossip!" she said.

"But we are playing the Ban Jia Jia game where you are my patient instead of a doll and now I'm giving you a body check-up. Don't worry! Nobody will see us as I have drawn the curtain. Now as your doctor, I am examining your body. I demand that you take off your clothes and lie on the bed."

"Oh, no! Are you crazy? I would be ashamed to death to do so. I would rather commit suicide than take off my dress to show my body to someone."

"To take off your clothes for a medical check-up is not shameful. Besides, when you get married one day, you will have to undress for your husband!" teased Bao Bao.

"Rubbish! Don't talk nonsense! Chairman Mao said that young people should get married in order to serve our country better. Stop your nonsense. Why is your mind so dirty and filthy today? This kind of nonsense should not come out of your mouth!"

"No! I don't speak nonsense. I just want us to play the new Ban Jia Jia game. By the way, have you ever heard the whisperings in the middle of the night? Your parents make a noise on their mattress! Their bed is not far from yours," pressed Bao Bao.

"No! You are talking rubbish with your imagination! I have never heard anything like that! I fall asleep as soon as I lie down. I am a good student of Chairman Mao and I follow his instructions immaculately: 'Good learning, good health and good work.' You are acting oddly today, why are you talking nonsense all the time?" asked Lin Lin.

"Lin Lin, as your doctor I have a request to make; I want you to take off your dress and let me examine your naked chest."

Bao Bao started to unbutton her cotton jacket. Lin Lin shoved Bao Bao away and slapped him in the face and said, "You dirty little guy! You can examine your female teacher. Don't

142

touch me! I remain pure, pure like the blue sky of our Motherland, pure like the blue water in the China sea. You have cheated me to play this Ban Jia Jia game and brought me to your room. You just want to seduce me." Her cheeks became red. Her face and her neck were hot. She cried and ran through the corridor into the bathroom. She locked herself inside the bathroom and sobbed vigorously.

That was horrifying! It is a nightmare that I have just experienced. Why has such misfortune fallen upon me? thought Lin Lin. She continued to cry and asked herself, Am I still pure? My female teachers and Ma Ma have always warned me to stay away from boys and not let them touch my body as they would make me lose my virginity. Have I already lost it? she wailed.

It was Chinese tradition that young women had to safeguard their virginity until they got married. In old China it was a scandal if, on the wedding night, the groom was to find out that the bride was no longer a virgin. Lin Lin continued to cry, as she thought she was no longer a virgin and that she would die of humiliation because she had been touched by Bao Bao. "Chairman Mao will be so disappointed with me!" she wailed.

"Lin Lin!" called Bao Bao outside. "Please forgive me! I had no bad intention. I was just trying to play Ban Jia Jia with you. I just wanted to examine your body medically! Lin Lin please forgive me for bringing you such embarrassment. Lin Lin, forgive me, please don't tell anybody what has happened just now. It would be bad for you as well as for me, Lin Lin, please promise me, I beg you."

Bao Bao begged and begged but no response came from the bathroom. He heard his young cousin still sobbing. He could not understand why a small girl was so vulnerable and could be hurt so easily. After all he had done nothing! He couldn't stand it, so he went out for a walk to get some fresh air.

An hour later, at five o'clock in the afternoon, Auntie finished her meeting with the residential women's committee and came back home. She heard the loud sobbing from the bathroom, "Is that Lin Lin?" she questioned as she hurried to the bathroom.

She grasped the doorknob and called, "Lin Lin! What are you doing inside? Open up the door!"

Lin Lin heard her Ma Ma's voice and opened the door. When Auntie saw her daughter's tearful face and unbuttoned jacket, she urged, "What happened?"

Lin Lin rushed into her Ma Ma's arms, "Bao Bao interfered me," she choked.

Auntie flung her hand across Lin Lin's mouth to silence her, glancing anxiously over her shoulder to see if anyone was around, forgetting she was in her own home. She took her little daughter into the living-room. She wanted Lin Lin to tell her everything.

Bao Bao came home late in the evening, because he was embarassed to sit with the family at dinner, and he was particularly ashamed to face his little cousin. Why did I try to examine her? If my cousin was as curious as I am about sex, it would have been a different case. Then we could have examined each other. Now everything has gone wrong and I have made a complete fool of myself! Now in Lin Lin's eyes I am a dirty, low and cheap boy. She will never respect me as an elder brother. Was the devil inside me and was it he who drove me to act so insanely?

Bao Bao intentionally skipped dinner because of his bad feeling. He could not believe what he had done earlier that day. He did not want to go home. However, on second thoughts his face brightened up. Perhaps little cousin has kept everything to herself? As a girl she must be uncomfortable with this topic – girls are generally more shy than boys. That's why there are never any girls near the 'Health Section' flipping through those books! I doubt Lin Lin pays any attention to her parents at night. Yes. I must take the view that she is too shy to make a fool out of herself by describing today's episode to the family!

The moment he entered the house however, he was panic-stricken to find that the atmosphere was unusually tense. He knew something was wrong. But he had no choice now but to continue to walk forwards.

Bao Bao regretted that he had underestimated the situation. Had he known the atmosphere was so tense, he would not have come back home. But if he hadn't come home where would he have gone? Now he felt as if he had been convicted of a crime and was waiting to hear the verdict from his uncle. He admitted that he was not only guilty to his uncle and to his family but also to the Party and to Chairman Mao. They had all guided and educated him to be a good person and to devote his loyalty and life to the Party and the country.

Auntie noticed that Bao Bao had returned home and ushered her little daughter out of the room. Uncle stared at Bao Bao in disbelief; his face was crumpled up in fury and Bao Bao thought he saw foam forming at the sides of his uncle's mouth. Auntie closed the door of the living-room gently. Bao Bao sank his head and gazed at the dirty wooden floor, which had not been polished with wax for the past ten years. Bao Bao killed time by counting the number of wooden planks that made up the floor. The room was quiet but full of tension. Finally, Uncle broke the silence and said, "Bao Bao, do you know what sin you have committed today? We adults call it 'interference'."

Bao Bao was shaking with much fear – he had heard this word before; but it was always associated with crimes and misdemeanors. And he himself had never had any intention of coming close to any such things. Upon hearing his uncle's words, Bao Bao trembled and dropped to his knees. "Please forgive me, dear Uncle," he begged. "It was absolutely not my slightest intention to touch my cousin. The devil drove me there."

"Huai dan! Bad egg!" cursed his uncle. "What are you talking about? There is no devil in our new socialist society! Chairman Mao has taught us not to be superstitious! We rely on our human power only! The unconquerable, almighty human power of six million Chinese! Together we are building a new country, a country free of superstition," cried his uncle.

"Dearest Uncle, I really did not have the slightest intention to interfere with my small cousin," cried Bao Bao.

"Bao Bao, do you know that I promised your dear parents that I would do my utmost to educate you to become a useful and great person in the new society? We have always been proud of you and your academic performance. Do you know that your father and I have hoped that you could lead a different kind of life, the life of a renowned scientist, well respected by all? You are the only son of our two families. So, on your shoulders you carry two families' hopes and dreams for the future."

His uncle continued, "You know that nowadays we get less food due to the distribution of ration coupons. However, the whole family saves food for you because you need more food. You need food to grow up and to study hard. We hope that one day you will be sent to Moscow, or East Germany, to further your studies. Alright! Stand up!" ordered his uncle.

Bao Bao stood up and thought it was better to let his uncle go on talking without interrupting him.

"Bao Bao, we will let bygones be bygones. We will all keep quiet about what has happened this afternoon. Fortunately, none of our neighbours knows about this episode. We will keep it within our family. We are after all one family. What's bad for you will not be good for us." Bao Bao looked up at his uncle. He had not expected such generosity from him.

To show his gratitude, Bao Bao sank down on his knees again and kowtowed to his uncle, "Please forgive me, Uncle," he said. Then Bao Bao raised his right hand. "In the name of God, I swear never to repeat such a foolish act of sin again. I promise that I shall endeavor my utmost to fulfill the family hopes. From now on, I will get the best grades at school so that I will be sent to Moscow one day."

Uncle lifted Bao Bao up from the ground and made him sit on a chair. "Our country belongs to us now," he said. "Every one of us has an equal opportunity to move forwards. Before, under Chiang Kai Sek, only a handful of children from rich families were allowed to study abroad. Now the situation is reversed. Now it is our turn to attend universities." Although Uncle said this, in his mind he was not sure if it was possible. He knew that the family background would be a hindrance for Bao Bao. Nevertheless he felt it was his responsibility to encourage Bao Bao.

Bao Bao raised his head and slowly peered into his uncle's eyes. He very badly wanted to give his uncle a big hug to express his gratitude, but Confucian tradition forbade him from doing so. His uncle belonged to the older generation and there was a big gap between the young and older generations. Bao Bao had to show his respect to his uncle. The boy was glad that his uncle was not too angry with him now. In old China, a nephew would have been punished with a whip or a ruler. But now, in New China, these punishments were all forbidden and instead persuasion and confession-writing was used.

"Bao Bao," Uncle continued in a fatherly voice, "as your uncle and deputy father, I would like to advise you not to damage your health. It is unpleasant and humiliating to touch on this subject."

Bao Bao wondered why his uncle mentioned the damaging of health. He felt that his health was alright, except that sometimes he felt weak.

"Your father should tell you about this, but he is not here. So I must talk to you. You know something about sperm? We Chinese consider it the 'essence' of the human body. Chinese doctors often compare a drop of sperm to a glass of blood. If you play with your penis with your hand, you are likely to create an outpour of sperm. In other words, you are damaging your health. If you do it as frequently as you implied when you told Yuan Yuan about your shooting down American spy-planes, you will ruin your health. You will not grow taller and you will become weaker and soon you will look sick."

Bao Bao recalled what he had read in the medical book at the bookstore and responded, "In the eyes of the western doctors, sperm is nothing but protein similar to the vitamins contained in egg-white."

Uncle shook his head, "Chinese and Westerners are constituted differently," he said. "This is why you rarely see a Chinese team winning a world football competition or a field competition. We grow up with rice and vegetables, whereas westerners are fed with nutritious food, such as wheat, beef, milk, honey, eggs, cheese, steak, lamb, pork, chicken, etc. and lots of vitamins. They can afford to lose sperm, whereas we Chinese cannot. If a young man such as yourself is accustomed to masturbate, it won't take long for your health to deteriorate. This habit is like a demon that will devour your soul, as well as your body, and destroy you."

Bao Bao desperately wanted to tell his uncle that he was always pestered by this demon lately. No, no, for God's sake, no! he warned himself. Uncle belongs to the older generation. I cannot tell him this. To decent people I cannot confess my dirty thoughts. How can I disclose to him that I listened to him and Auntie in the night!

Bao Bao was pleased that he was not blamed or punished by his uncle. But he told himself, I must not show my happiness to my uncle, at least not in my face. I must show deep regret. I must keep my head low. I shall keep on counting the narrow wooden planks on the dirty wooden floor.

"So do not rid yourself of precious sperm, as it is the essence of your existence," his uncle was continuing. "Don't forget!" his uncle emphasized the point.

At this point Bao Bao finally mustered up courage to ask, "When should a young man get a lesson on sex?"

"Not at your young age. You should not be bothered with it, as sex will distract you from your studies and your peaceful life. You will know this kind of thing without teaching as you grow up to become an adult. Sex is an adult matter which has nothing to do with you and you should stay away from it." Uncle finished his warning, then got up and walked out of the room.

Bao Bao sat silently on his chair and thought about what his uncle had just said. Suddenly he recalled a photograph of sperm that he had seen in a medical book in the bookstore; it had a big round head and a long squiggly tail like a baby frog. He remembered how he had gathered together the money he had received from his relatives as Li Shi, in the small red packets given to children to celebrate Chinese New Year, and bought himself a small microscope. He had gone into the bathroom and got some of his own sperm out and spread it under the lens. He had seen nothing. He had thought that the light in the bathroom was too dim and he taken the microscope close to the window to look again in the daylight. Again to his disappointment, he saw nothing. The toy microscope was not powerful enough to see any sperm underneath the lens.

After a while, Auntie came to his room and brought Bao Bao his dinner. "You should not miss any of the three meals a day; otherwise it will be bad for your stomach," she said. Auntie placed the tray on the table and left him alone. Bao Bao had no appetite but still picked up his chopsticks and chewed his food for a bit. It had been a long day for Bao Bao.

CHAPTER TWELVE

# HUNDRED FLOWERS CAMPAIGN

In a spacious room on the second floor of Shanghai Wu Ai Middle and High School, Song Ping, Bao Bao's uncle shared an office with three male and two female teachers. On the white painted walls hung a large portrait of Chairman Mao and underneath the photo was a long wooden bookcase that contained the complete works of Chairman Mao, a few volumes of Karl Marx's translated work in Chinese and a pile of newspapers. Six wooden desks were arranged in two parallel rows. Uncle Song had chosen the last row for himself. He felt more secure with no-one sitting behind him, so he would not be watched from behind. It was unavoidable, of course. Some prying eyes would look at him from time to time. Uncle Song would rather have his own personal office, but who had their own office at a time like this? In Mao's eyes, Chinese intellectuals were suspicious elements, for they were constantly associated with upholding bourgeois ideals. Even the school director was required to share an office with the Party Secretary. It was the Party's idea to let people watch each another on a daily basis.

On Uncle Song's small wooden desk stood a penholder with pencils and fountain pens and a teacup with a bamboo cover. Adjacent to the cup, there were two bottles of ink – red and blue – a small empty plastic box in which there were a few paper clips and a black and white photograph of Auntie Ying and Bao Bao's cousin Lin Lin.

One morning before school started, all the teaching staff were gathering in the office. Uncle Song sipped his morning tea and flicked through the newspaper while waiting for the bell to ring.

Suddenly, Party Secretary Cui appeared at the doorway of the faculty office and said, "Good morning comrades, today at five o'clock after school a very important meeting will take place in our conference room".

Secretary Cui went from office to office, notifying all teachers personally. The teachers were all annoyed that they could not go home after school. Uncle was especially annoyed, as he had to take Lin Lin to the hospital later to get rid of inflammation in her right eye. Nowadays Auntie was always preoccupied with the intensive political studies that were organized for housewives and she was rarely at home. Since they had no telephone at home, Uncle Song had to make a trip home to notify his wife of the changes in his schedule for the day.

Always these stupid meetings after meetings and campaigns after campaigns! When will the Communists ever give us a break?! So he cursed in his mind and glanced around the room at his colleagues. No-one seemed to be pleased at the news of today's meeting, but no-one dared to say anything. Silence hung over the room, every single breath could be heard.

By lunch-break, Uncle Song was very upset for, by going home at this time, he would lose his siesta. Alternatively, he could contact his wife through the phone service at the phone kiosk. It was very inconvenient as the phone service would have to notify his wife of his first call and then request his wife to walk all the way to the phone kiosk to wait for his second call.

The meeting as announced by the Party Secretary personally must be an important one, so it would not be possible for Uncle Song not to attend. Normally Song Ping would enjoy sharing his problems with his colleagues; but, after living under the red flag for about a decade, he had learned not to trust anyone, not even his best friend. To be betrayed was a common phenomenon, as denouncement was highly recommended and encouraged nowadays. Perhaps all six teachers in the room were annoyed with the announcement of the meeting, but they had all chosen to remain silent about their ruminations. After all, silence was the only way to survive in the new era.

After the meeting, at the dinner table at home, Uncle Song told the family that today's important meeting was about Chairman Mao's four-hour speech, addressing the right solution for the contradictions between the people and the Party. The solution proposed by Chairman Mao was very democratic this time. Instead of using force to remove dissatisfied and rebellious people, Mao was to employ open criticism forums to ease the political tensions between the people and the Party.

In response to Chairman Mao's address, Party Secretary Cui invited all teachers and staff to criticize the Party cadres. As soon as Uncle paused to take a breath Auntie interrupted, "it would be difficult to criticize the Party openly in public, because in the past decade everyone living in the new regime has learned only to please and to praise the Party under any circumstance." Uncle Song agreed and said to Bao Bao, "You are so lucky not to be involved with the Hundred Flowers Campaign, because you are too young." Hearing this, Bao Bao silently made a resolution to find out as much as he could about this adult campaign, simply because he was so curious about everything.

In fact, all intellectuals across China were astonished at such a generous offer by Chairman Mao; to be able to criticize the Party openly was unheard of. Mao's approach had brought a mixture of feelings to the intellectual world. While some read the news with great pleasure, others believed that this might be a trap set by Mao. The majority of people chose to remain tight-lipped. Finally after two hours of encouraging teachers to criticize the Party, Secretary Cui brought the meeting to a close.

A few weeks later, Uncle came across in the newspaper an article by the famous sociologist, Fei Hsia Tung, who compared Chairman Mao's speech to early springtime weather. Sometimes it was warm and sometimes it was cold, so cold that flower buds could easily freeze on a whim. This description represented the overall opinion of the intellectuals about being invited to criticize the Party. No-one understood or knew the real motive behind such a friendly invitation. Thus, in order to avoid misery, everyone preferred to keep their mouths shut. When it was absolutely necessary to speak, they would simply praise the Party again. The Party was like a beautiful woman who needed to be praised all the time. This situation lasted a couple of weeks until the first criticism broke out.

One evening, Bao Bao read in a newspaper that the only source of news was from the government's "New China News Agency", which had no competition and released news after a lot of delay. News was always released to the Party's newspaper in the first place and the non-Communist newspapers were never allowed to publish any news articles before the Party's newspaper did so. At many press conferences only Party newspapers' reporters were allowed to attend. There had been a long history of fighting between newspaper publishers and the Communist leadership. The former always wanted to report everything accurately, but the latter prevented them from doing so.

Teacher Ho and Teacher Wang at Uncle Song's school were not interested in communist activities and had never showed their enthusiasm in previous campaigns. However, this time they were active. They copied Chairman Mao's famous phrase, "Let a hundred flowers bloom and let a hundred schools of thought contend," in calligraphic writing and distributed the calligraphy to all the teachers at the school. Their aim was to get the teachers to pay attention to Mao's encouragement to speak out.

Teacher Ho and Teacher Wang came to school early every morning and brought a pile of newspapers and distributed them to the teachers. Bao Bao read the newspaper brought home by his uncle. It contained an article by Ke Pei Chi, a courageous lecturer at Beijing University. He wrote:

> *When the Communist Party took over the city, Shanghai, in 1949, they were welcomed by the people. Now, the people have turned against the regime. In retrospect, it seems remarkably similar to how one welcomed Chiang Kai Shek at first and later on rebelled against him. Now, Party members act like secret policemen and keep ordinary people under surveillance all the time. The Party attitude of "I-AM-THE-STATE" cannot be tolerated. If the Party is to work to our satisfaction, it will be acceptable. If not, the masses will punch the Party to the floor and overthrow the Communists. That is not being unpatriotic. It is because you Communists have failed to serve the people. The downfall of the Party does not mean the downfall of China.*

Bao Bao was shocked and went on reading:

> *Where is our pork?! We never get any pork and Communists bullshit about how we enjoy high living standards. Everyone is suffering from a shortage of food. But Party members on the other hand, sit in luxurious sedans and smoke expensive cigars. We, the public are very angry at the Communists and want to annihilate them.*

152

Bao Bao read another article – by Zhu An Ping, the chief editor of *Guang Ming Ri Bao* – who criticised the regime as follows:

*Only Party members are assigned leading positions in work units across China. These work units range from government departments to school institutions, to factory compounds and farm land. Every matter, no matter whether it is big or small, must be approved by Party men; but although these Party men occupy the top positions, they possess neither expertise nor knowledge. They have neglected diligence and hard work and have caused damage to the country.*

Bao Bao lifted his head from the newspaper and thought for a while. This reminded him of a sentence that Stalin had once used, "We Communists are people from special moulds and we are made of special material" – a sentence offered as justification of the situation that Communists held all the leading positions in society. Nevertheless, was this true? Bao Bao doubted it.

The fierce attacks on the Communist Party continued in the newspapers as well as in meetings for weeks. It was reported that, once, the Party Secretary reproached all non-Communist teachers, telling them, "Don't think that you are indispensable to us. In three years, we will have harvested new teachers and we will not need you any more!"

The more Bao Bao thought of these unpleasant events, the more frustrated he was. He often wished that he could discuss the current political situation with a friend. But Bao Bao found himself in the same situation as millions of intellectuals in China: he had no friend. Why are friendships such difficult things? Why must the Party require all human contacts and relationships to be contained within the framework of Party ideology? Bao Bao failed to understand this.

Hu Feng, a famous writer, modern literary critic, poet and translator was a leader in the literary world for thirty years. His strong belief in realism prompted the publication of a report on recent art and literature known as the "Three Hundred Thousand Word Book" – "Sanshiwan Yan Shu" – which was directed against Mao Ze Dong. He was arrested in 1955 and thrown into prison. His friends, acquaintances and relatives were all obliged to submit their personal letters and correspondence with Hu to the authorities. These were confiscated and used as evidence to denounce Hu. Those who refused to denounce Hu were automatically labelled as his supporters and were punished or sent away to remote places for Reform Through Labour. Under such circumstances, it was better to have no friends.

The open criticism from Ke, Chen, Zhu, and other brave scholars soon received support from their fellow intellectuals. Encouraged by them, high school teachers Ho and Wang both began to attack the Party Secretary fiercely. This time, the content of the meeting went far beyond its usual boundaries. Uncle Song and his fellow colleagues found it more exciting this time, as it was not full of routine propaganda statements. Teacher Wang said, "The relationships between teachers and students have been affected negatively. How can a young man learn from a teacher, who may later become a possible target for students to struggle against and denounce?

"I remember," Wang added, "During the Three-Anti and Two-Anti Campaigns, high school students gathered information about the private life of their teachers and used this to attack them. Teachers have to be extremely careful of what they say and what they do."

Lu Yun, the geography teacher, voiced his complaint, "Why did our big brother, the Soviet Union, remove all big factories from Manchuria to Russia shortly after the end of World War II? And why did China venture into war with Korea without help from Russia? Why did the Russians insist on collecting interest from the loan for economic aid whereas the US cancelled their loans to third world countries?"

Uncle Song noticed that Party Secretary Cui's leading position for this meeting was taken over by teachers Ho and Wang. They became "heroes" in the teachers' minds because of their courage and lack of regard for the consequences. Today's meetings did not take too long as Ho and Wang let everybody go home. The teachers were grateful that they could now go home early. They wanted to say "Thank you" and praise them for their courage, but no-one dared to get close to Ho and Wang in the presence of Party Secretary Cui. Most of the teachers did not know how to react as nobody could predict the ultimate outcome of this campaign.

While the adults were busy with the Hundred Flowers Campaign, something very unusual happened at Bao Bao's school. One morning, Wang Ming, one of Bao Bao's class-mates, a progressive student and a member of the Youth League, entered the men's toilet and discovered a Da Zi Bao announcing, "Down with Communism in China!" glued to the toilet wall. He was utterly shocked and he could not believe his eyes, so he read the Da Zi Bao over and over. He wanted to tear it down, but he refrained from doing so. Instead, he rushed into the teachers' room and reported his finding to Teacher Ma, who followed Wang Ming hurriedly to the toilet. When Teacher Ma saw it, he was frightened. He asked Wang Ming to stay calm, and stand outside the smelly toilet to guard the Da Zi Bao, while he, Teacher Ma, ran to the Party Secretary's office to report this criminal case.

At that moment, Bao Bao was passing by. Bao Bao saw that Wang Ming was pacing back and forth in front of the toilet. Bao Bao looked at him curiously. Hmm. What is he doing I wonder? Seeing the toilet reminded Bao Bao that he had to go in anyway. So why not now? he asked himself. Bao Bao walked up to the entrance of the toilet, as if he did not see Wang Ming.

"Excuse me, you are not allowed to go in!" Wang Ming said.

"But I must use the toilet. I have to go in. It's urgent," pleaded Bao Bao.

"Do you not understand that you are not allowed to go in right now?" Wang Ming raised his voice.

Bao Bao avoided Wang Ming's gaze and demanded in a soft voice, "Please let me through, otherwise I will piss here!" as he pushed himself forward into the toilet.

Wang Ming had no alternative but to let him in. Inside, Bao Bao saw the counter-revolutionary slogan and was horrified also. Bao Bao could not understand why – amongst students, who had all grown up under the red flag – a bad element still existed, critical of the Party. The Da Zi Bao was written in block Chinese characters to avoid identification of the handwriting. Hearing the commotion between Bao Bao and Wang Ming, other students came and demanded to enter the toilet. Bao Bao and Wang Ming could not refuse them.

When Bao Bao was leaving he saw the Headmaster, Party Secretary Huang, and other high ranking school officials arrive at the toilet with a camera. The Headmaster stopped Bao Bao and other students from leaving the area. After taking photographs of the Da Zi Bao, the Headmaster told the few students who had just came out of the toilet, including Bao Bao, that they should not mention this incident to anyone, not even to their classmates. This was when Bao Bao realized that the reason why he had never heard any bad news from the media was because all bad news was treated as a national secret. In the mass media, one could read only good news. Bao Bao presumed that many counter-revolutionary Da Zi Baos had appeared across the country. This was why Chairman Mao started the Hundred Flowers Campaign – to encourage everyone to speak out bravely.

At noon, Bao Bao walked home with Li Yong. "Where were you? I did not see you in the last two classes" asked Bao Bao.

"I was detained at the Headmaster's office."

"Why? Were you alone?"

"No. I was not alone. Some politically backward students, or so called 'bad elements' from other classes were with me. The Headmaster wanted to find out who had written that hideous Da Zi Bao and stuck it on the wall in the toilet."

"Has he found out who did it?"

"No. Nobody has admitted it."

"Of course, nobody would admit to it so easily. Did they all go to the toilet this morning, prior to Wang Ming's discovery?" questioned Bao Bao.

"According to them, not everybody in the group went to the toilet early this morning."

"They may have lied. How about yourself? Did you go to the toilet early this morning?"

"Um…What do you…mean?" Li Yong stuttered while quickly looking down at the ground.

Bao Bao grabbed Li Yong's thin shoulders with his bare hands and shook him vigorously, "Come on, Li Yong, you know you can trust me. Tell me, were you at the toilet this morning?" Bao Bao urged.

"To be honest with you, I did go to the toilet this morning," Li Yong said, with hesitation.

"Did you see the Dai Zi Bao there?"

"No, I didn't," Li Yong stumblingly answered.

Hearing Li Yong speak so haltingly Bao Bao demanded, "Did you write this counter-revolutionary Da Zi Bao?"

"No... No!" shouted Li Yong.

As soon as Bao Bao heard Li Yong's half-hearted reply, Bao Bao began to suspect that perhaps Li was the person who did it. However, Bao Bao did not want to interrogate Li. Instead Bao Bao changed to a soft tone and said, "Li Yong, I am not interested in finding out who did it, because I am not the school authorities. But whoever did it should never admit it. We must be aware of the regime's usual trick of pressing everyone to admit their faults in order to receive a lenient penalty!"

Li Yong was amazed to hear Bao Bao say this and added, "But that's the way it has always been! The Party promises us that they will treat us leniently if we admit to our wrongdoings! Why do you think the opposite?

"Li Yong, don't be so naïve! The moment you admit everything you will lose all your bargaining power. Don't you remember the ungrateful person, Gao Si Yan? The day he admitted his guilt he could do nothing, but wait for his verdict." Bao Bao added, "As long as you don't admit your wrongdoing, they can't do much to you legally. I would never stupidly admit a crime or a wrongdoing which I did commit unless I was caught on the spot by the authorities!" Bao Bao thought he was saying too much, as if he were teaching Li Yong, so quickly he changed the subject, "Did the meeting with the politically backward students came to any conclusion today?"

"No, it was as I said before." Li Yong's voice had returned to normal.

"Do you boys have to meet again?" asked Bao Bao.

"Yes, the meeting will continue this afternoon after class. The Headmaster said that, from now on and until the authorities catch the person who posted the counter-revolutionary Da Zi Bao, we have to meet every day after school," Li Yong said.

Bao Bao regretted that misfortune had fallen upon Li Yong. This was what he did not want to see.

In the evening Bao Bao sat in his chair and began to flip through the newspapers which his uncle had brought home that afternoon. Just at this moment, someone knocked on the door, "Who could it be at this hour?" Bao Bao thought. It was strange for a visitor to come to their home at such hour. Auntie opened the door and saw Teacher Ho and Teacher Wang at the doorway. Their visit was completely unexpected.

Bao Bao jumped up from his chair and rushed to the doorway to welcome them. It was odd to receive non-family guests in the evening. However it was considered acceptable in China to pay a personal visit to a person's home without advancednotice, since most domestic phone-lines were inactive.

Teacher Ho and Teacher Wang came to see their colleague, Uncle Song, who was startled to see them, since he did not know these two teachers well. At school, he rarely spoke to them. Their contact would consist of no more than an occasional "Hello" and "Good morning".

What is happening? Why are they intruding on our privacy in the middle of the evening? Bao Bao wondered, asking politely, "May I pour you some tea?"

"No thank you," Teacher Ho replied swiftly as he looked at Uncle.

Soon after they sat down, the teachers handed over to Uncle a page from today's evening paper. Out of politeness, Bao Bao slipped out of the door, along with Auntie and Lin Lin, since it was an adult discussion.

"The Party is encountering a serious crisis," Teacher Ho said in a solemn voice. He pointed his index finger at the front page of the newspaper. "The twelve butchers in the pork lane at the marketplace have been reduced to two butchers. When pork is unavailable, it is difficult to convince people that our living standard is increasing. The prices of our vegetables have skyrocketed. They have gone up at least six times. People are losing confidence in the Party. Life nowadays is harder than in the old days under Chiang Kai Shek's old regime." Bao Bao eavesdropped behind the door and agreed with Teacher Ho that he hardly ever had meat to eat, but he consoled himself, We have to suffer now in exchange for a bright future. As Chairman Mao said, Teacher Ho is just too shortsighted.

Teacher Wang said, "We are leaving this evening's newspaper here for you," and he folded up the newspaper and put it on the table. He added, "By the way, a visitor from Wuhan told us that on 12 and 13 June, thousands of high school students demonstrated on the streets. They called out slogans, "Welcome Kuomintong! Welcome Chiang Kai Shek!" Other demonstrations of similar scale have taken place in quite a few Chinese cities over the past few weeks. It's astonishing to see so many complaints thrown at the Party." Teacher Wang was becoming excited.

The two teachers exchanged glances with one another; Teacher Wang said, "Complaints have been suppressed for many years and all of a sudden we are encouraged to speak up against the Party. We must take advantage of this opportunity to reorganize the Party at our high school. Our immediate goal is to relieve Party Secretary Cui of his power. As far as we are concerned, his job can be performed by School Director Fu."

"I would also prefer Director Fu to run the school but it is a castle in the air," remarked Uncle. He glanced at their faces and suddenly realized that he was saying too much to the two strangers.

"Nothing is wishful thinking," Teacher Ho said. "This afternoon, Teacher Wang and I attacked the Party Secretary and now we need your help. That is why we have come to you. It is certain that you will have a lot of complaints too. You may put your thoughts and grievances together and speak out tomorrow at the meeting. We are counting on you," added Teacher Wang and then the two men left.

There was no-one else aside from Uncle and the two guests in the room. However, behind the closed doors hovered the rest of the family, pressing their ears against the door to listen. Now that Teacher Wang and Teacher Ho had gone, Auntie quickly entered the room. Bao Bao hid behind the door, curiously waiting to hear what Auntie would say.

She said to her husband, "I was eavesdropping on your conversation. I hope you will continue to remain silent and not be influenced by these two men. The Party Secretary will remain as the Party Secretary; whether be it yesterday, today or tomorrow. This campaign will pass as previous campaigns have done. Chairman Mao and the Party Secretary will not step down because of criticism from intellectuals. This campaign is a test from Chairman Mao to measure how successfully he has won the confidence of intellectuals through his series of campaigns. I can only imagine that your two colleagues are seeking trouble. They think that if a million intellectuals are against the Party, then the Party cannot take revenge easily. This is wrong. Dear Song Ping, you must think of our little daughter and me. If anything happens to you, our lives will be hard. I know you have a lot of anger that you would like to give vent to, but think of us and try your best to be tolerant and remain silent. Being tolerant has been a Chinese virtue for thousands of years. You should uphold this virtue!"

His wife's words touched Song Ping, who realized that he had underestimated his clever wife and his wife had a clear overall view of the entire situation. He was grateful to her and said, "Thank you for guiding me out of this muddled situation. I will remain silent. Please don't worry. Shall we go to bed?"

As a high school student, Bao Bao had heard a lot about the Hundred Flowers Campaign and he had been asked to express his hidden dissatisfaction against the Party, though he was never directly involved with the campaign. Tonight he was dumbfounded to hear so much and such severe criticism against the Party. What the adults mentioned about the price of the pork and vegetables was correct. A year ago, the supplies of meat, fish and cooking oil were not as rare, but nowadays a piece of meat had become such a luxury that one had to wait in a long queue at the market long before dawn in order to obtain some, even with a ration coupon.

Bao Bao conjured up in his mind a bright, socialist China with abundant food and spacious accommodation for everyone – the picture that the Communist Party had often painted in everyone's head. Bao Bao thought, It won't be too long that we have to suffer. In fifteen years, China will overtake England. The intellectuals should not be so harsh on the Party. Why don't they share Chairman's perspective?

Bao Bao was confused over the intellectuals' reaction towards the Party's governance. When the Communists took over

China, Bao Bao had just started his education in primary school. On that historic day in September 1949, when the Communist Red Army took over the city of Shanghai, as Bao Bao recalled, he was asked by his primary school teacher to go home early. That night, the soldiers of the National People's Party – the Kuomintang[20] – retreated and all city inhabitants were asked to switch off all lights and pull down all curtains, as whoever tried to peek through the curtains would be shot immediately by the angry retreating troops. Bao Bao's Ma Ma held him and his sister tightly and stayed in darkness away from the windows. The next morning Bao Bao saw some soldiers wearing light yellow uniforms with stars on their hats. They were busy setting up telephone poles and wires on the streets. Ever since that historical day, Chairman Mao had been painting a beautiful and shining New China in Bao Bao's mind.

Bao Bao remembered that Chairman Mao had said, "On a blank sheet of paper, free from any mark, the freshest and most beautiful characters can be written, the freshest and most beautiful pictures can be drawn." It is no wonder, Bao Bao thought, that intellectuals are harsh towards him. They have gathered much experience in life. They are complicated. They are no longer blank sheets of paper on which Chairman Mao can write whatever he wants.

Now Bao Bao had grown up and become a teenager. He eavesdropped on Uncle's conversation with the two visitors, and also with Auntie earlier in the evening. He was surprised that Uncle had suppressed his anger against the new regime. Usually Auntie was very careful in conversation with her husband in front of the children, but today she was too nervous to handle this emergency and forgot the presence of the children. Now Bao Bao was certain that it was not only other intellectuals, such as Teachers Ho and Wang, who had a lot of complaints. Even his dear Uncle was upset with the government.

He thought of the Wuhan high school student demonstration mentioned by the two teachers. Can it be possible that young students are rebelling against our new regime? How can it be? I myself am a high school student, but I have never thought about demonstrating against my own Motherland. This must be a rumour! Bao Bao thought. And Chairman Mao has always taught us never to believe in rumours! He paced around the room and decided to verify the "rumours" with Chef Wang or by listening to the Voice of America. But unfortunately today was Tuesday. He had vowed that that he would not wake up at midnight during week-days. It was a discipline that he had vowed to follow.

According to Teachers Ho and Wang, the Party had lost control of the current political campaign. Both teachers seemed in a good mood the following day. Uncle Song supposed that their household visits last night were successful. Yes, he was right. At today's meeting, not only Teachers Ho and Wang spoke fiercely, but all the other teachers expressed their dissatisfaction with the Party.

Teacher Li said, "We have been friends with some colleagues for a long time, but as soon as one becomes a Party member his views change dramatically, as if he belongs to another planet, and our friendship is discontinued. I don't know why there is a clear line between Party members and non-Party members. Only Party members belong to the powerful inner circle of our Communist regime and non-Party members are considered as outsiders. Among Party members, they address each other as 'Comrade so and so'. However, non-Party members they simply call by their names. I feel that it is not good to discriminate against non-Party members."

"Also," Teacher Li continued, "Our Premier Chou started his speech with, "Comrades and friends". The former he addressed to Party members and the latter to non-Party members."

Teacher Feng added to Teacher Li's criticism. "It seems that friendship among people has been wiped out by the Party's doctrine. Human relationships are deteriorating day by day. Old friendships are disappearing because many are being labelled Counter-Revolutionaries. It is difficult to make new acquaintances, let alone new friends. Furthermore, to greet a Counter-revolutionary on the street could bring trouble to oneself."

Teacher Yu anxiously voiced the following: "In the past, we received a salary increment regularly and allowances for lunch and transportation, etc. Now after the revolution, all allowances have been cancelled and we have heard nothing about a salary increment for years."

Since everyone was speaking fiercely and angrily, Song Ping felt uneasy sitting there silently. Teachers Ho and Wang glanced at him from time to time to remind him that it was his turn to speak. After long hesitation, Song Ping finally came out with a mild attack against the Party, "Once a group of foreign journalists visited our high school and the authorities forbade us to talk in private. In our library we still have quite a few English books and magazines but no-one dares to borrow them because books in Western languages are classified as 'poisonous'". As soon as Song Ping said his few words, he felt much better. What he said was nothing but facts. He had no intention of attacking the Party. He was just responding to Chairman Mao's call to let a hundred flowers bloom and a hundred schools of thought contend. He felt better, now that he had fulfilled his duty and not let his colleagues Teacher Ho and Teacher Wang down. It was because of Auntie's warning that he made only a very mild statement.

Party Secretary Cui stood up, bewildered. He was humiliated by the open criticisms of his subordinates. It was the first time that he had ever heard such attacks on the Party and on himself. Nevertheless, he was grateful, as seen from his face, for the criticism from all the teachers. He promised that all comments would be carefully considered as guidance for future improvement and in the meantime he would forward these criticisms to his boss, the Party Secretary of the district.

Teacher Ho and Wang's original intention was to overthrow the Party Secretary, but the attacks were not severe enough to pull him down from his seat, especially as they were not directed against Party Secretary Cui himself personally. Teacher Ho was disappointed and stood up to give a closing speech. "The life of intellectuals under Communist rule can be summarized in one word – fear. Fear dominates intellectual thought. One fears to offend Communist Party members when speaking; and one fears to be denounced, whether one does something wrong or whether one does nothing wrong. I am sure many colleagues are still afraid to speak out in the presence of the Party Secretary and Party members."

Teacher Ho had pinpointed precisely the element which Song Ping suffered the most from – the fear to speak out. Traditionally, Chinese intellectuals praised only those who were courageous enough to stand up against repression. The most prominent heroes were those who had no fear of losing their lives. Now Song Ping felt himself to be a coward, who had spoken only a few insignificant words. As soon as the meeting ended, he ran out of the room, for he had no face to see his colleagues. He repeatedly said to himself, "I am a coward". The next day, he did not show up at school. He reported sick, in order to avoid more fierce confrontations at the school meetings.

In order to qualify for sick leave, teachers had to submit a doctor's certificate, but this time it was easy to get approval. Song Ping called both School Director Fu and Party Secretary Cui, the one right after the other. They were both very friendly on the phone. It was not unusual for the School Director to talk politely and courteously on the phone; but the Party Secretary was friendly this time as well, which was quite unusual. Song Ping knew it was the criticisms given by the teachers that had altered his arrogant attitude. Thinking of Teachers Ho and Wang made Song Ping feel conscience-stricken. He had not contributed anything to educate the Party Secretary. This time, nobody asked him for a doctor's certificate, nor did anyone question the duration of his sick leave. Song Ping was glad that he had been diplomatic, calling both the Party Secretary and the School Director, one after another; as one of them would remain in power at the end of the campaign. Who knows? Perhaps one day they will think of my polite gesture during turbulent times, thought Uncle Song.

CHAPTER THIRTEEN

# CHEF WANG'S BIG SECRET

During class that day Bao Bao found his mind often wandering to the news regarding the student uprisings in Wuhan. Absent-mindedly, Bao Bao preoccupied himself with his own thoughts, asking himself repeatedly, How could high school students, like myself, possibly demonstrate against our country? Don't they love our country, our Communist Party and our most respected Chairman Mao?

As soon as class finished, Bao Bao hurried over to Chef Wang's coffee shop. Chef Wang was engrossed with his cooking, so Bao Bao decided to return home first. At home, Bao Bao completed his homework assignments, then returned to visit Chef Wang after dinner. Chef Wang was now sitting in his wicker chair and listening to Shanghai Opera on the radio.

When Bao Bao knocked on the door and entered his room, Chef Wang said, "My boy, you came to see me before. Tell me, what do you have on your mind?" Bao Bao closed the door and sat on the edge of the bed. Then he said, "I have heard a rumour that high school and university students were demonstrating in Wuhan. Do you know anything about it?"

The Chef answered, "Not only in Wuhan, but in many cities, such as Beijing, they have organized mass-demonstrations against the Party's arbitrary allocation of jobs. In Hanyang, thousands of high school students gathered together to boycott classes. They destroyed the offices of Party members and stuck up Da Zi Baos and wall-posters everywhere. They demanded that Chairman Mao should step down and welcomed Chiang Kai Sek to return. Many posters read, 'Mao Ze Dong, Step Down!' 'Down with the Communist Party!' They even assaulted Communist cadets."

The brightness on Bao Bao's face vanished and he turned pale from Chef Wang's confirmation of the horrifying news. Bao Bao was scared. Chef Wang, however, was excited by this topic and wanted to demonstrate how well-informed he was about unpublished and little-publicised news. He added with pride, "The uprising was not organized only by students, but by workers and farmers as well. In Guangdong Province, the workers damaged government buildings and five Communist officials were killed. More than this, a series of anti-Communist underground organizations was discovered."

Bao Bao was taken aback to hear that an uprising of such great magnitude had taken place. Previously, he had thought that it was a small group of high school students only that had been causing such a nuisance. He felt sorry that his beloved country was in trouble. He found it difficult so quickly to upgrade into reality what he had believed to be a rumour. It was a dilemma. Should he, or should he not, believe Chef Wang? In confusion Bao Bao asked Chef Wang another question, "What is your opinion of Mao's Hundred Flowers Campaign? Are intellectuals supposed to criticise the Party?" Chef Wang smiled. "It was Mao's tactic to entice the snakes to come out of their caves." Bao Bao did not follow his meaning.

Seeing Bao Bao's confused face, Chef Wang asked, "Why don't we change the subject? We should talk about something more interesting and entertaining." He pulled a large brown envelope out from underneath his bed. He came close to Bao Bao and said, "Let me give you a lesson about sex". Bao Bao could not believe his ears. "Sex" was a forbidden word. He knew of its existence but to hear someone saying the word out loud was a first for him. It was as though a bolt of lightning had struck him. He remembered that Chef Wang had mentioned it before and he had decided then not to take lessons on the subject from him. He wanted to leave immediately. Even so, he was curious to see what was inside the large brown envelope.

Without uttering another word, Chef Wang pulled out from the envelope a number of black and white photos. Bao Bao was flabbergasted. – They were all photos of men and women, stark naked. – The erotic scenes were far beyond his imagination. He could not believe the existence of such things! Bao Bao's muscles became tense, and he grew restless looking at the photos. Chef Wang inched closer towards him, then wrapped his arms tightly around Bao Bao's shaking body, proceeding to unbutton Bao Bao's shirt and unbuckle his waist belt.

"STOP IT! Let go of me! Aiyaah! Let me go!" Bao Bao yelled as loudly as he could.

Bao Bao's voice echoed so forcefully that Chef Wang was afraid that the neighbours would hear. So he stopped interfering Bao Bao. Bao Bao dashed to the door. Just as Bao Bao was about to open the door, Chef Wang rushed to stop him, pleading, "Do not tell anybody about the photos! Please! Promise me!"

Bao Bao nodded hurriedly, "Okay! I promise. Let me go now!"

"If you ever need a lesson on sex, come to see me. I know such things bother many of you young people. I can give you all the lessons you need and let you know about everything that parents and teachers try to hide from you! Just do not tell anybody of the incident between you and me. Can you promise? Promise me!" insisted Chef Wang.

"Yes, yes! I promise!" answered Bao Bao as he pulled the door open.

Bao Bao rushed home, taking the shortest route possible. What did he want from me?! If I were a girl, he could have raped me, but I am a boy. Though I don't exactly know what 'rape' is, I can figure out from the Chinese characters that it must have something to do with a man and a woman having sex by force. Since I am a boy, what did he want from a boy? What could he possibly do with me!?

Lying in bed that night, Bao Bao could not sleep. There were too many things on his mind. First the student uprisings; then the unexpected interference from Chef Wang. Why did Chef Wang do that to me? Why was he unbuttoning my shirt and unbuckling my belt? What did he want? Did he want to see me naked like in those photos? How awful and filthy he is to think like that!

Suddenly an idea occurred to Bao Bao. He could easily denounce Chef Wang for interfering with him! If he did so, his political standing would increase a hundred times. He would be invited to join the Communist Youth League and get admission to a good university. Later on, he could become a Party Member and be sent to Russia or East Germany for further study. His future under the red flag would be secured. This would be a big, big step forward in his career and his entire life!

"No, I cannot do it! If I did, they would interrogate me to such an extent that I would have to tell them everything that Chef

Wang has told me! They might send him to a remote province for Thought Reform. He is a good man. No I cannot do it! He was trying to do me a favour by giving me a lesson on sex. He should not go to gaol because of me. I would never under any circumstance denounce him. Never! Never! A hundred times Never! That's for sure!

Do I need sex lessons? I don't think so. If I need them, Chairman Mao and my uncle will certainly provide them for me. No, I don't need them, Bao Bao concluded. I am going to wait until I am old enough to get married and it still won't be too late for me.

Deep into the night, Bao Bao was still thinking. He thought again of the speech by Chairman Mao, saying that the country had never before been so united, that now a bright future stretched out before our eyes. Who has united the country? Bao Bao asked himself. Without doubt it was Chairman Mao and the Communist Party that had done so. He had read that, in the late nineteenth century and beginning of the twentieth century, China had suffered tremendously. People had compassion for China because of what she had gone through. China was like a plate of loose sand and never had been so united.

After the Liberation, under the correct leadership of the Communist Party and Chairman Mao, China had made enormous progress in every aspect. It was clear to Bao Bao that China's quick progress in heavy industry was at the cost of light industry and the people's living standards. The more he thought about it, however, the more he was grateful to Chairman Mao and the Party. Bao Bao was aware that the Party's policy could not please every one of the six hundred million Chinese citizens. In the same way, a mother of six children at home could never cook a meal to please six children at the same time. Bao Bao had no doubt of his absolutely full support for Chairman Mao, who was quickly turning China into an industrial world power. Compared with this, the shortage of pork and of light industrial products were not issues for complaint.

Oh! For the hundredth time! Just remember Chairman Mao's saying, "Work hard, be a good student and contribute scientific knowledge to the country!" Bao Bao reminded himself.

No-one but Chairman Mao could have planted such strong determination in a young soul like mine!

As a Communist, one's head should be full of ideology and Party doctrine. One's two feet should march steadily forward, following the Party's orders, and one's eyes should look only straight ahead. Bao Bao was not ready to do this yet. He could not fully follow Communist doctrine and sacrifice his friend, Chef Wang. He was, after all, Bao Bao's only friend in the older generation, who willingly responded to his curiosity. Furthermore, if he had to please the Party, the second person that Bao Bao could denounce would be his uncle, because Bao Bao had heard the conversation between Uncle and Auntie after Teacher Ho and Teacher Wang left their home, and he knew that his uncle nursed a lot of rage against the new regime. If his uncle were denounced by him, the regime would force his uncle to vent his fury in public and he would be punished severely. "No!" Bao Bao shook his sleepy head. He would never do such stupid things. Merely thinking of it was frightening.

Bao Bao would never denounce Chef Wang. However, if Chef Wang were to be denounced by someone else, he would be forced to confess the names of all the people associated with him, which would inevitably include Bao Bao. In this case the Party would be angry with Bao Bao, asking why he did not denounce Chef Wang earlier, himself. Bao Bao would have lost the trust of the Party and could possibly run into trouble. Bao Bao was confused. Should he or should he not denounce Chef Wang? He had chosen not to do so. But he had determined also that he would never visit him again.

Bao Bao felt a huge sense of relief as he reached this resolution. He envisaged that Chef Wang might encounter some sort of trouble one of these days, since he talked so freely, without thinking that he was being watched by everyone, as everyone was spying on everyone else in the new society. Furthermore, he had collected a great many dirty erotic photos, and this activity was prohibited by the Party. With these thoughts in mind, Bao Bao fell asleep.

At midnight, the alarm clock began to ring, Bao Bao switched it off quickly to keep it from waking his sister, Yuan Yuan. It was time for "The Voice of America". Tonight Bao Bao had set the alarm clock to midnight so that he could listen to the latest news of the student uprisings. He hurried out of bed and peeped through the window into the dark night. There was nothing unusual. He put on his earphones and tuned in to "The Voice of America" in Pu Tong Hua[21] It was not difficult to tune in, but the buzzing introduced over the broadcasts in order to block short-wave transmissions was incredibly annoying.

Usually Bao Bao was able to receive about forty to fifty percent of each broadcast. On a lucky day, he could even receive sixty to seventy percent. Tonight, it was not so good and he only received half the broadcast. Nevertheless, since the stories from Chef Wang had served as background information, it was not so difficult to understand the broadcast, despite the constant interruptions. It mentioned the workers who had gone on strike in Guang Dong Province and the students who had demonstrated in Hanyang and in Beijing etc. This proves that Chef Wang, Teacher Ho and Teacher Wang were right! Bao Bo thought. This verification disappointed him, because he did not want Chairman Mao to step down and Chang Kai Shek to come back. He preferred to endure present suffering for the sake of a bright future for his socialist society. Bao Bao was upset that students had caused such commotion across China. Gradually he went back to sleep.

# CHAPTER FOURTEEN

# DOWN WITH THE SPARROWS

At four o'clock in the early morning, Bao Bao was awakened by the sound of his alarm clock. He pushed the off button and continued to doze. A few minutes later, the deafening noise of gongs and drums aroused Bao Bao from his sleep.

"What is the matter!?" he murmured. "Must I get up so early on a December morning?" Bao Bao complained. He was trying to ignore the noise, and continued to lie in bed. But Auntie came into his room and cried, "Bao Bao! You must get up now! Don't forget that today is the day on which we will write history. Across our Motherland we are launching a war against all sparrows. Our country is determined to exterminate them, until the very last sparrow is removed from our territory!"Hearing his auntie speak, Bao Bao had no excuse and dragged himself out of bed.

Recently, Chairman Mao had introduced a campaign against the "four pests" – flies, sparrows, mosquitoes and rats. Millions of Chinese people were called upon to exterminate them. Today was the first day of the "Great Sparrow Campaign". Sparrows were considered enemies of the farmers, because they consumed valuable grain. The Party concluded that the harvest results would look much better if there were no sparrows around to eat the grain. For an entire week, millions of Shanghai inhabitants were occupied with studying the various methods that one could adopt to kill sparrows. Everyone in China was following the famous saying of Chairman Mao that we "do not enter into a war that we will not win". In order to conduct the war, "sparrow campaign headquarters" were established in different districts across the cities. A leader, group leaders, sub-group leaders, small group leaders and team leaders were appointed to map out effective battle strategies.

Bao Bao was reluctant to participate but he had no choice. When the Party announced a campaign, the entire population – from six to eighty years old – was required to take part. Only those who were seriously ill or those who were lying on their deathbed were exempt from the campaign. If someone was unwilling to echo the Party-line, he would be in serious trouble. In this case his colleagues, neighbours, peers, relatives and family members were obligated to enlighten him, and to argue him from morning to evening, day in and day out, until he changed his mind and participated in the campaign. Every Chinese knew the importance of following the Party's calling. Bao Bao was no exception. So he got up from bed to take part in this historic campaign.

When Bao Bao entered the dining room, he saw that breakfast was already on the table. Uncle was checking his throwing net and bamboo poles, as if he were a soldier checking his rifle before going to the front. At five o'clock sharp, everyone gathered outside the house. It was still dark, so they carried flashlights and some people lit torches.

Workers were called to take part in this campaign at their own leisure. Many came directly from their nightshifts. Drivers of trams and trains, ship's-captains on the Huangpu River – all honked their horns to create a monstrous, ear-splitting noise to scare their enemies. The streetcars and buses moved as fast as possible to transport inhabitants to the front. The People's Liberation Army was also invited to shoot sparrows down, using their professional shooting skills. All schools were closed because of Chairman Mao's view that students learn more from the streets and fields than from books in the class-room.

If a foreigner had happened to visit Shanghai on 14 December 1958, he would have wondered what the millions of Chinese were doing in the darkness before daybreak. Everywhere on the streets, people were carrying red flags, bamboo poles, shooting gear, throwing-nets, gongs, drums and trumpets. Seen from an aeroplane, it would have seemed as if Shanghai was celebrating a festival in the darkness – the young and old, the strong and the weak, men and women – all marching in unison towards the People's Square. This had become the headquarters where the Vice-Mayor of Shanghai, Jin Zhong Hua, the commander-in-chief of the campaign, was to announce its opening. This was to be followed by an explosion of noise from thousands of canons, gongs and drums to terrify and shock the birds. Every loud speaker was switched on to maximum output. The noise was intended to drive the sparrows to certain areas

172

across the city where poisonous rice had been spread on the ground. A great many sparrows would die after consuming the lethal grain.

In the afternoon, the people reaped the benefits of their hard work. Loud-speakers across Shanghai announced that an estimated number of four hundred and forty thousand sparrows had been killed on that first day. A military jeep was decorated with thousands of sparrow corpses. At the top of the jeep hung a banner on which were written the big, red character words, "Congratulations." The jeep drove slowly to the city's headquarters to report the triumph of the war. Behind the jeep followed tens of thousands of marching Chinese – everyone held a bamboo pole, on which hung numerous sparrow corpses. The great triumph brought immense joy and pride to the inhabitants of Shanghai and smiling faces were seen everywhere.

The people smiled partly because they had successfully accomplished a mission and had proved to the Party that they were good citizens. They also smiled because they were looking forward to a good meal of stewed sparrow for dinner. Although the regime forbade them to eat the dead sparrows, Auntie picked up a few that were shot down or caught in the nets, or killed by bamboo poles. Only the ones that were killed by eating poisonous grain were put into a victory bag and submitted to the authorities as proof to the new regime of their victory.

Throughout the day, Bao Bao was sad to see so many small creatures being exterminated. He felt that men were cruel to use so many different methods and devices to kill the poor harmless creatures. He knew it was unfair, yet he was powerless in the face of the brutal campaign. Though Bao Bao was holding a long pole all the time to hit and to kill the exhausted sparrows that dropped down from above because of the increasing unbearable noise, he just pretended to attack the little creatures. In fact he did nothing and did not kill even a single sparrow. Fortunately, amongst the crowded group, nobody was watching him.

Back at home, Bao Bao decided to dissect a dead sparrow to satisfy his scientific curiosity. He placed one sparrow on a cutting board and opened its belly with Auntie's sharp knife. Bao Bao felt nauseous as he found a pile of intestines and a small heart stuck together with blood. Ugh! Bao Bao thought as he pulled open the sparrow's stomach and peered curiously into its inner organs.

Among the sparrows in the bag, Bao Bao found a crow and a blackbird. He picked up the crow and blackbird and hurried to Uncle's side. Uncle was lying in bed with his eyes half-open. Apparently he was worn out from the morning's activities.

"Uncle, can we eat these?" Bao Bao asked, holding up the crow and the blackbird in his two hands.

"Yes, yes, of course. Give them to Auntie," replied Uncle softly.

While Bao Bao occupied himself with rummaging through the bag of sparrows that they brought home, Auntie was preparing to clean the birds and said to Bao Bao, "Let me show you how to cook a couple of dozen birds! We must work quickly." She swiftly dumped all the birds into an aluminum pot half-full with boiling water. A while later, she took the birds out and removed the feathers one by one. Then she used a pair of scissors to open their bellies and remove everything from the birds' insides.

Lin Lin came into the kitchen with good news. She said, "Ma Ma, our neighbours are also cooking sparrows and we need not be afraid of getting into trouble."

"Good. But we still have to be careful. Many people did not manage to get any dead sparrows to eat and they will be jealous of us. They may denounce us. So tomorrow you children should not tell anyone at school that we ate any sparrows. It is forbidden, as you know," Auntie said.

After cleaning the sparrows one by one, Auntie put them into a pot and added two spoons of soya sauce and a little sugar as she stewed the birds. She would have loved to fry them for the crispness and better taste, but they did not have the cooking oil to do this. The rationing scheme allowed only a little cooking oil for each family.

At dinner, Bao Bao found the dish of sparrow to be delightful. He had forgotten the taste of this delicacy. It had paid off to get up so early in the morning. Regardless of the Communist campaign, fried sparrows were widely regarded as a delicious dish and were included in the speciality cuisines of many provinces. Although Bao Bao felt ashamed that he did not contribute to the killing of a single sparrow, he was happy to share the delicacy at the dinner table.

The following day Bao Bao came across Li Yong on the way to school and Li said, "Bao Bao, did you have delicious cooked sparrow for dinner last night?"

Bao Bao, should have said "No", according to Auntie's warning. But it was difficult to lie to his best friend. He knew that Li would never betray him. So after a few seconds hesitation, he admitted the truth. "Yes, we did. The taste was very good. I had forgotten how delicious it was. How about you? Did you enjoy a good dinner too?"

"Yes, we did." Li Yong added, "When we cooked the dead birds in our shared kitchen, I used wet soap on the window so that our neighbours could not see what Ma Ma was cooking."

The war to exterminate sparrows lasted for a few days until the commander-in-chief broadcast an announcement that Shanghai residents had attained complete victory. Everyone was happy that they need not get up at four in the morning any more and that their ears would not have to tolerate the deafening noise of the gongs and drums.

Two weeks after the combat, Bao Bao was still thinking of the succulent dish of sparrows. One morning he told his teacher, "I saw some sparrows on a cable pole this morning. Weren't we aiming to annihilate all sparrows, down to the very last one?"

The teacher knew that this had been the Party's original goal but did not know how to answer Bao Bao. After careful contemplation, the teacher replied, "I have not received any further instructions from the school authorities in regard to the extermination of sparrows, nor have I heard or read any news of a further sparrow campaign."

A few months later, a distant relative of Uncle, a farmer, came to visit. He complained about the shortage of food. "Oh! I know! If you are hungry, you also can catch sparrows to eat! I am sure there are still many more sparrows in the countryside than in the city," said Bao Bao.

The farmer answered, "Bao Bao, although sparrows do eat grain, they eat more insects, flies and ants than any other species. Our scientists in the China Science Institute have anatomized a great number of sparrows and from the content of their stomachs, they have concluded in a scientific report that a sparrow's diet consists only one fourth of grain and three fourths of insects. So, basically, sparrows are good birds. Since we have got rid of the sparrows; all kinds of insects and ants are now thriving to a point beyond our control. Insects devour and destroy far more grain than the sparrows. Furthermore, sparrows spare our trees from infestation by preventing white wormy cocoons from forming in trees." The farmer continued, "Did you know that our government is arranging to have sparrows imported from foreign countries right now? We are importing twenty thousand sparrows from Russia for an experiment!"

At a meeting held towards the end of 1959, Chairman Mao finally revealed his reluctant decision to cease killing sparrows but to keep on annihilating insects.

A few months after the Sparrows Campaign, Bao Bao still craved the good taste of the delicacy. One day Bao Bao said to his neighbour, Jia Gen, "If I had another chance to eat the sparrow dish I would keep every bit of it in my month for a long time, so to enjoy the delicious taste and flavour." Bao Bao was shocked at Jia Gen's unexpected response, "Have you tried to eat mouse?"

"No. Never! I cannot imagine that anybody could eat mouse. It's disgusting!" Bao Bao answered and his body quivered from the shock.

Jia Gen replied, "Don't say that! If you starved for three days you would eat anything! A farmer who once suffered starvation told me about this. So one day I caught about a dozen mice, each about eight to ten centimeters long. I cleaned them, peeled off the skin, took their innards out, and stewed them in a pot. The taste was even better and the meat much more tender than the sparrows. The most important thing for me is that I can always catch some mice whenever I have a longing for delicious food. As you know, mice are one of the four pests that Chairman Mao wants to exterminate.

Bao Bao did not know how to respond. From then on, he stayed away from Jia Gen. Perhaps he did not like his mouse-like smell. Nevertheless, Bao Bao admitted, "I have never experienced real hunger. If I starve for three days, will I eat mice to fill up my stomach?! I can't imagine it!"

CHAPTER FIFTEEN

# PAYING A VISIT TO DAN DAN

Today for the first time Bao Bao went to visit Dan Dan at home to give her private tutoring in geometry. Already since last Thursday he had been looking forward to being alone with her at her home. He put on a Chinese-style cotton jacket which he had ironed yesterday. Ironing clothing was not popular these days because it was thought to be a bourgeois habit. Since the Party took over China, nobody paid much attention to clothing. Shirts, pants and cotton jackets were not to be ironed and shoes were not to be shined. The Party demanded only the heart, and nothing of outward appearance from her citizens.

Even uncombed hair and unwashed faces were perfectly acceptable. If someone wore neatly pressed clothes and stylishly-combed hair, that person would be regarded with suspicion in the new society.

For the first time, Bao Bao was to visit Dan Dan and he was looking forward to sitting close to her. He did want to leave a good impression and so he did not dress too shabbily. He had ironed his jacket yesterday, although only two thirds of it. He cleaned and partly shined his shoes and coarsely combed his hair. He wished to leave an impression with Dan Dan that he was neat and clean, quite well-groomed, but still in line with the Party's dress code.

Bao Bao entered the alley to Dan Dan's house, a traditional Shanghai Shikumen residence of solid grey bricks, built in the twenties. It was a systematic construction: all the neighbouring houses in the alley were identical in size and shape. Above the alley dwellers' walkways, outside the windows on the second and third floors, clothes hung on long, thin, bamboo poles, four or five metres long. Each unit was guarded by a big black gate and inside that gate resided many families.

About half of Shanghai's inhabitants lived in such Shanghainese style houses. In other alleyways Shikumen houses were built of brownish orange and red bricks and the gates were painted a vermillion colour.

Bao Bao came to Dan Dan's house, Number 7 and stood a few minutes in front of it. Dan Dan's family lived on an upper floor. There was a doorbell at the gate. However, like most door bells, it was not working. In the new regime, doorbells, like many light industrial items, were no longer manufactured. He wanted to telephone her, but like most inhabitants she had no private telephone at home. Usually he would simply cry out a name and wait for the person he wanted to see to stick their head out of the window and rush to open the door for him. But Dan Dan was a girl. Bao Bao was hesitant to yell out loud for a girl, as he had never done so before. So, Bao Bao stood there for a couple of minutes, not knowing what to do. He could not retreat, because Dan Dan was waiting for him and he had been looking forward to this moment since last Thursday. As he was about to muster up the courage to yell out Dan Dan's name, an elderly lady appeared, so Bao Bao immediately refrained from calling out. Now he stood there, waiting for the strange old lady to pass by, so that she would not hear him calling out a girl's name. Finally, when the elderly lady had vanished out of sight, Bao Bao called, "Dan Dan!"

Bao Bao's voice was so gentle and low that no-one noticed it. He cried out again, "Dan Dan," raising his voice. This time, a lady stuck her head out of the first floor window and craned her neck forward. She looked down and peered curiously at Bao Bao, whose cheeks immediately turned pink. A couple of seconds later, another window on the second floor was thrown open and an old woman stretched her neck out of the window. Bao Bao stood there, panic-stricken. Before he could utter a single word, another set of windows was thrown open on the third floor as an old man walked out onto his terrace.

Bao Bao presumed that the old man was Dan Dan's father, as he knew that Dan Dan lived on the third floor. He raised his arm with a book in his hand and called out loudly, "About Math, I would like to speak to Dan Dan!"

Soon Dan Dan appeared on the terrace behind the old man. She responded, "Wait! I am coming down to open the door for you."

Bao Bao's heart started to pound even faster. He did not want to look up at the curious eyes above him. Luckily I have a

178

book with me! They will all look at my book and see that I am here for business! Contact between teenage males and females was only accepted for business in the new society.

Dan Dan opened the door, but hid half her face behind it. Her face showed shyness. She was not accustomed to receiving a male guest. Perhaps it was her first time. Politely she smiled at him, but dared not meet his eyes. She led him up the staircase. The older woman who had opened the window on the first floor now stepped out of her room, glancing at Bao Bao, as he followed Dan Dan on her way up the staircase. The lady was about seventy years old. Her shining silver-grey hair was cut short above her ears. She had small, bound feet belonging to the days before the Republic of 1911. Bao Bao avoided meeting her eye, as he believed that there were too many idle and curious people in China who enjoyed fabricating and creating sensational stories.

The book in Bao Bao's hand helped to prevent a lot of gossip. In fact, Bao Bao didn't have to bring the book, since Dan Dan had the same book at home. But if Bao Bao had had no book in his hand, the old lady might have whispered to the other old ladies that Dan Dan at the age of fifteen already had a boyfriend. This would have caused a commotion in the neighbourhood. In China, when a girl grew up, everyone was curious to see whether or not she had a boyfriend. Usually, it was acceptable to have a boyfriend if she was twenty years or older. If a girl changed boyfriends more than three times, she would be considered not a serious or decent girl. As for Dan Dan, she was much too young to have a boyfriend. Bao Bao awarded himself an imaginary pat on the back to congratulate himself for being so smart as to bring a book with him.

The staircase was narrow and steep. Even with the light on, it was still very dark inside. For Bao Bao, it was particularly dark, since he had just entered from the sunny bright exterior. He grasped the railings firmly as he followed Dan Dan up the staircase. She was wearing a pair of sandals, a black sweater and a pair of long cotton trousers. She ran swiftly up the staircase, while Bao Bao had to climb the steps one by one. Dan Dan waited for him in the corridor. As soon as Bao Bao reached the third floor, she switched off the staircase light and then led him into a bright living-room. Bao Bao could now see daylight again. The living-room was small with simple furniture. On the table there was an ancient American electrical fan by Westinghouse. It looked like a product of the nineteen-thirties. One door in the living-room led to a small terrace and another door led to a bedroom. Dan Dan introduced her father to Bao Bao. Her father greeted him and said a few polite words about the weather. Then Dan Dan brought tea for everybody. Her father excused himself and left Dan Dan alone with Bao Bao for the private tutoring.

As soon as her father left the room, Bao Bao took out from his pocket a green-coloured plastic hairpin which his Ma Ma sent to Yuan Yuan from Hong Kong. Bao Bao had borrowed this from his sister. Dan Dan was delighted to receive such a small souvenir. The plastic hairpin was not a valuable gift, but it was so delicately made, like a piece of real jade, that one could not find such a thing in Shanghai even for a lot of money. Dan Dan said, "Thank you, Bao Bao. I can wear it only when I am at home. If I put it on at school or on the street, I shall be in trouble, as this nice piece belongs to the bourgeois class. I don't want to be criticized. I promise you that I shall wear it as soon as I come home and have it on when I go to sleep."

Bao Bao sat across from Dan Dan and let her try to work out the solution for herself. Her face was round like a full moon. Her eyes were large and showed a dream-like naïvety. Her hair was shining black and she wore two long pigtails over her shoulders. Bao Bao had never had the opportunity to look at her so closely before because he had always been too shy to look into her eyes. Now that he was sitting across from her, he thought that she was like a fragile bud which was about to open and become a beautiful flower.

It suddenly occurred to Bao Bao that he had not seen a single real flower for months. Only in spring or summer could people see a small number of flowers blooming in the parks. Buying cut flowers and then placing them in a vase at home or in an office was a non-existent practice in society, because it was regarded as a bourgeois enjoyment. Bao Bao had never seen a flower shop, nor did he know whether any flower shops were still in business. Farmers grew vegetables more than flowers, as flowers were considered useless. Furthermore it was said that Chairman Mao hated cut flowers. He thought that they were a waste. Bao Bao could not imagine what kind of pleasure one could derive from choosing and arranging flowers in a vase. But now Dan Dan was sitting before him, and she was a thousand times more beautiful than any flower. He was grateful to Teacher Feng who had put Bao Bao and Dan Dan in the same group – the same *xiao zu*.

"Where do you think Teacher Feng can be?" asked Bao Bao. "He has not come to class for quite a while."

"I don't know. I only know that many of our teachers have been replaced," replied Dan Dan.

Bao Bao was sad to hear her response. He figured that Teacher Feng might have become an outcast. They might have labelled him a Rightist and sent him to a remote area in the North. However, he said nothing to Dan Dan.

Bao Bao was grateful to Chairman Mao who had emancipated Chinese women so that they now had an equal chance of studying in schools with male students. The Father of the Chinese Republic, Dr Sun Yat Sen had ushered Chinese society into the modern era, abolishing the foot-binding of women and allowing females to attend school, etc. Unfortunately, in the old days it was only those who were rich enough who could send their daughters to school. Nowadays, in Communist China, girls were treated as importantly as boys. Girls no longer stayed at home to do the cooking, sewing, and serving. Now they attended schools with the boys and learned subjects such as geometry as well.

Dan Dan shrugged her shoulders in distress and Bao Bao knew she needed him. "Try again! – If you extend the line BC and use CE as a fictitious line," he said in a voice that sounded soft and caring.

She followed his suggestion and drew a line with her pencil. As soon as she attempted the problem, following his suggestion, she smiled with much satisfaction. The solution became visible. She said, "Bao Bao! Why are you always so clever?"

"In order to solve a problem, one has to ascertain how to attain the solution. If a fictitious line is needed, then put one in. If ten more lines are needed, then add in the necessary lines. The more you practice, the easier it will be to envision the answers," Bao Bao answered as humbly as he could.

"Here, try to solve another problem!"

Bao Bao then placed a new exercise before Dan Dan and asked her to show him the washroom. Dan Dan led him out of her room and pointed to the door opposite the staircase. Bao Bao entered the toilet and found three wooden buckets painted a bright vermillion. Each bucket was about forty centimetres high and about thirty-five in diameter. He realized that Dan Dan lived in an old traditional Chinese house without a flush toilet. There were three wooden buckets for collecting human excrement – Ma Tongs – in the toilet and Bao Bao knew right away that these belonged to three different families. He did not want to use the wrong bucket, so he returned to Dan Dan's room and asked, "There are three Ma Tongs in the toilet. Which one should I use?" "Use the first one on the right hand side when you walk in," answered Dan Dan. She seemed embarrassed and perhaps she felt inferior, as most classmates, including Bao Bao, had flush toilets at home. Only poor people living in old Chinese-style houses had no flush toilets.

Every morning around four to five o'clock, an old truck would come by to collect human excrement. The truck driver would shout out loudly, "Empty the toilet buckets!" – "Dao Ma Tong!" Housewives and girls, including Dan Dan, would queue up and hand over the buckets to the driver, one by one. He would throw the contents into his truck. The truck driver would then return the empty buckets to the owners, who would wash them with a brush, rinse them with water and place them back in the toilet for the day. The stinky smell was absolutely unbearable. But for housewives there was no alternative. Some housewives wore mouth masks while others used their hands to cover their noses. The poor truck drivers must have been numb to the malodorous smell.

After "Dao Ma Tong!" it was time for every housewife to light her coal oven with coal balls – a mixture of coal-dust and yellow earth pressed into the form of small tennis balls. Housewives had to use paper and pieces of wood to start their fires and it would take a while to get them going. Once the stove was lit, however, it would continue to burn throughout the day.

Returning to Dan Dan, Bao Bao continued to help her with different problems until it was close to lunchtime. Although he wanted to stay longer, he knew it was time to leave, so he gave the excuse of being expected at home for lunch. Had he not said so, Dan Dan's family would definitely have invited him for lunch. He thought, I don't want to give her family trouble, especially nowadays when there is a shortage of food and not really enough for guests.

Bao Bao would have loved to ask Dan Dan to go out for a walk or invite her to a movie. But he found it inappropriate to do so. According to custom, one should work hard first before thinking of pleasure; or one should work and work and work and never think of pleasure. Whoever thought of pleasure did not make a good impression. Bao Bao did not know Dan Dan well, so it was better for him not to ask. Furthermore, it would be painful if his request was rejected. Nothing mattered more than his *face* which he could not lose under any circumstance. Another reason was, that they were both too young to go out together. Dating was for those who intended to establish a serious relationship and eventually get engaged. It was a primary rule in Chinese socialist society that all young people had to focus on work and not think of enjoyment. Bao Bao disliked such restrictions. Nevertheless, if Uncle Song Ping were to find out Bao Bao's reasons for going out with Dan Dan, he would be very disappointed. To Bao Bao, it seemed as though there was an arbitrary line between what was permissible and what was prohibited; between what was good and what was bad, as judged by society. Who set forth such restrictions? wondered Bao Bao. – Confucius? (479 BC) And now, of course, Chairman Mao?

CHAPTER SIXTEEN

# CAUGHT IN A NET

Three months later, things turned upside down. Auntie was right when she said that the Hundred Flowers Campaign was one of the many campaigns which would end with Chairman Mao remaining in power. Now the famous Mao saying was used again, "Power comes from the barel of a gun". Countless Party members had sacrificed their lives in order for Communists to attain power in China. The Communists would not step down and hand over power to the handful of intellectuals who had criticized them. So Chairman Mao hit back and this time he launched a new – "Anti-Rightist" – campaign. Those who had attacked the Communist Party and its representatives during the Hundred Flowers Campaign were labelled Rightists and severely punished by the Party.

Bao Bao was aware that this campaign had little to do with high school students like himself, but his curiosity drove him to find out what kind of punishment the intellectuals would be given by the Party. So he browsed through the *Guang Ming Ri Bao* (*Bright Daily*) which published the confessions of those celebrities in society who had sharply criticized and attacked the Party half a year ago. These individuals hoped that they would not be punished by being sent away to remote labour camps, never to come back:

Cheng Po Chun was removed from his positions as Vice-Chairman of the Democratic Union, Transportation Minister and Managing Director of the *Guang Ming Ri Bao*. Under the title, "I hate myself", he confessed as follows:

"I bow down to the people and admit my sin. Today I am a guilty man who has committed serious political crimes. I am now striving to reform myself. In past years, my political ambition increased immensely. I expanded my reactionary political programmes and put them into effect by means of conferences, forums and personal talks, so taking advantage of my official title and position. All these wrong expressions and publications were Anti-Party, Anti-People and Anti-Socialist. I cannot shift responsibility for my abominable wrongdoing. I beg the people of the whole nation, the Party, and the government to punish me appropriately. I hope, also, that the people of the whole nation will struggle against the Rightists and against me. I wish for a new birth for myself under the education of the Party, as well as Chairman Mao.

A similar confession was written by Luo Lung Chi with the title, "I have shamed myself", which was published across China. He admitted that with Cheng Po Chun and numerous intellectuals, they had formed an alliance that was a focus for Rightists. Luo was discharged from his posts as Minister for Wood Industry and Vice Chairman of the Democratic Union.

Cheng Nai Chi lost his position as the Minister for Nutrition and wrote, "I am a bourgeois individualist. I surrender myself to the people. I am taking off the ugly mask of a bourgeois maverick and opponent of the Party."

Lu Yun confessed, "I am ashamed that I never loved the Soviet Union, nor did I make a distinction between friends and enemies. The Soviet Union is our greatest ally. If we don't rely on her, we will be isolated. Before, I was angry at the Soviet Union for dismantling factories in Manchuria and removing them to the Soviet Union. Now I know this was a great favour that the Soviet Union did for us. They took the factories away, so that Chiang Kai Shek had no access to them. I feel ashamed and I deserve punishment by the Party and the government."

During the Hundred Flowers Campaign, Bao Bao's favourite newspapers were *Guang Ming Ri Bao* and *Wen Hui Bao* which had been accused of being used by the Rightists as political tools against the People's regime. Prominent people who held leading positions in these two newspapers were removed. The Party took the newspapers over and also suspended publication of magazines such as *Wen Yi Bao* (Literary Studies).

The poet Xiao Qing, editor of the magazine *Wen Yi Bao* (*Literary Journal*), was relieved of his position.

One of the most distinguished writers of modern Chinese literature, Ding Ling, Chairman of the Writers' Association and the winner of the Stalin Award, was expelled from the Party and the Writers' Association. Bao Bao felt sorry for Ding Ling, as she was one of the writers he admired very much. Amongst her works, the most famous was a book called, *The Sun Shines Over the Shanggan River.* Ding Ling encouraged every young person to write a book. She said, "Once you have written a good book, you will be valued differently. You will be treated as a writer and you will be able to establish your position in society." After she expressed this kind of wrong thinking and her dissatisfaction against the Party, her works were censored. She was labelled a Rightist and downgraded to working as a cleaning lady at the Foreign Office.

The famous professor, Ma Yin Chu, Chancellor of Beijing University, who had disagreed with Mao's population expansion, was dismissed and condemned as a Malthusian, a follower of Malthus. He was tagged a Rightist as well.

On 6 August 1958, *Ren Min Ri Bao* (*The People's Daily*) – the official Communist newspaper – after two months' delay, published an article admitting the Hanyang student riot. It reported that the student leaders involved in the uprising had been arrested and labelled Counter-Revolutionaries for organizing the students' riot against the people's regime. Consequently, the leaders of the students' uprising, Wang Qin Guo, Cheng Yu Wen and Yang Huan Yao, were executed.

To Bao Bao, this meant that the news from Chef Wang and the Voice of America was reliable. Since he would not be seeing Chef Wang any more, the only means for him to verify the news was through the enemy's shortwave broadcasts. Though the Hundred Flowers Campaign had not involved high school students directly, the struggles against the Rightists had called upon young people, again, to denounce their parents, relatives, teachers, etc.

At a struggle meeting, Bao Bao was asked to express his views about the Hundred Flowers Campaign. Bao Bao dared not mention Teacher Ho's and Teacher Wang's conversation with his uncle. If he did, he would be forced to confess everything in detail. His unnecessary statement would easily destroy his peaceful life and possibly bring disaster to his family and Teacher Ho and Teacher Wang, with whom he was not personally acquainted.

In response to the Party, Bao Bao had no alternative but to repeat his old story at the struggle meeting. "If a mother of six prepares a meal for her six children, she can never cook a single meal to satisfy six mouths at the same time. Since our country has a population of six hundred million, it is inevitable that some of us are not happy with the policies of the new regime. It was correct that Chairman Mao's Hundred Flowers Campaign let all intellectuals express their dissatisfaction with the Party and helped the Party to improve her work in the future."

Since Bao Bao was too young to be the Party's target for this campaign, and neither Uncle Song Ping nor Auntie Ying was a Rightist, they let Bao Bao go, although they knew that he had just repeated the old story about the six children.

Li Yong, being a backward element, was also not the authorities' target because his father was already in gaol and his poor mother was already working as a cleaning lady who was harmless to the regime. Unfortunately, he was suspected of having written the counter-revolutionary Da Zi Bao which was found in the male toilet. Although he was a tiny fish already caught in the net, the authorities would not let him go. Perhaps the Headmaster needed a guinea pig to report to the Party Secretary of the District, in order to close the file on this criminal act. The authorities targeted Li Yong, but in spite of the pressure imposed on him, Li Yong denied his involvement with the Da Zi Bao. Perhaps Li remembered Bao Bao's warning, "As long as you don't admit your wrongdoing they can't do much to you legally".

Seeing that they were not getting much from Li Yong, the authorities changed their strategy. Bearing a red banner, a small group of students paraded outside Li Yong's home, accompanied by noisy drums and gongs. The banner was inscribed with big Chinese characters, including the word, "Congratulations," suggesting that Li Yong had agreed to move to the commune in the remote Qinghai Province where his father was gaoled for Thought Reform Through Labour. When he saw the words on the banner, Li Yong was annoyed because he had never agreed to leave his mother, his high school and his city, Shanghai. However, after many repetitions of these unwanted and noisy home visits, Li Yong finally gave in and agreed to join a commune in Qinghai. Why Qinghai? It had been selected to give Li Yong the illusion that he might eventually find his father there. In reality, the chances of meeting his father were miniscule, as Qinghai Province is even bigger than Europe!

Where could he find a prisoner in the countless labour camps? For Bao Bao, it was painful to lose his good friend.

Bao Bao was astonished to find that, most unexpectedly, another close friend, Wu Hai Bin, had become a target at the struggle meetings. Wu's father had been identified as a Rightist.

Wu and Bao Bao had recently visited a few of their school teachers in their homes. They had been absent from school during the Anti-Rightist Campaign.

Three months earlier, Bao Bao had visited his art teacher, Wang, at his home. On one of the walls he noticed a large charcoal drawing of Lenin. Lenin was standing upright before a podium, giving a speech during the October 1917 Revolution. The drawing was quite large, about one by one and a half metres. Bao Bao said that the portrait was so lifelike and imposing that it looked like Lenin was standing right before him. Before Bao Bao had finished praising the drawing, Teacher Wang swiftly removed it from the wall, rolled it up and gave it to Bao Bao as a gift. Bao Bao was surprised and gratified as he did not expect such generosity from Teacher Wang.

At home, Bao Bao hung the portrait on a wall to cover a big spot where the old paint had come off. Whenever Bao Bao looked at the drawing, he thought of his kind-hearted Teacher Wang.

Since Teacher Wang had not showed up at school for the past two weeks, Bao Bao decided to visit him. This time, he asked Wu Hai Bin to come along, as Teacher Wang was also Wu's favourite teacher.

An elderly lady who looked like Teacher Wang's mother opened the door and told the youngsters that the teacher was not at home.

"Then, when will Teacher Wang return to school?" pressed Bao Bao.

The grey-haired lady was baffled by their question and seemed to be at a loss for words.

Bao Bao and Wu stood there in the doorway, waiting for an answer.

"Is he sick or out of town? When will he come back to the school? I have finished two paintings in his absence and I would like to show them to him." Bao Bao said. "All students are asking where Teacher Wang is," he added. "The art class is everyone's favourite and we all love Teacher Wang."

The old lady continued standing there without saying anything. Bao Bao thought he could see a tear forming in her right eye. After a while, the boys had no choice but to turn around and leave.

On their way home, Bao Bao said, "Wu, don't you think that it is odd that Teacher Wang has disappeared? He is not ill, nor is he at home. Where could he be?"

"Oh, Bao Bao! You think too much. We youngsters should not care too much about adult affairs. I'm sure he is fine. Perhaps he has just gone somewhere with friends? He will be back soon," Wu said.

"I doubt it. His mother seemed so sad. It looks as though something bad has happened to Teacher Wang. Let's hope that nothing bad has happened to him," Bao Bao added.

A few days later, Bao Bao and Wu Hai Bin decided to pay their Chinese literature and form-teacher, Mr Fang, a home visit. It had been two weeks since Bao Bao and Wu last saw him. They were told that Teacher Fang had fallen ill and if they would like to visit him at home, this would make the teacher very happy.

This time another old lady opened the door and informed the youngsters that Teacher Fang was not at home.

"Which hospital is he at? We would like to pay Teacher Fang a visit," said Bao Bao and Wu.

"No. He is not at a hospital," her grey-haired head shook slightly.

"But why did the school announce that Teacher Fang is sick?" questioned Bao Bao

The old lady felt uncomfortable and did not answer. "When will he return?" Bao Bao inquired further. "I don't know" the old lady stuttered as she closed the door. Bao Bao and Wu were perplexed.

A couple of weeks later, the school authorities announced that Bao Bao's Art Teacher Wang, Chinese literature Teacher Fang, Political Science Teacher Ma, and some other teachers had been removed from their teaching positions. Art Teacher Wang, Math Teacher Feng and many teachers at Bao Bao's school, as well as some teachers at Uncle Song Ping's Wu Ai Middle and

High School – Teacher Ho, Teacher Wang, Teacher Li, Teacher Yu and Teacher Wen – were all arrested and sent to the wild and barren Northwest for Thought Reform. Other teachers – the minority – who were fortunate enough to remain at school in Shanghai, were demoted from teachers to cleaners and they had to go through a series of other humiliations.

Amongst the "fortunate" minority were Bao Bao's most highly respected teachers, Teacher Ma and Teacher Fang. One morning, Bao Bao and his schoolmates were brought to the neighbouring school's large football ground to attend an accusation meeting against the Rightist teachers. Around eight-thirty, these teachers were brought onto a stage. Bao Bao was upset when his favourite teacher, Teacher Ma, and his form-teacher, Teacher Fang, were forced to kneel down on the stage, facing thousands of students and wearing ugly dunce's caps on their heads. A cardboard cartoon, drawn on A3 size paper, was hung around the neck and displayed on every teacher's chest. In Chinese writing, were the sentences, "I am a big enemy of the Chinese people," "I am a wang ba dan (a turtle's egg)," "I have betrayed my country, my people." Bao Bao was appalled by the scene. He could not understand why such a misfortune had befallen his teachers. Teacher Fang was such a kind lady who treated every student like her own child. Bao Bao recalled once when Teacher Fang, as form-teacher, led a group of students to do voluntary labour, moving bricks to a construction site by hand. As a teacher, Teacher Fang did not need to work herself, yet she worked harder than any student. Wearing gloves was not allowed, as they belonged to the bourgeoisie. Without them, Teacher Fang cut her hand accidentally on the rough surface of the bricks and, in spite of the bleeding, continued with the hard labour. Bao Bao was very impressed and felt that such a good teacher was rare. Bao Bao was miserable to see both Teacher Fang and Teacher Ma suffering from such psychological torture on the stage.

Soon Bao Bao's class leader, Zhou, went up on the stage as an accuser with a burning desire for revenge. Being a member of the Communist Youth League, she denounced Teacher Fang, "Rightist Fang has criticized me in the past for devoting much of my time and energy to political events instead of studying hard! She has no respect for our Chairman Mao who has said that our students should actively participate in political campaigns instead of burying their heads in books. She paid no respect to members of the Youth League, such as myself.

As soon as Zhou finished her accusation, she spat on poor teacher Fang, as well as on Teacher Ma, whom Zhou criticized for erroneously praising Song Bao Bao for doing a good job at writing Da Zi Baos. "That's all?" wondered Bao Bao, "For such miniscule matters, poor Teacher Ma and Teacher Fang are to be humiliated and tortured on the stage? The world has turned upside down! This is so disgusting, so inhumane and so revolting! Zhou is so ungrateful!"

Zhou and other members of the Youth League forced Teachers Ma and Fang and about fifty teachers from different high schools to parade out onto the street. The parade was followed by thousands of students bearing countless red flags. The noise of beating gongs and drums clashed with the shouting of slogans, "Down with the Rightist teachers!" "Long Live Chairman Mao!" The commotion attracted the attention of many pedestrians. Soon crowds of people gathered at both sides of the street to watch the parade of Rightists in dunces' hats. Bao Bao was furious at the beastly way the new regime was treating his honourable and innocent teachers. He wanted to jump up to save them from their humiliation, but he refrained from doing so, as one wrong move would find him alongside his Rightist teachers. The long parade dragged the teachers along the streets for two and a half hours until it was time for the Communist cadets to have lunch.

After the parade and humiliation, Teachers Ma and Fang were released. Fortunately they were not sent to a labour camp. Instead they were downgraded to work as cleaners at their school. They scrubbed the floors and cleaned toilets for their former colleagues and students. Nobody in school ever dared to greet or say "hello" to them, because they were "Rightists".

The Rightists were treated as if they were sick people with an infectious disease. Others thought they had better stay away from them. Bao Bao was sad to come across the Rightist teachers from time to time at the school. He would like to say something to comfort or to encourage them, but they urged him to go away as it would be bad for him if he was seen showing sympathy to them. For Bao Bao it was heartbreaking! He wished that he could run over to Chef Wang's place and vent his anger. Unfortunately Chef Wang was no longer available. Whom could he see when he was so depressed? Nobody. I can't trust anybody, thought Bao Bao.

Song Ping survived the Anti-rightist Campaign without a big problem. He had said little at the meeting, and that had been only to please his colleagues Ho and Wang, after their visit to his home. Now, it was time for Song Ping to pay for what he had said. When foreign visitors came to visit their school, Song Ping was merely an English teacher who was not supposed to talk or communicate with the foreigners in private. This instruction was given to him clearly by the Party and it showed that the Party trusted him. Nevertheless, how could he reveal such an 'insider's secret' to all the teachers?

Soon, the target shifted to Song Ping. Everyone in Song Ping's social circle was summoned to condemn and vilify Song Ping. At the end, it was unanimously agreed that it was Song Ping's fault that he had failed to follow the Party's instructions strictly.

The Party Secretary, Wang, still remembered the phone call from Song Ping requesting his permission for sick leave. At that difficult time, the Party Secretary had appreciated the fact that someone like Song Ping had respected him. In all, the attacks against Song Ping were not severe, for they had found no evidence of any counter-revolutionary act on his part.

A few days after the struggle meeting, Song Ping was asked to see the Party Secretary alone. Party Secretary Cui said to him, "Considering your overall performance, we are not going to label you a Rightist. However, we have to give you a punishment by no longer keeping you at our school."

Song Ping felt as though he had been punched in the stomach when he learned about his misfortune. He never imagined that this day would befall him. Now he regretted ignoring his wife's warnings. She was absolutely right when she said that Chairman Mao would never step down and the Party Secretary would always remain Party Secretary. Now it was time for the Party to take revenge and rid itself of those it considered bad elements. Song Ping had no idea what he could do if he was fired by the school. China was not a free market where one could get a job through filling out an application, or being interviewed. There was no such thing as choosing an occupation. All jobs were assigned by the Party. If one was unemployed, this meant that no unit would be responsible for that person and that he was a good-for-nothing, a rogue. Being jobless was dangerous. At any time, the police van could come and collect the jobless and send them off to the barren Northwest. Under such circumstances, one rarely ever returned to Shanghai. Furthermore, to be jobless meant that there were no ration coupons for one to survive on. Song Ping could not bear the thought of all the unfavourable consequences that would come with losing his job. He fell on his knees before the Party Secretary and said with tears in his eyes, "Please, Secretary, please forgive me for saying something that I should never have said. Please keep me in this school. I don't want to become a jobless rogue in society."

The Party Secretary held out his hand and gestured towards the chair, asking Song Ping to sit.

"For you to leave our school is not my decision. It is the decision of the Party Secretary of our District. I can only obey his orders and swiftly execute them."

"But what shall I do? I have a family. I am a decent person. I don't want to become an unemployed person. Please help me! Please save my life!" Song Ping wailed in despair.

The Party Secretary looked at the desperate man and felt somewhat sympathetic for him. Again he reminded himself that this fellow had shown him respect in the past.

"I remember you told me about your mother-in-law in Suzhou who needs your care. Is that true?" asked the Party Secretary.

Song Ping nodded.

The Secretary added, "I have an idea, I know it is hard for you and your family to return to Fuzhou, but what would you say if I recommend you to teach in Suzhou?"

The suggestion to relocate to Suzhou was so sudden and unexpected that Song Ping had difficulty coping with it. The Secretary continued, "I know you feel uneasy all the time and that your old mother-in-law lives alone in Suzhou. The Party Secretary of Suzhou Second Normal School happens to be an old friend of mine in the Red Army. If you accept my suggestion, I shall write to him and get you a job in Suzhou as an English teacher. Although America and Great Britain are enemies of China, our schools still continue to teach English. So we can still make use of you. Let me know your decision in a day or two."

Song Ping was excited but nervous at this sudden proposal, "Thank you. Thank you so much. You have saved my life. I need not think any further. I accept your offer and your help. I am extremely grateful to you and your compassion."

Coming out of the office, Song Ping remained baffled. It was all too much for him to take in. Everything had happened so suddenly. Fortunately, he did not suffer from heart disease, or else he might have had a heart attack. Song Ping could not decide whether the offer from the Party Secretary was "good" or "bad". The advantage was great for his mother-in-law, who was eighty-six years old and living alone. In China, children are usually filial to their parents. If possible, they always want to live with and take good care of their elderly parents until they pass away. Now the biggest headaches were Bao Bao and Yuan Yuan. Song had promised his brother and sister-in-law to look after them. Now, who would take care of these teenagers? Who would cook and do the laundry for them?

Song Ping rushed home to discuss the problem with his wife. He knew it would not be bad news for her. They would all return to Suzhou to look after mother-in-law.

When Bao Bao found out that his uncle and family had to leave him, he felt as though the sky was falling. It was not his fault, but whose fault was it? That night, the alarm clock woke him up. It was time for "The Voice of America" again. The broadcast reported that half a million intellectuals had been classified as Rightists. Most of them had been sent to labour camps in the northern wilderness and would never come back to cities again. Mao was afraid that an uprising, similar to the one that took place in Hungary in 1956, would eventually occur in China. To eliminate half a million intellectuals in China would help Mao sleep better at night. – He constantly suffered from severe insomnia, according to his personal doctor, Li.

Mao set a trap for people to criticize the Party, and they were caught by their own criticisms. This was what Chef Wang had meant when he spoke of enticing snakes to come out of their caves and then chopping off their heads. The broadcast confused Bao Bao a lot. He did not know what to think. He told himself that he should cease thinking and go back to sleep.

A couple of months later, Bao Bao found out that the mother of his close friend Wu Hai Bin had divorced his father, after the latter was labelled a Rightist. Intellectuals who did not attack the Party were not touched. The life of a Rightist was not easy. Wherever he went, whatever he did or said, and whoever he associated with, all would be monitored closely by the regime. Life for Rightists' families was harsh and they were ostracized by society. Rightist children had no chance of entering good educational institutions. Often, wives divorced their Rightist husbands in order to continue leading normal lives and to protect their children.

At school, Wu's classmates stayed away from him. It was heartbreaking for Bao Bao to see that his good friend Wu had suddenly fallen into such a disastrous situation. He missed walking to school with Wu. But Bao Bao knew that he could no longer do so. If he continued, he would be labelled as a person who showed "Compassion to a Rightist's son" or "Compassion to an Enemy's son". Bao Bao did not have many friends. Now the Rightist Campaign had taken his good friend and his favourite teachers away from him.

After much thought, Bao Bao concluded that it was better to accept that destiny was against the half a million Chinese intellectuals who had received higher education and contributed a great deal to Chinese culture. Now they were all living in despair. If they had killed someone, stolen something, raped a girl or committed a serious crime, there would be a reason for punishment. But what had they done? They had merely responded to Chairman Mao's call to speak out frankly from the bottom of their hearts. They had fulfilled Mao's wish. In consequence, some of them had ruined their lives and their families.

CHAPTER SEVENTEEN

# GREAT LEAP FORWARD

Uncle Song came home late, about two hours after other family members had finished their dinner. As soon as he came in, Auntie brought rice and other food, and invited him to eat. But Uncle was so excited that he forgot his hunger. Earlier in the day, he had spent four hours, listening to a broadcast speech by Chairman Mao regarding China's recent rapid development. Uncle told the family that under the great leadership of Chairman Mao, China would soon catch up with industrial nations like the United States, England, and France and become a world superpower.

"Tell us, Uncle! Tell us more! What was the conclusion of the speech?" Bao Bao asked.

"The conclusion was that China needs to double its output of steel and increase her grain production drastically. If these two goals coan be achieved, China will overtake England in fifteen years!" said Uncle.

"Wah!" Auntie and Bao Bao exclaimed in unison as they took in the news.

"What a miracle if it were to happen! If dear Chairman Mao's goals were to be accomplished! Just think – it has taken fifty to a few hundred years for the western nations to become industrialized and it will take us only fifteen! China will need only fifteen years!" cried Bao Bao.

That night Bao Bao was ecstatic about Chairman Mao's decision. He was grateful to be living at what was soon to be the pinnacle of China's history.

How lucky I am to be so fortunate to live at this time, to be a part of such a grand scheme and to witness the turning point of China's history. I support you, dear Chairman Mao! I will do anything to support any of your directions for China's industrialization! What a genius! Almighty Chairman Mao has not only established a brand new China but is leading our country to become the number one world power in a very short period! In fifteen years my career as a scientist will reach its first climax when I win the Nobel Prize!

That night Bao Bao could not suppress his desire to find out what the enemy had to say about China's swift march to becoming a world power. Although it was not the weekend, he set the alarm clock to wake him up at midnight. Unfortunately, the atmospherics on the short-wave radio were very noisy and he could catch only a few sentences. Among them, Bao Bao was unhappy to hear attacks on Chairman Mao, saying that he was too idealistic, that his Great Leap Forward was a Utopian scheme which would never be realized. Bao Bao's response was to think that the country's enemies were jealous of China's swift move into industrialization.

The following day, Teacher Yang, who had taken over Bao Bao's class as the new form-teacher, went into detail about Chairman Mao's Great Leap Forward plan. Bao Bao could not stop thinking of his previous form-teacher, Teacher Fang, his Rightist teacher.

Teacher Yang smiled warmly at the students and said, "Mao's Great Leap Forward Plan proposes that on the industrial side, China is going to double its output of steel from its current 5.35 million tonnes to 10.7 million tonnes by next year (1958). On the agricultural side, grain production is to increase multiple times and all farmers are to be encouraged to join communes. This has always been a goal of Communism and the dream of our Chairman Mao since he was young.

"Recalling the 64th Party meeting, Mao stated that in fifteen years Russia would overtake America, and China would overtake England. According to Chairman Mao, England's current steel output has reached twenty million tonnes, which is far beyond China's output. Therefore, to please Chairman Mao, the Minister of Mettalurgical Industries has worked out a plan for China to reach twenty-five million tonnes by 1959, thirty million tonnes by 1962, seventy million tonnes by 1967 and 120 million tonnes by 1972 – so in less than fifteen years England will be overtaken!" Teacher Yang shouted enthusiastically.

"Long live Chairman Mao!" shouted the students.

When the cheers and excitement gradually subsided, Bao Bao raised his hand and asked, "How can we achieve such an ambitious goal when we have limited steel mills in our country? We cannot double the number of our steel mills overnight and we have less than twelve months until the end of 1958! How are we going to increase our steel production to 25 million tonnes by 1959?"

"Good question!" Teacher Yang praised him. "Chairman Mao is mobilizing millions of people to produce iron and steel from small furnaces, using *tufa liangang* (a primitive method for producing iron). Soon we will see *tufa* furnaces (home-made furnaces) in backyards in the cities and everywhere in the communes in the farms. You students will participate in this exciting project in one way or the other."

Bao Bao shared a smile with his fellow classmates. Everyone seemed curious and enthusiastic to learn about the home-made furnaces.

Cheng Li raised her hand, "Teacher Yang? How does the *tufa* method operate?"

"Don't be so anxious! You will have ample time to learn about the method. But a general idea is that you students will gather metal pieces and throw them into a blast furnace to help create iron!" said Teacher Yang

"Oh!" sighed some students hearing this answer.

Although Bao Bao was delighted to learn that China was on the right track to overtake Great Britain, he was slightly disappointed that the introduction of this new political movement – The Great Leap Forward – would mean that he and his schoolmates would have no class for a couple of weeks and/or months. He was becoming impatient and complained to himself. If things go on like this, how can I become a scientist? But immediately he reproached himself. Stop it! Stop being so selfish, Song Bao Bao! Be selfless like Dr Norman Bethune. I should only think of my country and remember that this is another revolution – an industrial revolution.

A few days later, the school authorities selected from each class a few strong, tall students to work in the furnaces of the nearby high school. Bao Bao looked more like a scholar than a labourer, so he was not chosen to join the production team. Instead, he and his classmates were given an assignment to collect iron material for the furnaces. Bao Bao was relieved that he was not qualified for production work, as he feared that he would easily injure himself if he worked at a furnace with steel and fire, because he was constantly absent-minded when performing labouring-work.

Towards the autumn of 1958, about one million "backyard furnaces" were set up across the country. These were manned by over ninety million people, plus indirect labour. A total of over one hundred million people, or one sixth of the Chinese population, were recruited to participate in Mao's Great Leap Forward Campaign. In order to support a national movement on such a grand scale, people were organized to look for iron material and coal, to cut trees to make charcoal for the furnaces. Due to the lack of minerals, the workers took everything they could find, such as window frames, door handles, iron bedsteads, pots, iron heaters, cooking utensils, iron farm tools and iron doors and melted them to produce steel.

In a neighbourhood school, about thirty furnaces were set up by professional workers. Each of the furnaces occupied three square metres of ground space and was more than two metres high. One day, someone asked the school authorities what would happen if it rained – the iron-producing process would be interrupted. So in fear of rain, all tables and chairs were removed from the big school canteen to make room for the relocation of twenty furnaces from the school playground. So, even in the rain, thousands of students had to eat outdoors while standing in the playground, as no canteen was available for dining. With the goal of achieving the national target of 10.7 million tonnes for Chairman Mao, no-one dared to complain.

As a consequence of the large-scale production of iron by "backyard furnaces", the ratio of farmers to industrial workers dropped from thirteen point eight to one in the first half year to three point five to one in September 1958, because ninety million farmers started to produce "steel" by *tu fa* (the primitive method). Bao Bao heard that, on the farms, only old people, children and women worked in the fields during harvest time as all the men were busy with iron production. He thought of the danger of shortage of grain for the winter.

One night after dinner, it was time for Bao Bao to listen to the local news from Uncle's radio, which he usually did with the family. It seemed as though China was undergoing many changes and Bao Bao wanted to hear how well China was progressing.

"Good evening! This is the voice of Xinhua Broadcasting Station. Welcome to our daily evening broadcast. Tonight, we have some excellent news for you all! This afternoon, China finally launched our very own satellite, a satellite of 3,290 catties!"

Bao Bao's hands froze on his headpiece. Satellite? he thought in amazement. Satellites, I have heard of these. They have something to do with science and space technology. Have we made a leap forward in space technology as well?

Bao Bao hopped off his chair and walked towards the window. He pushed the thin curtain to his right and stared out into the dark, starry sky, trying to look into space. Space! Satellite! Bao Bao silently screamed with exhilaration. He continued to search the dark night sky, as if staring longer and harder would allow him to catch a glimpse of a satellite. But then Bao's fascination was suddenly interrupted by his own voice in his head, But why a satellite of a couple of thousand catties? What does space have to do with agricultural products? I must ask Teacher Yang tomorrow.

"Well, as you know, in 1957 our big brother Russia successfully launched two satellites," Teacher Yang explained then. "For the first time, a man-made satellite entered into space and this ushered in a new era for mankind. This news was surprising to the world and our supreme leader, Chairman Mao, was particularly envious. Since Chinese technology is not so advanced as to enable us to launch our own satellite into space, certain cadets came up with the idea of borrowing the name 'satellite' to report a high harvest figure, to flatter our Chairman Mao. After all, to hear about launching satellites and to receive news of a good harvest are two goals that Chairman Mao is deteminedly looking forward to."

So one after another, "satellites", with higher and higher totals of grain, were announced by radio and newspaper headlines every day. The average production of grains was 350 catties per Mu (0.17 acre). On 26 June, a satellite from Jiang Xi province was announced, of 2,430 catties. On 18 July, less than a month later, Fujian's satellite was announced, of 7,275 catties, followed by Hubei's 15,361 catties. The highest grain-production satellite – of 36,956 catties – was launched by a commune in

Hubei, one hundred and four times more than the average production. Bao Bao was curious to know how production could increase so many times on the same piece of land. Later on, he received the explanation that the farmers had adopted Chairman Mao's method to cover all paddy-fields with drainage systems and to dig the earth as deep as four metres prior to seeding. When visitors came to such satellite launching farms, the cadets pressed a few bunches of wheat together tightly and showed these to the visitor as if they were cut freshly from the field. Bao Bao was happy that Chairman Mao's Plan was hailed as a tremendous success both in steel production and agriculture. Surely China was on the right track to overtake England.

CHAPTER EIGHTEEN

# GIVING THE PARTY HEARTS

Immediately after the Anti-Rightist Campaign, a new campaign, "Handover Heart to the Party", followed. Chairman Mao feared that certain intellectuals had sympathy for Rightist colleagues who had been severely punished by the Communist regime and sent to gaol. So the regime brought forward a new campaign called "Handover Heart Campaign", during which thousands of students, pupils, teachers, professors, writers and artists were mobilized to deliver their hearts to the Party. Probably Chairman Mao remembered the Chinese saying, "One should catch fishes that escaped the net as well", even though the intellectual fishes had showed no animosity against the Party.

Today, Bao Bao and all his schoolmates were asked to stay behind after class to produce paper hearts. They cut out from thick carton paper the shape of a human heart, symbolizing the real hearts of students, workers, and soldiers. They were then asked to hold up their paper hearts in their hands and march from every corner of the city towards the People's Square in Shanghai. They sang revolutionary songs and cried out revolutionary slogans mixing them with the noise of gongs and drums along the way. It looked as though another festival or celebration was taking place in Shanghai.

The small and big crowds marched with all sizes of hearts towards the government buildings, into directors' and principals' offices, delivering countless hearts to the Party Secretaries in different sectors, and the Party Secretaries then forwarded these hearts to the Central Committee of the Party. But to give hearts to the Party was not everybody's business. Only those intellectuals who had fulfilled the prerequisites of the Party were qualified to do so. In Bao Bao's school every class was divided into *xiao zus* – small groups – to produce paper hearts. Because Bao Bao had a good record in writing Da Zi Baos, he was asked by his new form-teacher to be the leader of one of the small groups. Bao Bao was artistic, creative and innovative, and he invented a new three-dimensional heart, instead of a conventional heart cut from simple carbon paper, as seen everywhere else. He showed the group how to produce a big three-dimensional heart shape by sewing many pieces of red material together and filling them with cotton. The heart was more than one metre in diameter and his group worked late into the night.

The next morning, the teachers were impressed to see the innovative product of Bao Bao's group. All other students had merely cut out hearts from sheets of carbon paper and painted them red, while Bao Bao's was like a solid sculpture.

"My original idea was to make a heart connected with a pump which could be squeezed by the human hand. Once it was pressed, the heart would expand and shrink. That would really look like a functioning heart," Bao Bao said.

"It is unfortunate that we have to deliver the hearts this morning, otherwise we could employ your idea to make a big heart that measured up to three metres in diameter to represent our entire school in the parade," replied the new form-teacher, Teacher Yang.

Since Bao Bao had contributed immensely to the making of an unconventional heart, he was invited to the boardroom to listen to the speech of the guest speaker, Professor Gu from the famous Fudan University. Only teachers and student representatives were usually invited to such important meetings.

As soon as the boardroom had filled with students and teachers, Professor Gu entered with a smiling face. He was about fifty years old, half bald with a few remaining – half grey, half black – strands of hair. He wore a pair of metal-framed glasses with small round lenses. After being introduced by the Party Secretary, Professor Gu started to talk about his personal experience. "Only after I had given away my heart to the Party did I began to feel relieved. The whole process can be summarized in one sentence, "The Communist Party heals sicknesses and rescues people, while individualism ruins people."

Assistant Professor Gu added, "My individualism was so strong that it damaged the country. After the Revolution, I did not earn as much as I did before. I was not satisfied and tried to leave the University. I had written a book which a publisher wanted to publish at a minimum remuneration. I refused the offer.

"I was furious with my title as Assistant Professor because my colleague, though less qualified than I, was promoted to full professor.

"Furthermore, I wrote a personal letter to Chairman Mao, in the hope that he would help me to fulfill my malicious individual greed. Out of my individualistic desire, I treated the People's knowledge as my own property and refused to show my files to my associates. I thought it was the fruit of my personal efforts. Why should I share my achievement with those who had contributed nothing? If I were to relinquish my discoveries, all young teachers and researchers would soon be better than me. So I organized my files in such a way that others had no access to them. Do you see how dreadful that was?" Professor Gu said.

"My individual thoughts had driven me so far that I even had sympathy for the Rightist Counter-Revolutionaries." Ko lowered his voice and added, "At that time, I had lost all sense of direction. At one point I even supported the Rightists' attacks on the Party which I believed were justified. When the Anti-Rightist Movements began, I was uncomfortable. I felt as though they were attacking me and I had difficulty holding up my head as I feared to face Communist Party members. I did not sleep well at night and often woke up distraught. I sometimes hallucinated that I had been arrested on account of being a Rightist. When the Anti-Rightist struggle came to an end, I was relieved. Deep down inside, I felt sympathetic towards the Rightists. I thought they were mishandled by the Party. But in spite of my inner thoughts against the Party, the new regime has trusted me and honoured me as an Anti-Rightist scientist."

Upon hearing Professor Gu's story, Bao Bao realized that the Party found him useful and thus did him no harm, because he was a scientist who could do things that Mao could not do. If Professor Gu were a writer, he might be in trouble these days. Even the most famous writer in modern Chinese literature – Lu Xun, whom Chairman Mao had admired and praised – might not survive the Anti-Rightist Campaign. The Chairman was a writer himself and he might not want to be challenged by another writer. Besides, Chairman Mao had to rely on scientists to make an atom bomb as soon as possible, which was priority number one in Mao's mind. Bao Bao thought back to a recent photo of the famous American Chinese missile scientist, Professor Qian Xuesen, who sat proudly next to Chairman Mao at a state dinner Party. "If only I were a scientist!" Bao Bao thought. Bao Bao was glad that he had chosen to be a scientist as his goal in life, otherwise disaster could easily fall upon him, as it had upon the famous writer Hu Feng, now in gaol. How long will Hu Feng be kept in gaol? Bao Bao questioned in his mind. Perhaps until Mao dies or until Hu Feng himself dies. It all depends on whoever dies first.

Bao Bao sat there with all the teachers, the Party Secretary and a few political activist students. He did not feel proud or honoured, to be at one table with the "prominent figures" of the school. Instead, he felt uncomfortable. He paid full attention to Professor Gu's speech. Gu was his idol. If Bao Bao's career progressed as he anticipated, he would be a scientist like Professor Gu in ten years time. So Professor Gu's speech could be a valuable experience for Bao Bao.

Professor Gu sipped his tea and continued, "The Handover Heart Campaign provided a good opportunity for me to reveal my unfortunate individualistic thoughts. But the fear of losing face and prestige prevented me from doing so. In the end, my suffering was aggravated. After the Anti-Rightist Campaign, my political consciousness improved, so I volunteered to be 'red' (a politically advanced person). I found it extremely difficult to do this. I wanted to be 'red', but I was neither 'left', nor 'middle', but 'right' (a less politically advanced person). How could I make plans for myself if I was not 'red'? Fortunately at that critical moment, the Party Secretary came to me and helped me make plans."

"Afterwards," Professor Gu continued, "I found out there were too many restrictions in the proposed plans and I could not see any way to cross these barriers. Gradually I recognized that pernicious bourgeois thoughts were a poisonous tumour, which must be cut off as soon as possible. Only when poisonous bourgeois thoughts are absolutely removed, can there be room for proletarian thoughts."

Professor Gu took another short break to sip tea and added, "Now, I have found my sickness. It is time to be cured. Our university required us to deliver our hearts. Although I was determined to get rid of individualistic thoughts, I had no courage to speak out at the initial discussion. Soon many colleagues came to help me. At this point, I realized that the restrictions were the Party's measurements and I asked myself, 'why did I avoid speaking the truth?' Without telling the truth, how could I deliver my heart to the Party? At the subsequent second and third meetings, I encouraged myself to speak out my bourgeois thoughts from the bottom of my soul. First I thought my colleagues would mock me, but on the contrary, my confession was accepted with encouragement. After the meetings, I felt much relieved, as if I had recovered from a serious sickness. The Party Secretary came to talk to me, so I felt that the Party still trusted me. Now I feel as though the gap between the Party and myself has disappeared. Before, I was afraid to be close to the Party. It was as if I was stinking. Now I feel as though I have taken a bath and I am clean again. So I can be close to the Party now."

Professor Gu became more lively and concluded, "I shall deliver my book together with my heart to the Party without asking for any reward. I shall reorganize my files so that they can be understood by others and disclose them to everyone. I shall spend more time to teach my assistants, in order to show my gratitude towards the Party. I have recovered from the sickness of bourgeois individual thoughts and am ready to be criticized." Bao Bao wondered if Professor Gu's confession was really from his heart or if he was forced to make it under pressure.

Early in the morning, Professor Gu presented his paper heart together with the paper hearts of his students and delivered them to the Party Secretary of the university. From now on, he would not forget that he had given his heart to the Party and he had no heart left for himself.

The teachers and students all clapped when Professor Gu finished his touching story. Bao Bao applauded as well. If one had judged by Bao Bao's calm body and relaxed facial expression, one would never have known that the youngster's mind had been turned completely upside-down from listening to Professor Gu's confession, as Gu was someone whom he had admired. If he was ten years older, Bao Bao would be a scientist like Professor Gu, sitting there to be criticized, with no alternative but to confess his bourgeois thoughts. While Bao Bao clapped, he felt enormous inner disappointment. Suddenly he felt as though he had lost his goal.

That night, Bao Bao lay in bed and thought about Professor Gu's confession. "But what am I thinking about? If the political campaigns continue one after another without pause, perhaps I will never go as far as Professor Gu in the future. Where is the time for study? Professor Gu went to school in the old days, when schools were strictly places for learning, and no politics was involved! But I have no time to study! That's my biggest disadvantage! The many political campaigns are taking away all my time and energy. Every night I am exhausted."

That night, Bao Bao suffered from insomnia. He no longer knew what to do with his future. He found it difficult to sleep but eventually dropped off, thinking about his friend, Wu.

Bao's friend Wu's father had been labelled a Rightist, removed from his work unit and sent to a labour camp in the barren Northwest. After this, his wife had divorced him and Wu, as the son of a Rightist, became very isolated at school. Wu was Bao Bao's best friend, but Bao Bao did not dare to speak to him in public. Wu knew that, because of his father, he had become a black element in school and everyone stayed away from him in order not to be contaminated. Bao Bao wanted very much to speak with Wu and walk home with him everyday but he could not do so any more.

The next morning Bao Bao woke up with the idea that he could visit Wu at his home. He waited until he had finished dinner that evening, before making his way to Wu's house in the dark, as in daylight, he would easily be recognized by his schoolmates as he walked in and out of the lane where Wu lived.

Bao Bao arrived in front of Wu's house. He picked up a tiny pebble from the ground and threw it at Wu's window. Right away, Wu opened his window and looked at Bao Bao with his eyes wide open. He was surprised that Bao Bao was standing at the entrance of his house! He rushed downstairs and opened the door quickly. Wu could not believe that, at such a tumultuous time, Bao Bao still dared to visit him. Is he courageous or is he merely stupid? Doesn't he know that I am under surveillance at all times?! What would happen to him if someone saw that he had visited me at home? Is he looking for trouble? Wu questioned himself in disbelief.

Bao Bao followed Wu up the creaking staircase. The house was old and very dirty. As Bao Bao walked up the old staircase, he thought, "Why doesn't Chairman Mao build new houses for his Chinese people? All the nice houses and tall buildings were built before the Liberation by the notorious foreign imperialists in the Foreign Concessions. Perhaps it is Mao's doctrine to execute Thought Reform through many campaigns first, then to build new houses for the masses? Or perhaps it is his plan never to build houses and buildings for his people? This could be plausible, judging from the living standards in Yan'an, a Communist base where people used to live in caves, and where Chairman Mao started his peasant revolutions in the nineteen thirties. Is life too good for those who dwell in Shanghai? Do people need Thought Reform more than houses?"

When Bao Bao entered Wu's room, he saw that Wu lived with his mother in one small room and they shared a kitchen and bathroom with two other families. Soon after they entered the living-room, Wu's mother retreated to the washroom to let the youngsters have an intimate conversation.

"How come you are here? Don't you know that I am a bad element now and you are not supposed to come near me? Aren't you afraid of being contaminated?" muttered Wu.

The smile on Bao Bao's face disappeared as he looked seriously into Wu's eyes. "You are my friend," he said. "No matter what happens, you are still my friend. Now, tell me what happened to your Dad! I remember him as a very well-respected intellectual in our community. What kind of crime has he committed? Where is he now?"

"Bao Bao! We shouldn't speak about this. It is a dangerous topic!" whispered Wu.

"Hurry up and tell me the story of what happened to your dad!" pressed Bao Bao.

"My father obeyed Chairman Mao's call to criticize the new regime. So he published a few articles. One of the articles was written against the one-party system prevailing in our country. Unfortunately he erroneously cited our enemy number one, the United States of America, as a good example of a country with two major parties. He was accused of praising our enemy and thrown into gaol. About two months ago, just before he was to be sent to the remote northern area, the authorities allowed Ma Ma and me to visit him in gaol for fifteen minutes. Behind the bars he looked terribly old. – Within the past two to three months, he has aged ten to fifteen years and he has lost about ten kilos in weight. It looked as if he had been tortured. He even had difficulty with walking. He could not stand up straight and could only limp towards us. To what extent he has been physically hurt, it was impossible for us to find out, because two guards were standing next to us and listening to our conversation attentively."

"Where is he now?" Bao Bao asked.

"As to where he is specifically, we have no idea. So far, we have not received any letter, nor any news of him. Every day we ask the postman, but our efforts are in vain. After my father was sent to a remote place, I started to gather information about living in the barren Northwest. So I know that three factors must be making my father's life unbearable. First, the climate is scorching hot in the summer, while in winter the temperature drops to minus ten or minus twenty centigrade. The prisoners do not have adequate clothes to be able to survive the cold. The second major problem is the lack of food. Our regime does not have sufficient food to feed ordinary farmers so why should they care about prisoners? Many prisoners die of starvation. The third factor is the hard, strenuous work that they have to do for more than ten hours every day. My Dad is a scholar. How can he endure that amount of physical labour? We can only pray every day that he still survives."

"How about your Ma Ma, is she alright? I heard that she has divorced your father. Is that true? Why would she do this, at this critical time?" Bao Bao asked.

"Yes, she did. Soon after my father was labelled a Rightist, the neighbourhood authority wanted to kick us out of this three-room apartment. The school authorities were going to expel me from high school. Ma Ma had no alternative but to divorce my Dad, just to show the Party that she had drawn an immaculate line between herself and her Rightist husband. So they let us continue to lead our lives as before, living in the same apartment in Shanghai, but instead of the three-room apartment that we had for our family previously, we had to let two other families move in to share our apartment. Now Ma Ma and I are allowed to live in one room only. When the two other families moved in, we three families had to share the bathroom and kitchen. Only through divorce has Ma Ma saved herself and me. I sincerely hope that my Dad, whether alive or not, will pardon Ma Ma. It was a very difficult decision for her to divorce her beloved husband, especially since they have shared a harmonious and happy marriage for the past eighteen years."

"So what are your plans for the future?" Bao Bao continued to question his friend.

"As the son of a Rightist, I have no future. No university will accept me even if I get straight "fives" (equivalent to straight "As"). It is a wonder that they have not kicked me out of Shanghai High School. Thank goodness, I have never uttered a single word against the Party. The school authorities even forced me to denounce my father and asked me to accuse him of being a traitor to our Great Motherland. I had no choice but to say something bad about my dad. Had I not done so, I would have been expelled from school and I would never have seen you and our other classmates again. My denunciation was from my mouth only and in my heart I love my father deeply. In despair I was thinking of escaping to Hong Kong or Macau..." Wu's voice gradually trailed away.

"How would you do it?" asked Bao Bao curiously.

"I have studied the geographical location of these two places. Unfortunately Shanghai is too far away from Hong Kong or Macau. It takes two nights and one full day to travel to Guangzhou by train and from there it is an additional four-hour train ride to get to Shenzhen, the border city adjacent to Hong Kong, or one can travel from Guangzhou by an overnight ferry to Macau. If we go to these cities and do not speak the local dialect, Cantonese, we might be suspected and most likely arrested for interrogation. The worst part is that I don't have any relatives or friends in Guangzhou or Shenzhen, otherwise I would try hard to join them there," murmured Wu.

"Hmm. Not everyone living in Guangdong Province, where Hong Kong and Macau are located, has access to these two foreign cities. The border controls are unusually strict. Once a person passes through the border control at the Chinese side, he still has to produce another permit, allowing him to enter Hong Kong or Macau. The permits to enter Hong Kong and Macau are issued by the British and the Portuguese authorities respectively. Even supposing you had a relative in Guangdong, you would still be unable to enter Hong Kong or Macau due to the lack of a permit!" Bao Bao reasoned.

"But I was thinking of swimming there!" whispered Wu.

"Do you know how to swim?" Bao Bao asked.

"No!" Wu answered. "But I can learn to swim and I can practice it day in and day out until I become an excellent swimmer. I have the will-power to achieve this."

"You would have to be more than an excellent swimmer! It would require over ten hours of swimming, depending on the wind, waves and currents. Some people have tried and died before reaching their destination."

"Bao Bao, you might be able to go to Hong Kong yourself if your parents could get you an entry visa to Hong Kong, but, on second thoughts, it is impossible to get an exit visa from the Public Security Bureau in Shanghai. They won't issue a visa; nobody is granted an exit visa these days. Furthermore, you can't even try to apply for one. If the authorities find out that you have the slightest intention of leaving China, you will immediately be downgraded to the position of a traitor! They will ask how come you do not love our country and why is it that you want to leave us to go to a deteriorating capitalist society. In this case, Bao Bao, your position would not be better than that of a Rightist in the eyes of the Communist Party," Wu argued and then continued, "Bao Bao, you are in a little bit of a better position than me, but after all not that much better. The reason I say this is because your parents are currently in Hong Kong, an evil and capitalistic society, so your family background is grey if not black. I say again that you are not in a much better position than me and you will not be able to get into a good university either. University education is restricted to those who come from good families, such as the children of Party members or of war heroes who dedicated their lives to the Party and to overthrow Chiang Kai Shek. Also eligible are the children of poor farmers or workers.

Since family background plays such a dominant role, the academic records of our high school are insignificant."

Bao Bao was shocked. He looked at his friend who had broken such awful news to him. All along Bao Bao had indulged in the dream that, with his stellar grades, he would be able to conquer the world. He quickly snapped out of his own thoughts as he remembered that Wu's Ma Ma was hiding in the washroom while they two youngsters spoke in private in the bedroom.

"Goodbye!" Bao Bao shouted as loudly as he could, to ensure that Wu's Ma Ma would hear him leaving and could finally come out of the washroom. Wu was incredibly grateful for Bao Bao's unexpected visit and clasped Bao Bao's arms tightly in appreciation. Wu walked Bao Bao down the narrow staircase.

As soon as Bao Bao left Wu's place, he felt saddened. He wanted to smash his head against a wall. He was ashamed of having neglected to consider the impact his family background could have on his future. For as long as he could remember, Bao Bao had always done everything to please the Party and had worked hard in school to obtain excellent grades. But these two factors combined together were insignificant when compared with his family background. Only now did he realize that his own future was in jeopardy. Yes, from time to time, he had been warned of the importance of family background; yet in his mind, he had always believed that performing well in school and participating enthusiastically in all political movements and helping out his comrades would persuade the authorities to take a more lenient view towards his weak family background. There was no way he could change his origins.

The conversation with Wu had made Bao Bo well aware of the momentous weight family background carried in Mao's China. Bao Bao felt light-headed, as there was no remedy for his birth. He could not ask his parents to return to China. Even if they returned, they would be considered grey elements, because by living in Hong Kong they had already been contaminated by capitalism. Good family background required three generations of proletarians in the family.

That night Bao Bao suffered again from insomnia. Now he had to face reality, the cruel reality that his future dreams had burst like a balloon. It was not Wu's fault that he had pointed out

Bao Bao's poor family background, but Bao Bao had misjudged his weak position in the eyes of the Party. Perhaps he had been too busy with his studies all the time and with his involvement in the Party's political activities. Or perhaps he was so egocentric that he had taken no notice of what the Party might be willing to give him. Now it was clear to him that the Party would not give him much, on account of his family background.

A few days ago, when he attended Professor Gu's confession, Bao Bao had thought that he would be able to accomplish more than Professor Gu by the time he reached Gu's age. Now he realized it would be difficult – even impossible – to do as much. If he was not admitted into a good university, how could he move forward in his career? Now Bao Bao began to face the fact that, in the eyes of the Party, he was nothing but a tiny cog, like one of a hundred millions of Chinese. Thinking of the tiny cog, he remembered a song that he used to sing when he was younger:

*I would like to be a tiny cog,*
*So that I can be set where they can use me,*
*In a complicated machine,*
*Or in a simple wheel,*
*Where they can screw me in tightly.*

*And I shall remain there, with peace of mind.*
*For the rest of my life.*

*Perhaps people do not know*
*That I exist.*
*But I know that in the roaring of the big machine,*
*The tiny cog is needed.*

Bao Bao sang this childhood song to himself twice and thought for a while. He concluded that to be a small cog was the Party's plan for him and that the Party had never endorsed any bigger plan for his future. To be awarded a Nobel Prize and to be a respected scientist and to study in Russia were simply his and his uncle's dreams. If he were rejected for university, which his dear friend Wu believed might be the case, he would have to accept any job offered by the Party and remain there for the rest of his life in China. Any change in career after such a beginning seemed highly unlikely. Perhaps this was the Party's plan for the millions of people at the bottom of society. Only those who had excellent family backgrounds, such as the children of Party leaders and heroes, were admitted into famous universities. Later on they would graduate and lead the country and the millions of mediocrities.

Bao Bao could not tolerate the thought that he was one of the millions of mediocrities and repeatedly told himself, "I only live once. I cannot waste my life. It is too precious to me." With his great self-confidence, he could not wait to grow up to grab the globe in both hands. Bao Bao was determined to do his utmost to make his life meaningful, as Nobel Prize-winners did, who made immense contributions to mankind. If someone were to say to Bao Bao that he was not talented enough to achieve such great things, Bao Bao would jump up and contradict them. "How do you know I can't do it? Prove to me that I am not talented!"

Now, from what his friend Wu had pointed out, Bao Bao realized that he was at a dead-end in his life. He now understood that there was a huge gap between how far he wanted to go and how far he would be allowed to go. Life as a mediocrity would be too boring for Bao Bao. He knew that he would never be able to lead an ordinary, mediocre life. If the Party imposed such a boring life upon him, he would have no way out but to end his life.

The word "suicide" had never occurred to him before, as he had never encountered such agony in the past. Life had treated him well. His parents regularly remitted a hundred Hong Kong dollars for him and his sister to share, equivalent to forty-two Chinese yuan, about the income of an average family. He paid a little for rent, and a small amount for food, and let his uncle and auntie keep the rest of the money. If he took his own life, what a nightmare it would be for his parents! How would Auntie and Uncle explain this act to his parents? Bao Bao would leave his poor younger sister alone in the world. No, I cannot die! Bao Bao shook his head. I cannot end my precious life so soon and so easily. I need to struggle and fight my way out, as many great people have done in the past, struggling to overcome hardships in order to achieve their goals in life. I should follow their path. He began to realize that he had never had a hard time in his life up to now. Perhaps now was the time for him to stand on his own feet. Yes, I've got to be strong! I must find a way out for myself, Bao Bao said to himself. But now is the time for sleep and tomorrow will be another day.

CHAPTER NINETEEN

# A DATE AT THE MOVIES

Bao Bao had been waiting for Dan Dan for a while in the foyer of the Mei Qi Cinema House on Nanjing Road. Two days ago, he had handed her a white envelope with a cinema ticket inside and then run away quickly. He was too shy to talk to her about where they should meet today to go to the movie. Now it occurred to him that Dan Dan might decide to arrive late so that no-one would recognize her in the darkness. So Bao Bao entered the cinema house by himself and took a seat. He need not worry about Dan Dan, because all the seats were numbered. Dan Dan would be led to her seat next to him by an usher. The movie was going to start in fifteen minutes and it was quite empty inside. Sitting there in the cinema, Bao Bao thought of today's movie, *Awara Hu (The Wanderer)*, an Indian film that he had seen about four years ago, in the same cinema house. A couple of weeks before, when Bao Bao was giving private tuition to Dan Dan, they chatted about the film and she told him that she had not seen it. So Bao Bao bought two tickets, knowing that she would not reject them.

*The Wanderer* was the story of an Indian lad who was kicked out by school because the school authorities found out that he worked as a shoe-shine boy after school. Later, he stole bread for his sick mother who was lying on her bed whimpering from hunger. He then found a job at a factory and worked there for a while, but he was soon fired. As an unemployed person, he had nothing to do but wander. After a while, the daughter of a rich lawyer fell in love with him. The father was furious that his daughter had become involved with a penniless wanderer. The luxurious villa in which the lawyer and his daughter resided was a spectacular sight for the Chinese, who, living in Mao's China, could never have imagined the existence of such grandeur on earth. Bao Bao especially admired the scene where the Wanderer roamed freely in his casual shirt and jeans along a country road under bright sunshine. According to the new regime, after seeing this movie one should condemn Indian capitalist society – especially since the young man was starving, had no schooling

216

and was without a job. However, deep inside his mind, Bao Bao admired the freedom and independence that the Wanderer enjoyed. He found life in China boring and monotonous; such an adventure – indeed an adventure of any kind – was unheard of.

The film had not begun and Dan Dan had not yet arrived. Bao Bao's mind drifted off as usual, this time to the film business in Hollywood. He had recently read that Hollywood was suffering from a financial setback. The number of spectators had dropped drastically from a staggering eighty-two million in 1946 to a mere four million in 1955. This was due to competition from television and low quality films. The number of films produced had also reduced from 509 films in 1951 to 230 films in 1956. Furthermore, Hollywood film manufacturers no longer owned the cinema-houses. They had either sold off the cinema buildings or converted them into offices.

In order to turn their fortunes around and rescue the deteriorating film industry, film-producers were devoting large sums to movies with spectacular scenes and longer playing times, films such as *Around the World in Eighty Days* which lasted for two hours and fifty-nine minutes. Paramount's *War and Peace* lasted for three hours and thirty-nine minutes and the production had cost thirteen point five million US dollars. Another strategy the film businessmen were using was to hire out older films to television companies. Due to the huge decline in audience numbers, three to four thousand cinema houses had closed down.

During the time when Bao Bao was growing up, he had heard from some old people that the film, *Gone With the Wind*, had been shown in Shanghai, where it had created a sensation, as one of the most magnificent films ever shown on cinema screens in China prior to the Liberation. Bao Bao was just a baby back then.

The lights in the cinema finally dimmed and Dan Dan appeared. Bao Bao was overjoyed. He asked if she had been sitting behind, waiting for the lights to go off, because she was afraid of being seen.

"No," she replied. My father caused the delay. He insisted on having a talk with me before I left home for the cinema." Bao Bao felt relieved and they both smiled at each other. The movie started and as usual, the first ten minutes before the feature film was full of trailers for future films. During this time, Bao Bao paid more attention to Dan Dan than the screen. He noticed she was wearing a sweater with a floral design, but in the darkness he could not distinguish the colours. He wanted to hold her hand, but he decided to wait.

Suddenly, *The Wanderer* came onto the screen. The Wanderer himself made an exciting jump over a high wall as the police were chasing him. The audience was taken aback and some even screamed. Seizing this opportunity, Bao Bao quickly grasped Dan Dan's hand. Although he was afraid of being rejected by her, his emotions were out of control. Contrary to his fear, Dan Dan held onto his hand tightly. This brought immense ecstasy to Bao Bao. Things were working out much better than he had expected.

Dan Dan's left hand was holding tightly onto Bao Bao's right hand. Bao Bao felt the softness of her skin. It was the first time that he had ever touched a female's hand. His body was quivering as he was electrified by the feminine touch. This feeling was unknown to him. Now he began to recognize the power of a woman. What made him happy was that Dan Dan was holding his hand tightly and not letting it go. Bao Bao wanted to leave his hand with her forever. He knew that her gesture was a sign that she liked or even loved him. So he turned his shoulder slightly to the right, closer to Dan Dan and stretched out his left arm so that his left hand could join his right hand in caressing her hand. Bao Bao felt wonderful. Now he began to understand why young men were always looking for girlfriends and why they eventually married them. Bao Bao scarcely looked at the screen, as he had seen the film before. Dan Dan on the other hand was engrossed in it, while at the same time she let Bao Bao caress her hand.

A little later Bao Bao forced Dan Dan to open her left palm at the same time as he opened his right palm. He inserted his four fingers into the spaces between her fingers in her palm, then closed his palm into a fist. Dan Dan was smart enough to close her palm as well, so their ten fingers were tightly crossed. The tighter they held on to each other's fist, the more pleasure they derived. Having so much fun with Dan Dan's hand, Bao Bao wanted to hold her body and kiss her, but his common sense stopped him. He wanted to leave a good impression on her. He knew everything should take time. If a relationship developed too fast it would eventually collapse. Bao Bao was more than satisfied that Dan Dan had responded positively and this was much better than he had dared hope for. Now he was sure that she liked him too and he knew that he had a chance to develop the relationship with her into a long-term one. He could visualize in his mind a picture of a happy life with Dan Dan and he felt as though his life was already happier and more meaningful.

Suddenly Bao Bao and Dan Dan were dazzled by a flash of light and they were both shocked. Bao Bao immediately grasped that it was a warning from the theatre usher that he should behave, so he turned his body swiftly away from Dan Dan and straightened his back so as to face the screen. Fortunately, the film was approaching its end and Bao Bao had had a lot of fun already. Bao Bao had learnt that even in dark cinema houses lovers were being watched. In contrast to the park, the dark cinema was not a paradise for lovers.

As soon as the movie was over, the cinema hall lit up. People began to stand up and move towards the exits. Bao Bao and Dan Dan remained in their seats until the majority of the audience had left. They stood up reluctantly, partly because they were having so much fun touching each other's hands and also partly because they were afraid to be seen in public.

"How did you like the film?" asked Bao Bao.

"It was great. I'd heard of this film before and now I've finally seen it. Thank you, Bao Bao. I just can't imagine that there are rich people in India, who live in such a rich and luxurious villa, just like a palace."

"Yes, the huge house made an incredible impression on me too, when I saw the film for the first time four years ago," said Bao Bao.

"What did you think of the film this time?"

"This time around, I admired particularly the freedom that the Indian boy enjoys. Did you notice that the boy is able to wander freely from here to there and that he can change jobs as he wishes without obtaining any permission from the Party? Do you remember that sunny day when he walks confidently along the country road? I wish I could do the same."

"Yes, you're right. We in China are not allowed to change jobs and move from one place to another," Dan Dan said regretfully.

"I can't imagine that my thoughts have changed much during the past four years. All I remember this time is the freedom that he has and not the beautiful house they reside in."

Bao Bao added, "Four years ago *The Wanderer* was shown at the Asia Film Festival, which lasted for two weeks. During the festival a queue of a thousand people lined up outside the cinema to buy admission tickets; some people even spent the entire night waiting outside, to see a film from capitalist India and Pakistan. The admission tickets were marked up ten or twenty times in the black market". Bao Bao paused for a while to study Dan Dan's peering eyes and then continued, "There were a number of films from the Soviet Union and Eastern European countries, but people were not interested; nothing fascinated the city as much as a film from a capitalist country. Along with the Indian film was a film from Pakistan, where the pretty female movie star donned a pair of denim jeans. I was younger and didn't try to obtain an admission ticket. I thought I could see more films from capitalist countries at the next film festival, but I was wrong. Now I have been waiting for four years and the film festival has never shown the Pakistani film with the girl wearing jeans again. Only this Indian film has come back."

As soon as they left the cinema and walked on the street, Dan Dan asked, "Why have your thoughts developed so much over the past four years? Do you think my thoughts will change when I watch this film again in a few years' time?"

"You may focus on some other details," Bao Bao replied, "such as the big house, the actors and actresses, who are very different from those in our films. I am not sure if you will think of 'freedom' as I did. For me 'freedom' has become very important lately. The following small poem has become a motto in my life, and I think of it day in and day out:

*Life is precious,*
*Love even more.*
*If it is for freedom,*
*Both can be thrown away.*[22]

Dan Dan said, "I'm also familiar with that poem. Speaking of freedom – have you heard that renowned Chinese pianist Fou Ts'ong has run away and sought refuge in England, our number two enemy? They said he did it for freedom. What do you think?"

Bao Bao answered right away, "I know, I know. Let me tell you, I have followed Fu Ts'ong's story closely. He was the son of the famous translator Fu Lei, who is a highly-esteemed Chinese scholar, who has translated Voltaire, Balzac and Romain Rolland into Chinese. Fu Ts'ong started to learn the piano at the age of four, under the superb guidance of his intellectual father.[23] He later became an excellent pianist. In 1953, at the age of nineteen, he was sent by the Party to Poland to study the piano at the Warsaw Conservatory. Two years later he won the Mazurka Prize at the Chopin Piano Competition. – My sister Yuan Yuan has been playing the piano for many years, and this is why we are very keen on pianists.

"Do you have a piano at home?" asked Dan Dan.

"Of course we do!" answered Bao Bao with pride, because it was rare that someone owned a piano at home.

Bao Bao added, "My Ma Ma used to play the piano before she left for Hong Kong…. But to continue with the story of Fu Ts'ong. After winning his prize, Fu Ts'ong was supposed to return home in Shanghai, but instead he sought refuge at the British Embassy in Warsaw. Because he was such a talented pianist it was no problem for him to enter the United Kingdom and remain there. When we heard this news in China, we became very angry. We all accused him of being a traitor who had betrayed his Motherland."

"How about his parents? Does his father ask him to return to Shanghai?" asked Dan Dan anxiously.

"We don't know. We are not his relatives. But, for sure, life is going to be harsh for his parents. How did his scholarly father face the Party when his son became a traitor? Will his parents survive? How will they survive? We don't know yet. But I agree with you that the young Fu Ts'ong did it for freedom, for which he has sacrificed everything including his parents, his girlfriend perhaps, his friends, his city Shanghai and above all, his Motherland." Bao Bao spoke with emotion in his voice.

Deep in his heart he admired Fu Ts'ong greatly for grasping this unique opportunity and for his courage and bravery.

"Do you think people living in England can move from one place to another place and change from one job to another, without obtaining permission from the Party, like the Wanderer did in India?" asked Dan Dan.

"I believe they have the freedom to move around and to change their jobs whenever they want. Because there is no Hu Kou Bu system – no registration system – to control the movement of the inhabitants," replied Bao Bao.

"Bao Bao, it is not necessary for you to walk me home."

"In the dark streets, it isn't easy for us be seen," replied Bao Bao as they walked side by side together towards her home. In public, Bao Bao dared not touch her hand, even though the street-lighting was dim. After walking for about a hundred metres, Dan Dan felt uneasy and said to Bao Bao, "If you insist on walking me home, you may follow me. Walk three to four metres behind me. Otherwise just go home and we will see each other at school tomorrow."

Bao Bao obeyed the order and kept a distance of at least three metres behind her. He understood it would be very bad for her, as well as for him, to be seen walking together in the night. Neighbours would be glad to have a new discovery to gossip about. Life was monotonous under the new regime. Gossiping was perhaps the only entertainment that housewives had. Neither Dan Dan nor Bao Bao wanted to be their target.

After a while, they arrived at Dan Dan's house. She pulled the house key out of her pocket and turned her head backwards as if to say "Goodbye" to Bao Bao. He watched her entering the house and then turned around and walked along the same street back home. This time he nearly jumped into the air in celebration of his great success in love. He felt as though Dan Dan was already part of him. He was thinking of the next step. He would hold her tightly, conquer her step by step until she surrendered her heart to him. He conjured up this wonderful picture as taking place in the not too distant future.

At the same time, he felt that what he had in mind with Dan Dan was not in line with Chairman Mao's education or his family's expectations. But he quickly comforted himself. I have done so much for the Party and I have worked very hard to live up to my family's expectations of me. My relationship with Dan Dan is just a small favour to myself. Besides, he continued, my feeling for Dan Dan is beyond my control. I have done nothing wrong. But he knew that the timing was not right. His feelings for Dan Dan had surfaced a couple of years too soon. But after all he was precocious for his age. There was nothing he could do about it!

The following morning, encouraged by last night's success, Bao Bao approached Dan Dan during the class recess. However, Dan Dan's attitude towards him was cool, and this was incomprehensible and unexpected. During the following class session, Bao Bao could hardly concentrate on his study. On a small piece of paper he wrote, "Why do you ignore me? Didn't we have a lot of fun last night? I need to talk to you desperately!" Then he folded it and, when Teacher Liang turned her back on the class to write on the blackboard, he threw it onto Dan Dan's desk, which was two rows ahead of his. Dan Dan unfolded the small piece of paper and read the message. Without turning back, she tore the piece of paper into many small pieces and shoved them hastily into her schoolbag instead of throwing them away into a rubbish bin. Apparently she wanted to make sure that the message would not fall into a third person's hand.

During class break, Bao Bao approached her again and tried to speak to her, but she kept on talking to some other girls and ignored him. This annoyed Bao Bao. He could not figure out why her attitude had changed so drastically overnight. He could not recall whether he did anything wrong. "No," he thought, he had done absolutely nothing wrong. Bao Bao thought of a writer's description of womens' moods as being as unpredictable as clouds in the sky.

After school, he chased after Dan Dan and followed her on her way home, as he wanted to clarify with her what he had done unknowingly which had annoyed her.

"Tell me, why won't you talk to me today? Have I done anything wrong, to upset you?" asked Bao Bao anxiously.

Dan Dan continued walking, as though she did not hear a word.

"Tell me Dan Dan. Why are you angry with me?" pressed Bao Bao.

"I am not angy! You did nothing wrong," Dan Dan said, suddenly turning around.

Bao Bao stared at her. Dan Dan looked Bao Bao straight in the eyes and said, "Last night, I came late to the cinema because my father asked me where I was going and I told him. He tried to forbid me to go out with you. We had a small argument and I said to him, 'If you forbid me, then I will leave this house and never come back.' So he let me go. That's why I came late to the cinema.

"When I came home, he was waiting for me and talked to me again. This time his eyes were full of tears. He said, 'When your Ma Ma was dying, she made me promise to get you a good husband. So I am extremely concerned about who you associate with. In this society, there are only two types of men who are suitable for you: The first are scientists, whom our regime never struggles against. Scientists belong to a privileged class. The second are the children of Communist officials.'"

"But I...," Bao Bao began.

Dan Dan interrupted, "My father reminded me of a remote and poor relative of mine, named Li Li, who married a son of a high ranking officer in the army and the authorities immediately allocated to the young couple a two-bedroom apartment in the exclusive Hua Shan Road and her family moved out of the slums right away. Li Li is no longer the poor girl she was a couple years ago. Through marriage, Li Li is now leading a comfortable and wealthy life."

Bao Bao grew impatient and said, "I shall be a famous scientist. So I am the right man for you." He said this loudly and proudly as Dan Dan's two round eyes filled with tears.

She replied, "No. My father said you are a decent young man but unfortunately your family background is so poor that you will not become a scientist. In the first place, you will never gain admission to a good university, and then they will never send you off to Russia or East Germany. You are just a day-dreamer. How can you become a scientist in China if you get no support from the Party? The accomplishments that will result from your personal struggle will be very limited. My father said it is crucial that I marry one of the two types of people he mentioned. He regrets that he has no dowry for me and indeed the opposite is true. He counts on my support for the rest of his life. So he forbids me to see you again. He said that at our young age, I could easily get involved, even if I just go out with you once in a while."

Bao Bao stood there dumbfounded. He could not believe that Dan Dan had spoken such jarring words to him. A flush of embarrassment crept up his body and his face turned burning red. Dan Dan's words hit him badly. He could hardly walk. He asked her to stop walking for a while. "You mean your father will not allow you to see me any more. How about the tutoring?" asked Bao Bao.

Dan Dan replied, "My father said, 'Forget the tutoring!' The worst scenario is, I fail geometry, but he will not blame me."

All of Bao Bao's enthusiasm for females and his zeal for life were suddenly extinguished. He felt so weak that he could not walk any more. He could never have imagined, last night in the cinema, that his heavenly pleasure then would turn into hell today.

A few minutes later, he decided to pull himself together and declared out loud and clearly, "I will be a famous scientist one way or the other." Abruptly he turned around and quickly walked away from her. This was totally unexpected by Dan Dan who cried out loud, but he did not turn his head back. He walked away quickly, ignoring Dan Dan's weeping, until he came to an empty spot in a park and started to Fang Sheng Da Ku (wail loudly). He could not care less for the pedestrians who watched him in the park. They thought that perhaps the wailing young man was mourning the loss of someone in the family. Nobody imagined that he was crying over losing his lover at such a young age.

That night was indeed a sleepless one for Bao Bao. Never had he felt so miserable and sorrowful in his life. He thought that he needed to change his living environment and everything else around him. He knew that he could make as many changes as he wanted in his mind. Nevertheless in reality, he was in a dismal situation. He could do nothing, not even move to another city or transfer to another school, unless it was approved by the Party. If

225

he took off on his own, he would not survive without ration coupons.

That night, he racked his brains to think what he could possibly do with his future. After thinking about it the whole night, he came to the conclusion that he should struggle in a foreign territory and then come back to China when he had achieved some fame. But how could he execute this plan? As his close friend Wu Hai Bin had warned him, the moment the Party got the message that he had the slightest intention of leaving China to visit his parents, he would be suspected and labelled a Rightist, or even as a traitor. Now he realized it was impossible for him to alter his environment. Every move could potentially ruin his fate. Just one wrong step could hurl him into an abyss and he would never, ever, be able to raise his head to see daylight again.

CHAPTER TWENTY

# YOUNG AND ALONE

The next day, after school, Bao Bao returned home around half past four. The moment he pushed through the entrance door he heard his sister Yuan Yuan sobbing. He rushed to her. She handed him a letter to them from their uncle and auntie. Bao Bao knew immediately that Uncle and Auntie must have left Shanghai. Tears sprang from his eyes spontaneously as he read:

*Dear Bao Bao and Yuan Yuan,*

*Forgive us for taking off without saying a proper "Good Bye" to each of you. The reason why we were so inconsiderate and rude was to avoid a sorrowful farewell. You know nothing in our lives is worse than parting and dying.*

*Had you known that we would leave this morning, I am sure that neither of you would have slept well last night. Then today you would both have taken leave of absence from school. We would have cried painfully at the train station. But what for? In order not to distract you from your intense studies we decided to take French leave. Please excuse us!*

*Auntie has cooked dinner for you for tonight. Starting tomorrow, you will both take breakfast, lunch and dinner at our next-door neighbour's place. You know that our neighbour, Mrs Yang, always treats you both as if you were her own children. So don't be shy and treat her as Auntie Ying or your Ma Ma. I have paid twenty yuans to her for this month's meals and the rest of the money is in the savings book underneath the mattress of your bed. Furthermore, we have also hired Wang Ma, the old lady you know, to clean the apartment and do laundry for you once a week on Mondays.*

*We deeply regret that we have to leave you alone like this, and this is also bad for Lin Lin who will lose all the friends that she has made in Shanghai during the past year and now she needs to adapt to small city life. Nevertheless, you know well that we have no other choice. In any case, we are better off than being labelled "Rightists".*

227

*Please accept our sincere apologies again and we will write to you as soon as we get to Suzhou. One day you both may visit us, or we will come to visit you. Suzhou is not very far away from Shanghai.*
*Forever loving you,*
*Uncle, Auntie and Lin Lin*

As soon as Bao Bao finished reading he started to sob too. He held Yuan Yuan tightly and they wept together. For quite some time, Bao Bao had been aware that his uncle's family would be forced to leave Shanghai one of these days, but why today? Why particularly today? Today was an awful day, because his heart had just been broken by Dan Dan. Now he witnessed the bitterness of the old Chinese saying, "Huo Bu Dan Xing", "Misfortune does not come alone".

After a while, both brother and sister started to quiet down. Bao Bao said to Yuan Yuan, "Sorry to have spent such a little time with you in the past. You are a wonderful sister."

Yuan Yuan replied quickly, "You are such a good brother too." Bao Bao added, "When walking on the streets together, all of our acquaintances, friends and neighbours have always remarked, 'such a handsome brother and pretty sister', and since we are both in the best high school in Shanghai, Ma Ma has always been so proud of us and our relatives are very envious of us. Too bad Ma Ma is not here with us."

"When is Ma Ma coming back?" asked Yuan Yuan. I really miss her. I dream of her sometimes."

"One day for sure! But maybe not very soon." Then Bao Bao changed the subject to distract his sad sister from thinking about their absent Ma Ma. "Starting tomorrow, how about we walk to school and back home together? If I am late, you wait for me; and I will wait for you, if you are late."

"Great! It's a good idea," said Yuan Yuan, smiling. She stretched out her hand and clasped Bao Bao's palm with her palm, so the deal was closed.

"With the money Uncle has left us I am going to hire the best piano teacher in town for you. Are you willing to continue with your hard work?" asked Bao Bao. He knew that Yuan Yuan had lost her piano teacher recently due to the Anti-Rightist

Campaign. It looked like her teacher, Mr Sun, was in trouble now, because he had not shown up for the tutoring during the past few weeks.

"Of course, I will work hard," Yuan Yuan answered with a cheerful and smiling face. I'm delighted that you will find me a better teacher. I'll play the piano for you every evening. I know how much you love the piano! I won't disappoint you."

"Yes, I love the piano, but I don't have the talent for it myself. What a pity!" Bao Bao replied. In fact Bao Bao had once taken piano lessons, but he could not keep up with his tutor so he dropped the lessons. He felt regret whenever he thought about it.

"Bao Bao, you need not play yourself! Let me play for you. A king need not play the piano himself. He just sits there and enjoys the music, as we have seen in the movies. Have you ever heard of a king trying to learn the piano? Am I right?" Yuan Yuan tried to please Bao Bao. They both laughed. She knew that he felt inferior for not being able to play the piano himself.

~~~

One day, Bao Bao saw an ambulance come to collect an old lady from his backyard alley. He asked himself, What would happen to me if I became seriously ill? Would the ambulance come for me and take me to hospital as well? They would first notify my parents. My Ma Ma would rush back for sure. If she came back, she would never be allowed to leave again. My chances of leaving for Hong Kong would be diminished. Suppose I was sick – he pursued this line of thought – but not so seriously sick that Ma Ma had to rush back to see me. Would the government on humanitarian grounds grant me an exit visa to let me join my family in Hong Kong?

In Shanghai he officially lived alone with his younger sister, with no-one to look after him when he was sick. Yes, it could possibly work if he had a good reason. He became excited. He considered himself a good student and a good ex-Pioneer. He was a teenager, harmless to society. So Bao Bao decided to give it a try. So far he had been quite lucky with doctors and clinics, as he had always received notes from them whenever he needed one. Using medical reasons to excuse himself for being absent from some of the political campaigns was his expertise. Now he would try to invent a medical reason to accomplish his ultimate goal of obtaining an exit visa. Whether he would succeed or not, he could not say at this initial stage, but one thing he was very sure of. His intention to leave the country must not be detected in any way by the authorities. So even if he failed, he would be safe and he would never be condemned.

To find a suitable sickness was a daunting task. He briefly thought of cutting a piece of flesh off his leg, but that was too obvious. He would not be able to answer the questions if they interrogated him. If he said he suffered from stomach-ache, it was not so serious that he would have to leave for Hong Kong. If he complained of intestinal bleeding, which he could attain by eating excessive chicken blood the day before, a doctor would arrange for him to stay in hospital for a couple of days for observation. No. None of these were suitable for his purpose.

One day, he passed by Hua Shan Hospital and registered as an outpatient. He complained that he was suffering from chest pains. The nurse checked his blood pressure and said that it was slightly higher than normal. The doctor came to check his chest with a stethoscope and asked him to breathe in and out. After examining him for a few minutes, the doctor said to Bao Bao, "You have no serious sickness. Perhaps it is the cold congested in your chest area that is causing you pain. We will give you some pills and syrup to fight against your cold and you will be fine in a couple of days." With that, the doctor walked out of the hospital. Bao Bao was disappointed.

During the next couple of weeks, Bao Bao went from hospital to hospital after school. He discovered that high blood pressure was an interesting sickness. To find out more, he went into the big bookstore that he had patronized on several occasions. This time in the Health Section he took out a book regarding blood pressure and turned the pages. He flipped through the pages slowly until he read that blood pressure rose when one got excited, angry or depressed, or after the body went through a quick succession of movements, or an emotional disturbance. He thought that he would try it out.

He went to the nearby Second People's Hospital of Shanghai and paid one yuan to register as an outpatient, receiving a ticket numbered "ninety-eight". Then he heard them call the number, "fifty-five". He asked the nurse how long it would take to wait for about thirty patients. The answer was, "At least two hours". So he went out to take a walk. Two hours later, before he returned to the hospital, he ran about the last three hundred metres up to the hospital gate. He wanted to see if his blood pressure had risen. However, they were calling number seventy-eight. So he guessed he had to wait another one and a half hours or so. To wait longer was not a problem, but what did annoyed him was that his blood pressure would drop by the time the doctor saw him. He was not interested in going out again, as the Bund was the Bund. He had seen it a hundred times. So he sat there nervously until they called the number ninety. Then he went back outside. He walked slowly for about two to three hundred metres and then started to run as quickly as he could. When he entered the hospital again, they were just calling number "ninety-eight".

Bao Bao headed into the consultation room, where the nurse checked his blood pressure and said, "Your blood pressure is very high – it is a hundred and sixty over a hundred". A few minutes later, a female doctor, about fifty years old, came in and examined Bao Bao's chest with a stethoscope. Again he was asked to breathe in and breathe out. She asked, "Do your parents have heart disease?" Bao Bao had never heard there was any problem with his parents' hearts, but his father had high blood pressure and diabetes. After hesitating for a few seconds he lied to the doctor in a sad voice, "Yes, my Pa Pa has been suffering from heart disease and high blood pressure since he was a teenager."

The lady examined his chest with her stethoscope again and again. Finally she said, "The pump in your heart works irregularly. This is caused by your high blood pressure. Maybe you have inherited these diseases from your Pa Pa. I am writing down your diagnosis and the prescription. Take each pill once a day after meals and come back to see me in three months; one pill is to reduce your high blood pressure while the other is to cure your heart disease. If your condition does not improve, you might need heart surgery. Your heart disease is genetic. There is not much I can do for you at the moment". Bao Bao stood up from his chair and took the diagnosis and the prescription. He thanked the doctor as he walked out of the hospital.

The moment he came out of the hospital, he was overwhelmed with joy. "This is much much better than I expected!" he said to himself, running a few steps and jumping up in the air. He continued to run and jump for quite a while, to express his happiness. He carefully put his diagnosis into the inner pocket of his jacket. He could not believe things had gone so smoothly for him. He thanked God for helping him. Instead of going home right away, he went to his Great-Auntie's place. The old lady lived with her daughter on the second floor of the same house where Kai Kai lived.

He knew his distant uncle, the son of the old lady, was a physician and the owner of a small private clinic. Bao Bao guessed correctly that, based on the diagnosis of a leading government hospital with an official stamp, the son could easily write him a sick leave note for six months. Bao Bao was smart enough not to ask the female doctor at the Second People's Hospital to write such a note. Had he done so, the doctor at the government hospital might have suspected his intention and might not have given him the note containing the diagnosis. Also, she might have asked him to return in a week to have another check, because she might have been afraid that Bao Bao was taking advantage of her. Also, without the official confirmation of Bao Bao's heart disease from a government hospital, the son of his elderly relative would never give out a sick-leave note for such a long period. Bao Bao was careful not to present himself at his relative's clinic, because if he did so, he would definitely have his blood pressure measured and his chest checked once again.

Things worked out exactly as Bao Bao had predicted. The next day, Da Jie,[24] the daughter of the old lady, delivered him a sick-leave note for six months. After school, when Yuan Yuan came home, Bao Bao showed her the diagnosis. Yuan Yuan was surprised. She said immediately, "How come you have high blood pressure and heart disease? I know Pa Pa has high blood pressure but I have never heard about any heart disease in our family. Where did you pick up the heart disease?"

"Doctor said it's genetic. I have no idea. Perhaps I worry too much! You know, our parents are not here and being the elder brother, all burdens fall upon my shoulders. Perhaps my young heart cannot handle such a heavy load. Anyway, let's not discuss where the heart disease comes from. I need your help to present this six-month sick-leave note from the doctor to Party Secretary Huang. Can you go to see him for me tomorrow?" Bao Bao asked.

"I have never talked to the Headmaster, or the Party Secretary. I am afraid to see him."

"Please, Yuan Yuan, you must do me this favour. I need him to grant me sick leave for six months. He is the only one who has the authority to do so. Without official approval of my long six months sick leave, I will have to go back to school. I heard our Party Secretary Huang is a veteran of the Long March of Twenty-five Thousand Miles. He is a very powerful political figure and also a sympathetic, friendly and kind man. He treats students like his own children. Yuan Yuan, I think you are the only person who can help me. If you don't do it for me, I will have to go to school and see him myself. But I am sick and I am supposed to stay at home," said Bao Bao.

"Alright, Ge, [25] I'll go to see him tomorrow. I'll do everything for you."

Bao Bao added, "When you see him, don't say too much, alright? Just show him the doctor's note and let him make a decision on my case."

Yuan Yuan nodded and looked at her brother, "Yes, I won't say anything."

"Now listen! It is very important that you see him in person. Don't give the sick leave note to his secretary or his deputy," warned Bao Bao.

"Yes, I will insist on seeing him in person," Yuan Yuan assured him.

Unfortunately, the Party Secretary was not in. So she tried again the following morning. This time, she was able to see him in person at his office. After Secretary Huang read the diagnosis and the sick leave note for six months from the private doctor, he questioned Yuan Yuan, "Who cooks for you at home?"

"Nobody cooks at home. We eat at our neighbour's place."

"Who washes your clothes and cleans the house?"

"We have an amah who comes once a week to wash our clothes for us. We clean the place ourselves."

"How old are you?"

"Fourteen, and my sick brother is sixteen."

The old Communist Party official thought for a while. Then, showing sympathy for the sick student, he said, "I suggest that your sick brother, Song Bao Bao, should go to Hong Kong to join your parents and let your parents take care of him. I will write a letter to the Public Security Bureau to support his application for an exit visa. Tell your brother it is very important that if he goes to Hong Kong – that deteriorating and rotten capitalistic society – he should refuse to go to any night-club, dance-hall or horse-racing course. He should refrain from bad habits such as smoking and gambling. He should not forget the teaching we have given him and he should continue to be a good student of Chairman Mao."

Yuan Yuan came home and told Bao Bao the news. He felt so exhilarated that words could not express the happiness he felt. Things were really working out well for him. His initial plan had been to get the six months' sick leave from his school first and then later, at an appropriate time, raise a request to go to Hong Kong for his parents to look after him. Now one stone had killed two birds. What a miracle! He could only believe that God was on his side.

Two days later, Security Officer Ye came to visit him and brought him the official application form for an exit and return visa and asked him to fill it out right away. While Bao Bao was filling out the form, the officer murmured, "In a week's time, when you get the exit visa, you will no longer be sick." Bao Bao was scared of saying anything. It seemed that the PSB officer saw that his sickness was not genuine. What could Bao Bao say? So he did not answer and the officer left. For Bao Bao, it was already a triumph that the application for an exit visa was delivered to him at home. He remembered how his poor Ma Ma had gone to the Public Security Bureau for two long years, day after day, crying most of the time and nobody cared! How fortunate he had been! The officer told him that he would get the visa in a week. Bao Bao felt it was too good to be true. Should he believe it or should he not? He did not know what to say. Good things seemed to be arriving too fast. Soon he came to the conclusion that he should believe it, so he could sleep at night.

For seven consecutive nights, he slept like a baby. He did not think of his sickness, his visa, his school or the PBS officer. He completely escaped from his world. How had he managed to do this? He had gone to the library, where he borrowed the complete works of Shakespeare in Chinese translation. Now he was deeply involved in the plots of the plays, in the writing and in the dialogues of this mastermind. In the hustle and bustle of life, after a battle like he had been fighting, it was great for Bao Bao to have a break, to do the things that he had been looking forward to doing for years. The more he read Shakespeare's work, the more he admired him, a real genius.

With Shakespeare's company, day and night, a week passed by quickly. On the eighth day, Bao Bao was debating whether he should go to the Public Security Bureau to collect the visa, or whether he should wait at home until the officer came to deliver the exit visa to him. In the end, he decided to wait until the officer came. So he paid special attention if anyone knocked the door. He read the play, *Hamlet*, for the second time, but his inner mind was not so peaceful. The question, If I fail to get the visa, what will happen to me? lingered in his mind all the time. But Bao Bao soon came to a comforting conclusion. Nothing will happen to me, because my attempt is covered up well. It was not me who wanted to go to dirty, corrupt, capitalistic Hong Kong. It was the honourable Party Secretary's suggestion. So if my application is rejected, life will go back to normal, just like before. I would have lost nothing, except two week's schooling – actually one week's classes at the most, because half the time would have been devoted to ongoing political campaigns and voluntary work on a farm, or in a factory, or in cleaning the school premises.

Nevertheless, it was a fruitful break for Bao Bao, since he used the time to plough through the major works of Shakespeare, which he had wished to do for a very long time. This reading convinced him of Shakespeare's greatness as a writer, and persuaded him that he should spend more time to study his plays in the future. Perhaps one day he would be able to read the work in English, the mother-tongue of this great master. It would be fantastic if he could do so. English was one of his favourite subjects. Unfortunately his favourite English teacher, Sun Yue, had been labelled a Rightist and was removed from her post. Bao Bao was not so familiar with the new English teacher, a graduate from the Shanghai Second Foreign Language School.

CHAPTER TWENTY-ONE

# CHAIRMAN MAO MEETING

It was early morning and someone was knocking at the door. In the past few days, Bao Bao had been paying close attention to the door as he was hoping that Security Officer Ye would appear to deliver the exit visa to him. He opened the door quickly. It was indeed Officer Ye. In his heart, he was delighted, but his outward appearance remained calm and expressionless. Officer Ye said, "Put your clothes on and come with me quickly! Chairman Mao wants to see you."

Bao Bao was taken aback and replied, "Chairman Mao is in his residence in Beijing Zhongnanhai. You mean I have to go to Beijing?"

"Chairman Mao is now in Shanghai. Don't ask questions. Come quickly!"

Bao Bao was rushed out of the door by Officer Ye and ushered into a black sedan. They drove for more than an hour and then the car entered Xijiao Park. This Park was unknown to Bao Bao, as the park was not open to the public, but reserved exclusively for foreign state guests and government heads from Beijing. The park was huge and the car continued to drive for a long time on a road alongside a small river. Bao Bao saw picturesque scenery inside the park with beautiful green trees, bushes and lawns and occasionally some white swans swimming placidly on the river under the willow trees. He found it strange that there was not a single person in such an immense park. In a crowded and busy city with millions of inhabitants, it was astonishing that there could be any such huge and silent place. Bao Bao asked the officer, "Why does Chairman Mao want to see me? I am not the most politically conscious of students. He should see Zhou and Wang Ming."

"Don't ask questions! Just follow me," replied Officer Ye.

The car stopped in front of a large villa and they entered and walked through the corridors, passing one room after another. Bao Bao could not have imagined it was so big inside. Officer Ye handed Bao Bao over to a guard who led him to another room. In the room a nurse dressed in white uniform inspected Bao Bao.

She demanded that Bao Bao take off all his clothes, except his underpants, and lie face-up on a narrow bed while she placed a dozen rubber rings around his head, chest and upper arms. The rubber rings were connected by wire to an enormous white machine. Bao Bao wondered, "Is the nurse checking to see whether I am really sick?" Then he thought, Whatever, whatever! There is nothing I can do now. In the worst scenario, I die.

After a while, the nurse pulled out from the machine a few A4-size sheets of paper, which she stapled together and passed to the guards standing nearby. Bao Bao craned his neck to see the contents of the report but in spite of his best efforts he could not make out what the diagrams meant. The guard left with the report and the nurse told Bao Bao to stand up and put his clothes back on. After a few more minutes, the guard came back and asked Bao Bao to follow him to a larger room and then asked Bao Bao to wait outside.

Bao Bao was very frightened. He just stood there motionless and sweated. After a while, the door opened again. Another guard came out and escorted Bao Bao into the room. In the middle of the room, a tall, big man was sitting in a chair and smoking. He did look like the most honourable Chairman Mao. Next to him was an old man who kept a record of the entire conversation. Bao Bao was not offered a chair, so he stood there, trembling and sweating.

"Are you Song Bao Bao?" asked Chairman Mao.

"Yes," Bao Bao replied.

"How old are you?"

"Sixteen."

"Why do you want to leave your wonderful country and go to the deteriorating British Colony of Hong Kong?"

"It was not my idea. It was the suggestion of most respected Party Secretary Huang of my school."

"Silence! It was you who wanted to betray us and escape to deteriorating Hong Kong. Don't you dare blame your bad intentions on our good comrade, Huang. I have always known that we can never trust those who are from a poor background. Your case has proved once again that our policy is correct."

The Chairman spoke with a raised voice. It was apparent he was angry and he shouted, "Now tell me why! You have grown up under our red flag. How can you betray your Motherland?"

Bao Bao uttered in a low voice, "I did not betray you and my beloved Motherland. I am sick, so Secretary Huang suggested to my younger sister that I should join my parents in Hong Kong where they can look after me."

"Silence!" Chairman Mao shouted.

He slammed his right fist on the table and spoke loudly and sternly again, "Don't think that you can fool us. Take a look at the report from our lie-detector!" Chairman Mao snatched the stack of papers from the corner of his desk and threw them at Bao Bao. "We know you are a liar! We know that every word from your mouth is a lie. You, Wang Ba Dan, you rotten egg, you bastard!" This time Chairman Mao slammed both his fists on the table and stood up.

"Take this Wang Ba Dan and liar out! And send him to gaol!" Chairman Mao hollered at his guards.

Immediately two guards stepped forward, grabbed Bao Bao by the arms, and dragged him out of the room.

Bao Bao was frightened and scared to death!

At that moment, he woke up. It was a nightmare. Bao Bao felt very lucky to be lying on his own bed. But his underwear was wet.

Since the day Bao Bao had received the doctor's sick leave note for six months, he had stayed mainly at home, except for visiting his neighbour's for meals. Nobody had ordered Bao Bao to stay at home all the time, but he decided to do so himself. He told himself, I'm sick, so I'm sick. This is the discipline that I must follow! Since I don't go to school, I shall refrain from all outdoor activities in order to give the authorities the impression that I am seriously ill. I think I must follow this discipline, as I am being watched by everyone.

Today Bao Bao went to his neighbour's place for lunch and heard that Chef Wang had been arrested. "What shocking news!"

Bao Bao immediately turned to his neighbour and asked, "Why?"

"Chef Wang was charged with sodomy."

Bao Bao had no idea what "sodomy" meant. He finished his lunch quickly and went out to the courtyard to read the "Da Zi Bao", the big character poster, about his friend, Chef Wang. The Da Zi Bao accused Chef Wang of being a Counter-Revolutionary who had been constantly against the new regime. He had sodomized many youngsters. The Da Zi Bao also called for those who had been taken advantage of by Chef Wang to denounce him. Chef Wang had been arrested and was waiting in gaol to receive the verdict on his case. For Bao Bao this was shocking news. Bao Bao hurried home to check the dictionary. Soon he found out that the word "sodomy" means to have "sexual intercourse with males". "Sodomy", written in Chinese characters, "Ji Jian", literally meant, "sex in chicken style". Bao Bao was confused, as he had never paid attention to the sexual intercourse of chickens. He could not figure out how two males could make love. This was another piece of the puzzle to which he could find no answer anywhere. If I were to go to the bookstore, would I be able to clarify it? No, no, I had better stay at home as I am sick. This time Bao Bao was not in the mood to investigate the mystery of male sexuality. The timing was not right.

The news of Chef Wang's arrest had a great impact on Bao Bao, since he was to a certain degree acquainted with Chef Wang. Right now was the most critical moment in Bao Bao's life as he was waiting for his visa. If Chef Wang mentioned Bao Bao's name, he would have a problem getting his exit visa. How can I stop Chef Wang from mentioning my association with him now? He is in gaol, with no access to the outside world. According to Chef Wang he has no relative in Shanghai. If he did have someone visiting him in gaol, I could possibly send a message through the visitor, asking Chef Wang not to mention me under any circumstances. Now I can do nothing. How fortunate I was that I left Chef Wang's room as he was trying to unbutton my shirt and loosen my belt! Our regime was right to arrest him. Now he cannot interfere with any more youngsters to make them victims of his dirty sexual desire. Again Bao Bao admired Chairman Mao's wise saying, "The eyes of the masses are immaculately bright." The regime knew everything about everyone.

If he was interrogated, Chef Wang might not survive torture. Bao Bao had heard that sometimes victims had to endure a straight forty-eight hour period in a dark room with no sleep and with strong voltage lamps shining in their faces. If they did this, they would encourage Chef Wang by telling him, that the more he said, the more lenient any punishment would be, he thought to himself. Bao Bao was very nervous, like an ant crawling on a hot plate. Everything seemed negative, especially if Chef Wang were to give in and offer up Bao Bao's name. Bao Bao could do little to stop this. So he could only turn to God, But to which God? Bao Bao asked himself. Yes, that is a good question. During the ten years of the new regime, there have been several campaigns organized against religions and superstitions. Gradually Mao has become the new God in the minds of millions of Chinese. Nevertheless, since Mao has rejected me in my nightmare, I have no choice but to turn to another God – a real God. But which religion? Should it be Buddhism, Hinduism, Mohammedanism, Christianity, Roman Catholicism or any of the many others that I have read about?

These days, people were not allowed to talk about God or religion because "Religion is the opium of the people", as Karl Marx had pointed out. So some people prayed to God in the dark of their private rooms, while most of them prayed in their minds. Bao Bao was born in a Catholic missionary hospital. His grandmother said, "When the Catholic priest surgeon made a sign of the cross with his fingertips in blessing, Bao Bao entered into the world, and he was baptized at birth." So Bao Bao should worship the God of the Roman Catholics and adore the Virgin Mary. This was a secret that Bao Bao kept to himself because among all the religions, Catholicism was the most notorious in Communist eyes. Catholics were constantly supporting Americans, Chiang Kai Shek and Counter-Revolutionaries, with the intention of overthrowing the Communist regime. Now that his Grandma had passed away and Bao Bao's Ma Ma was abroad, no-one could reveal the secret of his birth, so he had little to worry about. He had heard that there was a Catholic church in Shanghai; but he was not interested in finding out its location nor did he have the slightest intention of visiting the church. The church can only get me in trouble, Bao Bao warned himself. God is almighty, the creator of the universe, and he does not need to be worshipped. Everyone is a child of God and everyone is equal in his eyes. I trust God will forgive me for not going to church.

Suddenly he saw a glimmer of hope in the darkness. The worse scenario was that Bao Bao would have to assume the role of witness to denounce Chef Wang. After all, he could be classified as a victim of Chef Wang, if he were called by the authorities to serve as a witness. However, Bao Bao was certain that Chef Wang would not be so childish as to believe in the sweet words, "The more you confess, the more lenient your punishment will be". The situation isn't that bad after all. So Bao Bao comforted himself.

CHAPTER TWENTY-TWO

# SHOCKING FAMINE NEWS

Due to excessive sleep over the past few days as a result of staying at home, Bao Bao was not sleepy at night. One night he got up from bed and took a quick peek at the backyard. Outside, it was pitch dark and Yuan Yuan was sound asleep. There was no sign of any police surveillance. He quietly reached for his headphone and tuned it into his favourite channel, "The Voice of America". As usual, the Voice was interrupted by loud atmospherics. Sitting close to the radio for more than an hour, Bao Bao listened patiently to the broken sentences in Mandarin from "The Voice of America". While doing so, he was careful not to forget to look from time to time to see if there was any movement in the quiet alley underneath. The message he received was shocking, a personal attack on Chairman Mao; saying that, after Stalin's death, Mao was ambitious to become Head of the Communist Bloc. In order to achieve his goal he was exploiting the entire nation's resources to modernize China by exporting excessive foodstuffs, such as rice, wheat, soya beans, oil, eggs and pork to Russia and East Germany, in exchange for machinery. He was donating enormous amounts of agricultural products to third-world countries such as Albania, North Korea, and North Vietnam, to gain their support in nominating him as leader of the third-world countries. The agricultural products which were supposed to feed Chinese people, especially the Chinese farmers, were shipped abroad. Chinese farmers had no rice or other grains to eat. Instead they had to eat sweet potato leaves, tree bark, and wild herbs, etc. Millions of farmers were dying from starvation.

Another Mandarin broadcasting channel that Bao Bao tuned into was from Taiwan, mentioning that in some provinces the starvation has aggravated to such a disastrous situation that even cannibalism was seen. A woman cut the flesh from a corpse and ate it to fill her stomach. A married couple ate their own baby who had died a day or so previously. Bao Bao was really astounded and furious to hear such shocking news, as it was utterly unbelievable.

In his daily life, he had noticed before, that his ration had been reduced from thirty to twenty-five catties a month and it was now down to twenty catties per month. He was fortunate to share his meals with Yuan Yuan, who ate very little. Besides, Bao Bao's parents sent regularly, twice a month, parcels of canned food such as luncheon meat, ham, sausages and lard to feed the family in China, in addition to their monthly remittances of money. Bao Bao had heard about the famine in China, but he could not imagine the extent of the terrible famine in the vast rural areas, which had now become even worse.

The news of cannibalism from the Taiwan broadcast was horrifying for Bao Bao. He felt sick and his face turned as white as a sheet of paper. He doubted the reliability of the news from this enemy's broadcast. Usually he would seek verification from Chef Wang. However, he had nobody to check this information with now, and nowhere to find out the truth. He did, however, recall a remark made by the Barefoot Doctor, Wang at the moon-festival dinner-table, "The farmers are suffering from hunger and some have even died from starvation". Furthermore, didn't Uncle's relative from the countryside say something about starvation? No, Chairman Mao could not be so cruel. He loves us, especially the farmers. I hope he would not let millions of farmers die, simply to fulfill his dream of becoming the leader of the Communist Bloc. After all, Chairman Mao is from farming origins himself. He was born into a wealthy farmer's family. Millions of Chinese farmers supported him, to help him succeed in the Revolution and make him the supreme leader of the country. Mao should show his gratitude to the farmers and not kill them by starvation.

The following morning, Bao Bao left home immediately after he had taken breakfast at his neighbour's house. He could not stick to his self-imposed discipline of not going out during his period of sick leave, because this news about the farmers was far too important. He could not stop wondering whether what he had heard last night from the enemies' broadcasts was true or not. He had to find out whether millions of farmers had died or were dying due to Mao's ambition. He no longer cared about the exit visa, which Security Officer Ye might come to bring him at any time. His mind was preoccupied with finding out the truth.

He went first to the old three-story house in Yan Dang Road, where he had stolen the copper handles to build his radio and where the owner of the house had fled to Taiwan and let many of his distant relatives move in to occupy the big house.

Bao Bao went straight to the second floor where his Great-Auntie and her neighbour Kai Kai's family lived.

His Great-Auntie was in her sixties and still quite healthy and active. She had three sons and one daughter. The eldest son, Da Guai,[26] was a general physician with a small clinic in Shanghai. He was the doctor who had issued a six-month sick-leave note for Bao Bao. Her second son was Er Guai, who fled to Taiwan with the owner of the house, shortly before the Liberation of Shanghai in 1949. For nine years, there had been no mail, nor long-distance call between mother and son. It was heartbreaking for Great-Auntie to think of her second son. Nobody was more eager than the old lady to hope for reunification between mainland China and Taiwan. However, the word "reunification" could not be used in China as it offended the new regime. The proper terminology at that time was to "liberate" Taiwan under Chiang Kai Shek, as the Communists had liberated the whole of China except the island of Taiwan. His Great-Auntie's third child was a girl, Da Jie, who was now a secretary at a factory. She was the only person who lived with his Great-Auntie and who really looked after her. The youngest son was San Guai, who had become a farmer a couple of years ago. The true purpose of Bao Bao's visit to his Great-Auntie was to find out from her how his distant uncle, San Guai, was doing as a farmer and perhaps gain a true picture of the farmers' famine.

In 1955, San Guai had tried to gain admission to university but he failed miserably, due partly to his poor family background – as his second brother was in Taiwan, a sinful place – but also because of his poor academic record at a Tier Five high school. When he was rejected by the university, he did not dare to return home. He wandered for two full days on the streets of Shanghai. Finding that nobody would take him in, he had no alternative but finally to return home. His father, Bao Bao's Great-Uncle, was furious with him. The moment his father saw him, father and son had a big quarrel and San Guai left home at the age of nineteen. He saw no future for himself and was thinking of committing suicide.

In the same year, Mao promoted the idea of communes. Within a few months, about sixty percent of all farmers across the country had signed up to join one. Not surprisingly, at this point there seemed to be a shortage of experienced managers, organizers, and in particular, accountants to help with the administration. But Mao had an answer to this problem. "Where can we find accountants?" he said and then answered his own question. "We do have people. We can motivate the graduates of high schools and middle schools to do this job. The issue is that they have to be trained quickly and improve their skills on the job in the future." Speaking of future farms and communes conjured up a bright picture of Russian farms in San Guai's mind. He saw vast lands where the wheat was like a golden-coloured ocean shining under the sun. He saw gigantic mowing tractors roaming the wheat fields freely and he saw grain piled up like hills. In this picture, there were no buffaloes pulling plows through the fields and no farmers working barefoot on the wet soil of the rice fields.

After Mao's call for communes, many people from different occupations decided to devote their lives to farm-work. San Guai found many advertisements in the papers, seeking young graduates to work as accountants and as clerks for the farms. He responded to a farm in Lan Zhou. There were two reasons why he did this. Firstly, he knew that, in Lan Zhou, there were many Muslims, and so he thought that beef would be abundant there. San Guai loved beef, but in Shanghai, he had not had tasted beef for years! Secondly, he had quarrelled with his father, so this was an opportunity for him to leave home. The further he could go, the better for him. He determined never to come home again, and applied to the Head of Communes in Lan Zhou in the following terms. "Although I come from a capitalist family, I am still a good young man and I am responding to Chairman Mao's call to join a commune. So please allow me to become a farmer. I will not disappoint you," he wrote. Soon the Head of Communes replied, accepting his application to join the ranks of the farmers. San Guai bought a ticket and boarded the train to Lan Zhou. After three days and four nights of sitting in the train, he arrived at Lan Zhou.

His first impression of Lan Zhou was the brown, dusty sand and earth covering the whole city. He also saw the Yellow River, which he had heard praised so much, the great river where the Chinese race was supposed to have originated. Now he was standing on its shore, looking into the dark, muddy colour of the endless Yellow River and began to understand why their ancestors named it the "Yellow" River. The Head of the Commune took him to his living quarters. He was assigned to live in a big cave with ten other men from all over China. San Guai was curious to see people residing in all kinds of caves. A cave unit was like an apartment with one, two or three bedrooms. The advantage of a cave was that it was cool in the summer and warm in the winter. However, it was miserable inside the cave. There was no window and the air did not circulate at all. San Guai recalled that Chairman Mao was living in a cave when he started the farmers' revolution in his earlier days in Yan'an. Now to live in a cave was a privilege for San Guai and the other young newcomers to Lan Zhou, as it meant they were following in Chairman Mao's footsteps.

Soon Bao Bao arrived at Great-Auntie's place. There were two beds in her large room, one for Great-Auntie and Great-Uncle and one for her daughter. The moment Great-Auntie saw Bao Bao, she asked, "How is your health?"

"Fine, thank you, not better and not worse," Bao Bao answered indifferently.

"Are you staying home every day due to your sick leave? If there is anything your Uncle Da Guai can do for you, please tell me," said Great-Auntie. Then she asked, "How are the meals at your neighbour's place?"

"Fine," Bao Bao replied, with no interest at all. "Great-Auntie, do you have any news from Uncle San Guai in Lan Zhou?" he asked.

"Why are you asking about San Guai? Have you got any news of him, or has anything happened in Lan Zhou?" asked the old lady anxiously.

"No, no, I do not have any news from Lan Zhou. But I heard that farmers are suffering from severe starvation. Is this true? Uncle San Guai is a farmer there. Could you tell me something about his life?"

The old lady hesitated for a while. Apparently she was thinking what to say or what not to say.

Bao Bao noticed her hesitation and explained himself a little. "I just want a true picture of the life in a commune in remote China. Whatever you say to me will be kept strictly to myself. I am smart enough not to tell anyone else what you tell me. The reason for my question is my concern for my dear Third Uncle and also I am thinking that if I don't get admission to university, I may have to follow his path to become a farmer."

The old lady was pacified when she heard Bao Bao's explanation. Quickly she said, "Don't follow San Guai's path. He has made a big mistake. Now he is in a terrible situation." Tears came into her eyes as she talked. Bao Bao reached out to pat her shoulder to console her. She repeated, "Don't ever, ever follow his path to become a farmer. You know you are my favourite great-nephew. I cannot let you fall into Mao's trap like San Guai did and destroy your life!" Great-Auntie began to sob. Bao Bao was touched by her.

Suddenly Great-Auntie realized that the door of her room was open, so she stood up and went to the door. She looked left and right outside the door. Fortunately, there was nobody outside her room. She closed the door and walked back to her chair and continued her conversation with Bao Bao. "San Guai is a problem child, a so-called black sheep in our family. As a child he did not like to study, therefore, he went to a Tier Five school. After he graduated, he could not get into any university, nor could he find a job. So in desperation, he believed in Communist propaganda, that a wonderful bright future for him lay within a farm. So he felt that to become a farmer was a good response to Chairman Mao's call."

"How is his life in Lan Zhou?" Bao Bao asked.

"His life as a farmer is miserable," Great-Auntie replied. "The moment he arrived in Lan Zhou, he found that things were completely different from what Communist propaganda promised. He was put into a dormitory inside a cave with no toilet. They had to do their things in the open air or in the bushes. Showers are unknown to the farmers, who take baths only once or a few times each year. They eat in the commune's canteens. San Guai likes beef but he has never tasted beef in Lan Zhou! In the canteens, they serve rice mixed with tree leaves and roots, just to fill their stomachs. At night, San Guai cannot sleep because of hunger and he suffers from constipation all the time. We asked him to come back, but it is impossible because his Hu Kou Bu – his registration – was transferred to Lan Zhou."

"Can't his Hu Kou Bu be transferred back to Shanghai?" asked Bao Bao.

"No, in no way can his Hu Kou Bu come back to Shanghai. In order to solve the problem of over-population in the cities, the regime only transfers Hu Kou Bu out of Shanghai and never lets people come back," answered Great-Auntie.

"How is Uncle San Guai's health?" asked Bao Bao.

"Poor, very poor. Due to malnutrition, his body is swollen, which is a common phenomenon among people there, due to lack of food," said Great-Auntie.

"How much is his Ding Liang – his fixed ration – for food?"

"His ration for food has gone down from fifteen to ten catties per month. For this reason, we – Da Guai, Da Jie and I – save ten catties a month for San Guai. Every month I exchange a local ration coupon to a national coupon for ten catties to be mailed to San Guai, who wrote to us that, without our help, he would die."

Bao Bao felt it was unfair that he himself, as a student, received twenty catties, whereas his uncle got only ten on a farm where he had to do hard physical work. "It is too bad that he gets so little rice at the farm," he said and added, "I doubt Uncle San Guai could use your ration coupon because, according to Chairman Mao, they all eat together in the canteen at the communes. There is no private kitchen where Uncle San Guai could cook a meal for himself."

"You are absolutely right," said Great-Auntie. "But perhaps he could use the national ration coupon in exchange for something to eat, such as mantou. Anyway, he wrote to us that these ration coupons have saved his life."

"Do you know how many farmers are suffering from hunger? And how many have died?" pressed Bao Bao.

"I am sure all farmers are suffering from hunger. You have just seen that our own fixed ration – our Ding Liang – has been reduced. I can't tell you exactly how many farmers have died from hunger. This is not what a commoner at our level should know. As I have heard, many have been dying from starvation. Every night, I pray to Buddha that San Guai will not die."

While Great-Auntie was talking, Bao Bao asked himself, Shall I mention cannibalism? ... No, no, I should not scare her. She should not know about such a horrible thing. If I mentioned it, she would insist that I tell her the source of this horrifying information. This would only create a problem for me! Perhaps I should change the subject. Should I tell her – a sympathetic and thoughtful lady just like my own Ma Ma – that I am applying for an exit visa to join my parents in Hong Kong?

No, no, he answered himself. I'd better not. My suspicion is that it is better to keep it secret, otherwise I may not succeed. Great-Auntie is nice, but how about the people around her? What would Da Jie and Da Guai think of it? Would they think that I am taking advantage of the six-month sick leave? But if I don't say anything, and then I do get an exit visa tomorrow, she might think that I am an ungrateful person. No, no, Great-Auntie is so kind and she loves me so much, as much as she would love her own grand-child. She will be happy if I can get out of here. Now, let me keep my fingers crossed and I will come back to say goodbye to her in a few days if I am lucky.

Upon leaving, Bao Bao said a few words to console his Great-Auntie. "Don't worry too much! I am sure my Third Uncle will be fine in the end." Bao Bao did not know what more to say. He really could not think of any nice words to make his Great-Auntie happy. He was angry that he was unable to ascertain the truth or otherwise of the enemy broadcast, that many millions of Chinese farmers had died of starvation. Later on Bao Bao found an answer to his own question. I cannot know the number right now, as farmers are continuing to die. A few years hence, everybody will know it as history, and we will have an accurate number of the victims. Now one thing is for sure and this is that all the farmers are suffering from starvation. Why? Why is Chairman Mao doing this to his own people? Is he out of his mind? Bao Bao was furious.

After a while Bao Bao cooled down and he gave himself another explanation. Chairman Mao is not aware of the desperate situation throughout China. He is surrounded by high-ranking officials who try to please him and flatter him. So he may still erroneously believe in the great success of his Great Leap Forward Campaign. He may believe that steel and grain products have increased many times and that, even after exporting immense quantities of food abroad, there is still abundant food left for domestic consumption. Yes, Chairman Mao has travelled extensively in his private train to many places in the country on tours of inspection. Everywhere he is surrounded by loyal subordinates who love him so much that they report only good news to him and hide from him the grim cruel but true picture of destitute China.

Nevertheless, everywhere that he visits, Mao is greeted and welcomed by at least a few hundred healthy males and females of different ages and from all social classes, including cheerful children, wearing red scarves and with colourful paper flowers in their hands. Perhaps the same welcoming group arrives by train or by aeroplane at each place he visits, one or two days, or just a few hours, before Mao's private train pulls in.

CHAPTER 23

# SISTER YUAN YUAN

As soon as the piano lesson was over, Bao Bao rushed out to meet and to greet the new piano tutor, Comrade Lu. Lu was a tall man, about six foot tall or more. He wore a blue Mao suit and a pair of glasses with transparent plastic frames. Bao Bao had read Lu's resume. He was a graduate of the Shanghai Music Institute and had recently been accepted by the Shanghai Symphony Orchestra as assistant concert pianist. The moment Lu stepped out of the door, Bao Bao asked Yuan Yuan, "How was the lesson?"

"Excellent. I really liked him. He is by far the best teacher I have ever had."

"How much does he charge?" asked Bao Bao.

"Two yuan per lesson or eight yuan per month."

"So keep him."

"But he is too expensive. We cannot afford so much."

"Yes we can," Bao Bao tried to convince her. "Ma Ma remits forty-two yuan to us every month. We pay twenty yuan for our three meals and less than ten yuan for rent, electricity and water bills and we have, on average, twelve yuan left. So to pay eight yuan a month to Lu is affordable. Why do you say that we cannot afford it?"

"I think it is an awful lot of money to pay for a piano tutor."

"I don't think so," replied Bao Bao. "Just imagine! One day you may become a famous pianist. Who would think then about this small amont of money? Just consider it as an investment."

"I am comparing him to my previous tutor, whom we paid only four yuan a month. Lu wants double that amount. Maybe he thinks that we two live in a big house and our parents are in Hong Kong. He may consider us capitalists and want to exploit us."

"Yuan Yuan, you are really funny. We are told that only capitalists exploit people. How come you say capitalists are being exploited? Your political conscience is questionable. If Lu wants a few yuan more, then just let him have it. He has better qualifications. The main thing is that he has to do a good job. I hope to see the fast progress of your piano skills within a short space of time."

"Ge, you are really treating me well. I shall work very hard to learn more pieces to play for you." Yuan Yuan was extremely happy.

"Yuan Yuan, you know, these days I have been preoccupied by the thought that I will have to leave you if my visa is eventually granted. I would really hate to do that, but on the other hand, it would be an enormous pity if I don't leave. I really don't know what to do. If I don't get the exit visa, this wouldn't be a problem."

She immediately replied, "You should go to our parents, because you are so sick. Don't worry about me. I shall be alright. I shall go to school and eat at our neighbour's place. Life will be the same as before. I will survive. Don't worry!"

Bao Bao was sad and restless. He repeated, "I really hate to leave you alone."

"Don't worry, Ge, I shall be okay," Yuan Yuan reassured Bao Bao.

"I have an idea! What do you think if we invite our Younger Uncle, our father's youngest cousin – the one who is working at the shipyard in Pu Dong – to move in to stay with you? Our Younger Uncle is in his late thirties and still a bachelor. If he comes, we will give him the noisy living-room and you can stay in our bedroom facing the courtyard. I shall put a lock on the door for you. At night, you can lock your door."

Yuan Yuan looked at him with surprise and said, "How did you come to have such a brilliant idea? We see him only once a year during the Chinese New Year when he comes to distribute Li Shi – red envelopes. But I guess he is after all not a bad man."

"I can't think of any other relative who is single, and I don't want a whole family to move in to our place. Once they move in, they will never move out. If one day our Ma Ma comes back, then we three would have to squeeze into one room. Ma Ma would blame me. I cannot make such a mistake."

"Have you asked Third Uncle?" asked Yuan Yuan.

"No, it is too early because I haven't received my visa yet. If you have no objection, I shall call him at work and invite him over to have a talk. I am not like Ma Ma, to ask him to move in by writing a letter." Then Bao Bao added, "I think it's a good idea to ask him to move in to our big place. You just mentioned that Lu saw our big apartment. I do worry that, after my departure, the neighbourhood committee might send another family to share our apartment, because they might not tolerate a small girl living in a spacious two-bedroom flat alone. According to the living standard after the Liberation, our two-room flat should be shared by two families and each family should consist of four to five people."

"But I wouldn't let anybody move in. My argument would be that my Ma Ma and Ge will come back soon," said Yuan Yuan.

"Yes, I know you would do it. But you can never manage to handle these men, nor can I. First they will try to convince you. Then, if you don't agree, they will just move in by force, promising that they will move out when your Ma Ma and Ge come back. Their promise will mean nothing! Once they move in they will never, never move out! That's for sure! Now with our uncle here, he will fight against them. The best argument not to let another family move in is that you and Younger Uncle cannot share one room! With this argument they can do nothing, absolutely nothing! That's our trump card and we will be safe."

Yuan Yuan admired Bao Bao's cleverness and thoughtfulness and said, "I have no problem about living with our Younger Uncle. You are always so smart. Do what you think is best for our family and please go ahead to install a lock on my bedroom door."

"Any news about your exit visa?" All of a sudden, Yuan Yuan thought about this and then added, "I know you are restless because Officer Ye was supposed to deliver it to you a few days ago. So far there is no news. Do you want me to go the Public Security Bureau to ask for it for you?"

There was no reply from Bao Bao for a minute, because he was contemplating.

"Why don't you answer me?" Yuan Yuan asked again.

"No, don't go to the PSB, it's an unsympathetic place, where Ma Ma has shed many tears. Let me wait a couple of days and if it is really necessary I'll go to the PSB myself." This is what Bao Bao said, but in his mind he was very anxious to get his visa, because waiting was like hell to him.

Soon Yuan Yuan went back to practising her piano and Bao Bao continued to read Shakespeare to distract himself.

~~~

"Pang, Pang, Pang!" Bao Bao heard a noise at the door. Who can be here to visit at such an early hour? he wondered. He quickly got up and opened the door. It was Security Officer Ye, from the PSB. Bao Bao did not believe his eyes. He asked himself, "Is this real or is it another dream?" He squeezed his leg to see if he could feel pain. "Yes, this time it's real."

He dared not say "Good morning," to Security Officer Ye, because greetings like, "Good morning, Good afternoon, Have a nice day", belonged to the tradition of the bourgeoisie. Without speaking, he led Officer Ye into the living-room. He asked him if he could offer him a cup of tea or water.

"No."

Officer Ye opened his briefcase and handed over a most precious document – Bao Bao's exit visa. This exit visa would enable him to leave China legally. Bao Bao was overjoyed, yet he put on an expressionless face. Bao Bao took the visa from the officer. Again he was not allowed to say, "Thank you", for the same reason. The visa was a small folded piece of paper, twelve by fifteen centimetres in size, a light green colour with black Chinese characters splattered across it, and containing the bright red round chop of the Shanghai Security Bureau. Bao Bao unfolded the visa with shaking fingers. Inside was his photo; the date of his birth; the place of his birth, a validity statement and date. Officer Ye opened his mouth this time, "The visa is valid for return within six months. If you need to stay longer you can extend it in our Foreign Affairs Office in Hong Kong upon presentation of a new doctor's certificate. One thing you must bear in mind," he emphasized, "You should never, ever, say anything bad about our country.

"There is nothing bad I can say," Bao Bao replied immediately. "I am very grateful for the care our new regime has given me. Everything I say about our country will be good. Trust me."

Officer Ye added, "You should never repeat anything that you hear in China, such as the farmers' lack of food, the fact that we have to use ration-coupons for meat, oil, clothes and material for clothes, etc. These are national secrets, which cannot be revealed to outsiders in Hong Kong."

"Yes, I swear I will not say anything about our Great Motherland." Bao Bao assured Officer Ye of this, repeatedly.

As soon as Officer Ye left, Bao Bao jumped up and down, shouting, "I've made it! I've made it! I must let Ma Ma know that it was easy for me to get a visa. I didn't even have to visit the Public Security Bureau, not even once! Bao Bao took another look at the visa. It said that the bearer could leave China within thirty days from the date of issue, but Bao Bao thought he should leave as soon as possible.

Now Bao Bao was debating whether or not he should leave the day after tomorrow or three days later. It all depended on how many things he had to settle and how many people he had to say "goodbye" to. In any case, he would buy the train ticket tomorrow.

Now the first and most important thing was to call Younger Uncle to come over and then ask him to move in. If he could not move in, it would be difficult for Bao Bao to leave, as he could not leave Yuan Yuan behind, all alone. He also wanted to notify a few schoolmates about his impending departure. What about Dan Dan? Bao Bao wondered what he should do about her. Finally, he came to a conclusion. No, I'd better not see her any more! If I see her, it might jeopardize her father's plan for her. According to her father, she should follow her relative Li Li's path to marry a son of a Communist Officer to enjoy a wealthy life. If I see her, Dan Dan might promise to wait for me until I return. It would not be fair for her to wait indefinitely. And also it is good for me not to have unnecessary pressure to become rich and famous quickly. As a matter of fact, I don't know what I am getting into. My life might be miserable in the capitalist society that I am heading to.

Upon hearing that Bao Bao was going to Hong Kong, Younger Uncle rushed over to visit them the same evening. With no hesitation, he agreed to move in during the next few days, to live with Yuan Yuan. Soon after Younger Uncle left, Bao Bao asked Yuan Yuan again, "Are you sure that I can leave you alone?"

"No problem, Ge. You see I manage my life well without you. In fact I need no help from you. Now that Younger Uncle is moving over here, I will not be alone. As long as I am not alone, I am fine. Go to join our parents and make a rapid recovery in your health!" So Yuan Yuan reassured her brother.

The next morning, Bao Bao went to say "goodbye" to Great-Auntie, who was shocked to learn that Bao Bao was leaving and was on his way to the train station to buy his ticket.

"How come you did not mention it to me before? How did you manage to get a visa so quickly?" the old lady questioned him.

"I did not know it myself. Yuan Yuan went to the Headmaster of my school to get my long sick leave and the sympathetic Headmaster and Party Secretary offered me the chance to leave Shanghai and join my parents because there is nobody to look after me here," Bao Bao answered.

"When do you leave?"

"Tomorrow evening?"

"Why so soon?"

"Yes, I know it is soon. But I think the sooner I am with my parents, the better it will be for my sickness." This is what Bao Bao said, but in fact he was afraid of Officer Ye, who could come back and withdraw his visa if he discovered anything wrong.

"Now do me a favour, take a letter from me for Er Guai in Taiwan and mail it in Hong Kong."

"Certainly, I will do anything for you."

"I shall deliver the letter to you tomorrow morning," said Great-Auntie and she gave Bao Bao a big hug. Bao Bao saw her eyes were full of tears.

When Bao Bao walked out of her room he heard her sobbing. Is Great-Auntie happy for me or is she sad that she will not see me any more? Bao Bao asked himself. When I come back with a Nobel Prize she will no longer be around. Bao Bao turned his head round, to give her a quick final look and walked slowly down the staircase with a melancholy feeling.

In the afternoon, Wu came to see Bao Bao at home. Wu held Bao Bao's hand tightly and said, "You made it. I really cannot believe it! Congratulations, anyway. Tell me, how did you do it?"

"I'm sick, so kind Party Secretary Huang is letting me join my parents in Hong Kong," replied Bao Bao.

"Ha-ha, how can a healthy person like you suddenly become sick? Tell me what kind of trick you employed to fool the authorities?"

Bao Bao did not like his friend questioning him and thought, "There is no way I can tell him the truth. First of all, I'm still in China. They can take back my exit visa easily. Secondly my sister, Yuan Yuan, is still here, so the authorities could give her a hard time if they find out that I have been dishonest with them. However, if I insist that I am sick, nobody can challenge me!"

So Bao Bao replied with confidence, "I really am sick. The People's Hospital has written me a diagnosis. Do you want to take a look?" As Bao Bao spoke, he pulled out the doctor's note from his drawer and handed it over to Wu.

As Wu read it, his face became serious and he said, "Wah! You really have high blood pressure and heart disease!"

Then Wu said, "Bao Bao, do you think you will ever come back? If I were you, I would never come back to this awful place! Here, even if you are successful, it doesn't mean a thing! This place belongs to the offspring of a handful of Communist leaders only. You have no chance here, no matter how great you are! My father is a good example for you to remember. Whenever you think of coming back, think of my poor father."

Bao Bao was touched by Wu's sincere warning, but he did not want to attack the Party, so he answered, "Wu, my mind is really confused these days. Perhaps I should concentrate on my sickness and when I get rid of it I will see what to do with my life. We should keep in touch and I will let you know my progress and you let me know what's going on at school."

"Sure, we can communicate by letter. How long does it take to mail a letter to Hong Kong?" asked Wu.

"If only distance is considered, three to four days by surface or one to two days by airmail. But in reality it takes fourteen days or longer," Bao Bao answered.

"Why so long?" asked Wu curiously.

"My friend told me that every overseas mail is read and checked to ensure that there is no leak of our 'national secrets,'" Bao Bao answered.

"What is considered to be a 'national secret'? wondered Wu. "Do we, ordinary people, know any 'national secrets'?"

"Yes, we do. Things like writing Da Zi Baos, killing sparrows, fighting against Rightists, the Great Leap Forward, communes and farmers' starvation, these are all considered to be national secrets."

"How do they check the mail?" Wu questioned him further.

"They have a special machine that opens the envelopes by adding humidity that dissolves the glue or rice paste. After checking the contents, they seal the envelopes again, and make the opening invisible," replied Bao Bao.

"How do you know?" asked Wu.

"My friend told me." Bao Bao did not want to mention Chef Wang to Wu and continued, "So be careful of what you write. I don't want you to get into trouble because of our correspondence, as happened in the well-known case of the famous writer Hu Feng."

"Yes, I remember Hu Feng, the poor literary intellectual, who was denounced by his correspondence with his friends and associates."

"I always feel sorry for writers who are denounced and thrown into gaol. I have a great deal of sympathy for them," said Bao Bao.

"Now you will soon be in a good position, able to speak and write whatever you want. As for us, we still have to be extremely careful," Wu said.

"By the way, is there any news from your father?" Bao Bao asked.

"Yes, we finally got a letter from him. The letter was hand-carried by someone who came back from the remote Northwest. We are comforted that he is still alive. As long as he is alive we have a glimmer of hope that we will meet again one day," said Wu.

"What is his life there like?" wondered Bao Bao.

"Miserable, absolutely miserable! He had nothing to eat and nothing to wear in the cold winter and as an intellectual, he was forced to do ten hours of manual work and four hours studying Mao and Marx's works daily. My Ma Ma gave the messenger, his friend, some warm clothes and some national ration coupons for him to take back to my father. I also enclosed a letter from myself."

"What did you write?" Bao Bao was curious.

"First of all, I let him know that we are fine and we miss him every day. And then, I encouraged him to put up with the suffering – for the end of this darkness is the beginning of light. He has to survive darkness in order to see twilight and sunrise. Of course in the letter I could not mention that the sunrise means the end of Mao's rule in China, but I believe my Father will understand it," said Wu.

"Of course you should not say such a thing! Are you crazy? If you say that, they will execute you. You should be extremely careful!" said Bao Bao without any hesitation.

"Now about the letters you write to me," he continued. "You must be careful what you write in these, as well! I reiterate that I don't want to see you get into trouble. I have seen too many sad cases in the past years. That's enough for me for the rest of my life! Now I cannot afford to lose you, dear Wu, my dear friend and friend forever," said Bao Bao and his eyes dimmed with tears.

Wu held onto Bao Bao's arms tightly for a while and left sadly as if they would never see each other again.

CHAPTER TWENTY-FOUR

# FAREWELL TO FRIENDS AND RELATIVES

After dinner, Yuan Yuan started to play the piano. She practiced one of her favourites that night, Beethoven's Moonlight Sonata. Sure, she was sad. To play the piano was a way to escape from the reality that her dear brother, Bao Bao, was to leave the following day. Bao Bao also avoided speaking to her. What he wanted to say to Yuan Yuan had all been said. To repeatedly rake over the same topics would eventually cause both brother and sister to feel more upset. Bao Bao knew that the best thing for him to do was to leave Yuan Yuan for a while. Perhaps he could say goodbye to other friends or relatives. He wished Chef Wang was still at home, so that he could just run over to say goodbye with a sense of pride in his achievement. However, he did not want to go too far. Leaving Yuan Yuan all alone for their very last night together was something he would never do. In other words, he wanted to go away from Yuan Yuan and yet remain close to her physically at the same time.

Finally he chose to say goodbye to his neighbour, Dr Sun, a general physician who lived on the fourth floor of the same apartment building. Dr Sun was in his late fifties, living with his wife and two sons. Bao Bao chose to say farewell to Dr Sun because he would still be in close vicinity to Yuan Yuan and also because doctors, like intellectuals, would do no harm to Bao Bao.

"Hello, Bao Bao, we have not seen you for a long time. How are you? Have you had dinner?" Mrs Sun said while she opened the door.

"Yes I have, thank you."

"We heard that you and your sister take your meals at your neighbour's place. How is the food?" asked Mrs Sun.

"The food is so-so. What can we expect these days?"

"You must have something to tell us. What can we do for you?" Mrs Sun asked in a straightforward manner. Though they lived in the same building, Bao Bao had not visited them for at least a year. Bao Bao used to play with Dr Sun's younger son, but since they went to different high schools, they had a different circle of friends.

261

"I just came to say 'goodbye' because I shall be leaving for Hong Kong tomorrow."

Mrs Sun's eyes shot wide open. She screamed so loudly in the house that everyone could hear, "BAO BAO IS GOING TO HONG KONG TOMORROW!" Her husband Dr Sun, and their two sons all came running into the living-room. They all gazed at Bao Bao admiringly. And in a second, the house fell silent.

"Nobody is allowed to leave China these days. How come they are letting you go to Hong Kong?" It was Dr Sun who broke the silence.

"Because I'm sick. My school Headmaster said I should go to my parents who will look after me," Bao Bao answered full of pride.

"What is your sickness?" wondered Dr Sun.

"I have high blood pressure."

"How old are you?"

"I am sixteen."

"It is impossible to have high blood pressure at your age," Dr Sun said and took out his blood pressure measuring gear and proceeded to measure Bao Bao's blood pressure.

Bao Bao wanted to escape, but it was impossible to run away. So he tried to make himself as nervous as possible in the hope that his blood pressure would rise according to the information retained from the medical book in the big book store. Unfortunately, it did not work this time. Dr Sun said, "See, you have no high blood pressure, as I said!"

This made Bao Bao nervous and he added quickly, "I also have heart disease as shown by a diagnosis from the People's Hospital."

Bao Bao felt embarrassed and stood up to leave. Mrs Sun came with him to the door and said, "Say hello to your Ma Ma for us."

"Thank you, thank you, Auntie Sun," Bao Bao said and left.

Outside, on the staircase down to his own apartment, Bao Bao hit his chest with his fists and blamed himself, How stupid I was to say farewell to Dr Sun. I have successfully stayed away from doctors so far. Why did I seek trouble tonight? Bao Bao continued to blame himself. Why didn't I insist that I do have high blood pressure? I should have lied to Dr Sun that I had just taken some pills to keep my blood pressure low. Why was I so stupid! Why? Why?

His thoughts raced. If anyone in Dr Sun's family were to denounce me tomorrow, I would be finished! Even if I was on the train, they could still catch me as long as I am on Chinese territory. One telegram to the border station and they could detain me there and stop me from crossing the border. I would be sent back to Shanghai for interrogation and then they would put me in gaol, as Chairman Mao did to me in my nightmare. Dr Sun's family member would get credit for this and become a hero, like one of the many new heroes in our society these days.

Now, what shall I do? Bao Bao asked himself. Nothing, there is nothing that I can do, except pray to God, to the real God! concluded Bao Bao.

Upon returning home, he found that Yuan Yuan was still playing the piano. Her back was facing Bao Bao and she was hunched over the piano, looking down at the keyboard. After a while Bao Bao went to his own room and got into bed. The question about whether Dr Sun or his family would denounce him had made him restless. Finally Bao Bao consoled himself with the following thought, Dr Sun is after all an intellectual. Intellectuals should help intellectuals during this extremely difficult time.

The next day Yuan Yuan had a half day absence from school because her brother was leaving. She had asked for a whole day's absence, but the school authorities had granted her a half day absence only, as the class discussion in the morning on "the crimes of American Imperialism" was compulsory for everyone. So, in the morning, Bao Bao went by himself to say goodbye to his relatives. When they heard the unexpected news that Bao Bao was leaving in the evening, everybody was shocked and said similar things. "How come you could get an exit visa?" "Why didn't you tell us before you submitted the application?" "Who is going to look after Yuan Yuan now?" Some relatives even expressed dissatisfaction, and others even cursed the Communist regime in the presence of Bao Bao. "Don't ever come back. The world outside must be hundred times better than here. At least they have food to eat."

"Mao is wrong to isolate us from the rest of the world and to tell us that people live very poorly and miserably in other countries. In reality, we are the ones who are poor and miserable. You are fortunate that you will be able to see it with your own eyes."

"You know, those excessive campaigns were Mao's and the Party's dirty tricks to make us so occupied and preoccupied that we had no time to think. We were dragged along blindly, made to follow the Party like animals."

"It is said that Mao, as a penalty to himself for his mistakes in the Great Leap Forward, refrains now from eating stewed pork, which previously he ate at every meal. Why is his penalty so mild, when millions of farmers are dying because of his silly mistake?"

Bao Bao was very surprised suddenly to hear so many unexpected complaints from his relatives. Why have they never expressed such complaints to me before? he wondered. Soon he found an answer for himself. We are all suffering from living under Mao's rule, but no-one dares say anything, not even during the "Let a Hundred Flowers Bloom" period when Mao invited us to speak out. Now, knowing Bao Bao was leaving China in a few hours' time, they could unload their complaints to Bao Bao, who would not have time to denounce them. That was for sure.

Bao Bao thought, After the Anti-Rightist Campaign, about half a million intellectuals were removed to the barren Northwest. Those remaining are "good people", totally obedient to Chairman Mao. Now unexpectedly he had heard so much dissatisfaction coming from the "good people", that he could hardly believe his ears. If it was not for his impending departure, he would never have heard so many complaints – complaints from deep in the hearts of the "good people". Now he started to ask himself, What has Mao done to China? Is he really the saviour of the Chinese people, as praised in the famous song, 'The East is Red'? Why does he run the country so poorly that we don't have enough food in the cities and the farmers are dying of starvation? He certainly deserves credit for fighting against Chiang Kai Shek and establishing New China, but why did he invent so many campaigns to destroy our private lives? Will his objective of converting six hundred million Chinese into Dr Bethunes eventually be achieved? We do not have enough food now for our present population. What will happen if our population doubles in ten to fifteen years as a result of discontinuing birth control as Mao wishes? One question after another came into Bao Bao's mind and he had no answers to them.

Bao Bao walked for some time, absentmindedly. He was obsessed with the question, Why do so many good and respectable people dislike Mao? Suddenly, he became aware of his surroundings and asked himself, Where am I? This is not the way home! Without any conscious decision on his part, he was in fact walking towards Dan Dan's home! – In fact, since leaving Dan Dan a little abruptly, he had felt uncomfortable, from time to time. Sometimes he had asked himself, Did I behave correctly towards a young girl who loves me? For the past few days he had been debating in his mind whether he should see her to say good-bye. Now he made a decision. Yes, I should say good-bye to her, otherwise I might regret it for the rest of my life, because once I leave this place, I shall not come back again.

"Dan Dan," Bao Bao shouted loudly underneath her house. – He was not timid this time, because he thought he did not belong to this society any more. – Dan Dan came down right away and Bao Bao followed her back up the old staircase. Bao Bao saw in her hair the green-coloured plastic hairpin he had given her and was deeply touched. She must think of me all the time! he thought. It is good that I have come to see her before I leave.

As soon as they entered her home, Bao Bao said, with a loud and proud voice, "I am going to Hong Kong this evening."

"No, it's impossible! My Pa Pa said that no young man, including you, would be allowed to go to capitalist Hong Kong. Only some old people over sixty are allowed to go there."

"Your Pa Pa is wrong!" Bao Bao raised his voice when he uttered the word "wrong".

To prove what he said, Bao Bao pulled out from his inner pocket his valuable Exit Visa. Dan Dan looked at the green-coloured exit visa with amazement.

Then Bao Bao embraced her tightly. His cheek touched her cheek. He could smell the pleasant scent of her skin and body. (He was to remember this for many years.) Then, abruptly, Bao Bao turned away from her and ran swiftly down the staircase. He did not want to hear Dan Dan make any commitment to wait for his return.

In Hong Kong later, in a film from a capitalist country, Bao Bao saw a boy kissing a girl and he regretted then that he did not try it out with Dan Dan before he left her.

At noon, Yuan Yuan came home. After a quick lunch at their neighbour's place, the brother and sister went out to shop for a gift for their parents. They took the street-car along Huai Hai Road and then switched to a bus heading for the busiest shopping street, Nanjing Road. Yuan Yuan suggested buying a piece of art work for their parents. They went into the Arts and Crafts store. But they could not find any nice piece of art work there. All "art works" were finished coarsely in the spirit of the new regime: it was not allowed to put too much effort and time into making such useless bourgeois items. "How about a traditional Chinese jacket or gown for Ma Ma?" Bao Bao suggested. The pair of siblings walked into a clothing shop, but they found no silk jacket nor gown there; only the popular Mao suits and jackets in blue, grey or green. However, when Bao Bao looked more closely at the purchase arrangements, he realized that people had to hand over their ration coupons for a cotton jacket – money alone was not enough. "It's such an ugly garment anyway. Who will wear such a thing in Hong Kong? Let's not waste our time here!" urged Bao Bao as he and Yuan Yuan came out of the shop and went into a confectionary store.

The biscuits looked stale and old in the window pane. They did not look the slightest bit fresh, and what's more, they needed ration coupons for these ugly biscuits as well! The candies were not as shiny and colourful as Bao Bao had remembered. "What can we buy to take to our parents?" became a huge problem for them. They walked and walked. They saw that most stores were empty and had no goods inside.

By chance, they walked by a food store where a few people were queuing up. "What are they buying?" Bao Bao and Yuan Yuan wondered curiously. Soon they found out that the people were buying melons from Xinjiang Province. Bao Bao turned to Yuan Yuan and said, "How about buying a big melon for our parents?" "Good idea!" Yuan Yuan replied. "It's better than taking nothing." So they bought a big melon weighing more than four pounds. The siblings felt very happy as their mission had been accomplished. Nevertheless, in the late afternoon their Younger Uncle came to see Bao Bao off and said, "How stupid of you to take such a heavy melon to Hong Kong! Don't you know that all our good things are exported to Hong Kong and other countries in exchange for hard currency? I am sure that such melons will be cheaper and even better in Hong Kong."

Bao Bao replied, "We are not stupid. We really cannot find anything else for our parents. If you can think of something for me to take, we can go and buy it. We still have time to shop. The train does not leave for a few hours." To this challenge, their uncle was speechless. Bao Bao added, "If we can buy something else, I will leave this melon here for you. In fact, I hate to carry such a heavy melon on such a long trip." But their Younger Uncle just stood there speechless, looking at Bao Bao with wide eyes.

At the crowded train station, it was a scene of Sheng Li Si Bie (Farewell in life is as sad as separation by death). Yuan Yuan sobbed very loudly and Bao Bao also cried. Their Younger Uncle's eyes welled up with tears at the painful sight of the siblings clutching each other affectionately and sadly. Only now did Bao Bao begin to realize how dependant Yuan Yuan was on him. Now he felt extremely sorry to leave her behind. He blamed himself and said to himself that he shouldn't do it. In order to punish himself, he said to Yuan Yuan, "Don't cry! I can change my mind and not go now! I will cancel my trip and go back home to stay with you." As he said this, Bao Bao thought, If I decide against leaving China now and return my visa to the PSB, I will be praised by the Party. If I do not do this, I may never get rid of the guilty feeling that I pretended to be sick in order to leave China. This guilty feeling will hover over me for the rest of my life, even on the day when I receive the Nobel Prize.

"No, no, you cannot do this," Yuan Yuan shouted inbetween her hiccups and sobs. "You should go to our parents and they will take good care of you." Bao Bao could tell that she was making a huge effort now to suppress her crying.

Their Younger Uncle became nervous and said, "Bao Bao, you cannot change your mind at the last minute. You should go. I will take good care of Yuan Yuan! Don't worry! You know it is a one in a million chance that you have got a visa! Getting a visa is even more difficult than winning a lottery!" Then he told Bao Bao, "Get into your compartment now. The train will leave at any minute!"

"Ge, you must get on the train!" exclaimed Yuan Yuan. "I'll manage to get a visa soon so that our family can be reunited in Hong Kong. If you don't go now, we two will never be able to get our visas at the same time and our family will never be reunited!"

Bao Bao thought for a little while about what Yuan Yuan had said and answered, "True, what you said is very true. We have to do it one by one. I did not realize you have grown to be so clever now."

On the bustling and noisy platform, Bao Bao was confused by all the advice given him by Yuan Yuan and his uncle. Yuan Yuan gave him a big hug, holding him tightly for a long time, until their uncle patted his shoulder, telling him to board the train. There was no more time to indulge his guilty feeling. He stepped reluctantly onto the train and turned to give Yuan Yuan and his Younger Uncle a final look. At this moment he saw Dan Dan among the crowd about fifteen metres away. Bao Bao rushed down out of the train and ran towards her.

"How long have you been at the station?" asked Bao Bao.

"You told me that you were leaving Shanghai this evening. My friends told me that the only way to leave Shanghai is by train to Guangzhou. Since I did not know what time train you would catch, I came here this afternoon. For the past three hours, I have been searching for you among the crowd. My eyes are dizzy now."

Bao Bao was deeply moved. He wanted to hold her tightly, but Yuan Yan and the Younger Uncle were urging him to re-board the train. He restrained his burning desire, as he did not want to show Yuan Yuan and his Younger Uncle that he had a girlfriend at such a young age.

As soon as he got back on the train, he stuck his head out of the train-window. He had said everything to Yuan Yuan already and had successfully avoided making any commitment to Dan Dan. Now he just wanted to look at them silently as long as he could. As soon as Bao Bao's eyes met his sister's once again, he felt warm tears pouring from his eyes. He could not help it.

Neither could Yuan Yuan and Dan Dan. They wailed at the thought of seeing Bao Bao for the last time. The Younger Uncle witnessed their sorrowful parting and began to cry too. Bao Bao felt nothing was worse than Sheng Li Si Bie. Bao Bao had not felt so emotionally disturbed when his Pa Pa and his Ma Ma left him. Perhaps Bao Bao was too young or perhaps he was not as involved with them as with Yuan Yuan and Dan Dan.

Suddenly, the train's horn blasted and the train itself began to rumble. The churning sound it made, at first faint, soon became louder and louder. The train began to pick up momentum and leave the platform. Bao Bao felt his heart drop a few hundred metres. His head spun loudly and his body trembled uncontrollably as he saw Yuan Yuan grow smaller and smaller in the distance until she disappeared from his sight. At this moment, Bao Bao thought back to when his Pa Pa had left the family a few years ago. Bao Bao, still a child, had gone to the train station with his Ma Ma, sister, and brothers, to see Pa Pa off. Ma Ma and all the children were crying. But his father did not cry. Instead his face turned red, bright red. Bao Bao did not know if his own face also turned red when the train pulled out, as he had no mirror to see himself with. Perhaps his face did turn red as both his face and his neck felt warm.

CHAPTER TWENTY-FIVE

# JOURNEY TO FREEDOM

Bao Bao started to look for his seat. He had bought a hard berth on the second level of the compartment. He had chosen the upper berth because it was quieter and he did not mind climbing up and down.

Today was another big day in his life and he had said farewell to many relatives. For the first time, he felt that Yuan Yuan was very close and very dependent on him. He regretted that he had not spent enough time with her when they lived together, especially since he did not walk with her to and from school every day before Uncle and Auntie's departure.

All of a sudden he realized that, not only was he feeling sad and guilty, but he was completely worn out. He needed some sleep, and he needed it immediately. He soon fell asleep in his upper berth as the train kept moving on. At twilight Bao Bao woke up. "Where am I?!" he asked himself. Last night, he had been exhausted and he had fallen asleep right away. This morning, the vibration of the moving train made him feel as though he was a baby, lying comfortably in his Ma Ma's cradle. Soon he realized that he was on the train. It's my first train ride and I like it! He was glad that he had two nights and one full day to spend in the train.

In Mao's China, there were no trips for ordinary people, no vacations, no holidays. School had sometimes organized small trips to work voluntarily on the farm or at a factory in the suburbs, but getting there was mostly by bus or by foot. So it was not unusual for a sixteen-year-old teenager never to have experienced a train ride.

Lying sleepily on the upper berth, Bao Bao looked back out of the window. In the faint half-light, he saw that the train was running over a bridge and he saw a huge body of water underneath. This must be the Yangzi River, the biggest river in China! Bao Bao thought. He was fascinated. He had read much about this famous river. He could not believe that, now, he was on it. Bao Bao conjured up in his mind a vision of the new Yangzi River Bridge in the faint distance, which was to be completed in two years time, and which would connect the North and the South in the east part of China. Bao Bao continued to speculate. I must be in Nanjing now. What a marvelous city! Formerly it was Chiang Kai Shek's capital! When I come back to China one day, I must not forget to visit Nanjing. Bao Bao thought back to his school, to the time when he learnt, in Teacher Ma's class, that, "The Nanjing Yangzi River Bridge will be entirely designed and built by Chinese engineers. When completed in a few years' time, the bridge will be a two-tiered road and rail design spanning 4,600 metres on the upper deck, with about 1,580 metres spanning the river itself." Bao Bao was proud of this future achievement. Now he felt that Mao had done the right thing in treating the scientists and engineers well and never struggling against them. Praise was always given to the Communist Party and Chairman Mao for the fast progress that China was making, but he realized that, behind the scenes, the contributions of intelligent and diligent scientists and engineers were significant.

A few minutes later, Bao Bao climbed down groggily from the upper berth, left his compartment for the corridor, and walked towards a window there. "Is this the Yangzi River?" he asked a train attendant.

"No," came the reply. "This is Qian Tong River."

This made Bao Bao wake up more fully. He had been thinking of Nanjing, to the west of Shanghai, but he was traveling south!

Bao Bao had been told that the train ride would be interesting because it stopped in many provinces and cities, which he knew only from his geography classes. He had also heard that everywhere farmers would bring their local specialties to the railway stations in an attempt to sell them to passengers. The train passed through a vast expanse of agricultural land. No small plots of land could be seen, since the commune had combined the small plots into huge pieces of land. In the autumn, the wheat would turn into a golden colour like the ocean shining under a blazing sun as their Third Uncle, San Guai, had once imagined. Even so, there was no tractor ploughing the land, no grains piled up like hills. Farmers still worked with their hands, barefoot, in the fields, relying on their buffaloes to pull the heavy ploughs. Bao Bao asked himself a question. "When will big farming machines be used on the farms?" "Probably not any time soon," he immediately answered himself. "We have an excess of human beings. How would people be occupied, if we used big farming machines instead of people to work on the farms?"

His thoughts moved to the question of China's population. It was frightening to think of the consequences, if the Chinese population began to expand rapidly again. Bao Bao found that Mao's directions were paradoxical. On one hand he urged China's modernization and on the other hand, he promoted the expansion of China's population. Bao Bao worried about China. What would China look like if we had double our present population and at the same time there was no increase in agricultural land? He thought further. There is no way we can increase our agricultural land unless we invade other counties, as Japan invaded us. Perhaps this will be another big mistake of Mao if he doesn't stop the population expansion. We cannot count on an atomic war to kill half of the world's population as Mao mentioned.

But his thoughts were interrupted. The loud-speaker announced, "Next stop, Hangzhou!" This name was familiar to every Chinese because of its beautiful scenery. But for Bao Bao the famous "beggar's chicken" [27] of Hangzhou was more interesting than its beautiful West Lake! Many years ago, one of his relatives journeyed to Shanghai from Hangzhou by train. He bought several of the famous Hangzhou beggar's chickens. He gave one to Bao Bao's Ma Ma and told her that the farmers sold the warm, freshly-baked chickens through the train windows to the train passengers. Bao Bao was excited at the thought that soon the train would stop and he could buy a chicken himself. Chicken had become a delicacy during the time of famine. The last time he had tasted chicken was about three months ago during the Moon Festival. Thinking of the delicious Hangzhou baked chicken made his mouth water.

Soon the train pulled in at Hangzhou Station. Bao Bao was too impatient to wait at the window, but stepped down from the train to go to try to buy a beggar's chicken. The moment he touched the cement surface of the platform, he realized that he had been very naïve. I'm so stupid! How could I think that there would be baked chicken? The farmers are short of grain. What can they feed the chickens with? He climbed back on the train empty-handed and disappointed.

A couple of stops later the train pulled into Jin Hua, the place famous throughout China for Jin Hua Hams. It would not be a bad idea if he could buy a piece of Jin Hua ham for his parents. He stepped down from the train in order to buy some ham. But there was no ham, only beggars begging for money or food from passengers on the platform. A young beggar of about ten years old, dressed in filthy, thin rags, told Bao Bao that he had not eaten anything for two days. Out of sympathy Bao Bao gave him one yuan. Immediately Bao Bao was surrounded by twenty to thirty beggars who begged from Bao Bao and then robbed him. The few yuan in Bao Bao's pockets disappeared. Swiftly Bao Bao forced his way through them and climbed back into the train. Fortunately his money for the trip was safe as he had sewed it, together with his exit visa, into the inside pocket of his jacket and others could not possibly get at it.

Bao Bao was depressed. He climbed up onto his berth and lay down there, quietly. Gradually his heartbeat became normal again. He was very sad. Not because the beggars had attacked him and robbed him of a few yuan, but because of the overall situation in China. Jin Hua is situated south of the Yangzi River, where the land is most fertile and fish are abundant in the lakes. For thousands of years it had enjoyed fame as, "a village of fishes and rice" – "yu mi zhi xiang".

Now Bao Bao saw with his own eyes that the farmers were indeed suffering from severe starvation. He sighed and said to himself, Chairman Mao, what did you do to China, especially to Chinese farmers? When we talk of you, we automatically think of you as the supreme leader who has established the New China; we unanimously agree that you are the saviour of the Chinese people. But all the time you have been using Chinese farmers to fight for you to make you the new "emperor" of China; and in return, what have you given them? You have given them hunger, starvation and communes in the place of homes. Bao Bao's thoughts travelled from yesterday's farewell with his relatives, where he incidentally discovered that so many "good people" were, deep in their hearts, against Mao, to the article by Ke Pei

Chi, the courageous lecturer at Beijing University, who wrote, "When the Communist Party took over the city of Shanghai in 1949, they were welcomed by the people. Now the people have turned against the regime."

How is it possible to turn against the regime? wondered Bao Bao. For he knew what Mao had said: "Power comes from the barrel of a gun".

Without arms and with zero mobility, farmers can do nothing, but wait to die from starvation. As for the brave lecturer, Ke, he has been executed, or is in gaol or the barren Northwest, if he has been lucky. Bao Bao was sad that there was nothing he personally could do to change the situation of his country. His thoughts went further. Actually the Chinese people are very easy to handle. Our obedience to the emperors for more than four thousand years shows this clearly.

But you have to provide the people with their basic needs, with food! Bao Bao emphasized to himself. Why has Mao failed to do this? Bao Bao asked himself. Is Mao a good leader or just another tyrant, like the many there have been in Chinese history?

After much contemplation, Bao Bao concluded, Mao is a great politician, a philosopher, a poet, a writer and a strategist. Unfortunately he is also a dreamer. It would be much better if he had not led the county, and had not been involved in planning. The leaders around him, such as Zhou En Lai, Liu Shaoqi, Deng Xiao Ping are much more capable to lead the country. This is what Bao Bao thought and this is what millions of Chinese also thought. But who dared to tell Mao this?

In the early morning, the train pulled in at Guangzhou Station, and this was the end of Bao Bao's train ride. He knew from a geography lesson that Guangzhou is the biggest city in Southern China. He had never imagined that he would have the chance to see it so soon in his life. Bao Bao was really excited. The train stopped. All the passengers were rushing to get their baggage and disembark. But Bao Bao remained sitting underneath his berth, watching his fellow passengers hurrying forwards. He took it easy, as he was not expected by anyone at the station and his boat for Macau was not scheduled to leave until night. He had a full day to kill in Guangzhou. On the one hand, he wished he could get an immediate connection for his onward trip, so he wouldn't have the headache of how to spend the day in a strange city with his big suitcase. But on the other hand, he thought that he should avail himself of this unique opportunity to take a look at this interesting city, as he might not come back again to Guangzhou.

Once the last passenger had disembarked, Bao Bao grabbed his suitcase and stepped down from the train. The station was so grand, so crowded, and so noisy with people coming from all over China, that Bao Bao did not know what to do and where to go. Then he decided that first, he should walk out of the station and find a place to leave his big suitcase. Soon he found a small hotel nearby. Walking in, he asked if he could leave his luggage there until the evening. The girl at the reception counter could not understand what Bao Bao said in his Shanghai dialect and replied in the local Cantonese dialect, which Bao Bao could not understand, not even one single word. Bao Bao was perplexed. But soon he asked her, "Do you speak Mandarin, the official Chinese language?" The girl nodded and said, "What can I do for you?" Bao Bao smiled when he heard Mandarin spoken, though the girl did not speak Mandarin well. Bao Bao presumed that she had learned it only recently. Now Bao Bao felt grateful to the Communist Party, for unifying the spoken languages of China and simplifying the complicated written characters of the Chinese language. Some of the characters containing twenty to thirty strokes had been reduced to five or six strokes. This would speed up the writing as well as the learning of the Chinese language. However, the side-effect might be harmful to the morality of society as Chinese people might tend to look for a simpler way doing everything in their life and work. In the other words, they might do things in a "ma ma hu hu" – casual and so so – manner, as human thought is influenced by the language people use. Bao Bao hoped that he was wrong.

After the Liberation, the Party had made great efforts to force everybody in China to speak the same language, Mandarin. Because China is such a huge country, there are several hundreds of dialects. Some provinces like Fujian have over a hundred dialects in that one province alone. Only the Party's iron hand made it possible to change China into a one-language country. Now Bao Bao took advantage of this accomplishment of the

275

Party and communicated freely with the girl from Southern China.

Bao Bao told her, "My boat to Macau leaves at eight tonight", and he asked, "Can I store my luggage here at your hotel?"

"No."

Bao Bao did not want to take "No" for an answer and asked another question, "I'll pay you for the storage. How much do you want?"

The girl said, "This is a hotel, not a baggage storage place."

"What am I to do now?" Bao Bao asked. "I want to get rid of my suitcase and see the city."

"Take your suitcase with you and leave the hotel or get a room in our hotel!" Apparently the girl was getting impatient.

Bao Bao realized that he did not have much choice and asked, "How much is a room? I want the smallest and cheapest room, just to store my suitcase."

"The cheapest room is five yuan a day."

"That is a lot of money," Bao Bao thought and explained, "I just need it to put my suitcase in until this evening. I will not sleep in the room."

"In that case you can take a day room. It's two yuan fifty. But you have to return the room to us by six this evening," said the girl.

"Can you make it a little bit cheaper?" Bao Bao tried to bargain with her.

"No. This is a hotel. Our prices are fixed."

Bao Bao had no choice and paid her two fifty. "That was a big rip-off!" Bao Bao complained to himself. But he soon overcame his unhappiness. "I should not let this small unpleasant matter ruin my day," he thought. "The great city of Guangzhou is waiting for me outside, under gorgeous sunshine!" Bao Bao took out a small map of Guangzhou and started his private sightseeing tour right from outside the hotel.

First Bao Bao went to visit the famous Yue Xiu Park. Inside the park, he walked up the hill, discovering that all the steps leading to the hill were built of grave-stones. How many graves has the new regime destroyed in order to build this long flight of steps! he thought. On each of the grave-stones one could read the details of the previous occupant of the grave.

Bao Bao discovered a small street where every shop was dedicated to the eating business. To his amazement he saw many cages with live animals in them, including cats, dogs, snakes, wild pigs, wild chickens, pangolins, hedgehogs and other wild animals, whose names were unknown to Bao Bao. Bao Bao found it appalling that people in southern China could eat such animals, something that the majority of Chinese people, including Shanghai inhabitants, would not even think of doing. On the other hand, Bao Bao was glad that, during severe shortages of food such as at present, people in Guangzhou could still enjoy such delicacies. Of course, one had to pay a huge price for them. For sure they were not meant for the man on the street in Guangzhou. These poor animals were mainly for tourists from Hong Kong and Macau and government officials to enjoy.

After a few hours of walking in the big city, Bao Bao felt tired. Although the city of Guangzhou had a big name in Southern China and a big population, to Bao Bao it was not impressive, nor attractive. Bao Bao saw only old houses, old buildings, and dirty and noisy streets. Apparently Guangzhou was like Shanghai. People in the past decade, here also, had been occupied with Chairman Mao's campaigns, while the construction of new buildings, new housing quarters, schools, hospitals had been totally neglected.

Bao Bao recalled that, in class, Teacher Feng had talked about Shamian Dao or Shamian Island at the southern tip of Guangzhou, a small island of only 0.3 square kilometres in size. In the nineteenth century it was divided into two Foreign Concessions, given by the government of the Qing Dynasty, one to France and one to the United Kingdom. Since Bao Bao was curious about western culture, he thought to himself, Why don't I pay a quick visit to Shamian Dao? Perhaps I can find some relics of colonial times. So Bao Bao got on a bus for Shamian.

In Shamian Island he found a quite different atmosphere. The island was isolated from the hustle and bustle of Guangzhou city. It was very quiet. The streets were flanked by tall, green French plane trees. He saw many historic buildings, but all lacked maintenance. They looked terrible; old, dirty and abandoned. Among the relics, the French Catholic Church, "Our Lady of Lourdes", was the most outstanding, but it needed restoration badly.

Bao Bao stood at the entrance of the church and wondered whether to enter or not. It would be quite safe for him if he went into a Catholic church as nobody would pay attention to him. Here he would not be denounced for his association with the notorious Catholic Church.

After much hesitation Bao Bao walked in and looked around. Everything inside the church was new to him, as he had never been in a church in his life. He was unaware that, as a Catholic by birth, he had to make a sign of the cross and kneel down and pray. Nor did he know that the Virgin Mary's statue stood just in front of him. The church was quiet. Only a few old ladies in black dresses were praying inside. For Bao Bao it was something special, as if he were in a fairyland. He could not describe his curiosity toward such novelty.

Bao Bao came out onto the streets again. Guangzhou was much warmer than Shanghai. Even in winter under the sunshine it must be close to twenty degrees centigrade. At a road junction, he came across a wooden street sign pointing in different directions: "Shamian North Road, Shamian South Road, Shamian 1 Street...." Bao Bao had no doubt that the street names had been changed after Liberation. He also noticed that many old mansions had been converted into government offices and churches turned into factories.

The boat to Macau was scheduled for departure at eight o'clock. However, at half past five Bao Bao went back to the hotel to get his suitcase. He paid the receptionist two and a half yuan and complained that it had been a very expensive way to store one piece of luggage. Later he found out, to his annoyance, that there was a luggage storage facility inside the railway-station, where it cost only a quarter yuan to store one piece of luggage for twenty-four hours. What could he say? Why didn't the girl at the hotel reception desk tell me this? Why didn't I ask at the station the moment I got off the train? Oh well, that's life! Bao Bao had to pay a price to gain experience in travelling. He made up his mind not to be upset and to let bygones be bygones. I have had a nice day in Guangzhou, which is a priceless experience. The ugly parts of the journey, such as unnecessary payment, I'll soon forget. So Bao Bao consoled himself.

Bao Bao was supposed to join his family in Hong Kong, so why did he take a boat to Macau, which with Hong Kong and Guangzhou formed a delta on the estuary of the Pearl River? Certainly, Bao Bao was going to Hong Kong. But with the short notice of only a few days, it was impossible for Bao Bao's father in Hong Kong to obtain an entry visa for him so soon. Certainly British law stipulated that children had the right to live with their parents and the British consulate was obliged by law to issue an entry visa for Bao Bao. However, the processing time to issue an entry visa was one month. Because of this and in order to see Bao Bao as soon as possible, his father had asked him to go to Macau first and wait there for a visa to enter Hong Kong.

At a quarter to eight Bao Bao boarded an old motorized boat for Macau. It was about thirty-five metres long, with a double deck. There were no cabins, and no berths; only reclining seats. The boat was quite empty. There were only about thirty passengers, even though the boat's full capacity was over one hundred seats. Bao Bao glanced at the passengers. They were all women in their sixties or older. He was the only young man among them all, and stood out in the crowd. He felt shy and uncomfortable among so many older people. He experienced the sudden fear that it was impossible for a young man like himself to leave China, even legally. He warned himself, Don't be so optimistic that you can leave China! You haven't passed the frontier yet. Wait until tomorrow morning! Sitting down on a reclining chair, Bao Bao took out his book of Shakespeare's works. But the light in the lounge was too dim to read by. And in fact he was too tired to do any reading. After a full day's hectic sightseeing, he was exhausted. Soon he fell asleep on the chair.

What time is it now? Bao Bao woke up suddenly on his reclining chair. It was pitch dark outside. Bao Bao walked to the toilet and saw a round clock hanging on the middle of the wall in the upper-deck lounge. It was about five o'clock. Another three hours to go, said Bao Bao to himself. I should get some more sleep, so that my parents will see me in good shape. He tried to doze off, but in a while he woke up again, because he was again bothered by the thought of his future. Bao Bao recalled vividly a conversation with Chef Wang.

"Can you tell me what you know about Hong Kong? Perhaps one day I may join my parents," Bao Bao had said once to Chef Wang, knowing that he was from Guangdong province where Hong Kong was located.

"Hong Kong is a terrible place," Chef Wang had answered. "I have relatives there and they have told me everything about it. Over four million inhabitants squeeze into about eleven hundred square kilometres consisting of Hong Kong, Kowloon Peninsula, and the New Territories, an area about one sixth the size of Shanghai. After the Opium War in 1842, the British brought their law to rule Chinese people there."

"How is life in Hong Kong? Bao Bao had asked.

"Terrible for the poor people, and heavenly for a few rich people and for the British rulers. The poor people are extremely poor. The rickshaws on the streets of Hong Kong illustrate how the rich exploit the poor."

"How about the chance of going to university there?" asked Bao Bao.

"No chance for you, because you are a newcomer. Your schooling in China will not be recognized. Besides the text-books are all in English. They learn English from kindergarten, whereas you have learned very little English, or even no English at all, at school," answered Chef Wang.

"If I cannot study in Hong Kong, can I study abroad?" Bao Bao was anxious to know the answer.

"Don't dream of it, my son. It's the privilege of those from very rich families to study abroad."

Bao Bao disagreed and argued, "I have heard that many great people have worked their way up through their college education."

"This is very difficult to do nowadays. The famous universities like Harvard and Yale do not give scholarships to foreign students unless you are the son or daughter of a minister in your country, or you can make a great contribution to the USA. Without a scholarship, you have to pay enormous school fees there. Even if you have the money, it doesn't mean that they will take you. Admission is absolutely impossible for you. Don't dream of it, my son. You are wasting your time." This was what Chef Wang had said, discouragingly. Then he added, "Bao Bao, you are a good teenager. Your problem is that you think too much and worry too much. You should take it easy, as most things are beyond your control. When you get older, you will agree with what I say now."

Chef Wang paused for ten seconds and added further, "In this world – I have to say it again – if you are born with a silver spoon in the mouth, you have everything. If not, you will have nothing! We always blame the notorious capitalist societies because rich people hand over their fortune to their own children. In reality, Communist society does the same. First of all, our regime says that you cannot be granted admission to university because of your poor family background. Then, to those from a hundred percent proletarian family background, the regime says, 'Do what your father did and carry on your father's glory.' This means if a father is a farmer or a worker, the son should inherit the virtue of being a farmer or a worker. Eventually university admissions, leadership positions and fortune all go silently to the children of Communist leaders."

Once again, as then, young Bao Bao was dominated by fear for the future. He could think of no answers to what Chef Wang had said, and all he could say to himself was, I'll see what I can do about my future in Hong Kong. Once again Bao Bao was convinced that his decision about his relationship with his girlfriend Dan Dan was correct. However, deep in his heart, Bao Bao missed her very much. How nice the world would be if Dan Dan were accompanying him on his trip to Hong Kong!

Bao Bao went out of the lounge. It was cold and windy. In the darkness of twilight, he could see nothing. He heard the sound of the river water being propelled by the motor as the boat moved forward. The cold wind fluttered against his cheeks and his head. Bao Bao thought this must be the darkest moment before the sunrise. He raised his head. Looking at the sky, he could see a line of faint light. This signalled the break of day. Suddenly a new idea occurred to him. What would happen to China if Chairman Mao died now?

The hypothetical question of Chairman Mao's dying excited Bao Bao immensely. If Mao dies today, Liu Shaoqi, Zhou En Lai and Deng Xiao Ping would run the country. The first task the new leaders would perform would be to stop exporting excessive food abroad. Farmers' lives would be saved; they would be liberated from the communes; and family life would be resumed. The farmers would have the incentive to work on their plots of land. There would be abundant food in the markets. The new leaders would immediately introduce birth control to reduce the birth rate. They would let younger leaders replace the old in the Central Committee. They would let many writers and Rightists, such as Hu Feng, come out of gaol. Bao Bao's favourite writer, Ding Ling, would no longer sweep the streets and do the work of a cleaning lady. Instead, she would return to the position of Vice-Chairman of the Writers' Association and write more good books. Many young people would follow her thinking and attempt to write a book. The new leaders would gradually open up China to the world, allow more students study abroad, and welcome foreign investors to invest in China. Soon we would see many new buildings, new dwelling quarters, new theatres, new schools, new golf-courses, and new stadiums emerging on Chinese soil. There would be no more idiotic campaigns, no more struggle meetings to take away people's time. Every Chinese would be entitled to get a passport to travel abroad. There would be no more disturbances, no more police surveillance against listening to broadcasts of "The Voice of America." The Hu Kou Bu registration system would be abolished and so would ration coupons. Family background would no longer be a criterion for university admission. Students would concentrate on their studies and be spared from joining crazy political campaigns which forced students out of their classrooms. Bao Bao would not need to rack his brains and waste his valuable time to find a way to leave his own country. He would go back to Shanghai to live with his beloved sister Yuan Yuan and go to the cinema with Dan Dan again. Their parents could come to visit them, or live with them, as they wished.

What a wonderful world! Bao Bao thought. As Bao Bao came back to reality, he realized that he had absolutely no idea how long Chairman Mao would live. Mao is now sixty-five, he thought. Bao Bao compared Mao with the previous emperors of

China. According to Chinese history the average life of the emperors was forty-nine.

Sixty was the official retirement age for Chinese males. Will Mao retire now and set a good example for future leaders in China, like George Washington did for America? Bao Bao wondered. But he recalled what Auntie had said to Uncle; that Mao would never step down. This was the same question that Bao Bao had asked Teacher Feng and to which he never got an answer. Millions of Chinese were concerned about this, as it was a matter of life and death for China. Chairman Mao has built the country and now he is destroying it to satisfy his egoistic ambition, Bao Bao thought and sighed.

The sun came out of the east in the darkness and started to rise slowly. In an hour, Bao Bao would arrive in Macau. Bao Bao went back to the lounge and bought himself some steamed bread (mantou) for breakfast. Even on the boat he had to pay for it with money as well as with the national ration coupon. Bao Bao left the lounge and watched the sunbeams shining on the endless Pearl River. He sighed and said, How big my country is! In the past two days he had seen much of his vast Motherland. China is such a big country that, although I have traveled two days by train, I have passed through only a quarter of it. In such an immense country, my role can only be that of a tiny cog. It's unfair to me!

Thinking of a tiny cog reminded him of the song he used to sing when he was a boy. This made Bao Bao furious. He clenched his fist and said aloud, "No. Chairman Mao. I won't go for it! It's not fair to me. Would you have agreed to be a tiny cog when you were a youngster like me? I don't think so! You have achieved a great deal because you had ambition. Why won't you let me seek to fulfill my ambition too?"

Now came the most crucial moment in Bao Bao's life. He was queuing up to pass the frontier. He saw the sixty-year old women passing through, one by one, without any problems, but he was nervous, and thought, But I am a young man, the only young man in a group of older people. How shall I answer if the officer asks me any questions? His heart beat fast and faster. He felt that perhaps his cheeks and his neck were turning rosy. He kept telling himself, Be calm and take it easy! Everything will be fine.

He started to pray under his breath to the real God, "God, let me pass the border. My parents are outside waiting anxiously for me. I promise that I shall go to church every Sunday in Hong Kong. There I will not be watched, nor denounced". He kept on repeating the same prayer, "God, please help me", until his turn came.

He stepped forward and handed his exit visa to the officer in green uniform. He tried to control himself, not to show the officer that he was extremely nervous and his hands were shaking. The young officer looked at the document carefully and raised his head to check whether Bao Bao was identical to the person shown in the photo. Then he took the chop, stamped it on the visa, and handed it back to Bao Bao, who stood there dumbfounded. The officer said, "You can go now." Bao Bao realized that he could leave China now. So simple! Bao Bao thought, as he walked forward. It's unbelievable! He really wanted to jump and exclaim aloud to the world, "I've made it, I've made it!" But he suppressed his triumph and excitement. He walked at his usual pace to leave China silently.

Outside the gate, his Pa Pa and Ma Ma were waiting. Bao Bao was wearing a black sweatshirt and a pair of black trousers. He wanted to declare to the outside world that he had nothing to do with the grey, green and blue Mao jacket any more. He ran quickly towards his Ma Ma, hugged her tightly and said to her with tears in his eyes, "My exit visa was delivered to me and I did not visit the Public Security Bureau even once! You see how lucky I was!" His Ma Ma sobbed from happiness. His Pa Pa was so excited that his face turned rosy to see his eldest son, Bao Bao, who was now as tall as he was. The last time he saw Bao Bao was when he himself left China, when Bao Bao was still a child. Bao Bao said to his parents, "I won't return to China unless Mao is gone, or unless I go back as a famous scientist with a Nobel Prize!"

NOTES

[1] Also called Big Character Poster, written in big characters in Chinese calligraphy to be mounted on the wall about two meters up from the ground for pedestrians or other members of the public to read on the street, or on a designated notice-board at school, factory or work unit. The size was usually a minimum of half a newspaper page to a full page. The content was usually a protest, an expression of opinion, or an announcement, or Communist propaganda.

[2] The Chinese Communist Party, founded in July 1921. After defeating Chiang Kai-Shek's Kuomintang regime, the Communist Party became the ruling party of Mainland China, beginning from 1 October 1949.

[3] Mao Ze-Dong (1893-1976), leader of the Chinese Communist Party, who led the Chinese peasants' revolution from 1927 until he established the People's Republic of China in 1949. He later endeavoured to transform China from an agrarian country to a world power in too hasty and damaging steps. However, he is still respected as China's supreme leader and founder of the PRC (People's Republic of China).

[4] Mahjong is a Chinese game played by four people with approximately 144 tiles made from wood, bone, bamboo, or ivory. Four players are involved and the objective of the game is to collect winning sets of tiles.

[5] The forerunner of the Chinese Communist Army, or the People's Liberation Army, the world's largest military force. The insignia of the Red Army is a roundel with a red star.

[6] The supreme leader of the Kuomintang, the ruling party of the Nationalist Government of the Republic of China beginning in 1928. He later retreated to Taiwan after being defeated by the Communists in 1949 and served as the President of the Republic of China in Taiwan until he died in 1975.

[7] Chiang Kai Shek led the Nationalists against the Communist forces and was driven from the Mainland to Taiwan in 1949.

[8] A famous Chinese liquor, distilled from fermented sorghum containing up to 53% alcohol. Maotai is an expensive liquor frequently served at state banquets.

[9] One of the highest grades of Chinese green tea.

[10] A Chinese Communist force and forerunner of today's People's Liberation Army.

[11] A mountain in China's Shandong Province, about 1,520 metres high. It has great historical significance.

[12] The First Five-Year Plan (1953-57) and The Second Five-Year Plan (1958-1962), each followed the Soviet Union's model, and aimed at

building up China's heavy industry and accelerating China's growth the emphasis on heavy industry and agricultural output.

[13] A Communist youth organization originating in the Soviet Union for children from six to fourteen years old. A Youth Pioneer can be by the red scarf worn round the neck. After they reach fifteen years of teenagers gradually leave the youth pioneer organisation and are ready join the Communist Youth League.

[14] "Liberation" was widely used in the fifties, to mean the takeover of China by the Communists in 1949, "liberating" six hundred million Chinese people from the oppression of the Chiang Kai-Sek regime.

[15] Kow-tow: to kneel and touch the forehead to the ground, to express regret, respect, submission, or worship, in Chinese tradition.

[16] The Kinmen (Quemoy) and Matsu island groups, situated in the Taiwan Strait.

[17] These cakes are made of wheat, and are twice the size of a pancake. Sometimes they are covered with sesame seeds,

[18] The state visit to Beijing and Shanghai made by Indonesian President Sukarno actually took place in October 1956. This novel places it at a different date.

[19] Thomas Robert Malthus (1766-1834) pointed out the dangers of an uncontrolled increase of population.

[20] Political party founded by Sun Yat-Sen in 1911. Its dominance in China lasted from 1928 to 1949 under the leadership of Chiang Kai-shek. It later became the official ruling party of Taiwan.

[21] Mandarin, the official Chinese language.

[22] By Hungarian poet, Sándor Petöfe (1823-1849).

[23] Fu Ts'ong's father, Fu Lei, a famous translator, was labelled a Rightist in 1957. In 1966, at the beginning of the Cultural Revolution, he committed suicide with his wife.

[24] Eldest Sister.

[25] Elder Brother.

[26] In Fujian Province, parents address a child, using the term "Guai", which means, "obedient, filial and well-behaved". "Da Guai" means "the oldest good son", "Er Guai" means "the second good son" and "San Guai" means "the third good son".

[27] A famous dish served in big restaurants in China. The chicken is wrapped in clay (or, nowadays, in kitchen foil) and then baked. Its origin is said to be as follows. Once a hungry beggar stole a chicken in the country-side, but had nowhere to cook it. He lit a fire, wrapped the chicken in mud, and placed it in the fire. After cooking, it tasted delicious!

## ABOUT PROVERSE HONG KONG

Proverse Hong Kong is based in Hong Kong with expanding long-term regional and international connections.

Proverse has published novels, novellas, fictionalized autobiography, non-fiction (including biography, history, memoirs, sport, travel narratives), single-author poetry collections, children's, teens / young adult and academic books. Other interests include diaries, and academic works in the humanities, social sciences, cultural studies, linguistics and education. Some Proverse books have accompanying audio texts. Some are translated into Chinese.

Proverse welcomes authors who have a story to tell, wisdom, perceptions or information to convey, a person they want to memorialize, a neglect they want to remedy, a record they want to correct, a strong interest that they want to share, skills they want to teach, and who consciously seek to make a contribution to society in an informative, interesting and well-written way. Proverse works with texts by non-native-speaker writers of English as well as by native English-speaking writers.

The name, "Proverse", combines the words "prose" and "verse" and is pronounced accordingly.

# THE PROVERSE PRIZE

The Proverse Prize, an annual international competition for an unpublished book-length work of fiction, non-fiction, or poetry, was established in January 2008. Unusually for a competition of this nature, it is open without restriction of nationality, residence or citizenship to all who are at least eighteen on the date they sign the entry form.

The objectives of the Proverse Prize are: to encourage excellence and / or excellence and usefulness in publishable written work in the English Language, which can, in varying degrees, "delight and instruct". Entries are invited from anywhere in the world. Long-listed writers to date include writers born or resident in Andorra, Australia, Canada, Denmark, Germany, Hong Kong, New Zealand, Nigeria, Singapore, Taiwan, The Bahamas, the PRC, the United Arab Emirates, the United Kingdom, the USA.

**Summary Terms and Conditions**
(for indication only & subject to revision)

The information below is for guidance only. Please refer to the year-specific Proverse Prize Entry Form & Terms & Conditions, which are uploaded, no later than 30 April each year, onto the Proverse Hong Kong website: <www.proversepublishing.com>.

The free Proverse e-Newsletter includes ongoing information about the Proverse Prize. To be put on the eNewsletter mailing-list, email:
info@proversepublishing.com with your request.

**The Prize**
1) Publication by Proverse Hong Kong, with
2) Cash prize of HKD10,000 (HKD7.80 = approx. US$1.00)

Supplementary publication grants may be made to selected other entrants for publication by Proverse Hong Kong.

Depending on the quality of the work in any year, the prize may be shared by at most two entrants or withheld, as recommended by the judges.

In 2017, the entry fee was: HKD320.00 OR GBP35.00.

Writers are eligible, who are at least eighteen on the date they sign The Proverse Prize entry documents. There is no nationality or residence restriction.

Each submitted work must be an unpublished publishable single-author work of non-fiction, fiction or poetry, the original work of the entrant, and submitted in the English language. School textbooks are ineligible.

Unpublished first translations into English (including those already published in the writer's mother tongue) submitted by the author are welcome. The submitted work will not be judged as a translation but as an original work.

Extent of the Manuscript: within the range of what is usual for the genre of the work submitted. However, it is advisable that novellas be in the range 30,000 to 45,000 words); other fiction (e.g. novels, short-story collections) and non-fiction (e.g. autobiographies, biographies, diaries, letters, memoirs, essay collections, etc.) should be in the range, 75,000 to 100,000 words. Poetry / poetry collections should be in the range, 5,000 to 25,000 words. Other word-counts and mixed-genre submissions are not ruled out.

Writers may choose, if they wish, to obtain the services of an Editor in presenting their work, and should acknowledge this help and the nature and extent of this help in the Entry Form.

## PREVIOUS WINNERS OF THE PROVERSE PRIZE

Rebecca Tomasis, for her novel, "Mishpacha – Family"
Laura Solomon, for her young adult novella, "Instant Messages"
Gillian Jones, for her novel, "A Misted Mirror"
David Diskin, for his novel, "The Village in the Mountains"
Peter Gregoire, for his novel, "Article 109"
Sophronia Liu, for her collection of sketches, "A Shimmering Sea"
Birgit Linder, for her illustrated poetry collection, "Shadows in Deferment"
James McCarthy, for his biography, "The Diplomat of Kashgar"
Philip Chatting, for "The Snow Bridge and Other Stories"
Celia Claase, for her essay and poetry collection, "The Layers Between"
Lawrence Gray, for his novel, "Adam's Franchise"
Gustav Preller, for his novel, "Curveball: Life never comes at you straight"

## PREVIOUS WINNERS OF SUPPLEMENTARY PRIZES

Victor E. Apps, for his young adult novella, "The Perilous Passage of Princess Petunia Peasant"
Rupert Kwan Yun Chan, for his autobiography, "Chocolate's Brown Study in the Bag"
Sally Dellow, for her poetry collection, "Wonder, Lust & Itchy Feet"
Patricia Glinton-Meicholas, for her poetry collection, "Chasing Light"
Lawrence Gray, for his collection of short stories, "Odds and Sods"
Patricia W. Grey, for her novel, "Death has a Thousand Doors"
Emily Ho, for her "Memoirs of an Ice-Cream Lady"
Henrik Hoeg, for his poetry collection, "Irreverent Poems for Pretentious People"

L.W. Illsley, for his young adult epic poem, "Astra and Sebastian"
Akin Jeje, for "Smoked Pearl: Poems of Hong Kong and Beyond"
Lelawattee Manoo-Rahming, for "Immortelle and Bhandaaraa Poems"
James Norcliffe, for his poetry collection, "Shadow Play"
Jan Pearson, for her novel, "Red Bird Summer"
Jan Pearson, for her novel, "Tiger Autumn"
Jan Pearson, for her novel, "Black Tortoise Winter"
Jason S Polley, for his poetry collection, "refrain"
Jason S Polley, for "cemetery miss you"
Shahilla Shariff, for her poetry collection, "Life-Lines"
Laura Solomon, for her young adult novella, "University Days"
Laura Solomon, for her novel, "Hilary and David"
James Tam, for his novel, "Man's Last Song"
Dennis Wong, for his novel, "Revenge From Beyond"

## NOVELS, SHORT STORY COLLECTIONS
## AND OTHER FICTION
### Published by Proverse Hong Kong

**A Misted Mirror**, by Gillian Jones. 2011.

**A Painted Moment**, by Jennifer Ching. 2010.

**Adam's Franchise**, by Lawrence Gray. 2016.

**Beyond Brightness**, by Sanja Särman. 2016.

**An Imitation of Life**, by Laura Solomon. 2013.

**Article 109**, by Peter Gregoire. 2012.

**Bao Bao's Odyssey: from Mao's Shanghai to Capitalist Hong Kong**, by Paul Ting. 2012.

**Black Tortoise Winter**, by Jan Pearson. 2016.

**Bright Lights and White Nights**, by Andrew Carter. 2015.

**cemetery miss you**, by Jason S Polley. 2011.

**Cop Show Heaven**, by Lawrence Gray. 2015.

**Curveball**, by Gustav Preller. 2016.

**Death has a Thousand Doors**, by Patricia Grey. 2011.

**HK Hollow**, by Dragoş Ilca, 2017.

**Hilary and David**, by Laura Solomon. 2011.

**Instant Messages**, by Laura Solomon. 2010.

**Man's Last Song**, by James Tam. 2013.

**Mila the Magician**, by Zhang Jian 章简. 2013. (English / Chinese bilingual)

**Mishpacha – Family**, by Rebecca Tomasis. 2010.
**Odds and Sods**, by Lawrence Gray. 2013.

**Paranoia (the Walk and Talk with Angela)**, by Caleb Kavon. 2012.

**Revenge from Beyond**, by Dennis Wong. 2011.

**The Day They Came**, by Gérard Louis Breissan. 2012.

**The Devil You know**, by Peter Gregoire. 2014.

**The Monkey in Me: Confusion, Love and Hope under a Chinese Sky**, by Caleb Kavon. 2009.

**The Monkey in Me**, by Caleb Kavon. Translated by Chapman Chen. 2010. E-book. 2010. (Chinese)

**The Perilous Passage of Princess Petunia Peasant**, by Victor Edward Apps. 2014.

**Red Bird Summer**, by Jan Pearson. 2014.

**The Reluctant Terrorist: in Search of the Jizo**, by Caleb Kavon. 2011.

**The Shingle Bar Sea Monster and Other Stories**, by Laura Solomon. 2012.

**The Snow Bridge and other Stories**, by Philip Chatting. Scheduled 2015.

**The Village in the Mountains**, by David Diskin. 2012.

**Tiger Autumn**, by Jan Pearson. 2015.

**Tightrope! A Bohemian Tale**, by Olga Walló. Translated from Czech by Johanna Pokorny, Veronika Revická & others. 2010.

**Tightrope! A Bohemian Tale**, by Olga Walló. Translated by Chapman Chen. 2011. (Chinese)

**University Days,** by Laura Solomon. 2014.

**Vera Magpie,** by Laura Solomon. 2013.

# FIND OUT MORE ABOUT OUR AUTHORS AND BOOKS, PRIZES AND EVENTS

**Visit our website**
<www.proversepublishing.com>
**Visit our distributor's website**
<www.chineseupress.com>

**Follow us on Twitter**
Follow news and conversation: <twitter.com/Proversebooks>
*OR*
Copy and paste the following to your browser window and
follow the instructions: https://twitter.com/#!/ProverseBooks

**"Like" us on www.facebook.com/ProversePress**

**Request our E-Newsletter**
Send your request to info@proversepublishing.com.

**Availability**
Most titles are available in Hong Kong and world-wide
from our Hong Kong based Distributor,
The Chinese University Press of Hong Kong,
The Chinese University of Hong Kong, Shatin, NT,
Hong Kong SAR, China. Web: chineseupress.com

All titles are available from Proverse Hong Kong
and the Proverse Hong Kong UK-based Distributor.

We have stock-holding retailers in Hong Kong (Growhouse,
Bookazine),
Singapore (Select Books),
Canada (Elizabeth Campbell Books),
Principality of Andorra (Llibreria La Puça, La Llibreria).
Orders can be made from bookshops in the UK and elsewhere.

**Ebooks**
Most of our titles are available also as Ebooks.

www.ingramcontent.com/pod-product-compliance
Lightning Source LLC
Chambersburg PA
CBHW051334020726
47501CB00007B/2087